Up Beaver Creek

A novel by

Sue Fagalde Lick

Blue Hydrangea Productions
South Beach, Oregon

Up Beaver Creek

Copyright 2018 Sue Fagalde Lick

All rights reserved. No portion of this work may be reproduced, distributed or transmitted in any form or by any means without written permission.

This is a work of fiction. Although some of the locations are real, all of the characters are fictional. Any similarity to real persons, living or dead, is coincidental and not intended by the author.

ISBN: 978-0983389491

Address orders, inquiries and correspondence to Blue Hydrangea Productions, P.O. Box 755, South Beach, OR 97366, (541) 961-4561, sufalick@gmail.com.

For all the widows and widowers starting over

1

IT'S HOT IN THE HOSPITAL waiting room, and I hate employment forms.

Married, single, divorced or widowed? What business is it of theirs?

Age? Old enough to know better.
Sex? Not lately.

Does anybody really care about my previous jobs or where I went to high school? Do I tell them I went to three different community colleges but didn't graduate from any of them because my first husband was allergic to work and I had to keep dropping out to pay the bills—until he became allergic to me? Do I explain I spent the past two years taking care of Tom and had to quit my job at the hospital in Missoula because I didn't have time to work? That I had only taken that job because we were running out of money and I had no intention of making a career out of it?

References? They can't call any of my references unless I give my real name, and I don't want to do that.

I don't want this job anyway. I just ordered business cards that say I'm a singer and piano player. Shiny white-on-black cards with my new name, P.D. Soares—SWARZ, not SORE-ez—across a keyboard. The girl at the print shop was all impressed, wanted to know where she could hear me perform.

I look up from the application, gazing at the patients in the waiting room reading old issues of *People* magazine. Haven't I spent enough time in hospitals?

Yes. I tear up the application and toss it into the blue recycle bin by the desk. I consider giving the lady in charge some excuse, but she's on the phone, staring at her computer, so I just walk out the door.

Let them wonder. They'll never see me again.

THE MAID is in my room at the Coast Inn, so I sit outside on this dirty white plastic chair, watching the cars go by on Coast Street. I always wondered what kind of people lived in these dumps, the ones you rent by the week, the ones with no pool, no continental breakfast, definitely no room service. The kind that probably have bedbugs and semen stains. The kind where the cops bust drug dealers. And here I am, all dressed up in my boots, black slacks, gray sweater, and silver jewelry. It's only 10:00. I never knew a day could be so long.

I'm having trouble getting this new life started. Oh, I've got the new name, the new look, and now I've got the business cards, but I'm stuck between the woman I used to be and the woman I am now.

"Widow brain," a friend of mine called it. You just can't quite get a grip on your thoughts anymore. I should call my friend, let her know where I am. But not yet, not until I have something good to report. I'll have to explain why I'm not "Cissy" anymore.

Don't do anything for a year. That's what all the how-to-grieve books say. It's a good plan, but you can't really do it. Everyone is after you to make decisions, take care of business, get over your loss and move on. It's not like the flu; you don't "get over" it. I just couldn't stand it anymore. So I put my stuff in storage, rented out the house, and hit the road, changing my name to P.D.

I had a little savings left, the rent pays for the house, and Tom left me some life insurance money. Good old Tom. When the insurance matured or whatever it was supposed to do in 20 years, we were going to do something extravagant, like tour Europe or take a cruise. Instead, I've been wandering around the Northwest in a white Chevy Volt, a little electric-gas hybrid car. Every now and then, I stop to recharge. If I get stuck between plug-ins, I use gas for a while.

Tom and I talked about buying a beach house.

Or opening a piano bar, starring me. We even had a name for it. Yes, you guessed it: P.D.'s.

Unlike the first husband, Tom always liked my singing. In fact, I was singing when we met back in my hometown of Santa

Cruz, California. This local coffee house had open mics, and I was doing a set with some friends when Tom walked in with a co-worker. They were both dressed in suits and carried briefcases. They sat way in the corner, drinking coffee and talking business, but I caught Tom staring at me. Our eyes met. He smiled. I smiled back. He was handsome in that dark-complected Italian-Greek-Jewish-Portuguese kind of look, dark eyes, dark hair. I almost lost my place in the song.

Afterward, I was getting some tea, and Tom came up to me. "You have a beautiful voice," he said.

"Thanks."

As the barista served up my tea, he reached for his wallet. "Let me get that."

"It's free for the musicians," I said.

"Oh. Well . . ." He pulled a business card out of his shirt pocket. "I'm Tom Soares. I'd love to have coffee or something with you sometime."

Cue the romantic music. "That would be nice."

So we met for coffee and then lunch and then we did the dinner-and-a-movie thing. It wasn't long before we wound up mushy goofy in love, all over each other like teenagers, spending every spare minute together. Six months later, we got married and I changed my last name from the first husband's name, Wilcox, to Soares.

At the time, Tom worked as assistant director in the planning department for Scott's Valley, a town a few miles inland from Santa Cruz. But five years after we got married, he was offered a job as the director in Missoula, so we moved to Montana. Hot summers and snowy winters. We bought a cozy house near the university and spent all our spare time fixing it up. Tom did the 9 to 5 thing, plus he had to go to a lot of night meetings. Boy, he could toss the initials around, EIR, RTP, UBC, P.D.—planned development, ha. That's me, P.D. I'm a Planned Development. No, that's not my name. Neither is Cissy, if you want the truth. I'm just not telling you what it is. It's too embarrassing.

So here I am in Newport, Oregon, on the coast about midway between California and Washington. The Cissy part of me is feeling guilty about blowing off the job at the hospital. I mean, is this better, sitting in front of this dump watching the cars go by? Oh look, there's a homeless guy squatting by the side of the road waving a cardboard sign. That could be me in a couple months.

The manager is coming. Old guy, face almost as pale as his hair.

"Good morning. Enjoying the sun?"

Actually I'm freezing, but I guess people around here would call this a warm autumn day. "Yeah," I lie. "Beautiful day."

He goes into my room. I hear him talking to the maid, telling her to hurry up. I'm wondering what I left in there for people to see.

The hospital here is different from the one in Missoula where I used to work. That one was huge, five floors, hundreds of beds. I think they have 30 here. You could put this whole two-story hospital in the lobby of St. Patrick's.

I wasn't a nurse or anything. If I was, I would have a lot more job possibilities. No, I was one of those people in admissions where patients scared spitless about their upcoming surgeries or procedures would give me their name, address, insurance information, and emergency contact. I'd have them sign forms promising not to sue us if they died or something, and I'd collect their co-pays. Most of these folks were old. They had lived at the same address for 50 years and had lost their husbands or wives and now they couldn't believe they had cancer or kidney failure or whatever ailed them.

From the outside, I usually couldn't tell that they had anything wrong. If somebody was really sick, a friend or family member checked them in. Toward the end, I was the one doing all that for Tom. I was his emergency contact and the one he gave power of attorney to make his medical decisions.

We were married for 12 years, but we never had kids. I suppose that's a good thing, considering what happened, although sometimes I see mothers and daughters together and feel sad. Then again, my child might be almost a teenager now, just what I need. A pimply-faced kid telling me I'm an idiot while I try to figure out how to pay for school clothes that he or she will refuse to wear.

My kid would never let me be P.D.

In truth, I feel like a kid myself, as if those years with Tom never happened, and I'm right back where I was before, except somehow I'm older.

And colder.

The maid is done with my room. I'm going to stand by the heater while I figure out what to do next.

I PICK UP some coffee at the drive-through and head for the beach. I really missed the ocean when I was in Missoula. Now I plan to spend as much time on the sand and in the water as possible.

When I was a kid growing up in Santa Cruz, my family was always at the beach. Dad and my brother Andy would go fishing while I'd putter around, digging for sand crabs, collecting shells or playing in the water. When I was older, a lot of girls my age put on their bikinis and lay out on their towels hoping some guys would notice them. But I was always overweight and more likely to be covered up in baggy clothes and reading a book. Or knitting or embroidering, for Pete's sake. Basically I was a clone of my mother. Except that I loved to sing. School choir, church choir, open mics, the shower.

After I lost Tom, I felt the beach calling me home. I didn't want to go back to Santa Cruz. Too many connections to the past. After that last Sunday at church in Missoula, when I finally couldn't take any more "poor Cissy" vibes, when I'd had enough of sitting around knitting and crying, I began packing. Put everything in storage. Charged up the Volt and started driving. I traveled west from Montana through Idaho, Washington, and Oregon, all the way to the ocean, then headed south. I took my time, explored lots of side roads, walked a lot of beaches. By the time I got halfway down the Oregon coast, I was tired of driving. My clothes were dirty, I was hungry, and I saw three places that advertised live music. The welcome sign at the edge of town declared this place was "The Friendliest." Underneath it was a sign advertising a jazz festival, so I thought, okay, let's stop here.

It was Oct. 1. I arrived wearing a tank top, shorts, and sandals. As soon as I got halfway between I-5 and the coast, the fog closed in and the air turned cold. I had left most of my warm clothes back in Missoula. I had to buy myself a jacket and some socks at the Fred Meyer store. Got some other things at Salvation Army. I didn't mind. At that point, I'd had enough hot weather to last me forever, although I'm starting to wonder about that now. I mean it's October, allegedly Indian summer, and the hottest temperature has only gotten to the low 70s.

I hear rumors it rains like crazy here, and the tsunami warning signs along the highway make me a little nervous, but everyplace has something. At least it doesn't snow.

Wait. The Agate Beach parking lot is jammed with people and cars, license plates from all over the U.S. and Canada. What's going on? Santa Cruz is probably still crawling with vacationers, but we're talking hundreds of people in a place most folks never heard of.

"Did you see it?" a chubby boy shrieks. "Did you see it?"

"Yeah, it's huge!" screams a smaller boy, scrawny and bare-chested in his baggy swimsuit. "Come on!"

Well, now I'm curious. See what? Is there a whale on the beach? A boat that ran ashore?

Feeling overdressed in my apply-for-work clothes, I follow the crowd through a graffiti-marked tunnel under the road. There's a scuzzy-looking guy standing near the far exit playing his flute. The sound reverberates all around me. I want to sing, try the acoustics, but he's scowling in a way that scares me. I search for a tip jar and see only a can of beer. As I pass, he pauses to take a swig.

"I like your music."

He looks right over my head and goes back to playing.

The tunnel lets out at Agate Beach. I don't see anything. At first.
"Holy shit." Yes, I say it out loud. I can't believe how many people are here.

Everybody is heading north, kids, couples, old people, all holding up their cell phones to take pictures of what seems to be a massive rectangular chunk of cement sitting on the beach. Shucking my boots and socks, I join the mass migration.

The sand feels so good on my toes I want to lie down and wrap myself up in it, but every body-sized space seems to be taken up with tourists trying to snap pictures of whatever that is and put it on Facebook or Twitter. Me, I left my phone charging back at the motel, and my camera, I don't know. It's probably in the car somewhere. I don't have a portable computer. I used to use the computer on Tom's desk. It's in storage now.

My coffee keeps sloshing out of this stupid environmentally correct pseudo-paper cup. If I slow down to drink it, I'll probably get run over.

To hell with this. I'm stopping. "What is it?" I ask an old couple coming toward me.

The man stares at his cell phone, messing with his photos, but the wife answers. "It's a dock, floated here all the way from Japan. From last year's tsunami. Can you imagine something that big coming this far?"

The husband looks up. "It's taller than my head. I'd say it's oh, about seven feet tall. Sixty-something feet long. It's got writing in Japanese on the side. You know, they said we wouldn't see any debris from that tsunami for another year, but here it is. They're finding other stuff, like bottles and Styrofoam, too. This keeps up, our beaches are gonna be a mess with all that crap from Japan."

I scan the beach, see the usual seaweed, crab shells and stray pieces of wood and plastic.

"Yep," he goes on, "Those damned Japs are going to get us after all. They lost the war, but they'll kill us with their crap."

"Albert!"

"Wait and see."

I remember sitting in Tom's hospital room watching the TV footage that showed entire Japanese towns turned to rubble and washed into the sea. We watched the news anxiously for backlash in Santa Cruz, where our families lived, but the waves weren't big enough to do more than nip at the docks a little bit.

"Thank you. Guess I'll go see it," I tell the old bigot, slogging on through the sand, inspecting every bit of litter that might be from Japan.

The crowd stands thick around the dock, a big old concrete block crusted with mussels and seaweed, Japanese writing on the corners. I join them, sipping my almost-cold coffee. Debris from Japan. A life coming apart and washing up on a distant shore. Sort of like me.

This guy nearby is so intent on his picture that he runs right into me. When I feel his bare arm against my arm, I flash on a memory of Tom and me rubbing arms, comparing his tanned hairy skin to my light freckled arms. Laughing. Once, joking, he called me a harbor seal. "You're a walrus," I shot back, tweaking his mustache.

"Well, this walrus is going to get you."

And he did.

Nuts. Tears behind my sunglasses. Okay, I've seen the dock. The dock of the bay. The Otis Redding song, get it?

2

AN HOUR LATER, I'm scanning the bulletin board outside the J.C. Market when I smell cigarette smoke and notice a chubby bearded man in a fedora coming my way.

"Anything good?" he asks. Boy, this town is friendly.

"No, not really. There's a guy selling a litter of pigs, if you're interested."

"Tempting, but no." He chuckles.

"Am I in your way?" I ask, moving over a couple feet.

"No. I drive that taxi over there. I'm just waiting for Mrs. Mead to do her shopping. I'm Jonas."

"P.D." I notice his black tee shirt has a picture of a guy playing saxophone. Jazz rules, it says. "You like jazz."

"Of course."

"Me too."

He smokes, checks to see if Mrs. Mead is coming out.

"That smells good," I say, waving the smoke toward me."

"Want one?"

"No thanks. I'm trying to quit." A lie. I have never smoked.

"Oh, I gave up on that. Too much waiting around. I never know what to do with my hands."

Awkward silence.

"I sing," I say.

"Cool. Where?"

"Well, nowhere yet. I just got here. I'm looking for a place to live."

"Ah."

A van pulls up behind us. A mother wrestles a screaming toddler out of his car seat.

"You looking for a house or what?"

"I don't know. I don't have much money, and I haven't found a job here yet. I'm kind of starting from scratch."

Jonas looks back toward the store, probably trying to see whether the old lady is at the cash register yet. "Well, you know,

I've got an uncle who's got this property out in the woods near Beaver Creek, and he needs somebody to kind of watch over the place. He lives in Portland part of the time and Tucson during the winter. It's not a bad place, the one in Beaver Creek. My wife and I stayed there for a while, but then we had the twins, and you know, we needed more space."

I nod. "You think he'd rent it out cheap?"

"Yeah." He glances at me and back toward the store. "I probably shouldn't say this, but I think maybe he'd let you stay there for free if you just took care of the place, you know maintained it a little and made it appear occupied so nobody robbed it or burned it down."

"Huh." Now I really wish I smoked. "I might be interested in that. Where is Beaver Creek?"

"You head south over the bridge, go about six miles till you get to Ona Beach. Instead of turning in to the beach, you go east on Beaver Creek Road and head up into the hills. The cabin is a couple miles up. It's a nice area. My mom lives nearby in Seal Rock, a little ways farther down the highway."

"That sounds good. I can't believe this is possible when we don't even know each other."

"You seem okay. You like jazz. Let me get your name and number and try to put you two together."

"Cool."

He writes my info on the back of a receipt he pulls out of his pocket just before the old lady emerges. "Hey, Mrs. Mead. Let me help you with that cart."

We're done. "Thank you, Jonas. I'll talk to you soon."

He doffs his hat before turning all his attention to the old lady, who is babbling about overpriced oatmeal.

Very cool. Time to buy some food.

So NOW I'M at the gym, carrying my cell phone from station to station, afraid I'll miss Jonas's call. He's probably busy doing his taxi driver thing, but who knows?

I've been working out every day since I got here. I signed up for a month-to-month membership at this little gym in Newport a few days after I got to town. After all that time in the car, I was aching to work out.

It's about 2:30 now. After the grocery store, I stuffed my food into my ice chest at the motel, added a new layer of ice from the machine out front, changed my clothes and came here.

This is a good time of day to work out, not too crowded, just a few diehards and people with no life. Come here at 5:00 or on weekends, and the place is jammed with big guys with buzz cuts grunting and sweating and cheering each other on. Listening to them talk, I figured out most of them are cops.

We're cordial. I say hello and go about my business. Sometimes I glance over and see how much weight they're lifting. It's usually lots more than I can lift, but sometimes, like on the leg weights, I can match them and beat them. Forty-two years old and a woman, ha.

This gym is smaller than the one in Missoula, basically just two rooms, a mat room where they do Pilates and aerobics and this room full of weights and cardio machines. Mirrors and motivational posters cover the salmon-colored walls. I keep re-reading them: "Strong is the new thin." "You can do it." "Wanna lift?"

Tom and I used to laugh about being "fluffy," something we read on a humorous greeting card. Pictures of sheep. "Ewe's not fat. Ewe's fluffy." Actually, Tom wasn't fat. He just had the typical guy gut. When he got sick, he shrank to just bones. Horrible. I think I ate twice as much that first year to compensate.

I started losing weight when Tom was in the hospital and I just plain didn't have time to eat. You know how it is. You don't want to leave him for fear something will happen. As soon as you decide to go to the cafeteria for breakfast or lunch, that's when the doctor shows up. Every time. I was so scared I couldn't eat anyway.

As the weight came off, I started wanting to get fit, to get as healthy as possible so that what was happening to Tom would never happen to me. So I joined this 24-hour gym. It cost a fortune, but at that point, with all our other bills, money was becoming irrelevant. I got this trainer, a real bitch. She drove me nuts, forcing me to do all these things. Sit up, pull up, throw up. Run, row, lift, go, go, go.

I remember after the first workout, I hurt so bad I felt like somebody had beaten me up. I staggered into the hospital and told Tom, "Move over. I need that bed."

He looked up at me and smiled around his oxygen tube. "Come on in."

His voice was so weak.

At first, the workouts hurt so much I wanted to quit, but they took my mind off everything else, and my body started to crave exercise. Does that sound weird?

Ugh. I can't let my mind go back to those days when Tom was dying. I need to focus on what I'm doing right now, and right now, I'm on the treadmill. Running and thinking, thinking and running. I've got my phone perched in the water bottle holder. I'll have to see it flash. The screaming music, the roar of the machines, and that guy over there who keeps clanking his weights make it hard to hear.

If I go live on this property for Jonas's uncle, maybe I won't need a job. But I do need something to do. I'm used to getting up and dressed and out the door early, being around people, working all day.

Beaver Creek. I'm not quite sure where that is. And is this something I want to do? Is it in the wilderness? Am I the *Little House on the Prairie* type? Without Pa to rescue me?

Cissy isn't. But maybe P.D. is. Ring, phone, damn it.

I finish on the treadmill and start with the weights. Mirrors line the walls of this gym, so I can't get away from seeing myself. But it doesn't look like me. I swear sometimes I think my former self was abducted by aliens and placed into this whole new body. I still can't believe it.

Head to toe, it's different. My hair is red and spiky. I'm thin and muscular in my shorts and tank top, and I've got this tiny tattoo on my left shoulder, Tom's name in a heart. I got it when he was sick. I just wanted to hang on to him somehow. He cried when I showed it to him.

Now I'm thinking I might get another one, a rose on my breast. Maybe.

That shaved-head guy is watching me as I lift this barbell, 90 pounds. Old Cissy could barely lift her grocery bags. She didn't have to. Tom was there. Then when he got sick, well, there was that time I attempted to lift Tom. He had tried to get up, his legs gave out, and boom, he was on the floor. I tried everything I could think of, tried lifting him from every angle, tried wedging pillows under him. None of it worked, and he screamed every time I touched him, so I called 911. Burly guys like these guys lifting weights picked him up like he didn't weigh more than a beer.

Now this big sheriff guy is walking over here.

I let the weight slide back down. "Do you need this station?"

"No," he says. "I just wondered if you wanted me to spot you. We usually spot each other."

"Oh." I realize I am the only one trying to do this without a spotter. There's strong, and then there's stupid. My trainer used to say that. "Yeah, that'd be great. I'm almost done though."

Could there be a more vulnerable position than lying on my back with my legs spread and this guy leaning over me so close I can smell his breath on my face? I can feel my heart thudding in my chest as I reach back, grab the bar and push up. Suddenly it seems impossibly heavy, but no way in hell will I wimp out in front of this guy. I imitate the men and grunt loudly as I push with everything I have. My spotter leans in close, his hands underneath the bar just in case. "I got it," I gasp.

"I know," he says.

My arms begin to shake and I start lowering the bar, almost lose control and then suddenly I feel no weight. The guy has taken it over for me.

I sit up. "I had it."

"Oh, I know. You were about to have it right in the middle of your forehead." He has a very sheriffy look on his face. Stern. Righteous. Fatherly. He probably has four kids and a wife. I check for a wedding ring. None. But maybe he doesn't wear it to work out.

"Well, thank you. I appreciate it. I'll spot you next time."

"Sure." He turns away, and I imagine him rolling his eyes at his buddy over on the other side doing free weights.

To hell with both of them.

I go to the aerobics room to do ab crunches on the padded floor. I lie down, fold my arms across my chest and pull myself up. One, two, three. This is hard, the hardest exercise in my workout, but I love running my hand across my waist and feeling muscles.

The warm room smells of sweat. From the other room, I hear the clank of weights, the hum of the fans, and the roar of hip-hop music turned up loud. Six, seven, eight. I never feel more P.D. than I do in the gym, even in this small-town gym. At least one of the three treadmills is always out of order, and the weights are chipped and discolored from wear and tear. There is no TV, no juice bar, no personal trainer. It isn't unusual to be the only person here. When that happens, I let myself in with my key card, turn the radio to the oldies station and work out until I forget about everything outside, past, present or future.

22-23-24. Oh God, I can't, yes I can—27, 28, 29, 30. I lie on my back for a minute, just breathing, my abs feeling the shock. Two more crunches than last time. I peel myself off the mat, dry my face and arms with my borrowed motel towel, take a big drink from my water bottle, and go back to the treadmill for my cool-down run. The men are gone. I change the radio to the oldies station, climb aboard, punch in my settings and start running.

I have just reached the top of the hill when the phone rings. I fight to catch my breath. "P.D. here."

"P.D.? What kind of way is that to answer the telephone?"

"Mom." I was so ready for this to be Jonas calling about the property at Beaver Creek. Nothing brings you back to earth like your mother. "Hi, how are you?"

"I'm fine. Relatively."

"What does that mean?"

"You know. I'm old, I'm divorced and I might as well not have any children for all I see of them. All my friends have grandchildren. Some even have great-grandchildren, and I've got Tootsie." Her dachshund. Like a Tootsie Roll, get it?

"I know. I'm sorry. I should call more often."

"Or just come home. How about that?"

"I'm not—" People are coming in, glaring at me standing here on the treadmill. I try to walk, slowly, so I can still talk, but that doesn't really work. I get off, wipe the handlebar with my towel. "I'm sorry. What?"

"Where are you?"

"I'm at the gym."

"I don't understand why you spend so much time working out. Last time I saw you I didn't even recognize you with your red hair and those muscles. And that tattoo. My God. Where did my little girl go?"

She saw the tattoo? Oh yeah, when she came to Missoula just before I left, it was hot, and I wore a sleeveless top. "She grew up, Mom." I'm standing near the bathrooms now, sweaty, starting to feel cold in the path of the fans. "Did you call for anything in particular?"

"I'm sorry if I interrupted your *workout.*"

"No, that's okay, I was almost done, but I'm kind of standing in the way here, and I need to take a shower."

"Well, I was worried about you. Your father even called to ask about you, and I didn't know what to tell him. I said you'd moved to Oregon, changed your name and your appearance, like you're a spy or something, and I don't know what you're going to do. So tell me, what are you going to do? I know you're sad about Tom, but you've got to move on."

This is going to take a while. I head for the exit, stopping to sign out on the sheet near the door. Outside, the cold air hits me and I realize I left my hooded sweatshirt in the dressing area. I go back in and grab it, enduring the stares of a woman who is running on the treadmill I just left. I try to tell myself my mother won't be around forever and I should be patient, but everything I say to her somehow comes out sounding snippy and sarcastic.

I fall into my car with a sigh. "I'm going to shower and then—okay, I don't know yet. I'm looking for singing opportunities. I have a lead on a job taking care of a house near here. It would give me both work and a place to live."

"Why don't you just apply at the hospital? You've got experience in that."

"I did. It—didn't work out."

"You could ask people from the hospital in Montana to vouch for you."

"Yeah, I know. But Mom, that's—"

"You can't just lounge around in a strange town and expect to be discovered. You know, you're too old for this singing business anyway. Those people on TV, American Idol, You've Got Talent, they're all under 30. You're not a kid anymore."

"I know." I struggle to pull my jacket on with one hand. I'm half in and half out when I hear a beep that indicates another call coming in. It could be Jonas. "Mom, I'm sorry. I have a call on the other line. It might be a job. I have to go."

"Okay, well, I love you."

"I love you, too." Click. "Hello?"

"As a registered Montana Democrat, you should know—" I punch the disconnect button. A recording. My phone thinks it still lives in Montana. At least it ended the call with my mother.

I haven't seen either of my parents in months. Mom's in California, Dad's living in his camper. Wyoming last I heard. When he retired from Boeing, he wanted to hit the road. Mom absolutely refused. He went anyway. After six months, she filed for divorce, demanding alimony to supplement her part-time job at a florist shop. It's been two years now. It didn't really change things much. They'd lived separate lives forever. I'm pretty sure my brother Andy and I were the only things that held them together. When we grew up, they had nothing left to talk about. I really think Dad had a couple of affairs. Nobody ever said anything about it, but I think he did.

Dad took Tom's death almost as hard as I did. They used to go fishing and hunting together. And now . . . yeah.

I know it hasn't been easy for Mom. Losing Tom was tough on her, too, but she's got to give me some space.

As I drive toward the motel, I have to admit my mother raises some good points. I can't sit around forever, and I'm going to go nuts waiting for this one phone call. It might not even work out. The uncle might be looking for a man or maybe for a whole family to watch his place. I might not want to do it. Jonas was just trying to be nice. It's not like he consulted with his uncle first.

3

THIS TOWN doesn't have a shopping mall or a grownup-sized hospital, but it does have a music store. No, not where they sell CDs and iPods. This is where they sell sheet music, guitars, and violins and give lessons to reluctant third-graders. It's time I made my acquaintance.

I've been telling people, well not too many people, mostly myself, I'm a musician. I've got business cards ordered, and I've talked to people at a dozen bars and lounges, but I'm not even singing with the radio and my piano's back in Missoula.

Ocean Harmony Music. They've got notices posted on the door. On some of them, the ink has faded so much it's almost invisible, but a couple look new. The guy working inside sees me and smiles as I study the flyers and 3 x 5 cards. Flute lessons. Symphony concert next weekend. Open mic Saturday night at Café Mundo. Okay, but it's Monday. What can I do today?

Brakes screech. I hold my breath, waiting for the crash, but it doesn't come. I look across the street and see a guy in a truck shaking his fist at a woman in a Honda. I can't quite hear what he's shouting through his open window, but I suspect it's not a compliment. While I'm looking that way, I see the karaoke sign at the Blue Whale Pub. Karaoke. Not my favorite. Not a job. But it's singing. When?

The light changes and the traffic clears enough for me to make out "Monday night" in smaller letters. Well. It's something to do. I'll walk over later to see what time. Meanwhile, my fingers are itching to touch that shiny black grand piano I see inside the music store.

A bell rings as I open the door. I nod at the lanky long-haired owner and head for the piano. I play a blues scale up and down. It sounds good. Then I feel the guy hanging over me. I say, "This is a nice piano."

"Yes. Top of the line. Are you in the market for a piano?"

I remember the old upright Tom brought home for me shortly after we were married. It had been a school piano, and it was pretty scarred up, but it had a sweet sound. Nothing like this, of course, but I loved it. It reminded me of the one I took lessons on with Mrs. McKenzie after school. While most kids hated their music lessons, I couldn't get enough. That piano Tom bought me was the best gift anyone had ever given me. When he got so sick, I stopped playing it, and when I left Montana, when I became P.D., I put it in storage. It's the first time in years I haven't had access to a piano.

"No, I'm actually looking for work. I'm a singer. Jazz, pop, light rock." I look around, still fingering chords on the piano. "Or I could work in a music store."

He grins, showing a missing tooth on the side, his front teeth stained and crooked. "I'm lucky to keep the doors open at this point. If it weren't for kids needing band instruments, I'd already be closed."

I figured as much. "Yeah, well. It doesn't hurt to ask."

"No, no, it doesn't. Um, do you have a band?"

I reluctantly leave the piano and wander over toward the sheet music, where I don't recognize any of the top 40 songs but wonder why every store still has the same old Beatles and Barbra Streisand songs I bought 20 years ago. "No. I'd like to have one."

"You can put a notice in the window."

"Okay. Let me think about what to say and get back to you."

"Sure." The phone rings, and he rushes to the counter, which is awash in receipts, cords, cables, and used guitar strings.

I walk out into the cool air and cross the street. Karaoke starts at 8.

God, I miss my piano. I miss my house with the big windows and the flowered curtains and stew cooking in the crockpot. I miss Tom sitting in his chair on a Sunday afternoon humming while I play. I miss being able to leave the piano, go to Tom and kiss him hard, feel his arms come around me, feel him cradle me in his lap, feel him kiss his way down my neck.

Oh, nuts. If I don't stop this, I'm going to cry. I hurry to my car and drive back to the Coast Inn, dashing away tears as I shove the card in the slot three times before the green light comes on and the door actually opens.

This is not very P.D.

I had a house. I had a husband. I had a job. I even had a dog, Harry, but he ran away while I was doing the hospital shuffle. A neighbor's kid had volunteered to walk him because I was so busy. He left him alone in the park for a minute while he went to the restroom. When he came back, Harry was gone. He searched. I searched. I went to the animal shelter. I put up posters. I drove around the area for days looking for him. Useless. Harry was a beagle, cute. Somebody probably stole him. Meanwhile, Tom's condition got so shaky he could die any day, so I had to forget about the dog. Broke my heart. Tom had brought him home for me for my 38th birthday.

Damn. I can't sit here and weep all afternoon. Been there, done that. It's too Cissy. P.D. gets up and does something. I'm tempted to go to the animal shelter here and get me a new dog. But I can't do it while I'm living at the Coast Inn. I wish my stupid phone would ring. F'ing phone. Yes, unlike Prissy Cissy, P.D. swears.

And she hasn't been to church in a while.

Those people back at the church in Missoula are probably shaking their heads, saying it's a pity poor Cissy never had children. Now she's all alone. Yeah. Maybe. If I had kids, I don't know how I'd support them. Well, I guess I'd beg for my job back at the hospital, maybe have to take a position there that I didn't like as well as the old one. I'd have the life insurance money. I suppose my mother would help me. Maybe I could get two jobs, but then I'd never see my kids. I'd become one of those dragged-out single mothers who looks old at 42. Not a happy Cissy and definitely not P.D.

Why didn't we have kids? It's a long story. I can boil it down to this: spoiled eggs, slow-swimming sperm. We tried, but we decided not to go all high tech, and it didn't happen. We had filled out the papers to adopt a child through Catholic Charities. Then Tom got sick, so we couldn't do that either. End of story.

The Coast Inn is dead in the afternoon. It's the quiet time between checking out and checking in. I could go for a walk, but I'm tired from my workout and I already walked on the beach. Maybe

I'll go to the bank so I can buy a drink at the karaoke bar. I should have gotten cash at the grocery store, but did I think of it? No.

It's 7:00. Karaoke at the Blue Whale Pub starts at 8. I'm pooped. In this one day, I have almost applied for a job, walked on the beach, bought groceries, worked out, gone to the music store, and cried at least three times. My checking account balance is down to $152. That's not going to last me very long. I'll have to hit my savings again. Credit card, you say? Well, I finally added things up. I can't be sure until I get my statement or find a computer, but I'm pretty close to out of money there, too. Maybe they need a waitress at the Blue Whale Pub. Shudder.

Okay. What should I wear? I need to look good. No, hot. I've gone down two sizes since I became P.D., so I had to buy some new clothes, but I only have two decent outfits to choose from. I'm thinking I need another trip to the Salvation Army store. For that, I need cash. What if I sang *a capella* on the street? What do they call that? Busking. No. I don't know. Maybe. If I had a keyboard or a guitar-playing partner . . .

Okay, black silky shirt, black jeans with the silver belt, silver sandals. Eye liner. Eye shadow. Mascara. Red lipstick. The ruby necklace Tom gave me for our 10th anniversary. Dangly earrings. Yeah. Hello, P.D.

I'm walking tonight. Car needs a charge, and I don't want to waste my gas. Don't want to get busted for drunk driving either.

As soon as I step outside, I shove the key card back in the lock and go back in. It's cold. Foggy, too. I need my coat. In October. Why am I here anyway?

Oh yeah, I love the beach, and this seemed like a good place to sing. I was tired of being hot. Okay, less thinking, more walking.

These sandals were not a good idea. My toes are freezing, and I'm getting a blister, but I'm here. The Blue Whale Pub. Deep breath. Open the door into a narrow hallway. Dark. Noisy with music and talking and beer mugs clinking against each other. White board says the specials are fish and chips and sliders. I already ate at the motel, two granola bars and a peach.

"Can I help you?"

I startle as a sweating middle-aged man with a crew cut appears out of nowhere, holding a plasticized menu.

"Um, yeah. I'm here for the karaoke."

"That doesn't start for a while yet. It's in the bar. Do you want to have something to eat?"

"No. Thanks."

Down the hall and to the left, I see the bar. Darker than a 1950s confessional, lit by a few candles and 25-watt bulbs, it's crowded with couples and groups sitting at the tables. I'm trying to be P.D. and all, but this is one of those moments when Cissy starts whispering in my head, saying stuff like, "You can't go in there alone. You don't know anybody. You can't sit by yourself. Blah, blah, blah." I feel little zings of nerves in my stomach. But I'm here, and I'm not walking back to the motel until I sing.

I mosey up to the bar and find myself in line between two guys who are both at least a foot taller than me. I seem to be invisible until everybody in the whole f-ing room has been served. Finally, the lady bartender sees me.

"Can I get a beer?" I'm sorry for the edge in my voice, but it ticks me off, you know.

"Sure. What kind?"

Cissy would have had a daiquiri. Think P.D. "What have you got on tap?"

"Coors and Bud."

"Bud, please." As she fills the glass, holding it sideways to keep the foam down, I slide onto a stool near the right end of the bar. "What time does the karaoke start?" She shrugs. "I don't know. Whenever Collin gets here."

"The sign says 8:00."

"Does it? Well, he's on coastal time."

Some guys at the far end of the bar beckon the bartender. "Hey, honey, we're out of beer!" they holler. She goes. I like her tattoo. It covers her upper back from shoulder to shoulder, flowers, angels and waves above the band of cloth she's using for a top.

Could P.D. get one like that? I can just imagine what my mother would say. Does P.D. care?

I sip my beer and look around. My eyes have adjusted now, and I kind of like the dim lighting. Makes it easy to hide.

The walls are decorated with neon beer signs, lotto boards, and black and white pictures of the town in the olden days.

Scanning the crowd, I see some half-dressed barely-21-year-old girls. A couple of tourists drinking gin and tonic. A baseball-capped guy nursing his Jack Daniels at a little round table. Fishermen at the bar.

I wish they'd turn the music down.

At least it's not smoky in here. No smoking allowed. Up until they passed the new law a couple years ago, the smoke in Montana bars was like that fog outside. I'd take a breath and start coughing. But now, all I smell is beer and fishy grease from the grill.

The stool next to me is empty, but there's a jittery guy a couple seats over who keeps trying to talk to the bartender, who keeps trying to ignore him. I'm guessing he's here all the time.

I study my sweating beer mug and trace the drips along the flat spaces between the seams. Tom loved beer. Bud straight out of the bottle. Somehow that leads my mind back to a picnic we held for his 40th birthday. Two years ago. His cancer had already been diagnosed, and he'd started treatment. Oops, I wasn't going to tell you. Yeah, it was pancreatic cancer, one of the worst kinds a person can get. He'd had surgery, but the doctors weren't too hopeful.

His beautiful black hair was falling out from the chemo. I found it all over the pillowcases, on the bathroom floor, in the shower. He had taken to wearing a baseball cap all the time. His pants were so loose he wore his belt on the last notch so the end was sticking out. He covered it with a big old red Hawaiian shirt.

We, meaning his parents, his sisters, and I, went all out. His family flew up from California. We invited his co-workers from the city. The mayor of Missoula came with his wife. We hung balloons off the picnic tables and put up a sign that said, "Tom is forty and fabulous." We filled a whole table with cards and presents. The place was swarming with people who loved Tom, including lots of kids.

Anybody who ever thought we might still reproduce knew it was all over now. I could feel their looks, poor Cissy, whose husband is dying and no kids to keep her company.

Anyway. We brought out every food Tom had ever said he liked: Portuguese beans and linguiça, deviled eggs, potato salad, corn on the cob, brownies, chips and taco dip, cases and cases of Bud, along with jugs of wine for those who were too delicate for beer. Lemonade for the kids. And of course there was a giant chocolate cake with candles shaped like a four and a zero.

He smiled a lot, but he didn't eat more than a few bites. He got so tired you could see his face fading after an hour or so. Two hours in, he quietly asked me to take him home. His family followed us to the house, but I spent more time with them than he did.

The thing is, we didn't know if he'd have any more birthdays. We wanted to make sure we celebrated not only this one, but all the milestone birthdays he might miss: 50, 65, 70, 80, 90, 100. Nobody was saying that, but we were all thinking it.

Screech! The feedback makes me jump and brings me back to this bar. Somebody's testing a microphone. Hallelujah. The karaoke is coming. Give me too much time to think and I'll sink so deep into widow head nobody will ever find P.D. again.

Wait. That's who's running this? That teenaged kid? *He's* Collin? Great. I can just imagine what songs are on his list. Also, looking around, I don't see a lot of likely singers. But then, as my mother-in-law used to say to Tom's nephews when they complained they didn't like some food she served, "*Mais fica.*" More for me. Fewer singers, more songs for P.D.

Time to go to the restroom and warm up my voice.

When I come back, Collin is passing out song lists, blue sheets packaged in plastic just like the menus. I can see he's about to skip the bar, so I raise my hand. "I'll take one of those."

"Oh, you're gonna sing? All right. Can I get your name on my list?"

"P.D."

"Petey?"

"P period D period."

"Oh yeah. I get it. You'll be third, after Janey."

As he moves on, a sharp pain burns across my stomach. Nerves. I don't want any more beer. It's like pouring acid on an open wound. Besides, it defeats the purpose of lifting weights and eating granola bars for dinner. I push my glass aside and open the music menu. To my surprise, I actually know a lot of these songs. Maybe that's all people can buy for karaoke machines. I don't know. I honestly hate karaoke. Stare at the video screen and follow the bouncing ball, trying to sound just like Katy Perry or Beyonce or Blake Shelton or whoever. I'd rather sound like P.D. If I want to play around with the timing or the notes, I want to be free to do that.

The show is starting. A few more people have come in, including this older guy in a black suit with his white shirt half unbuttoned who's taken the stool next to mine. I have to strain to see the stage around him. He orders a shot of Johnny Walker. Maybe he just came from a wedding—his daughter's or the girl he loved. Maybe he was in court. Or maybe he's coming out of a date gone bad. Dating. Ugh. I have not gone out with anyone since Tom died. It's too soon. It would be weird and maybe make me feel worse, but I'm becoming more open to the possibility.

If I'm going to be really P.D., I should strike up a conversation with this guy. I don't have to date him. It would be nice just having somebody to talk to. Maybe I'll say something in a little while.

Collin takes the first song. "Love Shack" by the B-52s. He's not bad. Oh look, he's got colored lights synched to the machine so they flash with the beat. The kid has a good voice, and he's trying hard to get some reaction from the crowd, but nobody's even listening. Another thing I hate about karaoke. To everyone except your friends, you're just background noise.

He finishes, holds out the mic to the table of young women. "Janey?"

She's short and chubby with a head full of wild blonde curls and a low-cut blouse that shows her bountiful bosoms. And she's smiling like sunshine as her friends applaud while she dances up to the stage.

"I'm gonna sing, um, wait for it, I'm gonna sing 'Desperado.' Hit it, Collin."

From the first note, I'm mesmerized. Janey has the sweetest soprano voice I've ever heard, with just enough grit to tear your heart out. She doesn't even look at the screen. Doesn't need it. I rest my chin on my hand and wish with all my heart I was that young, that cute, and that free.

When she finishes, even the bartender claps and cheers. Now it's my turn. Is it too late to slither out the door?

"P.D.! Come on up," Collin calls. "Folks, we've got someone new tonight. Let's give her a warm welcome."

Three people applaud, including Janey.

I was going to do something sweet, but not now. I've got this low voice, almost a whiskey tenor, and I need to sing something totally different from what Janey just did. I choose "Friends in Low Places."

Collin gives me a look like, what? But he cues it up, and I sing the cowboy boots off that Garth Brooks hit. Janey is on her feet, hooting and hollering. Hot damn.

A fresh beer is waiting for me when I get back. The morose guy in the suit gives me a nod. As for my stomach? What stomach?

A few more people sing, badly, and then the rotation starts again. Janey gets raunchy and I go sweet this time. I'm looking at her, and she's looking at me, and we're developing a mutual fan club.

About two hours in, she starts into "Ain't no Mountain High Enough," and I can't stand it. I start singing harmony. She hears me and beckons me to the stage. Collin hands me a mic and we rock that bar.

Afterward, we hug. "Come sit with us," she says. She drags a chair over. Her young friends make room for me while I go get my beer. "You're really good," she says as I sink into the wooden chair.

"You too."

"I've never seen you here before."

"No. First time. I'm new in town."

Blah, blah, blah, boring, I know. It's too loud to say anything intelligent, and I don't want to be screaming over the singers, even that guy who couldn't carry a tune in a dump truck. I slide my sandals off my blistered feet, sip my beer, and enjoy not being alone. The next time I sing, I notice that guy in the suit is watching me. He even smiles, but then I see him answering his phone and he leaves a minute later. Oh well.

Around 10:30, Janey looks toward the door and there is Jonas, the cabbie I met outside the grocery store.

"My ride is here," Janey says, pushing back her chair.

"I know him," I say. "Jonas, the cab driver."

"Yeah, he's my brother. He comes and gets me when he has an opening in his shift. Hey, you need a ride?"

I can't believe this is happening. "Yes, I'd love a ride. I walked over, and my feet are killing me."

"Come on."

Jonas sees me coming, does a double take. "Hey, it's P.D."

Janey hustles me through the long dark hallway, waves at the guy behind the desk, and we're outside. It's even colder than it was before. I'm wishing for a thicker jacket. "P.D.'s a great singer," Janey tells her brother. "You ought to hear her."

"Really? Cool."

In a minute, I'm in the back of the cab. The sign above the meter says: *Thanks for riding with Jonas Peacock*. Janey is riding shotgun. There's jazz on the stereo, and it smells of cigarettes and French fries. For the first time since I left Montana, I feel like I'm home.

4

THIS IS MY CHANCE to ask about the place on Beaver Creek and whether Jonas has talked to his uncle—Janey's uncle, too, I suppose—but I kind of hate to kill the warm fuzzy feeling we've got going on right now as we head north through town, past the mom and pop stores, one of a kind restaurants, gas stations and cheap beach motels.

We'll be at the Coast Inn in just a few minutes. I open my mouth. "I was wondering—" I begin, but Janey interrupts. "So Joney, how are the kiddos?"

Jonas shakes his head. "Twice as much fun as a pack of puppies. Today we had two dentist appointments."

"Dentist? They barely have teeth."

"Tell that to the bite marks on my arm. Anyway, Molly wanted to get them started early. Since she's got the insurance from work, I didn't argue."

"I know how much you love going to the dentist for your own teeth. I'll bet this was loads of fun."

Jonas chuckles. "They didn't know what they were getting into until Ty was in the chair. He started crying, and then Tim started bawling. The hygienist got all freaked out, and I don't know what good it all did, but it wasn't cheap. And we just got the bill from the preschool. Next time, I'm getting dogs."

"No, you love them. I'll take 'em any time you don't want 'em." Janey turns toward me. "You should see them, P.D. They are the cutest things. You got any kids?"

I shake my head. "Nope."

"Oh. Me either. Not yet anyway."

I know she's going to ask me next if I'm married or divorced or what, so I change the subject. "I'm at the Coast Inn, just up ahead."

"Cool," Jonas says.

I'm about to ask him about Beaver Creek when his phone buzzes. I hear a one-sided conversation about a fare waiting at a house near the bridge over Yaquina Bay at the south end of town.

When I finally get the words out, we're already parking in front of the office at the Coast Inn. "Hey Jonas, I know it's only been a few hours, but did you have a chance to talk to your uncle about that property on Beaver Creek?"

"Oh yeah, Uncle Donovan. I called him. He wants to meet you."

His phone rings again. He assures whoever is calling he's on his way, then turns back to me.

"He'll be in town on Friday night. I'll call you to set it up. I've gotta go. Janey, you're riding along with me. This old guy is getting impatient."

I get out. It's so cold after the warmth of the cab I'm shivering. "Okay. Thanks for the ride. Bye."

I barely get the door closed before Jonas peels out of the lot and back onto the highway.

Well, I tell myself as I limp on my blisters past dark windows and other windows lit up with TVs flickering through the curtains, I sang, I made a new friend, and now I know Jonas's uncle's first name: Donovan. I just have to amuse myself till Friday night.

Another fight with the key card. Another victory. I switch on the box heater under the window and turn on the TV, cranking the sound up high so I can hear it over the fan.

I shuck my sandals and pull on some socks from the dirty clothes bag. I'm going to have to hit the laundromat tomorrow or start wearing dirty underwear. Suddenly I have this moment of reality. Call it a flash of Cissy-ness. Or maybe it's the beer wearing off. What the hell am I doing in this motel room by myself in this little town with no job, not much money, and this cockamamie dream of being a singer?

I run my hand through my hair. It's growing out, getting too long to stand up. Under the eye-blasting lights over the sink, I can see brown and a little gray along the roots. Sigh. Sometimes it's hard work being P.D.

I'M NOT GOOD at waiting. Not at all. "*Paciencia.*" Patience. Tom used to say it to me all the time. His mother put a religious spin on it. Have faith, she would say. Just wait and have faith.

Faith. I'm not so good at that part anymore either. I prayed myself silly when Tom first got sick, and it didn't do any good at all. I kept going to church, where everybody said they were praying for us. Well, thank you, but so what?

In the morning, I do the laundry, buy a fedora and a pair of jeans at Salvation Army, and go to the music store to put up the notice I wrote on motel stationery: *singer/keyboard player seeking band—jazz, blues, pop, anything but hip-hop.*

The store is closed, even though the sign on the door says they're open from 10 to 5 Monday through Saturday. I am never going to get used to the casual way business owners here treat their hours. Mostly one-person operations, they're closed whenever they decide they want to be closed. Tuesdays? Why not? Noon on a Saturday? Gone fishing. No wonder they're all going broke. At least Missoula businesses kept regular hours.

If I can't get any attention at the music store, maybe I should just go down to the waterfront, put my new hat on a bench and sing. But it's another misty cold day, and I don't feel like competing with the sea lions which bark incessantly while the tourists lean over the railing talking to them as if they were puppies. Oh, don't get me wrong, I like sea lions, but I can't out-sing them.

When in doubt, work out. The gym is empty. Mine, all mine. P.D. is in the building.

A GIRL CAN ONLY work out so long. While I was running on the treadmill, the sky outside turned black and it rained. I guess I'm just going to have to get used to the fact that it can rain here at any time, even on what starts out as a sunny day. Now it's clear again. A shower, some juice and a granola bar, and I'm driving to Beaver Creek. Just because Jonas's Uncle Donovan is not available doesn't mean I can't go look around by myself. I checked the phone book in my room, looking for a Donovan Peacock, but I found only Jonas and Molly. It would be helpful to know the address, but off I go, driving south out of Newport.

The 1930s bridge over Yaquina Bay is nearly a mile long, decorated with concrete towers and a big arch. Below, to the east, I see boats, restaurants and shops lining the waterfront. To the west, the bay stretches toward the ocean, with rock jetties on either side. A fishing boat heads out, its wake like a wide V. I can't believe I've been here for weeks and haven't crossed this bridge before.

I pass a seafood restaurant, a glass-blowing shop, and a few houses, then find myself on open road paralleling the ocean. South Beach. Lost Creek. Ona Beach. Turn left on Beaver Creek Road. I pass a boat launch area and head through miles of what looks like marshes with skinny white trees and some kind of yellow grass sticking up. A snowy egret fishes on the right. A flock of ducks, mallards I think, float along on the left. Elk crossing sign. Nice. Nature.

After a mile or so, I start seeing houses. Big houses up long driveways, with RVs and horse trailers parked out front. I could be happy in one of these. I pass the entrance to the Oregon State Parks Natural Wilderness Area. Something to check out later. As the road starts heading uphill, the houses grow more sparse, tucked up long dirt roads. Look at that shack, about to fall down. No, no, no. I hope that's not it.

Cattle, black and white. Why does this Uncle Donovan need somebody to house-sit? Why not just stop the mail, lock the door and have a friend drive by once in a while? Or rent it like I did my house in Missoula? Maybe he's got animals or exotic plants. Maybe he's growing marijuana. Maybe he has jewels or famous paintings or . . .

Pavement ends. Gravel road ahead. A narrow road to my right leads to Drift Creek Wilderness and Horse Creek trail. I need a map before I go off that way. This road is going to be challenging enough.

Gravel road plus wet weather equals mud. I can feel it coating my tires and the bottom of my car as I roll along. It's narrow, winding and mostly deserted. But little roads lead off here and there.

You have to look hard to see them. Wait, that's a nice house. That one, too. That one seems to have holes between the boards.

The road has turned north and keeps going uphill. It's marshy down below to my left, but there's a for-sale sign. Want to buy a swamp?

Great. There's a truck behind me, using headlights and fog lights in the middle of the day. The driver seems to want to go fast, but if I go any faster, I'll slide right off the road. Plus, is that rain? Oh yes. Little drops, then big ol' honkin' drops. Hold on, buddy, I've seen enough. I'm turning around.

Okay, a pullout. I'm turning, sloshing through the mud. Lord, don't let me get stuck. The truck flies by. I have no idea where Uncle Donovan's house is. I'm going back to civilization.

Do I want to drive this road every day? In the rain? My car is covered with mud. Some of it is even splattered on the windows. Maybe this is nuts. Maybe I should find a job in town and a nice normal apartment.

I'm tired. I'm staying in tonight and reading the trashy novel I bought at Salvation Army for 50 cents. Too Cissy? Who cares?

5

I'M STANDING JUST inside the door at Izzy's Pizza waiting for Jonas and his Uncle Donovan. I'm way early. I watch people come in and get seated and go through the buffet line. I swear every person complains they got too much at the salad bar and now they don't have any room on their plate for pizza or fried chicken. Everyone. Plan ahead, people.

I don't know. Maybe I don't want to stay here in Newport. It has been four days since the karaoke experience, and the charm is wearing off. It was raining cats and dogs when I got up, and I didn't get much sleep because my neighbors had this big fight, screaming and banging the furniture around. The police came, blue and red lights flashing through my curtains at 2:30 a.m., people shouting, doors slamming. I wanted to be back in my own bed in my own house in Missoula. When I finally got up, I didn't have anything to do except read and watch TV. Well, I did walk down the street to the Shilo Inn and ask if I could play the piano in the bar for tips. They said no, they only have music for Sunday brunch, and the same guy has been doing it for 15 years. How do I compete with that?

Where was *your* last gig, P.D.?

Bud Meyer's funeral. Back when I had brown hair.

Did I mention I tried to get my hair done this afternoon, but it cost so much I gave up and bought a box of dye at the Rite Aid store? I trimmed my hair a little bit with my nail scissors and got all ready to do the dye, but then I thought I'd get in trouble if I got orange stains all over the motel towels. Maybe I'll go back to Salvation Army and buy a towel or two. I know, it's very Cissy to even worry about this stuff. P.D. shouldn't care. Whatever. Get off my back. On a positive note, I'm wearing my new Salvation Army hat. It's black with a red beaded band and so cool.

Izzy's is up on a hill at the north end of Newport. Out the windows beyond the tables, I can see the ocean. The sun is heading toward the horizon, turning the shoreline silver. A couple guys in wetsuits surf nearby. A man runs with his dog. This isn't too far from where that dock landed. I wonder if any more tsunami debris has washed up on the beach.

The door opens, letting in a blast of cold air—what is it with the weather here?—and I see this giant, I mean giant. He's maybe six-six, with a graying brown beard, a leather watch cap and an earring in his left ear. He's wearing a white shirt with this amazing beaded vest and jeans.

Uncle Donovan? Lord have mercy.

I expected a clean-cut, married, golf shirt-and-khakis-wearing Republican, a corporate type who has enough money to own several homes. I got Santa Claus without his red suit. I'm pretty sure I'll be tending marijuana plants.

I should have known he wasn't the CEO type when he chose Izzy's instead of April's or some other posh eatery. Fine by me. This is cheaper, and I'm not sure who's paying.

"P.D.?" he asks.

"Yes," I say. "Hi. You must be Donovan. I love your hat."

"I like yours, too," he says.

"Thanks." I'm about to tell him how I found it at Salvation Army when Jonas comes in with his wife Molly and their two little boys, Tim and Ty, about three years old. Oh, surprise. I didn't expect the whole family.

Introductions. Molly is pretty, brown-haired, slimmer than I would expect anyone to be after having twins. She says hi, but all her attention is on those boys, who are like wild puppies eager to run.

"Why don't you go get us a table in the other room?" Jonas says to Molly. One of the boys, Ty I find out later—he's the one with the blue T-shirt, as opposed to Tim with the yellow T-shirt—jets out so fast he almost trips a waitress carrying a tray of drinks. Oh, this is going to be fun.

We hustle into the other room, and I wind up on the ocean side of the table between Jonas and Donovan while Molly wrangles the boys on the other side. Donovan doesn't even look at the menu. "How about the classic buffet all round?"

Wait. I still don't know who's paying. "I think I'll just do the salad bar," I say.

"What and miss the breadsticks and dessert?" Donovan asks.

"I want pizza!" screams Ty. Or is it Tim? Blue shirt. Ty.

"You'll get pizza," Molly says, pulling a spoon out of his hand just before he bangs it on the table.

I feel Donovan's big paw on my shoulder and peer up into eyes full of kindness. "This is on me. Go for it."

I notice a blue-green rock shining from a black cord at his neckline. Are those sparkles of gold?

"Okay. Classic buffet."

Maybe there's money in this marijuana business. I hear the plants grow like weeds. Ah, weed, get it?

As the waitress comes to take our drink orders, Donovan smiles at her. I see so much compassion in that smile I think about Tom and my heart hurts.

We're all getting up now, going to the buffet. Donovan nudges me ahead of him, and I load up on salad. Greens and beans. Potato salad. Grated cheese. Pineapple, strawberries, honeydew melon. I'm thinking I'll skip the pizza.

I glance back and see Donovan is taking almost as much salad as I am. Jonas is helping Tim pick out a few bites of fruit while Molly and Ty are already at the pizza bar. I scoot ahead to grab a breadstick, passing fried chicken, pork ribs, and macaroni and cheese. Donovan is right behind me.

"No chicken?" I ask.

"No, I don't eat meat."

Interesting.

A black man in motorcycle leathers walks up to Donovan and slaps him on the back. "Hey, Donovan Green, you old Irishman, I didn't know you were in town."

He turns and embraces him. "Good to see you. Yes, I'm here, hiding out as usual, but I'll be leaving soon."

"Well, call me before you go."

"I will."

I'm thinking, Green. Oh. He has a different last name. Of course. He must be their mother's brother. No wonder I couldn't find him in the phone book.

We get back to the table before the others. Donovan and I have both ordered iced tea. I would have figured him for a beer man. While I'm pondering this, he picks up his fork and sets it back down. "We probably ought to talk business before the others get back."

My stomach knots with nerves. "Yes. Good idea."

"So, I've got this place out on Beaver Creek. It's up the road apiece. I don't know if you've been there."

"I drove out yesterday, but I didn't know which place was yours."

"Well, it's 2.5 miles past the visitor's center and up a narrow driveway to the east. A little rustic, but I like it. Unfortunately, I can't stay here all year. I have a home and shop to tend in Portland and another place in Tucson. You see, I make glass art, sculptures, and jewelry, mostly from recycled items and natural materials like rocks and shells. I'd rather do it here, but I have to go where the galleries are and where the customers live. I also hate the rain. So come November, I head east."

I'm thinking *no marijuana*? But I have another question. "What about your wife?" It just slips out.

He sips his tea. "No wife. Not anymore."

The others are coming with their loaded plates. "So here's the deal. I keep a lot of my tools and jewels at the place on Beaver Creek. I've got a garden I'd like to keep alive. And I've got a couple cats who do not travel well. Plus, the place molds if it stays cold and damp. So I'm looking for somebody to keep it warm, feed the cats and make sure nobody steals the jewels and tools."

"What! You're telling her about the family jewels?" Jonas says as he sets down his plate and situates little Tim on his booster seat.

"Something like that." Donovan takes a big bite of salad. "So, P.D., do you have an actual name?"

"Just P.D."

Our eyes meet and I hold my breath. What if he insists on knowing my name?

"I like it," he says. "Jonas says you're a singer."

"That's right."

"I'd like to hear you sometime."

"Well, I'm doing the open mic at Café Mundo tomorrow night."

"Excellent. I'll go with you. If you don't mind."

He turns to his food with such gusto it appears our conversation is over. But that can't be it.

"What else do you want to know about me?"

He clears his throat. "I guess I should ask some questions, huh? Got a car?" I nod. "Available for the next seven months?" I nod. "Ever killed anybody?" I shake my head no. "Good. We'll work out the details later." He reaches out his hand to shake. I like the way my hand feels in his.

Donovan turns to his great-nephew. "Now, Mr. Tim, that's a big piece of pizza for such a little boy."

"I'm a big boy," the kid says.

Donovan ruffles his tawny hair.

I wonder if he'll grow up to be as tall as his uncle.

Suddenly I'm starving. P.D. or not, I'm hitting the dessert bar.

SATURDAY NIGHT at Café Mundo. He's here, this time without Jonas and his entourage. Donovan Green, Jonas' mother's brother, sitting beside me in this new-agey restaurant where you couldn't get processed food or a real Coca-Cola if you wanted it. I consider the hanging sculptures that look like oversized origami or out-of-control piñatas and wonder if Donovan's art is anything like this.

"They have some interesting art here," I try.

"Yes," he says, taking a bite of his fish taco without even looking at the art.

Does that mean . . . what does that mean? He hates it, he loves it, it's not worthy of his attention?

I'm acutely aware of being out to dinner with a man who is not Tom. But this isn't a date, is it? We both dressed up a little. Donovan bought me dinner. We both ordered the fish tacos and the weedy salad with raspberry vinaigrette. I had a taste for a glass of wine, but Donovan ordered iced tea, so I asked for the same. This kind of feels like a date. Or am I just meeting my new landlord? It's weird enough, but then I'm supposed to sing.

The stage is downstairs. We're sitting upstairs looking down on it. I hope I don't fall down the steps when it's my turn. I got permission to use the house band's electronic piano on the stage, but I haven't touched a keyboard in a month—except for that one at the store—and Donovan will be listening, and, and, and, that's whiny old Cissy speaking. I need to channel P.D. Fifteen minutes singing at a little open mic in this nowhere restaurant in this nowhere town is nothing for her.

Sure, that's why she spent all afternoon practicing.

Donovan hasn't told me much about himself. In fact, he has been much quieter than he seemed at Izzy's the other night. I tell him about Tom, about my house in Montana. I even tell him about my dog disappearing. Okay, I spill my guts. But he's a sympathetic listener. He doesn't get all gooey on me, all "poor you." Nor does he insist I have a plan. He just nods and listens. At one point, he kind of sighs, shakes his head and says, "Hard times."

That's it. "Hard times."

And what do I do? I make a dumb joke. "I think that's the title of a song."

Silence. I change the subject. "Tell me about your place at Beaver Creek."

"Well," he says, sitting back in his chair, thumbs tucked into his suspenders. "It's up in the trees, but I've got a great view of the valley and the creek from my studio in the back. You do any arts or crafts?"

I laugh. He's staring at me like he really wants me to say yes. "I used to do a lot of needlework, but I kind of let that go."

He shrugs. "Maybe you'll take it up again."

"Maybe. So how big is the house?"

"Not too big. It's—oh hey, aren't you next?"

On the stage, this guy with an English accent is reciting a pornographic poem. He's number four, and I'm number five. "Yes. I don't know why I'm so nervous."

"You'll do great. I know it." He winks and I blush.

Applause. Jesus, it's my turn. I do know why I'm nervous. The stairs, the piano, the songs, Donovan listening, wanting so bad to be a real singer. It was easier when it was just a hobby. But I'm also aware this is how I met Tom, singing at an open mic in Santa Cruz. As I cross the downstairs room to the stage, I can almost see him sitting at a table by the window, smiling at me. There's a little too much *Deja vu* going on.

We waste a few minutes with the M.C. futzing around trying to get the mic situated in front of my mouth. But finally he backs off and introduces me. "Here's P.D."

Two people applaud, the M.C. and Donovan. A few people stare at me while the rest keep eating and talking. A waitress with pink hair sets a dish of marionberry cobbler with two forks in front of a couple near the stage.

"Please, God," I pray, then strike the first notes of Billy Joel's "Piano Man." I make a mistake right away, but I play around it enough that I hope nobody notices. Shoot, half the people in here aren't even listening. I clear my throat and start singing. It isn't my best, but it isn't terrible. More people clap.

I start to calm down and get in the zone. For my second song, I do a heart-rending "Motherless Child," then completely change the mood with Tina Turner's "Proud Mary."

Big applause.

And I'm done. Three songs, and you're out. On to the young guys with the squealing guitars. The ones all the kids downstairs have been waiting for.

I wish they'd let me play all night. Someday, somewhere, I'm going to make that happen.

When I stand up, my legs are shaking. There must be a hundred steps.

Back at the table, where I'm hoping to collapse into a tall glass of wine, whether Donovan wants one or not, I find my "date" putting two twenty dollar bills on the table.

"Good singing," he says. "You ready to go?"

That's it? Go where? Is he thinking we'll go back to his place and fool around? He doesn't seem like that kind of guy.

As I put on my coat, he tells me he goes to bed early, likes to see the sun rise.

"Want to join me?" he asks after the waitress takes his money.

Wait? Is he asking me to spend the night with him? Whoa, big guy. I just came here to sing and get a place to live.

"If you come by about 7:30 a.m., the light will be just right to really appreciate the view from the cabin. Then I can show you around and give you the key. I have to head back to Portland in the afternoon."

7:30 in the morning? I look into those green eyes that seem to have glints of gold around the edges. He's serious. "Okay. Just tell me how to get there."

Ten minutes later, after a short ride in Donovan's red pickup, I'm back at the Coast Inn, asking myself, "What just happened?"

6

BY THE TIME I'm dressed, the sky is turning from black to gray. I've been awake since before my cell phone alarm went off. Too much to think about, all with "Proud Mary" playing over and over in my brain until I want to knock myself unconscious with my blow-dryer.

Channeling one of those stupid self-help books I read right after Tom died, I tell myself "one step at a time" and go through my routine: shower, get dressed, eat a granola bar and wash it down with coffee, brush my teeth, paint my face, shove my room key into my back pocket, grab my coat and bag, go.

What is appropriate attire for this? Beats me. I've got on my Salvation Army jeans and an old plaid shirt of Tom's with my tennis shoes and another necklace he gave me, a tiny beagle on a gold chain.

Thank God it's not raining. In fact, in fact I see a hint of blue in the western sky. It's 7:20. I'm probably going to be a few minutes late, but hey, come on. Drive through town. Over the bridge, past the fish shop, the auto repair place, the storage lockers, the trees, turn left at Ona Beach.

I see what Donovan was saying about the light. Now the sky is five shades of pink and red, and the water is practically on fire. A sliver of moon hangs over the hills. I'm looking around, noting the birds, the clouds, the creek, distracting my nervous self by wondering what the technical terms are for all this stuff, when I see something out of the corner of my eye. Something big. Eyes forward, P.D. There's an elk crossing the road right in front of me. I slam the brakes, skid a little and miss him as he nonchalantly strolls to the other side.

"Shit." My heart is pounding. I want to stop and calm down, but my car clock says it's already 7:34.

Onward, upward, visitor's center. Note the mileage. Rattle over the gravel road. At 2.5 miles up, I slow way down. I don't see anything for a minute. I have to turn the car around and look again before I see the driveway going into the trees.

It's almost quarter to 8. I'm surprised Donovan hasn't called me—until I check my phone. No reception. Deep breath. If it doesn't work out, I can look for something else, but here I go.

By now, the colors have faded into pillowy pink clouds on a bed of pale blue. They call Montana "Big Sky Country," but I never saw a sunrise quite this beautiful. It was worth getting up early.

Is that his cabin?

It's a log cabin with a totem pole out front, a rock-edged garden that appears to include stained glass flowers and weird sculptures made of sea shells and trash among the real plants, and a wide porch with two wooden rockers. Trees, mostly what I'd call pine trees, stand like sentinels guarding the house.

P.D. likes it. Cissy is still wondering about that road.

I chuckle as I think about what my mother would say. I'll send her a picture of one of those mini-mansions down the hill. Then I think about what Tom's mother would say, Gracia with her Portuguese accent. "It's cute," she would say. She grew up in a rock-walled hovel with dirt floors in the Azores, so she has slightly lower expectations. Tom's dad, a retired contractor, also Portuguese but back a generation, would shake his head. "It's going to fall down." My dad, on the other hand, my wandering father camping somewhere around Wyoming, would say, "When can I move in?"

What would Tom say? He'd gaze at me, stroke his mustache, and say, "Are you sure about this?"

But I'm liking it. The wood is still new-looking, and it seems like a cozy place to stay while I build my music career. Let's get out of the car and start this new adventure.

No one answers when I knock on the door. I remember what Donovan said about the view from his studio and follow a graveled path around the back. The ground slopes down, and the house hangs on stilts above it here. On a patch of grass at the edge of a cliff, I find Donovan in a heavy black coat looking through a pair of binoculars at the valley spread out below.

The dawn colors are fading, but it's still a great view. Beaver Creek threads silver through green pastures in which black and white cattle graze. It goes on forever.

I make plenty of noise with my shoes crunching on the rocks, but he doesn't seem to hear me. I clear my throat. Still nothing. "Good morning!" I semi-shout.

He turns. "Ah, you missed the best of it."

"No, I saw some wonderful colors coming in. Got so entranced I almost hit an elk."

He nods. "You have to watch out for them. Well, let me show you around."

He leads me first under the back of the house. I wonder if those stilts can really hold it up. "How long has this place been here?" I ask.

"Oh, I built it about six years ago. Lived here full-time at first. I was going through some stuff and needed to get my bearings. It's served me well." He turns away and sighs.

There's something subdued about him this morning. He seems to be moving slowly, reluctant to talk. Is he changing his mind about letting me stay here?

He continues the tour. "Now this, as you can see, is the woodpile. The fireplace is your main source of heat. Every year I stack up a couple cords of wood. Depending on how the winter goes, it may or may not be enough. You might have to get some more. I try to keep it covered so as to keep out the rain, as well as the squirrels and raccoons and other critters that like to nest in there, but it tends to be a losing battle."

Wood. Squirrels. Raccoons. Check.

"That's my kiln over there. No need to worry about that. Now, that locked cabinet is where I store tools to maintain the yard and house. I'll give you a key. I would like you to keep up my garden, such as it is. Have you got any experience gardening?"

Cissy does. Little Holly Housewife that she was. "Yes. I had quite a garden back in Missoula."

"Good." He looks around. "I guess most of this is self-explanatory. Let's go in."

He leads me up the back stairs. There's a small balcony with a wooden chair and a small round table. I can imagine sitting out here enjoying the view with a glass of wine.

The back door opens into his studio. Wow.

I feel like a kid who just walked into the toy factory. There's a giant table with what must be his current project on it. Rocks, shells, feathers, pieces of red glass. Beads of every size and color. The room smells of solder and glue. Oh my God, I want to touch everything at once. I want to sit here and make stuff. Put on some music, let me at it, and I'll talk to you in 20 years or so.

"I love this place," I say.

"Me too."

"How can you leave it?"

He shrugs. "Got to. But now you can see why I'd prefer to have someone watch over it."

"Sure."

He leads the way into the rest of the house. Our feet echo on hardwood floors decorated with Native American-patterned rugs.

It's not fancy. Just one bedroom, barely big enough for a double bed covered with a patchwork quilt, a nightstand with a lamp and a candle, and a shelf where Donovan's clothes are neatly stacked. There's a tiny bathroom, all wood-paneled, with a shower over a tub that can't possibly accommodate someone as tall as Donovan, and a living room-kitchen combination with a sink, stove and refrigerator along one wall, a counter in the middle, and two easy chairs and a wooden rocker circled around a fireplace at the other end. Donovan has a fire going, and it's warm. I'd like to curl up in one of those chairs and go back to sleep.

"I've got quite a bit of food stashed in the cupboards here, and you're welcome to eat it. I'd rather you enjoy it than have it go bad."

"Thank you. I appreciate that." That will save me a few bucks.

"Let's see. What else?" He's gazing around his house as if he just bought it. "Oh yeah. There's no sewer system up here, so you're on a septic tank. That shouldn't be a problem, but you ought to know. The water comes from a well, usually pretty dependable, but keep some extra water handy just in case. Now, the electricity is *not* so dependable. It tends to go out during storms, and we tend to be the last ones to get our power back. So I've got a lot of flashlights and candles."

I'm nodding, feeling little lightning bugs in my stomach. "You don't have cell phone reception here?"

He shakes his head. "No. I drive down the road apiece until I get a couple bars. I disconnected the landline because I'm hardly ever here. I hope that's not a problem. I guess you could hook it up if you need to, but you'd have to pay for it and put it in your name."

"Oh, no, that's okay." I lie. No phone? But who would I call? Oh, but how would people reach me if they want to hire me? I guess I'll drive down the road apiece.

"You have a computer?"

"No. I left it in Montana."

"Just as well. I don't have any hookups for that either. But they've got Wi-Fi at the diner in Seal Rock and at various places in Newport. I don't have a TV, so no worries about cable or satellite. The radio works pretty well."

I'm just standing here nodding like a fool. All I want to do is go to sleep in front of that fireplace. But what am I doing? Shouldn't I consider other options?

Now he's grabbing a set of keys off the mantel and handing them to me, along with a business card that lists several phone numbers for him.

That's it? No contract? No background check?

"You can move in this afternoon, if you want," he says. He's looking down at me, and I don't know what he expects now. A joyful shout? A teary thank you for giving this homeless widow a place to stay? A hug? I just don't know.

"I'll be gone until Memorial Day. Think you can stick it out that long?

Seven months. I shrug. "Sure. No problem." Cissy is shrieking in my ear. *Problem? Yes, there's a problem.*

I hear meows behind me and see a brown Persian cat sneaking up. When I reach to pet it, it runs away. "You said something about taking care of the cats."

For the first time since I got here, he smiles as he picks up the meowing ball of fur and cuddles her against his chest. "Yes, I'm sorry. This is Sasha, my little girl. She's skittish. Hernando, my male tabby, is prowling around somewhere. You'll find their food in the cupboards, and I'd appreciate it if you'd bring them in at night. It's not really safe. A lot of cats disappear around here with the cougars and raccoons."

I nod again. Cougars. Right. "Okay."

"Oh, and don't leave any kind of food out. It attracts the bears."

Bears.

He sets Sasha down gently. "All right, I'll let you go pack up. I'm leaving for Portland about 3:00." He holds out his massive hand. I give him mine and he holds it for a long time. "Thank you, P.D." Then he lets go. "Bye now."

Dismissed. Keys in my pocket. Driving my car back down that gravel road, thinking, *what have I done*?

IT'S SO BRIGHT I reach for my sunglasses as I come out of the trees and turn onto the paved road. Ah, quietness after the bumps and noises of the gravel road coming from Donovan's place. I can feel the keys in my back pocket pushing against my rump. I suppose I should put them on my chain.

Am I out of my mind? No TV, no Internet, no phone, no sewer, well water, frequent power outages, wild animals—hold the phone, Nellie. I'm not even sure he knows my last name. Maybe I should turn around and tell him I can't do this. The cabin is cute and all, but what am I going to do up there? I might go nuts being alone all the time.

What are my alternatives? Do I want to chase my renters out and go back to being the poor widow Cissy in Missoula? No. Do I want to go home to Mom, who tells me I'm too old to be a singer? Hell no.

It's a free place to stay. I can come down the hill every day if I want to. I can get a job in town. All I have to do is sleep there. It's very P.D.

Yes, I'd rather have Tom and the life we had planned. I'd like to have kids, a dog, and a house with a white picket fence. I also want to sing and play for a living.

But as the song says, "You Can't Always Get What You Want."

It's not quite 8:30. Ona Beach is right across the road. I'm going to stop, take a walk and clear my mind. For once, it's warm and sunny.

I park next to the only other car in the parking lot, a green Subaru wagon with a kayak rack on top. The owner is probably on the water. I picture myself stroking gently down the creek, looking at the birds and beavers. It sounds so peaceful. I wonder if Donovan has a kayak or rowboat stashed somewhere that I could use. I'll bet he does.

A muddy path cuts through the wet grass that leads to the banks of Beaver Creek. I don't want wet feet, but the river draws me. I hear it rippling against the mud and leaves on the banks. The sun sparkles off the current rushing west. I breathe in the cool air, smell the ferns and pines. It's delicious, so different from the dusty dry air in Missoula.

I'm still standing there when a ranger pulls up in his green truck and walks my way.

"Nice day," he says.

"Beautiful."

He hurries on toward the restrooms.

I wind along the path, crossing a wooden footbridge and coming out between the dunes onto a little beach with rocks on my left and Beaver Creek flowing toward the ocean on my right. The tide is way out. Gulls and pelicans congregate near the waterline as if they're having a meeting.

Not another soul on the beach.

I pull off my shoes. The sand feels cool on my feet, and a light breeze gentles my face. It's fine sand here, soft and Army blanket gray, dark where the water laps at it in big scalloped sections. Clumps of seaweed, rocks, shells and sticks decorate the beach. I fight against the memory of our honeymoon on another beach far away. Tom and I played in the water, collected shells and lay together on a Mexican blanket, touching each other's faces, amazed to have found each other. Do you know what that feels like, just to feel so blessed to love someone who loves you back?

No crying, no more crying. Deep breath. I dash away the tears and keep walking. *Keep moving* has become my mantra lately. Keep the body fit and busy, and the mind will follow. Somewhere up ahead is Seal Rock. Maybe a mile or so? Do I want to go that far? My stomach gurgles in answer. I need breakfast.

That's what I'm thinking when I see something sticking out of the sand. It glitters and I squat down to look. I scarcely breathe as I pull out a tiny bracelet. I'm pretty sure the writing on it is Japanese. The bracelet is silver, with pink hearts around the words. Is it from the tsunami? I can't imagine something coming this far to land on a beach in Oregon.

Clearly it belongs to a little girl. What happened to her? Did she die in the tsunami? Did the bracelet come off in the water? Or was this washed out of her bedroom while she fled with her family to higher ground?

If she's alive, is there some way I can get it back to her?

Of course, she could have come here from Portland with her family on vacation, but what if the tsunami really did carry it all the way from Japan?

I'm still squatting and not paying any attention to the ocean when a sneaker wave breaks from the pack and knocks me down. Cold! The current pulls at me as I scurry on my hands and knees to dry sand. If it were just a little bigger, that wave could have taken me out to sea. Just like those people in Japan. Time to turn back.

I'm soaked right through my pants, underwear, shoes and socks. Suddenly it seems like an awful long way to the car.

I reach the footbridge just as the ranger is pulling a big garbage can off the beach. Cissy would be too embarrassed by her wet clothes to say anything, but P.D. doesn't have time for that.

"Hey, is that from Japan?" I call.

He laughs and shakes his head. He's cute, all sandy-haired and freckled. Reminds me of my brother, if he were a little older. "Nope, it's all-American."

I catch up with him and hold out the bracelet. "I think this is from Japan."

"Oh?" He takes it from me, studies it. "Huh. I think you're right."

"What should I do with it?"

"Well, we've got some people working on things like this, trying to get items of monetary or sentimental value back to their owners. I don't know how they'll find them. Maybe the writing on here would give them a clue. I can turn it in for you."

"Good. Thanks. Can you maybe let me know what happens to it?"

"Yeah, sure." He pulls a notepad out of his breast pocket. "What's your name and number?"

I tell him, wishing I already had those business cards. Monday, they said.

"P.D.? What does that stand for?"

I smile. "Just P.D."

"Well, okay. I'm Dave. Thanks." He slips the bracelet into his pants pocket and goes back to hauling the garbage can up. As I start to walk back to my car, I hear the scraping of metal on pavement stop.

"P.D.?" I turn to see him studying my soggy attire.

"How'd you get all wet?"

"Sneaker wave."

He shakes his head. "Never turn your back on the ocean."

I know that. I grew up on the beach. They said the same thing in Santa Cruz. But he doesn't know where I'm from.

"People have drowned here in waves that caught them just a little bit higher. I'd hate to see that happen to you."

"Me too. I just got so caught up in the bracelet I forgot for a second."

"Well, take care," he says, starting to walk away.

It's mid-morning, and I've got an urge for biscuits and gravy. "Hey," I call. "Is there someplace good to eat around here?"

He stops. "Sure. Go south about a half mile and you'll come to the diner in Seal Rock. You won't find anything better around here."

"Thanks."

My stomach growls as I get back into the car and head south. I find the D & K Diner on the east side of the highway next to a real estate office and an antique store. The parking lot is crowded with American-made pickup trucks so big they make my little Volt look like a toy. Even in Missoula, this car stuck out as a yuppie commuter car, but here, oh my God. I might as well be carrying a briefcase and wearing high heels. Without Tom's income, it may be the last new car I ever have. I try not to think about that as I pull my wet pants away from my legs and push into the diner.

I find myself in a sea of men with baseball caps. A smiling woman with soft-looking blonde hair welcomes me.

"Good morning. Here for breakfast?"

"Yes."

I feel the men gazing at me over their coffee cups. Manly young men in their Carhartts and fishing boots, older men in flannel shirts. I guess these are going to be my neighbors, so I force a smile and follow the woman to my seat near the window. I want to channel a little Mae West and coo "Good morning, boys," in a voice that would melt butter, just for grins, but I don't want to call attention to my wet pants.

"Coffee?"

I nod, and she fills the cup already waiting there. It's warm liquid comfort. I start to relax. I feel a heater blowing near my feet. Good. My damp clothes are making me cold.

Somebody left a copy of the local paper on the table next to mine, so I grab it and amuse myself by reading about the water board, fishing regulations, a benefit for a kid in a wheelchair, and a tsunami drill. I swear these people are obsessed with tsunamis. I guess I won't have to worry about that way up the hill.

"P.D.!" cries a high voice. I look up to see my karaoke buddy Janey, wearing an apron over her red T-shirt and blue jeans, her curly hair corralled into a messy bun.

"Hey!" I can't believe how happy I am to see her. "You work here?"

"Yes, it's my mom's restaurant. She's Diana of D & K."

"I had no idea. That's fantastic. I'm about to move into your Uncle Donovan's place. Maybe I'll come here a lot."

Behind her, a guy is holding out his empty cup. "Darlin'."

She glances back. "Just a second, Uncle Rick. That's great, P.D. I'd love to talk, but we're slammed. What can I get you?"

I haven't even looked at the menu. "You got biscuits and gravy?"

She smiles. "Sure. Full or half order?"

"Full."

"With scrambled eggs?"

"Why not?"

And she's off, filling Uncle Rick's cup and several others, then disappearing into the kitchen.

Great coffee, biscuits and gravy, sunshine and a new friend. I feel good. I glance out the window at the sun sparkling on the ocean, then realize Uncle Rick, this forty-something guy with intensely blue eyes, is watching me. I smile and toast him with my coffee cup. He toasts me back. I feel my face turning red and focus my attention on an article about a Lutheran ladies pie social. Is he really another one of Janey's uncles?

7

A STACK OF LIBRARY BOOKS and my ice chest on the seat beside me, keys to my new home in my pocket, I head back up the hill to Beaver Creek a little after 3 o'clock. My tires crunch on the gravel, my white car gets another sprinkling of mud, and my radio starts to sputter as I watch the odometer. At 2.5 miles past the visitor's center, I turn up the narrow road to the cabin.

As I get out, I hear the whine of a chain saw from somewhere nearby. Pine tinges the air up here, where I can't see another house, just trees and wild blackberry vines. Compared to the weathered homes I saw on the way up, this one stands out with its reddish wood and its garden full of totems and sculptures made of stained glass and kitchenware. How odd. Is this the garden I'm caring for?

I park my car in the empty place where Donovan's truck sat this morning. A gray tabby cat runs up and circles my feet. Hernando, I presume. I reach down to pet him, feel him purring and grab him up into my arms. Oh my God, it feels good to hug something. As I cuddle this cat against my chest, I hear a yowling from the porch. The other cat. Sasha. Maybe a little bribe would help her to accept me as her new friend.

I set Hernando down, grab my bags and climb the front porch steps. Despite the sun and the hour, the steps are damp. Apparently the sun never quite gets through the trees.

The key fits rough, and I have to mess with it a while before I can open the door to my new abode. It smells of wood smoke, dampness, and cats, with a hint of coffee. This morning I was so sleepy I didn't even notice.

Hernando dashes in past me while Sasha hesitates in the doorway.

"Come on," I urge. "I won't bite." I put my stuff down by the door and squat so I don't seem so much taller. I mean, I'm Gulliver to her. I reach out a hand. She hangs back, twitching her fluffy tail. "Sasha, it's okay." She moves to the edge of the porch, squeezing herself into a tight brown ball. I think ahead to nighttime and wonder how I'm going to corral these cats, especially Sasha. If I just try to grab her, will she run away or turn all teeth and claws?

She's not moving. Hernando is pacing in front of the cupboard to the right of the sink. "Fine. I'm going to give your brother a snack. You do what you want."

So I go in, leaving the door ajar. Hernando swishes back and forth against my jeans as I open the cupboard and find a bag of Friskies and a bunch of little cans of kitty salmon, tuna and chicken. Hernando leads me to a spot by the back door, where two little bowls are arranged on a plastic mat with a picture of a cat on it.

I pour kibble into the bowls. He dives in, and I pick up my bags to haul them into the bedroom. Zoom. There goes Sasha. Obviously, bribes work.

Now that I've made my acquaintance with my housemates, it's time to look around. The fire is down to red coals. I'm going to have to figure that out real fast because it's nippy in here. But first I start snooping in the cupboards, cabinets and closets. This place reminds me of a ski cabin Tom and I rented once. All wood, bare-bone supplies, fireplace, snow falling outside, snuggling under a handmade quilt, trees brushing against the sides of the cabin. That was our second or third or fourth honeymoon; I lost track. We had some great vacations. One of the advantages of a government salary and no kids.

Having emptied his bowl, Hernando is staring at me.

"Yeah," I tell him. "You should have met Tom."

Tom would have made sure the fire was always roaring. He would have done all the driving on this scary-ass road. He'd have chased away the bears and cougars.

Or would he? He was a suit-and-tie guy from the suburbs.

Sigh. I'm romanticizing him. He wasn't perfect, but I still wish he was here.

Anyway. What do I find? Instant oatmeal. Crackers. Cans of Campbell's soup, all meatless. A box of crackers. Cans of peaches and pears. Several jars of homemade jam. Blueberry, blackberry, huckleberry. I don't even know what huckleberries taste like.

Pine Sol. Comet cleanser. Dish soap. Broom, dustpan, mop. Lightbulbs. AA batteries. A box of cinnamon-scented votive candles.

The refrigerator's disappointing. A nearly-empty carton of low-fat milk, half a cube of butter on a plate, three brown eggs in the slots on the door. That's it.

Looks like I'm going shopping.

If I don't want to use up every cent left in my savings account, I'm going to need to find a job just to eat. Maybe Donovan has a vegetable garden hidden somewhere. I like the idea of living off the land, even if I do have a sudden craving for a hamburger.

We didn't talk at all about money. I assume there's no rent and Donovan's paying the electric bill. If something breaks, who pays to get it fixed? Why didn't I insist on something in writing? A contract. That's where Tom would have come in handy. He was a real by-the-book guy. It would all be written out with detailed provisions in case disputes arose. Witnessed and notarized.

All I've got are the keys and these cats.

I do have Donovan's phone numbers. I can always call him. I also have his studio. I need to settle my stuff into the bedroom and get a fire started, but first I'm checking out the studio.

Open the magic door. It's freezing in here. I hadn't really noticed the big windows before. There's that view, late-afternoon sun on the pastures, blue sky with wispy white clouds.

But hey, what gives? Did somebody have a fight in here? I see bits of broken red, green, and clear glass on the table and on the floor, and there's a big dark stain on the rug I don't think was here earlier. Blood? Oh my God, I'm out of here. Wait, no. It smells like wine. I bend closer to sniff. Merlot?

What happened? I guess it's none of my business. But where are all those wonderful goodies that were out before? You know, those things I was supposed to be guarding? Aside from a wooden object in the corner that looks like a coat rack with a monkey face, they're all gone.

Something doesn't feel right. Was there a break-in between his leaving and my arriving? The fire didn't even have time to go out.

Maybe Donovan needed broken glass for a sculpture. Maybe he was just in a hurry and dropped something. A few things. Yeah, I don't buy it either.

He might have put his art projects in those closets to the left there. I try both of the keys he gave me. Neither one works.

Well, once I clean off the broken glass, I'll have a big empty table, a weird monkey coat rack, an amazing view, and oh, look at this, a portable electric heater. I'll be using that.

The bedroom looks pretty much the same as it did this morning. I push open the plaid curtains to let a little light in. Two of the shelves are empty now, but Donovan has left a pair of rubber boots and a couple of flannel shirts. I bet I'll be using those, too.

I'm putting my clothes on the empty shelves when I hear a noise behind me. Fear streaks through my chest. Intruders? Bear? Donovan? I turn and find Hernando gnawing at the zipper pull on my suitcase. "Yikes. You scared the heck out of me, cat." He keeps gnawing until I gently shove him away. "No."

He goes right back to it until I empty the rest of my stuff on the bed and shove the bag underneath. He curls up on one of the pillows. Fine. For once I won't be sleeping alone.

Now let's see what's in the living room.

Have I mentioned I don't really know how to start a fire? Maybe I can resurrect this one so I don't have to start from scratch. There's a poker thing here. I shove the remnants of the old fire around. Nothing. I lean in and blow like I remember Tom doing once in a ski lodge. I get a face full of ashes. I blow more softly. Nothing. I blow again, controlling the air as best I can. Ha! A tiny finger of flame rises up. We have fire! I grab a log off the pile in the box beside the fireplace and lay it on that flame.

The flame goes out.

Damn.

Newspaper. What about newspaper? I look around, and there isn't any. No magazines either. Doesn't this man read?

Okay. Desperate times. There's a blue recycle bin out back under the house. I go through the studio, across the little balcony and down the stairs.

There's the bin. I see newspapers in there, a little wet, a little smelly. As I'm leaning over the bin, a critter runs past me. Jesus. It's a rat. I think. Oh crap. What if there's one down in here?

I pull the newspapers out as fast as I can, go back up the steps, through the studio and into the living room, where the coals have turned black. Not even a hint of red. I glance up at the raw wood ceiling. "Not giving me any breaks today, are you, God?"

He doesn't answer, of course. So I shove in the newspaper all around that log and light a match. Whoosh, those papers go off like sparklers. I watch the blackness crawl across their surface toward the log. Please Lord, I pray.

The fire tickles the wood, blackens one little section. Come on, come on. The fire goes out, leaving the fireplace full of fluffy burned-paper ashes.

I try again. And again. Until I run out of newspapers. My hands are going numb. My nose, too. And my stomach is suddenly—oh Lord. I'm running to the restroom, wishing I had time to grab a library book . . . .

A little later, butt sore, guts unsettled, I open the medicine cabinet, hoping to find some Imodium or Pepto Bismal. I used to always carry them, but I ran out, and lately my stomach hasn't gotten this bad. There's nothing there but a bottle of aspirin and a rusty can of bandages. I check the kitchen drawers. No anti-diarrhea drugs. However . . .

I do find a nearly empty bottle of Prozac with D. Green printed on the label. It was prescribed in July by a local doctor. Interesting.

Of course it's no sin to be depressed. Living alone in this place could do it to you.

Oh. God. I'm running to the john again. Grabbing a book on the way. Making a mental shopping list. Imodium. Toilet paper. Meat. Fire.

THERE CAN'T BE anything left of my biscuits and gravy breakfast, but I don't trust my gut long enough to drive all the way back to Newport. So I make my acquaintance with the Seal Rock store. It's right out of the Walton's TV show. It's Ike Godsey's store, but without Ike and Corabeth. I mean wooden floors, bus route tacked up beside the door, racks of fishing gear, motor oil, cans of miscellaneous fruits, vegetables and beans, a cooler with milk and a few six-packs of beer. Heat pours out of a wood stove in the corner.

In a salute to the 21st century, they've got a Coke machine next to a juice machine and a microwave oven. Also a debit card reader and a sign noting they accept Visa and Mastercard.

A sign that says "Tamales $1.75" hangs over the counter. Tamales? And this string of triangular plastic chili pepper pictures dangles from the ceiling. The gray-haired woman behind the counter does not look Mexican. In fact, I can count on one finger the number of non-white people I've seen here—and he was a tourist.

"Can I help you?" she asks. She's sitting on a stool watching a television the size of a box of Kleenex.

"Well, I need some"—boy, I wish I had a less embarrassing problem—"Imodium."

"Over there across from the canned goods," she points.

Ah. It's the tiniest box I've ever seen, but it will do for today. Around the corner, I find a four-pack of TP. Okay. And then, near the counter, a bundle of kindling. Oh. Maybe that's what I need. I grab it. I can see I'm not going to find any meat—aside from the tamales—or fresh fruits and veggies here, so I'm going to have to go into town, but today I'm going to live on what I had in my motel room and what Donovan left behind. I sling my purchases onto the counter.

"Tummy trouble, huh?"

Now that's rude. But she's looking at me as if she actually cares.

"Afraid so."

"You know what's good for that?"

"No, what?"

"Agrimony. It's this herb—She says Herb, with a hard H—"that grows in the valley. My cousin makes a tea out of it, and boom, no more problems."

"Where does she get it?"

"Grows it herself. Says that's better than the stuff you buy in the store."

"Oh." I can feel trouble brewing down south in my guts right now. I look around, wondering where the restroom is. I don't see any hint of one.

"You camping round here?"

Great. She's chatty. "No, I'm staying at a house up Beaver Creek for the winter."

"Oh. Well, good to have you."

"Thanks."

My stomach is antsy, but I'm tempted to plant my butt by that warm wood stove over there and not move until spring.

Maybe old Corabeth could help me with my fire. "You know, I'm having some trouble getting the fire started in the house where I'm staying."

"Oh. You all by yourself?"

"Yes."

"Tsk. Tsk. Well, I've got just the thing." She reaches behind the counter and pulls out a rectangular package wrapped in paper. "You put this in the middle of your fireplace, light the paper in as many places as you can. Then slowly add kindling and work your way up to the bigger pieces of wood. Don't rush it. Let the fire find its own way. You'll have you a roaring fire in no time. It's the only thing that saves me. When my husband goes to Alaska every year to fish, I could freeze to death without my fire."

"Thank you so much. I'll take that, too."

As she rings up my stuff, she studies my credit card, the one I got with my new name just before I left Missoula. "What's the P.D. stand for?"

"Nothing. Just P.D." I grab my groceries. "Thank you."

"Come again soon," she calls as the screen door shuts behind me.

Oh my God. My guts are not going to wait for me to drive up that mud-packed hill. I get in the car, zoom across the highway—barely missing a northbound truck—and slide to a stop next to the restroom at Seal Rock State Park.

Thank God nobody's in there. It's like sitting on an ice floe, but I don't care right now.

My car crawls up the road, getting another coat of mud as rain streaks the windshield. I watch the odometer till I get to 2.5 miles past the visitor's center and turn up the tight gravel driveway to Donovan's house. Now, in my fantasies, this place would be all lit up, fire burning, soup simmering on the stove, a handsome man waiting to take me in his arms . . .

But no. It's dark. It's cold. There's no stew, no man, just two cats that streak out past my feet when I open the door. I guess I locked them in. Oops. Now I need to get them back in, but I decide to take care of business first. Imodium. Fire. Food. Uh-oh. I just noticed Donovan doesn't have a microwave. This will be the first actual stove I've used since I left Missoula.

Glass of water. Horse pill. Two. Okay, let's do this fire.

I should probably get all these ashes out of the fireplace, but I'm cold down to my bones. Also, I don't know where to put the ashes. I kneel down in front of the fireplace, take out the unburned log, lay one of my magic bricks inside, strike a match and light the paper like Corabeth said. Fire. I slide a couple sticks of kindling out of the bundle and lay them across the brick. The flame licks at the wood, and the wood lights. "Oh, thank you, thank you, thank you," I tell Corabeth in my head.

"Don't rush it," she said. I add more kindling, watching it burn, feeling a wisp of warmth. Then, holding my breath, I add the smallest log from the pile and cross my fingers. "Please, please, please." For a long time, nothing happens. I run to the bedroom and get Donovan's flannel shirt, putting it on over my shirt and sweater. It's so big it hangs almost to my knees and I have to roll up the sleeves to keep the cuffs from hanging over my hands. But it's warm. I resume kneeling in front of the fireplace.

Right now I could be warm at the Coast Inn. Or in my house in Missoula. Or at my mother's house, where she might make me a meat loaf covered in ketchup and cheese. I'm hungry. Good sign. Maybe the pills are working.

Finally, finally, the log catches fire. Orange and blue flames bathe my eyes in warmth. Thank God.

I stand, stiff from crouching and kneeling. It's going to be log by log, I think. I've won the first battle, not the war.

Now, food. I can't face another granola bar or more yogurt. Screw it. I'm eating some of Donovan's soup. Cream of potato. With saltine crackers. Tomorrow I'll have oatmeal. Then I'll go to the store.

I hate to walk away from this fireplace. But I've got to put something in my empty stomach. Okay, now where's a can opener?

AH, SOUP. IT'S WARM and tastes pretty good, although it would taste better with some meat in it. It's been so long since I could really cook anything. Microwaving prefab dinners in motel rooms does not count. I set my bowl, sleeve of saltines and a glass of water on a TV tray next to the easy chair and feel myself start to relax. I don't have to go anywhere or do anything tonight, just rest and enjoy the fire. I don't have to make any decisions. I don't have to be P.D. or Cissy or anybody else.

Maybe I've finally found what I needed. Just a quiet place to shelter in and take care of myself. A vacation from everything.

I think I'll put on my pajamas and read for a couple hours, then go to sleep in that cozy-looking bed.

No motorcycles or screaming neighbors to wake me up. No maid coming to clean. No checkout time to keep in mind.

My stomach has settled down, and the soup makes it feel content. Now, which book shall I read first?

The words blur together and I'm mostly asleep when I hear "Raaaaaaaa, yooooooowwwwwwooowl!" from under the house. Sweet Jesus, Mary and Joseph. I forgot the cats. If one of them is getting killed right now, I'm screwed.

I shove my feet into my shoes and step out into the cold.

I can't see anything. No lights anywhere. No stars, no moon. Just blackness. I go back in and grab a flashlight off the kitchen counter, turn it on and scan the area around the porch. Nothing.

It's raining, not too hard, but enough to start soaking though my clothes as I feel my way around to the back of the house and shine my light by the woodpile, afraid of what I'm going to see. Wild animals? Blood? Dead cats?

Two eyes reflect off my light, and my heart almost stops. But I take a step closer and catch a glimpse of brown fur. Sasha. Her back fur is standing up, and she's hunched in an arch, swishing her tail back and forth. "Hey, Sasha, are you okay?" I take another step closer. I don't want to scare her and have her run off into the darkness. "Come on, kitty."

The cat stares at me then settles down on her haunches, tucking her front paws under her chest. "It's okay, girl. We're going to be friends. I'll give you some yummy food when we go in." I risk another step and another. When I'm close enough to touch her, I squat down. "Now, will you let me pick you up?"

I reach out, touch a wisp of soft fur. "Okay, okay, we can do this." I ease closer, about to slide a hand underneath her when zap! Claws come out of nowhere, scratching my hand bloody. She runs off. Damn it.

So she's gone, and I have no idea where Hernando is either. I can feel blood trickling down my right hand, the wounds burning.

At least I know where I can find some bandages. I climb all the way up the back steps before I realize the back door is locked.

As I climb back down, I catch just a glimpse of the view. My eyes must have adjusted some because now I can distinguish different shades of gray and black. Nice. Hope I don't fall over the edge.

I follow my flashlight back to the front door, which I left open, probably a stupid move, and guess what? Both cats are back in, doing figure eights in front of the cabinet where their food is stored.

Luck? God? What they do every night? Whatever. I wrap a paper towel around my bloody hand, which has two long scratches but looks worse than it is, then fill those little buggers' bowls with kibble and canned kitty salmon.

"I don't know if you guys have a litter box. If you don't, you're going to have to hold it until daylight because I am not going out there again tonight."

They're not listening. They're eating, kibble crunching in their little mouths.

I miss my dog. You can reason with a dog.

My fire has gone out. I try to stir it back to life, but no. It's plum out. I have to start over. I did it once. I'll do it again. Or maybe I'll just go to bed.

Did you ever try to sleep with a cat pushing his claws in and out of the comforter all night? Then licking himself and getting up and purring in your face?

But he's something warm to pet when I wake up at 2 a.m. and have to pee. It's so cold my feet just about freeze to the floor and my butt to the toilet seat. My hand feels all stiff with bandages. What am I doing out here alone?

"Oh, Hernando," I sigh. I fall asleep counting how many days there are in the seven months until Donovan Green comes back.

8

I AWAKE TO THE pitter-patter of rain on the roof.

I don't want to get up. It's going to be cold, but I need the bathroom. I slide my feet into the flip-flops I'm using for slippers, put Donovan's shirt over my pajamas and get up. Brr. Through the door, I see the cats picketing the food cabinet again. How often does he feed these critters? My dog Harry ate twice a day, so that's what these guys are going to get.

The water coming out of the tap is ice cold. I splash some on my face, dry off, and pull on yesterday's clothes, topped by the flannel shirt. I straighten out the sheets and blankets on the bed, smooth the quilt into place, and go out to face the day.

"Good morning, cats. Did you make coffee?"

Right. Tom used to set the pot on a timer, so it was always ready when I got up. I rustle through the cupboards to find an ancient Mr. Coffee machine whose only control is an on-off switch. Thank God the coffee and filters are right next to it. I might do without a TV, but I am not doing without my coffee.

As I dole out the Folger's, Hernando swishes back and forth across my ankles. "Just a minute," I tell him. Sasha is watching me from the corner, doing that tail-twitching thing again.

Coffee on, I face my charges. "Let's get something straight. Coffee before cat food. This is not negotiable."

Their expressions give me the feline version of "whatever." I pour the kibble, spoon out the rest of the kitty salmon and leave them to their feast. Now, where's the morning paper? As if a paperboy could find his way up here.

Shoot. I have to build a fire again. What am I going to do when I run out of wood?

After breakfast, the cats run outside to do whatever cats do. I prepare to head down the hill. I'll check the phone. Arrange to get my mail forwarded to the box down by the road. Work out at the gym. Buy groceries. It's Monday, so there's karaoke again tonight at the Blue Whale Pub. All the way in Newport, five miles north and over the bridge.

Big day in Beaver Creek

It's a challenge to get into the car without getting the mud from the door all over me, but I mostly manage it.

The rain isn't helping the road. As I slip-slide down toward the paved section, I see a white truck and a couple guys with hardhats and surveying gear. They wave as I pass. I wave back.

This is not a mountain car; it's a city commuter car. Potholes lurk under the puddles of muddy water. Every time I hit one, I hope a wheel doesn't fall off.

The downpour is ramping up so I feel like I've got mud coming up and rain coming down. I'd sell my soul to be lounging on the sunny beach at Santa Cruz right now. Wait, did I really just say that? Lord, widow brain big-time. I don't know what I want.

Yes, I do. I want to get to the paved road in one piece.

Whew. At the highway, I turn on my cell phone. Two bars. Good enough. I have a message. I park in the lot at Ona Beach and check my call history.

Mom. I'll call her back later.

Next I hit the little post office in Seal Rock. I think my bedroom back at Donovan's house, barely large enough for a double bed and a shelf, is bigger than this. But they've got all the forms. The person behind the counter, who I think is a woman but who is so masculine looking and has such a deep voice I'm just not sure, is real nice and gets me signed up in a jiffy.

"How long are you gonna be stayin'?" she asks.

"Seven months."

She nods and reaches her bony hand to shake mine. "I'm Dakota."

"P.D. Well, you know that, I guess."

She/he holds my hand a minute too long. I carefully extract my girly fingers. "Thanks," I say and hurry out of there. What was that?

Okay. The gym. It's quite a ways from here, and I'm thinking I might get plenty of exercise just taking care of the house, but right now it sounds like the one place which feels like home.

Remember that guy who spotted me at the gym before? That sherrify guy with the shaved head? He's here, and he's right where I was then, lifting that barbell. With a lot more weight of course. And he's all alone.

I can't help myself. I sashay up to him and say, "Good morning. Need me to spot you?"

He lowers the bar and it clanks into place. His face is all sweaty, he's got sweat stains on the pits and the stomach of his gray tee shirt, and his legs are sticking out of his sweat-shorts. "No thanks," he pants, hauling himself to a sitting position. "I'm done."

"Oh, I don't want to scare you away."

"You're not." He gets up, rubbing a towel all over his face and mopping off the bench before heading to the free weights on the other side of the room.

Okay, fine. We're not going to be buddies. Not like me and the post office girl-guy. I shed my layers of coats and sweaters and climb aboard the treadmill for my pre-weights warm-up. Pretty soon I'm running, and it feels good. Just run. Forget about Donovan Green and the cats and everything in Missoula and Santa Cruz and everywhere else in the world. I set the treadmill for a varied program with all kinds of hills and valleys and focus on the red lights marking off each five-minute goal I accomplish. The music is loud, the gym smells like sweat, and there's a skinny guy grunting over at the shoulder press. I don't care about any of it. I'm finally warm, and I just want to run forever.

MY MUSCLES FEEL LOOSE and free and a little shaky by the time I dry off with a towel I borrowed from Donovan's cabin. I have lifted more weight and done more cardio on the treadmill and rowing machine than ever; I'm strong.

I grab my layers of clothes and head back out to the car. It only takes a minute to realize I can't walk around in a tee shirt and shorts, so I'm sitting in the car, engine idling, putting clothes back on, when I notice the little meter on the dash says I'd better plug this car in pretty soon. I haven't traveled far lately, but I have made several trips back and forth between Newport and Beaver Creek. I'll find a plug when I get home. Ha. *Home.*

I put the car into reverse and am just starting to back out of the parking lot when my phone does the little jingle jangle that tells me I have a message.

Probably Mom, I think, but no. It's from the real estate company that's managing my house in Montana. I park again and check my voicemail. Apparently they called me while I was in the gym, but I didn't hear it.

Here's what they say: "Mrs. Soares, this is Stella Brasch from Mid-Missoula Realty. I'm calling to let you know that the tenants in your house on Keith Avenue have given 30 days' notice. We need to know immediately whether you want us to seek another tenant. Also, there are quite a few repairs that need to be made."

What? They've only had the house for three months.

I don't want to think about this, but I'd better deal with it while I'm still in my post-workout glow. I push the "call back" button, listen to the phone ring in Montana, then hear a recording. Stella Brasch is not there. At the beep, I leave a message and hope I can hear my phone when she calls back.

Now, I could just say, "Take care of the repairs and find a new tenant." What kind of repairs could the house need anyway? I left it in good shape. "Quite a few," she said.

How much is this going to cost? The rent barely pays the mortgage. I'm using my savings to eat and pay for my insurance, phone, and credit card bill.

If my legs weren't already turned to butter, I'd get back on that treadmill and run until I actually got somewhere.

Now I'm freezing. I put on my jacket and zip it all the way up to my neck. I check my pocket for my grocery list. I need food. I also need a job. I'll buy a newspaper and start checking the help wanted ads. If God is really good, they'll have an ad for a singer/piano player.

Twenty minutes later, I'm buying groceries and stewing over this Missoula thing, churning over all the possibilities. I should be enjoying this trip to the store. After weeks living in motels, I can finally buy meat, vegetables and rice, things I can cook on a real stove. I could bake a cake if I wanted to. But now all I can think about is what's going on in Montana. Can I afford the repairs? What *are* the repairs? Are we talking hundreds of dollars or thousands? A couple light bulbs or a new roof? My inner Cissy is obsessing.

If I can't rent the house again without paying a fortune in repairs, I should just sell it and be done with it. I don't need a house in Montana. I love that house, but the only reason we were there was for Tom's job.

I wish he were here to talk to.

My brain is going like this as I loiter by the ground beef until this old guy pushing his cart stops and stares at me like *get out of the way*. So I pick up a package and move on to the fish, where I pick up a hunk of salmon on sale. I'm really not paying attention, not planning my meals, just grabbing food and throwing it into the cart.

My stupid phone rings again, and my heart jolts into higher gear, but it's just my mother. I consider asking her what to do about the house, but I know her answer. Sell it and move back to Santa Cruz. That's her answer for everything, like now the husband is dead, I can go back to being her little girl. Hello, I'm 42. I ignore the phone. I love my mother, but she just doesn't get it.

I will talk to the real estate agent, assess the damage and make a decision.

Fine. Cheesecake. My weakness. P.D. does not eat empty calories.

Or obsess about the past.

I toss a couple catnip balls into the cart. I'll make those cats love me yet.

9

DAY 5 AT BEAVER CREEK, Thursday. Halloween came and went. No trick-or-treaters up here. Fine with me.

It's a new morning. I've got my car plugged into an outlet on the porch with a long extension cord. It would charge a lot faster at a charging station designed for electric cars, but I haven't seen one here. A lot of the newer hybrids don't even have to plug in. They recharge themselves when you drive them. But around here, most people drive gas or diesel trucks. Big trucks, next to which my car only comes up to their tires.

I'm getting along better with the cats, have about a 50 percent success rate—up from zero—at starting the fire, and I got my first piece of mail yesterday. An advertisement for Papa Murphy's pizza. Tossed it. No pizza for P.D.

I've been looking at the job situation and learned something important about this "friendliest" town at the beach: There are no jobs, unless I want to clean motel rooms—"hospitality worker," drive a school bus—"child transportation specialist," or sell cars—"auto sales career." Maybe I should reconsider that hospital gig, but let me get this house thing settled first. I still have some money left. If I sell the house, I might have lots of money.

I have called the real estate agent twice a day since Monday. Nothing. Finally yesterday I got a message Stella was out of the office for the next two days. I left a message asking *anybody* in the office who knew what was going on to call me back. In a while, I'll go back down the hill to find out if anybody called. If not, I'll call them again every five minutes if necessary.

But first, I'm going to sip my coffee and enjoy the view from the back porch. There's more blue sky than clouds right now, and it's almost warm.

I had bacon and eggs for breakfast this morning. Not very P.D., but it tasted good. My stomach is calm now, and I don't want to mess with that.

I hear a vehicle down on the road, idling. Then I hear "Yoo-hoo!" Seriously. Yoo-hoo? Then I hear somebody call my real name. What the hell?

They're not leaving. The vehicle has a syncopated idle, like chunk-chunk-a-chunk-a. Heading back through the house and out to the driveway, I see down below a beat-up van with a rainbow on the side and a U.S. mail sticker on the back. Standing in front of it waving an envelope is Dakota, the girl-guy from the post office. Okay, she's female. She has breasts as well as gray-blonde hair hanging down her back in a skinny braid.

"Hi," I say, stumbling down the rest of the way. "What's up?"

She shows me an envelope. "Is this your real name?" I grimace and nod. "I've got a special delivery letter for you. You have to sign for it."

All kinds of things flash through my head, number one that Donovan Green is kicking me out or has decided to charge rent. But wait, he doesn't know my real name. Maybe it's something bad about my bank account or credit card. Or maybe Mom has decided this is the only way to reach me.

I sign, feeling Dakota's eyes on me. She hands me the letter. Her hands are so long, her fingers so bony. And the way she's looking at me . . . Hey, I don't swing that way.

Anyway, the letter, forwarded from my old address, is from the real estate company. It's thick.

"Thanks, Dakota," I say, which should be her cue to leave, but she lingers.

"So how's it going up here?"

Doesn't she have mail to deliver? Who's watching the post office? "It's going just fine. I'm figuring it all out."

"Well, if you ever need any help or just get lonely, I'm usually at the post office, and my house is nearby. I've got some friends you might want to meet sometime."

"Great," I say, nodding like I actually plan to join them. "Just don't tell them my real name."

She grins. "Nope. I wouldn't do that. Mine's worse, and ain't nobody gonna find out what it is."

"Thanks. Well, I'd better go read this."

"Hope it's not bad news."

I start walking up the driveway. Finally she gets into her van and drives on to the next mailbox.

Back in the sun with my cold coffee, I rip open the envelope. It's a list of the needed repairs and estimated costs. Holy crap.

> From: Stella Brasch, Mid-Missoula Realty
> Re: Repairs needed at 521 Keith Ave., Missoula, MT
> Dear Mrs. Soares:
> This is to notify you that tenants Ariel and David Johnson have given 30 days' notice. They will vacate the premises no later than Nov. 15 and turn the keys in at our office. We have inspected the house and will do one more inspection when we receive your instructions, but we have noted the following issues that need attention before the house can be rented again.
> * Paint: Due to smoke damage from a stove fire, the house needs a thorough cleaning and repainting. We will have to hire a professional crew at $50/hour for at least eight hours.
> * Plumbing: The shower does not drain properly, and all of the faucets drip, so we will need to bring in a plumber.
> * Carpets: All carpets are permanently stained and smell of pet urine. They will have to be replaced, at a cost of approximately $3,500.

This is where I stop reading and think I might be having a heart attack. Fire? Why didn't anyone tell me? And what happened to our no-pets policy? I thought the real estate company was supposed to be watching this. It has only been three months.

I read the rest. Somebody drove into the mailbox and smashed it, and the front porch light doesn't work. It comes out to about $5,000 altogether. Minus the $1,000 cleaning deposit and whatever my homeowner's insurance policy will pay, which I suspect is very little.

I remember when Tom and I first bought that house. We painted the inside together, playing our music loud, getting paint all over our hands and our clothes and in our hair, laughing and talking and making plans. And that mailbox. I loved that mailbox. It was shaped like a barn.

I wonder if any of those pet stains were from my dog Harry, the one who ran away while Tom was in the hospital. It's possible.

I sewed the curtains for that house with my own little Cissy hands. I can only imagine what Ariel and David have done to them in just three months. Damn, damn, damn.

Okay, think. Think like P.D. I can't afford the repairs, especially the carpet. If I went back, I could maybe take care of the little stuff myself. I could figure out how to fix a leaky faucet. I could install a new mailbox. I could clean and paint. But what about the carpet? I can't rent the house with smelly, stained carpets. Can I even sell it like that?

The cheapest thing to do is move back, stop this wandering around and let Donovan Green find somebody else to watch his pussycats. But I'm done with Missoula. I'm done with Cissy. I'm just getting started here.

If I sell the house and manage to make at least a little money, I can get my own place wherever I want. I'll buy my own P.D.-sized home, get my stuff out of storage, toss what I don't want anymore, and start my new life.

Hernando pads up the stairs and sits by my feet. I pick him up and hug him into my lap. I feel his purr vibrating against my thighs. "Oh, Hernando, I wonder if Donovan would sell me *this* house?" I laugh so hard Hernando takes offense and jumps off. I have no intention of building a fire every day and driving this muddy road for the rest of my life.

I'm standing up, about to go in when I hear the mail van again. It hesitates near my mailbox. Please don't yoo-hoo me again. I am not gay. Thirty seconds later, the van moves on.

"MOM. YOU'RE not listening."

"Of course I'm listening. As well as I can at this distance and with static in the background."

I walk a few more paces down the path to Ona Beach. I pass a family having a picnic on the lawn over by the creek. Fried chicken, potato salad, happy children, happy little white dog, happy husband and wife. Here I am on the phone with my mother.

When I mention the damaged carpets in my house, she goes off on all the carpets she's ever bought in her life. The braid, the shag, the mauve, the blue, the hi-lo. It's so not the point. I don't care if she covers her floor in woven-together banana peels. Or those newspaper mats I made in Girl Scouts.

At least the carpet talk got her off my living here at Beaver Creek. She's full of questions I can't answer. What if the cats get sick or hurt? Who's paying the utilities? What's to protect me from Donovan changing his mind? What if something breaks in the house? Why didn't I get our agreement in writing? Good points all. I'm thinking I need to call Donovan while I'm doing this spate of uncomfortable phone calls. Once I get done with them, I'm planning to hole up at the cabin and not talk to anyone for oh, about seven months.

She stops to take a breath or maybe a sip of her coffee.

"Mom. The carpets aren't the point. I can't afford to replace them. I'm thinking I should sell the house. What do you think?"

"You should have asked me that before you committed to this cabin in the woods."

"I know, I know."

"Well, don't move back to Missoula. Why would you want to live in Montana?"

"Right."

"And renters? Oh, the horror stories I've heard from my friends about renters trashing their houses. They say all the right things, but then they hold wild parties, put holes in the walls, make drugs in the basement . . ."

"So I should sell it."

"Yes! Sell it. Come back to Santa Cruz. Start fresh."

I skirt around a puddle on the path. I've left the picnic area and am walking the rutted path to the beach between salal bushes and sword ferns. "Mom, I'm going to be here for the next seven months."

I hear the oven timer beep in the background. Mom's baking again. Church bazaar? Book club? Charity sale? I don't want to ask. I see Ranger Dave up ahead and wave. He smiles and waves back before disappearing into the trees to the right. Is he just friendly or does he remember me and that Japanese bracelet?

"Mom?"

"Oh, my cupcakes are done. I'm sorry. I have to go. Call me again. Soon. Bye."

And she's gone.

I walk on, stopping on the sand-coated footbridge to lean over the rail and look down at the river. The water is olive green, forever rushing out to sea. How come it never runs dry? It keeps going and going.

THIS TIME WHEN I call the real estate company, Stella Brasch is actually there and has time to talk. She says she was starting to worry I'd gone AWOL, that she'd never reach me. It's happened before, she said.

I sit cross-legged on the sand. "No, no. I'm just—in transition. You know, after my husband dying and all."

"Sure. So what do you think? Find another tenant or put the house on the market?"

I dodge the question. "Are these repair prices really accurate?"

I can hear the clicking of computer keys. Is she calling up my file or doing something else while she talks? "Oh yes. They might be even higher. The cleaning deposit your tenants paid when they moved in will help some, but that still leaves quite a bit for you to cover."

"I can't afford it."

"There are ways of financing the repairs. Take out a loan. Put them on your credit card."

"No." I'm on the beach now. Holding the phone to my ear, I sink down to the cool sand. I wish I could dive into it like a sand crab and disappear. Clickety clickety in the background. "Stella, are you checking your e-mail while we talk?"

The clicking stops. "Sorry."

"So the question is this: Can I sell the house without making those repairs?"

"Well, you could list it 'as is.' Or you could include the cost of the repairs in the deal. Lots of people do that. Most buyers would rather pick out their own decor anyway. But people are more likely to buy a house that looks good, and this one doesn't right now."

It's my house, mine and Tom's. So many memories. I try to picture it with all the furniture out of it, bare the way it was when I left, but I can't stop seeing it with the old green sofa and the granny square afghan, the pictures of our parents and grandparents on the walls, our blue willow dishes on the wooden table, Harry sleeping on his pillow. . . Stop.

That's all over.

I stare at the waves rolling up and breaking on the surf, at the gulls gathered for a conference, at the creek running into the sea. It feels as if that whole life in Montana never happened. It's always been me sitting on a beach somewhere.

"Mrs. Soares. Are you still there?"

"Sell it," I say. "As is."

"Okay, but Mrs. Soares, I have to warn you that houses rarely sell within a month, and there are listings in your neighborhood with better curb appeal. Being near the university will help, but it could be six months or even longer. Are you prepared to carry the mortgage payments for as long as it takes? It's none of my business, but if you can't afford the repairs, can you afford the house payments? Property tax is coming up in a couple months, too. I'd hate to see you lose the whole thing to the bank."

I don't know which hurts worse, my head or my stomach. I summon up my inner P.D. "You're right. It is none of your business. And please call me P.D."

Did she just slam her pencil down on the desk? "It *is* my business if I'm spending time and money and not earning a commission. So let me be honest. I have other clients who are more willing to invest in selling their homes. I'm sorry about your husband dying, but we have to face reality. P.D."

I'm leaning my head over my knees now, my eyes closed as she continues her lecture. "Sometimes you can do a rent-to-own contract where renters' payments count toward buying the house. Of course you'd have to do the repairs for that. Frankly, I think you might need to take out a loan to tide you over."

Who's going to give me credit? I take a breath and try to sound calm and logical. "I understand. Just sell it as quickly as you possibly can for as much as you can get."

"Fine. Maybe we can do a little to improve its appearance without spending much money. I'll write up the listing and get back to you."

"Thank you."

Great. She's pissed, I'm pissed, and if that house doesn't sell in a few weeks, I'm screwed. Thanks a lot, Tom. Why did you have to get cancer and die?

I'M STILL CURLED UP in a ball of misery when someone taps me on the back and says, "Excuse me."

I gasp, tears stopped halfway down my face as I look up at Ranger Dave, all green and khaki clothes and blond hair.

"P.D. Are you okay?"

"Sure." I get up, wiping my face with my sweatshirt sleeves. He remembers my name.

"I wanted to share what I learned about the bracelet you found."

Montana fades away.

"You found something?"

"Yes. We have an expert from Japan we're consulting on some of these things. I e-mailed him pictures, and he said these bracelets are very popular with little girls there. His own daughter has one. The inscriptions are typically their first name and a saying like 'happy girl' or 'smart one' or 'princess.' They're so similar it would be impossible to track down the girl who lost it in the tsunami. In fact—"

I can see Ranger Dave going on about squirrels or beavers at a campfire talk. I interrupt with the question flashing like a red light in my mind. "Do you think she's still alive?"

He sighs. "I don't know, P.D. So many people died over there. We just have no way of knowing. I wish I could tell you more."

"So what happens to the bracelet now?"

"We've sent it to the Japanese consulate in Portland, along with some other things people have found."

"Like what?"

"More jewelry, a wallet, some pictures, a box of dishes. This is just the beginning. They say the big influx of debris is coming this winter."

"Wow. And the dock is still up at Agate Beach?"

"No, the state had crews chop it up and take it away. They were worried about somebody getting hurt out there." He glances back toward the bridge. He probably has others things to do.

"Well, thank you for telling me."

"No problem. You sure you're doing okay?"

"I'm fine. Tide's out. Guess I'll go for a walk."

"Watch those sneaker waves. Have you seen the eagle's nest?"

Eagles? On the beach? "No, I haven't."

"Shortly after you pass the rocks over there on the left, look up at the cliff, and you'll see it. If you're lucky, you'll even see the mom sitting on the nest."

"Cool."

I hesitate. He hesitates. "Well, have a nice day."

As I watch him walking away, I don't want to weep anymore.

I ENJOYED SEEING the mother eagle on her nest, but it's not that warm, so now I'm sitting in my car for my last call, to Mr. Donovan Green. I have written a list of questions about utilities, cat care, liability and such on the notepad I swiped from the Coast Inn. I'm all set for a long conversation that will tie all the loose ends left when he handed over the keys. I mean, who gives a stranger the keys to his house without a credit check, a background check and a reference check, without a written contract to make sure neither one of us gets cheated?

Sure, I get a free place to stay, but what's to say he can't take it away as easily as he gave it? Now that I've had a few days to think about it, this doesn't make any sense. For once, my mother is right.

Oh boy, is she right.

Donovan gave me four phone numbers, office, Portland home, Tucson home, cell phone. None of them are valid. That's right, none. The cell turns out to be a wrong number that hooks me up with some Chinese lady. The home numbers are both disconnected. At the office number, which gets me to something called "Northwest Productions," they haven't heard from Donovan Green in months.

Uh-oh.

P.D. stands for Pitifully Dumb.

He seemed so nice. Responsible. Smart. Pleasantly quirky. But what about that mess of broken glass and spilled wine he left in the studio? As they say with Waldo in those kid's books, where in the world is Donovan Green?

And what does this mean for me?

Who really owns this house? And these cats?

I STORM INTO the D & K Diner hunting for Janey or her mom. They would know how to find Donovan. He's Janey's uncle, Diana's brother.

There's a stranger working at the front counter. I have to wait behind a couple of old folks paying for their breakfast, praising the marionberry pancakes and wanting to know where they got those great sausages. Come on, people.

Finally, they're gone and I'm up.

"Breakfast or lunch?" She reaches for a menu.

"Neither. I'm looking for Janey or Diana."

She puts the menu back in the rack. "They're not here today. They drove to the valley for supplies."

Nuts. "Are you a relative, too?"

She smiles. "No, I'm Kelly, Diana's business partner. Who are you?"

"I'm P.D. Soares. I'm living in Diana's brother's cabin up Beaver Creek."

"Oh, yes, she told me about you. Is everything going all right?"

How do I put this? I study the fresh pies in the case. Marionberry, lemon meringue, Dutch apple, blackberry. "Well, yes and no. I'm not having any particular problems, but I had some questions and tried to contact Donovan, and none of the phone numbers he gave me works."

"Oh dear. He's done it again."

"Done what?"

"Disappeared." She leans forward, glancing toward the door to make sure no one's coming. "I shouldn't be telling you this, but since you're on your own and all, you ought to know. Donovan has some, um, let's call them issues. When he goes off his meds, he tends to drop out of sight."

"For how long?"

She shrugs. "It varies. A couple days. A couple months. Longer."

"So what do I do if I have a problem with the house?"

A car pulls up outside. Two men and a teenage girl approach the door. "I don't know. You'd better talk to Diana about that." The door opens. "Good morning, folks, three for breakfast?"

"Thank you, Kelly." I slip out the door.

Well, damn.

At the library in Newport, I do an Internet search on Donovan Green. I find a couple articles about his sculptures and some listings for gallery shows. I guess he really is an artist, but there's nothing newer than three years ago.

Crap.

10

I DON'T WANT to bore you. Let's just say days pass. A couple weeks. Cats, beach, open mic, karaoke with Janey, keeping the fire going. I put off job-hunting, hoping someone will respond to the singer/keyboard player cards I have plastered all over town.

I visit the Seal Rock store once a week or so and learn the owner I was thinking of as Corabeth from "The Waltons" is really Frankie. Her sister-in-law makes the tamales she sells, which are fabulous.

On my trips down the hill, I keep checking phone messages in the hope I'll hear my house has sold or Donovan Green has reappeared. Nobody knows where he is. Diana says she'll make some calls but can't promise anything. Jonas, when I run into him at the diner, shrugs and says, "That's Uncle Donovan; he'll turn up eventually. Meanwhile, enjoy the house."

Sure.

I'm using so many muscles hauling wood, and walking the beach and the trails around Beaver Creek I don't go to the gym much anymore. The weather gets colder and wetter, forcing me to spend more time inside. The grayness begins to weigh on me as I start to forget what sunshine looks like.

I get so bored I buy some yarn, needles and patterns at Fred Meyer so I can sit in the front of the fire and knit. It's not as Cissy as you might think. I'm using wild colors, orange, hot pink, chartreuse, and trying stitches I never tried before.

One day when I just can't knit anymore and I'm tired of reading my library books, I visit the music store. That big black baby grand calls to me like a lover. While Deuce, the store owner, is on the phone, I slide onto the piano bench. I play as quietly as I can and get so wrapped up in the music as I try to remember the chords to "Midnight Special" I don't even notice he's off the phone until I hear this amazing harmonica riff. I look up and see him grinning at me with his crooked teeth. He nods, and I crank up the volume while he blows and sucks along. We're rocking the house for a minute there, but I just can't remember that one chord. I try a D diminished. It sounds so bad we both burst out laughing.

When we get our breath, I ask, "What the heck is that chord?"

He shrugs. "I don't know. I don't read music."

"Really? You own a music store and you don't read music?"

"Nope." He reaches over to a shelf and hands me this fat music book, which boasts 500 songs. It's what they call a "fake book" because it's just words and chords and you get to figure out your own arrangements.

I look up "Midnight Special." Oh, it's a B7.

I'm about to hand the book back when he says, "No, play some more."

So I play and sing, and Deuce plays along. Pretty soon he's got half the instruments in the store out, guitars, drums, horns, and he plays them all. Occasionally he stops for a phone call or a walk-in customer, but not often. I wonder how he makes a living. Nobody's going to buy this eighteen-thousand-dollar grand piano, that's for sure.

This other guy—Deuce calls him Buddy—walks in, all fish-smelling and sunburned, with curly sun-bleached hair going every which way. A pit bull follows him in and lies down in the doorway. He picks up a bass guitar and joins in as the dog puts his head on his front paws and goes to sleep.

We jam until the fisherman's cell phone rings. It's his wife wondering when he's going to come home for dinner. That's when we realize it's dark outside, and the shop should have closed an hour ago.

"Busted!" Deuce hollers.

"Well, your old lady ain't gonna be too happy either."

"You got that right. I'll say it's your fault." Deuce hangs the guitar and bass back up on the wall. "What's your name anyway?" he asks me.

"P.D."

"That stand for something?"

"How about piano diva?"

"Why not? Well, Miss P.D., we got to go. But it's been fun. Where else you been playin'?"

I slide the cover over the piano keys and run my hand over the shiny black wood. "Cafe Mundo open mic. Karaoke across the street. Maybe church if I ever get religion again. Looking for other opportunities."

Buddy chuckles. "Mundo's okay, and church if you like it, but forget the karaoke. Come over here."

Deuce nods. "Definitely."

"Well, I sure miss my music. My piano's in storage in Missoula."

"I'll give you a good deal on a keyboard rental. Student model. I'll give it to you for $20 a month if you come demo this baby grand every now and then."

Money is tight. Every time I see those homeless guys on the street corners with their signs, I'm afraid I'll be next, especially if my house doesn't sell, but I'm already digging out my wallet. "Thank you so much. How much is this book?"

"That's twenty bucks, too."

"Give the girl a break, Deuce."

"Okay, ten."

I hand over the money, the last of my cash. It's back to the bank for me, but I feel so P.D.-licious right now I don't care. Life is short, but the days are long. There are 500 songs in this book!

We walk out together, Deuce, Buddy, the dog, and me carrying my keyboard and my fake book, wearing a giant smile on my face.

I don't even notice the drive back.

That night, I dye my hair. It comes out carrot orange. I love it. I trim it with nail scissors again and fluff it up. With the cats as my audience, I sing and play until my fingers feel bruised and my throat is sore.

Outside, it hails and blows like crazy. Inside, I've got food and drink, fire, cats, books to read, my knitting, and my music. Life is good. I can do this for seven months, no problem.

11

I WAKE UP on a Wednesday in mid-November to the wind blowing so hard I can feel it pushing against the house. Hernando is sitting like a sphinx, swishing his tail over the covers, making me cold with the breeze. When I grab the tail to stop it, he hisses at me and jumps off the bed. Okay. Somebody's in a bad mood.

I hate to get up. It's about 35 degrees out there, and though my watch says it's almost 8:00, it's dark as twilight. If I didn't have a full bladder, I wouldn't move.

I slide out of bed, go into the bathroom, flip the light switch, and nothing happens. The power is out.

So much for a hot breakfast. Or hot water. And, oh nuts, so much for charging my car. Or my phone. Time to build a fire and make like a pioneer woman.

THE CATS DON'T want to go out. I've been trying to read, but it's so dark I can't see the words. I've got some candles going, but I'm no Abe Lincoln reading by firelight. I could knit without looking, but I can't read the patterns. So I play some more music. I hate to wear out the batteries in the keyboard, but I'm not the kind of girl who can sit around doing nothing. Not Cissy, not P.D., got to keep busy. Idle hands and all that B.S. Blame it on my parents. Neither one could ever sit still. Of course my father took it beyond keeping busy to a permanent life on the road while Mom just focused on baking and volunteer work. I guess I'm a little of both.

So I'm playing by ear, every song I ever knew. Hernando's sleeping on the other chair while Sasha sits on the window sill, twitching her tail. It's so loud outside I have to crank up the volume on the keyboard. I tell myself the storm is like percussion, the wind like the swish of the brush on the cymbal, the rain like the rat-a-tat of the snare drum, with an occasional thunder boom from the bass drum. The lightning provides special effects. I wish I had a microphone so I could hear myself sing.

Donovan has this weird fish-shaped clock hanging over the kitchen sink. When I stop, I'm surprised to see it's already 10:30. I wonder what Deuce is doing down at the store. No customers, I'll bet. Maybe he just closed up. No doubt the businesses in Seal Rock, the shops, the store, the diner, etc., are all in the dark with no power either.

In a way, I like it. It feels like the world is taking a breather. Intermission.

My throat is getting sore. I have to quit caterwauling. I switch off the keyboard, sit back, close my eyes, and wonder if I can heat up some coffee somehow in the fireplace.

Bam! Something crashes into the roof. Over the bedroom, I think. Suddenly the rain sounds closer. Dreading what I'm going to see, I go look.

Hell. A pine tree has fallen on the house, and now it's raining on my bed. The top of the tree is sticking through a hole about a foot in diameter in the ceiling, and that's more than enough to create a waterfall.

Great. We have no working phone, the road is turning into mud soup, and I have no way of reaching Donovan Green. "God, if you're up there, please transport me to a sunny beach right now."

Nothing happens.

Obviously I have to do something. First thing is to push my bed away from the water. I shove it up against the wall near the door and strip off the covers. The mattress is only a little damp, but I'll have to hang the soggy blankets and sheets up near the fireplace and hope they dry by bedtime. I have not seen any other bed linens in the house. I guess I'd better knit me an afghan. Stat.

Water pours onto the wooden floor, making a puddle that spreads and threatens to turn the room into a lake. I grab the orange-stained towel I used for my hair and put it under the downpour. That's going to last about a minute and a half. I search through the cupboards and cabinets until I find a rubber bucket and shove it under the water, but it's coming down so fast it splashes over the sides. The bucket will be full in no time. I don't need a bucket; I need a swimming pool.

Right now I'm wishing for the cavalry to arrive. Or a neighbor. Or anybody, so I don't have to do what I know I have to do: Find a ladder and climb on the roof, move the tree, and cover the hole. I don't want to think about how much a permanent fix will cost. It shouldn't be my responsibility, but if I can't reach Donovan . . . Maybe I need to go back to the Coast Inn. Smuggle Hernando and Sasha in with me. Or maybe just Hernando and let the bitch cat Sasha fend for herself.

But I can't let the water keep coming in.

Living with Mom in Santa Cruz is starting to sound pretty good. But she wouldn't see me as P.D. Not a chance.

Son of a bug. Better suit up and get started.

I HAVE NEVER been on the roof of a house in my life. Whenever stuff needed to be done, the men in my family took care of it, and I was happy to let them. My husband was a government guy, but he still got up on the roof sometimes, I don't even remember why. I held my breath the whole time he was up there, praying he wouldn't fall.

I've seen men who work on roofs for a living walk on a pitched roof like it's flat ground. Makes me think of cows that walk on steep hillsides without falling off. Are their legs really longer on one side?

Anyway, I've got all my clothes on, plus my coat and Donovan's slicker and the orange hat I just finished knitting. I wish I had gloves. When I left Missoula, it was summer and 102 degrees.

As the wind tears at my clothes and beats on my face, I slog out to the back of the house, where I find a ladder. Big old silver thing, kind of bent and rusty. It's way taller than I am; thank God I've been working out so I can move it. But I wouldn't mind if that muscle-bound sexist sheriff from the gym showed up right about now. "Can I spot you, ma'am?" "Yes, please."

From here I can see the massive pine tree leaning on the house. It's huge. I have no idea how I'm going to move it by myself. The way these trees are swaying, another one could fall any second.

Donovan's yellow slicker hangs over my hands and past my knees. I take it off and throw it onto the wood pile.

By the time I drag the ladder around to where the tree is, I'm soaked and my hands ache with the cold and the hard metal edges. The wind is blowing at me, and I'm shivering. I make the ladder as steady as I can and start climbing. It occurs to me this roof is going to be slippery as snot.

I climb the ladder, kneel on the top and push at the tree. It's like trying to push a brick wall. It is not moving. The pine needles bite my hands. I push again, then stare at it. Remember the Ents in *Lord of the Rings*, those trees that were alive? I always thought they were pretty spooky. I stare at this one now, at the craggy bark and bushy branches waving in my face. "I need you to go sleep somewhere else. Help me out here."

A big gust. Pine needles scratch my face and the ladder shakes. Water runs down my collar and under my shirt. Shit, shit, shit.

What if I cut it into pieces? But how? If there was a chainsaw here, I wouldn't know how to use it. Maybe hack it with the ax? Could I just throw a tarp over the whole thing? There has to be a solution. What would a man do? What would that sheriff guy do? He wouldn't screw around with girly measures. He'd get out the heavy artillery. Maybe Donovan has a chainsaw down there somewhere.

Okay. I can do this. I'm going to climb down, take the tarp off the woodpile and tuck it around the hole, then hunt for a chainsaw. Lacking that, I'll get the ax and start hacking at this mother of a tree.

Another gust rattles the ladder, harder this time. I feel it rocking under me. I hold on and pray. After the gust passes, I start to slide one of my feet down to the top step. But my foot slips off the wet ladder rung. Suddenly the ladder is falling one way and I'm falling the other. I grab for the roof, but the shingle comes off in my hand.

I don't have time to see my life flashing before my eyes or even to holler a curse before I hit the ground. Crash. Pain. It was only two stories up, but I seem to have fallen on one of Donovan's crazy-ass sculptures, the skeleton of a whale, I think. I lie there in the rain and mud, hugging this pile of vertebrae made out of I don't know what, something hard as bone but not really bone. My right wrist hurts like crazy. Not a happy thing for a piano player. I think the ribs on my right side are cracked. It hurts to breathe. I'm scratched and bleeding from my chin and both hands.

Moaning, I roll over onto my back and stare up at the gray sky, at the rain pouring into my face, lightning flashing in the north. Thunder breaks almost simultaneously. The ground shakes.

Hey, God? I need a little help here.

NOW THIS IS WHERE Prince Charming comes and scoops me up. In the next scene, I'm cozy and clean in a hospital bed, right? With all my friends and relatives bringing flowers and chocolate. Right.

I'm thinking if I'm lucky, a bear or a cougar will put me out of my misery.

The good news is I'm probably going to live. The bad news is I have to pick myself up and get help. Also, the rain will continue to pour into the house. Why didn't I just look for something bigger to put under the hole?

I start to push myself up with my right hand and scream at the pain. It sounds like a whisper in all this weather noise. I switch hands and push. Oh Lord, Lord, Lord, it hurts. I think about broken ribs piercing my lungs or my heart and killing me dead right here on this stupid hillside. Did I mention Cissy was a hypochondriac? No time for that now. I tell myself to shut up and push with my legs. I'm up, standing near the fallen ladder. I kick it so hard I hurt my middle toe, maybe even break it, but who cares. The tree is still on top of my house, and I think I hear it laughing. "Heh, heh, heh."

F you, tree.

I'm shivering. Cold, hurt, probably a little in shock. I need to go to the hospital. I wonder if the neighbors have any working phones. I'm thinking no, and I don't want to waste time introducing my mud-covered broken self. I'll just drive down the hill.

When I hobble inside to get my keys, the fire is going. My keyboard, knitting and book wait for me. I'm dripping on the hardwood floor, and the water in the bedroom is already oozing toward the door. Both cats are pacing in front of their food cupboard. "Later," I tell them, grabbing my purse and keys.

I have to argue with the wind to get the car door open, but I shouldn't even have bothered. I don't know why God's pissed at me, but He surely is. When I reach around with my left hand to turn the key, the car won't start. Not enough electrical charge, and not enough gas. I was so busy thinking about the house in Missoula, I forgot to fill it up. I am screwed like a light bulb.

Time for plan B.

Oh my God, my wrist hurts. I can see it starting to swell, feel a weird numbness setting in along the side near my thumb. But my ribs hurt even worse. The middle toe on my right foot isn't too happy either. I guess I really did break it.

I imagine myself back working at the hospital in Missoula with somebody coming up to me holding their gut or cuddling a wrist like this with their other hand. I'd send them straight to emergency, get their insurance info later. I remember the scared expressions and the shock on their faces. One minute they were going along just fine, thinking about what to have for dinner, and then, boom, this happened.

If I wasn't busy, I'd come out of my cubicle and walk them to the ER, trying to assure them it would be all right, even if it wouldn't. I try this on myself now as I slip-slide down the driveway bent over holding my side. "It'll be all right, P.D., it'll be all right. These are minor injuries. You're standing, you're conscious, your vitals are good. You'll get fixed up, and somebody will repair the roof and dry things out. You'll be fine. If you can't play keyboard for a while, you can still sing. Or bang a tambourine."

But this doesn't sound too reassuring because my teeth are chattering and I can't stop shaking. The rain slashes at my face like razors. I clamp my mouth shut, hold my elbow against my ribs, and think, "God, I need a little help. Please."

Donovan's boots are too big and my feet slosh around in them. Blisters are forming on my heels. My toe hurts like crazy, but I don't think I can pull the boots off with an injured hand and busted ribs. I've got my purse looped over my left shoulder; it feels like it weighs a hundred pounds. Now that I've got it, I have to carry it.

On the road, I look around, head toward where I heard that chainsaw going a while back. Okay, there's a house. Small, white.

No cars. No smoke coming out of the chimney. Probably a snowbird, what the locals call people who flee this place when winter comes. I call them smart people. Just in case, I go up to the door and knock with my wrong hand. No answer. I think about breaking in, but what for? They wouldn't have electricity or a working phone either. I need to find a place with people in it to help me.

Back to the road, soaked, a shiver running all the way from my tailbone to my head. I wonder how long it takes before hypothermia sets in.

The next house is a long ways, probably about a mile, but I walk it, each step hurting from those damned boots and my broken toe, wind pushing at me, icy air hurting in my lungs, ribs hollering with every breath, blood oozing from my hands and dripping off my cheek. If this were a movie, the music would be really loud right now. Lots of cellos. I'd fall down a dozen times, but I don't dare because I don't think I could get up.

Oh God, no. What looked like a decent house from the road is just a broken shell, leaning hard to the south. I can't go any farther. I'm going to faint or throw up or both.

Wait. I see smoke from a chimney just over the trees. I might be saved. I actually chuckle, thinking about what my mother is going to say when I tell her about this little adventure.

And what fun I'm going to have screaming at Donovan Green if I ever find him. Not that it's his fault, but I have to blame somebody.

Just around the trees, I see a pink house, yes, bubblegum pink. And a van with a rainbow painted on the side. D. Wells and M. Davi, it says on the mailbox. God, you've got to be kidding.

I drag my bloody self to the door and knock.

12

LATER, I WILL NOTICE the frog wind chimes tinkling overhead, the yoga music playing somewhere in the house, and the scent of baking bread. Right now, I am only aware of Dakota from the post office, Dakota the woman who looks like a tall skinny hippie man, who held my hand too long when we met, who loitered at my mailbox the other day, who is now rushing toward me with her arms wide saying, "Oh sweetie, what happened?"

Then she's got her long monkey arms around me, and I'm trying to squirm away because my ribs hurt like hell. Finally she lets go and pulls me into the house, where it's warm, there's candlelight, and it's dry. I stand there dripping mud and blood and tell my sob story.

"I fell off the ladder. This tree fell into the roof, and I tried—and—I—the ladder—I fell."

"Oh, P.D."

"I think I broke my wrist and maybe a couple ribs."

"And you scraped yourself up good," says a short chubby woman standing in the kitchen doorway to the right. "I'm Maryann. You are . . ."

"P-P.D. Soares. I'm living in D-Donovan Green's place."

"Oh, Donovan. I'm sorry."

Later I will ponder what she means by that, but Dakota is hustling me toward the bathroom, telling me I have to remove my wet clothes and dry myself off. She'll loan me some sweats and take me to the hospital.

I FEEL LIKE A CHILD wearing a grownup's clothes in Dakota's gray sweatpants and black Rainbow Nation sweatshirt, but at least they're warm and dry, and my feet are almost comfortable in Maryann's pink rain boots.

It's weird in the rainbow van. I'm riding shotgun on what's usually the driver's side, next to an empty post office crate. The van rattles like crazy, and I wince at every bump, but soon we're back on pavement. I am so glad to see the highway. At the intersection, Dakota pulls a cigarette and lighter out of her breast pocket, lights up and takes a long drag before turning right, toward Newport.

"How're you doing, P.D.?"

I study the Chinese symbol tattooed on the back of her left hand. "Okay, I guess. I can't believe this happened."

"Yeah, well, I was pretty surprised to see you at the door. I wish you had called. We would have helped you."

I half-shrug. It hurts too much to shrug all the way. "Donovan disconnected the phone. The cell doesn't work." Also, I don't have Dakota's number. Didn't even know she lived up here. "And the power is out."

"Not unusual. That's why we have a generator. It's spendy, but it's worth it."

I watch the streets of South Beach passing by. Lost Creek. Thiel Creek. The airport. A rundown trailer park. Another post office. Turnoff to the community college. A bar. The bridge. "Are you taking today off?"

Dakota waves at a car passing us going the other way. "Sort of. The mail is all delivered. I can't operate any of the machines, and we didn't have a single customer, so I closed up the counter. I'll go back in a while to see if there's anything I can do."

In Missoula, the post office never closes during the day.

I study Dakota's profile as we cross the Yaquina Bridge over the bay into town. She must be older than I think, her hair nearly all gray, quite a few wrinkles on her face. Her eyes are pale gray like the ocean on a cloudy day. Her lips pout forward like she's thinking hard about something. I wonder what her story is.

"I sure appreciate your helping me," I say.

"My pleasure." She turns to smile at me.

She still thinks I'm gay, doesn't she?

YOU CAN PROBABLY imagine the next bit for yourself without my telling you. This is a small hospital. Besides me, they have two other patients in emergency, a pregnant woman who seems to be miscarrying and an old man who may have had a stroke.

I spent a lot of time in emergency rooms with Tom, and of course I worked at the hospital, so there aren't many surprises here. Meet with the nurse, fill out forms, get x-rays that show my wrist is sprained, not broken, two ribs are cracked, and my toe is just bruised, meet with the doctor, get my scrapes cleaned up and my wrist put in a brace, get a prescription for pain meds, go home with instructions to ice my ribs and my wrist and to make an appointment with my primary care doctor for follow-up. But none of this happens quickly. I spend a lot of time sitting on the edge of the bed watching my wrist and hand swell, dangling my legs and telling Dakota she doesn't have to wait around. But she insists. We listen to conversations from behind the other curtains, to nurses talking about some baby shower, to a heart monitor beeping somewhere. We don't say much to each other.

I get Dakota to plug in my cell phone. Yeah, yeah, there are signs saying no cell phones, but come on, it doesn't really hurt anything.

I am shocked to find . . . no messages.

Dakota's voice startles me. "Are there any electrical wires around that tree?"

Wires? "I didn't even think about that. I could have been electrocuted?"

She rolls her eyes upward and nods. "Yes ma'am."

"I don't think so, but I'm not sure." I try to remember the scene. I just keep seeing that ladder lying on the ground and that tree mugging the house. I don't remember any wires, but it's all a blur. When I think about it, I was probably out there less than 10 minutes altogether.

I scan the magazines in the rack. *Modern Baby. Parent.* A two-year-old *Good Housekeeping. Time.* I study the shelves. Purple rubber gloves in small, medium, large, and extra-large. A red box marked Hazardous Waste. An assortment of gauze pads, Ace bandages, tongue depressors, paper cups . . .

"Okay, Ms. Soares," a nurse says, hustling in with a pile of papers. "I have your discharge orders."

We have been here three hours. It's 2:30 in the afternoon now. In spite of everything, in spite of my ribs screaming every time I breathe, I'm starving. Also wondering how I'm going to cook and eat with one hand. And how I'm going to get off this damned hospital bed without help.

As soon as the nurse is gone. Dakota holds out her hand, helps me up, and leads me out with her arm around my shoulder.

"After the pharmacy, I'm taking you home to my house," she says. "You can't stay at Donovan's place alone."

"I—okay. Thanks." I hate to say it, but she's right. I'll look up Jonas's number, tell him what happened and put the whole tree-on-the-roof business in his friendly cab-driving hands.

"OH MY GOD, this is so good," I tell Maryann a little later as I sop up homemade vegetable soup with wheat bread fresh from the oven. Did the power come on? No, I hear a generator.

Eating with my left hand is a challenge. I've already slopped soup on Dakota's sweats, apologized and done it again.

"Don't worry," she says. "Maryann is a miracle worker when it comes to getting clothes clean."

I'm still kind of dazed. I didn't expect today to go quite this way. I thought I had my life put together for the next few months. Ha. God is up there laughing.

I've only been in Donovan's cabin for a couple weeks, but I was on the road before that, and spending all my time watching Tom die before that. I was so busy taking care of him I don't know when I last sat down for a civilized meal in a warm, pretty house with real silverware and friendly people.

These women have put together a home that reminds me of my grandma's house, before the dementia and all that ugly mess. When I was a little kid in my frilly dresses and patent leather shoes, I loved hanging out with my Italian grandmother. She taught how me how to knit and sew and cook. I'd help her in her garden, which was always loaded with blooming flowers, all kinds, all year round, or at least that's how I remember it. I guess I wanted to re-create that in my own home after Tom and I bought the house in Missoula. Then Tom died, and I didn't know what I wanted, so I ran away.

It feels weird being taken care of by Dakota and Maryann. I'm usually the one taking care of people.

After lunch, Maryann shows me the spare room where I'm going to sleep. It's plush, with a handmade quilt, watercolors on the walls, clean towels, the whole bit.

"I'll go to the cabin and get your things for you," Dakota says, putting on a jacket from the rack by the door, flipping her braid over the collar. "Then I'll see what I can do with that roof."

"No, no, I'll call Jonas. It's his family's problem."

Maryann shakes her head. "P.D., Dakota's a carpenter. She spent many years in the trades, and she can fix anything. She built this house."

I look around. "Really?"

Dakota rolls her eyes. "Yeah, well, we had to have a place to sleep and nothing I saw around here looked good enough for Maryann."

They exchange a look that makes me suddenly miss Tom.

"So give me your keys, and I'll go get your stuff while you rest."

I'm in pain here, there and everywhere, but I want to gather my own stuff. I don't know what I left out or how she'll know what's mine and what's Donovan's. "I'm going with you," I say.

"No, P.D., you need to rest. They said to ice your wrist and ribs 20 minutes of every hour for the first two days. Stay here and do that."

"I will. Later. Oh, and I have to take care of the cats."

Dakota smiles, showing a gap between her front teeth. "Sasha and Hernando? We know them, don't we?"

"Oh yes," Maryann says. "They come over here a lot. Sasha beat up our old cat several times, but Ginger showed her who was boss."

I look around. "I haven't seen Ginger."

Maryann shakes her head. "She's gone. Cougar, we think."

"Okay," Dakota says, handing me a coat. "Let's get going. It's going to be dark in an hour."

Country music plays in the rainbow van. Dakota lights another cigarette. I watch her suck in a long draft, her cheeks drawing inward, then blowing the smoke out. "I wanted to get to know you better, but not by you getting hurt," she says.

"Well . . ." I don't know what to say to that. In a second, we're there. The rain and wind have lightened up. Donovan's slicker is still on the ground where I left it.

Even unlocking the door gives me so much trouble Dakota takes the key away and does it for me. Grr. P.D. does not like being helpless.

Cats. Pacing. I can smell that one of them has decided to relieve him or herself in the house, but in the dim light I can't see where it is. I try to feed them, almost dropping the bag of kibble. I whimper in pain when I try to bend to pick up the pieces that fall out. Dakota takes the bag away and does it for me. Damn.

It's cold in here, the fire completely out. My keyboard is on one of the big chairs, my knitting on the floor beside the chair. Double damn. I can't play music or knit with one hand. I grab my library book and follow Dakota into the bedroom, where she's staring at the ceiling, her hands on her bony hips. The floor is soaked, the bed almost floating, water still pouring down from the hole where the tree sticks through. "You're lucky you weren't in here when it fell," Dakota says. She gazes around the room. "Did you notice the floor isn't plumb?"

"What?"

"It slants toward the north. See, there's less water on the south side. It's all draining the other way."

"Oh."

"Well, I like a challenge. I'm no roofer, but I'm going to see what I can do for tonight and hope it's dryer outside in the morning. Where's your suitcase?"

Oh crap. I left it under the bed and it must have ridden along when I pushed the bed over. So now it's wet, but my backpack, hanging from a hook on the door, is dry. As Dakota goes outside to look at the damage, I start throwing clothes into my pack from the shelves, topped by the rest of my library books and my miscellaneous junk from the bathroom. I'll get my food and whatever I forgot later.

I keep trying to use my right hand, but the brace stops me. Also the pain. Six weeks minimum, the doctor said. I may need physical therapy. I'm paying for the cheapest insurance known to man—or woman—so I don't even want to think about what all this costs.

Outside, I hear a rattling, scraping sound. Dakota is moving the ladder. Then I hear her walking on the roof. I leave my stuff on a chair and go out the back door to see what's going on. Can't see until I walk gingerly down the stairs and look up. Dakota is tucking a tarp into place.

"Hey!" I call.

She waves.

It's almost dark now. I hear a meow as Hernando brushes against my legs. I try to bend down and pick him up one-handed, but I can't quite do it; he rolls out of my hand and crashes to the ground. "I'm sorry, kiddo." He rubs my leg again, no hard feelings.

Dakota is coming down now, slapping the dirt off her hands. "That'll hold it for tonight. I'll bring my chainsaw out tomorrow and deal with that tree. We'll have lots of great firewood."

"We," she says. Not "you," as in P.D. burning it in the fireplace at Donovan Green's cabin. Considering everything, it doesn't make any sense to come back here. We don't have anything in writing to make me stay. These ribs hurt every time I move, so how am I going to keep that fire going? The pain is like a high whining in my ear that makes it hard to think about anything except going someplace warm, dry and soft and taking as many pain pills as I'm allowed.

"Okay, got your stuff?"

Dakota hauls my backpack out as I follow like a helpless child. Hernando watches us from the doorway. "What about the cats?"

"You want to bring them?"

"That one."

She grins. "I hear ya." As I climb into the van, she gets the cat food and grabs Hernando, handing him to me. I hope he doesn't turn all teeth and claws as soon as the van starts to move. "Where's the other one?"

"I don't know."

Dakota leaves me in the van with the engine running as she searches the cabin. In a minute, she comes out, locking the door behind her. "Couldn't find her. She'll be okay." As she gets in, I stare at her long, long legs. Her jeans, definitely made for men, are faded and stained.

"Did you lock the back door?"

"I did. Unless some burglar wants to come in through the roof, it's secure."

And off we go to the house Dakota built, Hernando needling my thighs through my sweats.

13

IT'S JUST BEGINNING to get light. I spent all night trying to find a comfortable position. Every time I moved, some body part sent a red alert to my brain, but I must have dozed off sometime. I awaken to the sound of a sewing machine and find Hernando purring against my neck. A candle burning in a red glass holder on the dresser offers a flickering rosy light. This bed is soft. I know it's going to hurt if I move, but I need to use the restroom. As I reach to move Hernando so I don't roll on him, he jumps off the bed and runs out of the room.

It hurts, it hurts, it hurts. I wrap my immobilized right hand around my ribs, barely breathing as I sit up and ease my feet to the floor. I stay there a minute, just inhaling and exhaling.

Sun shining in through the lace curtains falls across the foot of the bed like a white shawl. Beautiful. Oh, and some angel left my pain pills and a glass of water on the nightstand. They even opened the childproof bottle for me. I ease over, moaning, and take two. Okay, now I'm standing. Time to face my day. Bathroom, then coffee.

"Good morning," Dakota says from the long wooden table where she's writing on a yellow pad as I shuffle out into the front room.

"There's coffee and blueberry muffins," Maryann calls from her sewing machine. "Help yourself."

Muffins cooling on a rack on the counter. Granola and fresh strawberries. Hot coffee. Heaven.

I fill a hand-thrown ceramic mug with coffee and take a sip. Oh, thank God. Now if I could just make my screaming body shut up. Maryann has filled a couple plastic bags with ice cubes and left them in the freezer for me. I retreat to the easy chair, slap the ice against my ribs, then carefully unwrap my wrist and set it on top of the ice pack. My wrist is swollen and purple. I try to bend it, but the pain stops me. I try to flex my puffy fingers. Nope. Not today.

I close my eyes and almost fall asleep again, but the aroma of fresh muffins pulls me back to the surface. Breakfast.

I place blue willow dishes on a red quilted placemat, help myself to muffins, cereal and strawberries, pour myself a fresh cup of coffee, and settle into a chair across from Dakota.

Eating is a slow process. I reach out with my right hand, correct myself, and do it with the left, having to concentrate hard to do things I usually can manage without thinking about it. Just buttering a muffin with my left hand is a challenge.

But I plan to eat every heavenly bite. It's going to be hard staying P.D.-slim here. Too much good food. Plus I can't work out. But surely my body won't hurt this bad for long.

Out the window, I see the ground around the house is littered with pine needles and small branches, and the trees drip as if it's still raining. I wish I could go out for a walk.

"Are you getting enough to eat?" Maryann calls, stopping the sewing machine to cut the threads at the end of a seam.

"Oh my God. Plenty. It's all so good."

"I'm glad you enjoy it."

Dakota pushes her wooden chair back. "I'm going to go fetch some supplies and take care of that tree. Then I have to get to the post office."

I set down my fork. "Won't that make you really late?"

She shrugs. "It's a contract station, and I'm the boss. I called a friend to handle the counter till I get there. Gotta get that tree off the roof before the weather turns again."

"Well, let me help you." I start to get up, thinking I'll dress quickly and follow her down the road. Yeah, sure. Even my knee hurts. I scraped it pretty bad when I fell. I wonder if Dakota hears my little whimper of pain.

"No ma'am," Dakota says, throwing on her gray slicker. "You're grounded till you feel better. I've had busted ribs before. Hurts like hell, right?"

"Right." I sink back into my chair.

"So you stay here, keep Maryann company. Make some phone calls if you want. The landline works just fine."

"Thanks." I notice Hernando sleeping on the sofa. "I guess I should feed the cat."

"All done. I'll look for Sasha while I'm up there."

"Thank you for everything. How can I repay you?"

She smiles with her mouth closed. "No worries, P.D."

I don't know why, but I want to wail, and it's not from the physical pain. I guess it's that nobody has taken care of me for a long time.

As the rainbow van rattles down the hill, I lean back in my chair, staring out the window at blue sky, clouds, trees. I may not even get dressed today.

I have to notify somebody in Donovan's family about what has happened to the cabin, so I call Jonas's house from my station in the easy chair by the woodstove. Molly, his wife, seems to be dealing with a screaming kid as she answers. Apparently little Tim or Ty doesn't want to get dressed either. I explain what happened.

"Oh, I'm sorry. I don't know what to tell you. I'll have Jonas call when he wakes up."

I give her the number here, and then we're done. At least now the family knows about the tree trying to eat the cabin.

Time to check my cell phone messages.

Three from my mother, one from someone else.

As I'm dialing Mom, I notice a big yellow and red stuffed-animal-type turkey on a bookshelf near where Maryann sits sewing and realize I almost forgot Thanksgiving. It's only two weeks away. Crap. I'd like to keep forgetting it. I'm not looking forward to my first holidays without Tom. Mom's going to want me to hurry down to Santa Cruz because of course I can't be alone. Considering I'm struggling just to dial the phone with my left hand, I'm not sure how to make that work.

First I've got to tell her where I am. Well, sort of.

Ring, ring, ring, maybe I won't have to talk to her.

"Y'hello."

"Hi Mom."

"Well, finally. I've been calling and calling."

So much for "how are you?" "Remember I told you about the cabin where I'm staying. There's no phone and no elec—what?"

"Did you ever get it all down in writing?"

"No, not exactly. But—"

"That's not a good idea, dear. Anything could happen."

"I know. Mom, let me talk for a second. I'm calling from a friend's house." I'm aware Maryann is listening. I can tell because she has stopped humming.

"What kind of friend?"

Oh, for Pete's sake. "A girlfriend who lives nearby. Two women. Very nice, very helpful."

"Well, that's good. I hate to see you alone up there. So are you coming home for Thanksgiving? People have been asking, and I don't know what to tell them."

What people, I wonder. "Thanksgiving is . . ."

"A week from Thursday."

"I don't know, Mom."

"Well, we'd sure like to see you. I can make that pumpkin cheesecake you love."

Cissy loved it. P.D. doesn't eat cheesecake. Balancing the bulky phone between my neck and my shoulder, I pick at a loose bit of tape on my wrist brace and try to find the right words without telling her I'm busted up and staying with a couple of lesbians. "Mom, that sounds fantastic and I'd like to see you, but I can't leave here right now. Besides, the weather's not safe to drive in."

"I see." Now she sounds hurt. Maryann is staring at me.

"I'm sorry, Mom."

She sniffles. "Well, you have a family down here. Me, your brother, your aunt and uncle, Tom's folks. You can't keep ignoring us. We were there for you in your time of trouble."

Were they? Why is just sitting here, not even moving, making my cracked ribs hurt?

"I know. I'll come down in a few months, when the weather's better and things are more settled here."

"I don't understand what's to settle."

"I know, Mom."

"I could come up there."

"Oh no. That's too much trouble for you. Besides, everybody counts on you having Thanksgiving at your house."

"I suppose. But I miss my only daughter."

"I know."

And so it goes. Eventually I get off the phone, feel like an ax murderer for a while. I pet the cat, get another cup of coffee, check my cell phone messages one more time just because I have nothing else to do.

Deuce from the music store called, asking if I want to come jam. Nuts.

Sure, if he wants a one-handed piano player whose ribs hurt every time she takes a breath. But I don't want to lose the chance, so I'll call him back now and drop in as soon as I get my car charged and find the energy to get dressed.

"Ocean Harmony Music, home of beautiful sound and the best guitars in town."

Either he has no customers or he's goofing around with a friend.

"P.D. here."

"Hey, magic fingers."

Or he's high. Whatever. "I'm so sorry I missed your call, but I have no power and no phone service."

"That's what I figured. I just felt like jamming. Can you come down?"

I look down at my borrowed bathrobe and Technicolor wrist. "Um, no, not today. But soon. I hate to miss a chance to play music with you."

"Okey dokey, Smokey. I'll keep the piano bench warm."

As I hang up, I realize I don't hear the hum of the generator.

"Maryann, is the power back on?"

She pulls the pins out of her mouth. "Oh yes, it came back on sometime during the night. I'm glad it wasn't too long this time."

As she goes back to sewing, I just sit and breathe. Today that seems to be enough of a challenge to keep me busy. P.D. will not be performing today.

Phone calls done, I settle back in the easy chair with a book, but the pain pills make me sleepy. Pretty soon I've dozed off, lulled by Maryann's tuneful humming, the purr of the sewing machine, and, from the direction of Donovan Green's cabin, a chainsaw.

I AWAKEN TO PEOPLE talking and find myself looking into the cheery face of Jonas Peacock. Here I am in my night clothes, no makeup, hair probably flat.

"Hey, P.D."

I sit up as straight as I can, hoping I wasn't drooling or snoring. "Hi, Jonas."

"So a tree fell on Donovan's cabin."

I struggle to wake myself up. "Yeah, right over my bed. Good thing I wasn't in it." I stifle a yawn.

"This stuff happens up here. I'm sorry you got hurt."

"My fault. I probably shouldn't have been on the ladder, but I didn't know what else to do."

"You should have called me. With Uncle D. gone, I guess it's my problem. Definitely not yours."

Maryann interrupts. "Coffee, Jonas? Maybe a muffin?"

He grins. "Oh, yes please."

Soon he's sitting at the table drinking from another ceramic mug, this one shaped like a tree trunk with a handle. I wonder who the artist is, not that I'm into such things, but the Vicodin is making my mind wander.

I let Maryann refill my mug. "So Jonas, where the heck is your uncle?"

He shakes his head, chews a minute and swallows. "I don't know. He kind of does this. Disappears. He's—um—I probably shouldn't say anything." He scratches at his beard.

"Jonas. I'm sitting here with my wrist in a brace and broken ribs from trying to save his house. Tell me."

"Well, Uncle Donovan is bipolar, you know, manic-depressive. Plus he's an alcoholic. So he gets on a high, and he starts things and makes plans and does a lot of art, and then he goes into this dark place where he hides out from the world, doesn't talk to anybody, doesn't do anything but drink. I'm assuming that's where he's at now. We just hope he comes out of it all right."

"What do you mean?"

"After his wife left him a few years ago, he tried to kill himself. If Dakota hadn't come up to deliver a package and found him with the gun in his hand, he'd have died."

"Oh God." I'm trying to imagine this big man who seemed so mellow being so depressed that he'd kill himself. Then I picture Dakota wrestling the gun away from him. What if it had gone off?

I'm surprised to find I really care what happens to this man. I want to see him again.

Jonas sips his coffee and picks up the little crumbs left from his muffin. "Yeah, it sucks. I love my uncle, but I never know what version of him is going to show up. He was pretty calm last time he was here. I was hoping he had finally found the right drugs and would be okay over the long term. Guess not."

Outside, clouds have pulled across the sun. The sky is gray, threatening to rain again. Maryann quietly pins a seam as Jonas gazes out the window.

"Well, I ought to get going. Maryann, if you ever decide to open a bakery, I'll be there every day. And I'll be fatter than I already am." He pats his generous stomach as he stands and reaches for his jacket. "P.D., you came to the right place. Dakota and Maryann are ready for any disaster, right?"

Maryann nods as Jonas goes on. "I mean, have you seen how much wood they've got? And I'll bet Maryann has a hundred jars of food ready in case the big earthquake hits. The freezer is probably full of muffins, meat, fish, and homemade soup. Uh-oh, I'm making myself hungry again."

Maryann smiles. "Take another muffin for the road."

"It's not part of your doomsday stash, is it?"

"Go ahead and tease. If the earthquake does happen, we'll be ready with plenty of food."

"My mother owns a restaurant. We'll have food."

"Maybe."

Now that he mentions it, the rainbow ladies do seem to have an awful lot of wood stacked outside my bedroom window. And where did Maryann find strawberries in November?

Jonas is leaving. I have to ask him, "What about the cabin?"

"Well, P.D., here's the thing. First, I'm sorry I got you into this. I thought it would solve two problems at once. Instead it created several more. Knowing my uncle, you never signed a contract or anything. So, as far as I'm concerned, you don't have to worry about it. I went over and took a look at the cabin. That is a big tree and a dang big hole. I know a guy who will fix it up like new. I already talked to him, and he's got it on his schedule for a couple weeks from now." Jonas drinks the last of his coffee and wipes his beard with a cloth napkin. "In the meantime, I'm betting Maryann and Dakota will let you stay here for a while."

"As long as you need," Maryann says.

"Thank you."

"So if you still have stuff there, you can get it when you have time, and that's it."

"Yeah, my car is there, and a few other things."

"Cool. Well, I'd better get down the hill and back to work. Mrs. Mead is going to be needing her groceries again."

I feel a blast of cold air as he opens and closes the door.

Well, now I'm itchy to do something. The sky looks ominous, the clouds so dark it feels like twilight. Tom's Portuguese mother would have told me to keep *cou em casa*, my butt in the house, but I hate sitting still.

I ice my cracked bones again, watching the clock for 20 minutes to pass. The cold always feels good at first, but then it hurts, even through my nightgown.

Enough of sitting around in a bathrobe. I'm going to get dressed.

DID YOU EVER TRY to hook a bra with one hand? I have known men who prided themselves on their ability to *unhook* a bra with one hand, but it's not so easy when you're the one trying to wear it. Pants, socks and shoes are bad enough, but the bra is impossible.

I stand here half-naked for ten minutes trying to pull that thing around me and hook it up, but it keeps snapping out of my hand. I'm almost there, almost, almost, almost, I can feel the hooks approaching the eyes, then snap! I consider not wearing a bra at all, but I'm a 34C, and my breasts hang like water balloons without some support.

I come out, bra hanging off the front of me, the sides flapping in the back. "I need another hand."

Maryann looks up from her sewing and smiles. "Oh, you poor thing. Turn around." And snip-snap, I'm hooked. I want to just stand here and breathe for a minute because my ribs are killing me from all that dancing around with my bra, but I might as well get help with my shirt, too. She puts it on me, buttoning me up like I'm two years old.

I hate, hate, hate being helpless. A picture of me helping Tom get dressed tries to force itself into the front of my mind. I shake it off and try to make a joke.

"Well, I've had numerous men taking my clothes off over the years, but I haven't had anybody put them on me since my mom gave it up about forty years ago."

I force a chuckle, but Maryann is staring at me now. Uh-oh.

When she doesn't say anything, I add, "Thanks for helping me."

"You're welcome." She focuses on the seam she's basting. "I thought you were gay."

Suddenly the rain is pounding on the roof. "Oh. No. Never have been."

"I see."

"But it seems like a great way to go." God, I'm an idiot. "You and Dakota seem very happy together."

"We are."

"Is my not being gay a problem?"

"No, no. Of course not." But she doesn't look up. She's not humming or smiling anymore. "Dakota will be surprised. She wanted to introduce you to one of our friends."

Silence rises up from the floor like deadly gas, so I go hide in my room. That was awkward. Should I have lied?

I sit on the bed and cuddle Hernando. Male. He likes me. Sasha, female, hates me. Dakota . . .

It's my damned spiky orange hair, I decide as I do my best to arrange it with my left hand. I thought it made me look cool. I guess it just makes me look gay.

I plop my hat on my head and squeeze into my jacket, forcing my braced-up wrist through the sleeve, pulling the rest of the jacket around. It's almost as bad as the bra, but I manage it.

Maryann is doing something in the kitchen as I come out. Making cookies? She's got the cookie sheets on the counter.

"I'm going up to the cabin."

She turns. "Are you sure you're up to it? You need to keep your wrist elevated."

"I'm fine," I lie.

"Jonas said he'd take care of the cabin."

"I know. I just need to go for a walk. I'll see you in a little while."

Is it my imagination or is she beating those eggs with a little more force than necessary?

THE RAIN HAS STOPPED, but a cold wind thrashes the trees and beats on my face. My shoes crunch on the wet gravel as I move slowly up the hill. Yesterday morning I felt strong and buffed; now I feel like I've been sick in bed for a month. Still, it feels good to be outside.

The steep driveway is the worst part. When I breathe hard, my ribs talk to me. Well, it's not talking; it's more like cursing.

But I make it. The tree is off the house, replaced by a blue tarp, its edges flapping in the wind. Dakota is gone, but guess who's waiting for me? Ms. Sasha. And you know what? I don't have my keys. I don't have my damned house keys. They were still on the ring Donovan gave to me, and I gave it to Dakota. I do have my car keys. I was going to plug the car in to charge the battery, but I see by the cord running from the house to my car that Dakota has already done that. Of course. It's like having two moms, except one of them is more like a dad.

I pull the plug, get into my car, and turn the key. The engine starts right up. The cushiony seat feels good. I could just sit here for a couple hours. Or days. The cat is still hugging the front door, staring up at the knob as if she can make it open by force of will. Reluctantly, I get out of the car.

"Sasha, come on," I say, walking toward her. I hold out my good hand, make coaxing sounds with my tongue. "Come on, baby. Let me take you up to where there's food and warmth and Hernando." She's staring at me, seems to be listening. If she'd just let me pick her up—

As soon as I get within reach, just about to grab her under the belly, she slashes out with those claws again. I duck out of the way. Oh, my aching ribs! While she runs off to the woods, I stand there, hugging my elbow against my side. I exhale slowly and take in a gulp of cold air, then turn back toward the car. "Fine, cat. You're on your own."

I back out of the driveway and drive slowly down the hill, steering with my left hand and anchoring the steering wheel with my right elbow. I fully intend to drive into town, pain pills and all, but no. As I bump along the gravel road, the urge to curl up in a ball and let my car go where it will without me is so strong, I turn off at the rainbow house. Maybe tomorrow. Or the next day.

14

"WHAT HAPPENED TO YOU?" Deuce interrupts his transaction with a kid buying drumsticks to ask.

"Well, you see, there was this tree and this ladder and then I fell, and here I am, cuts and bruises, sprained wrist, cracked ribs, one-handed piano player."

"Damn. Wait a sec while I help this young man. $9.95 please."

The kid pulls a multi-folded ten-dollar bill out of his back pocket.

I sit down at the beautiful black baby grand and run my left hand over an E major scale. Oh man. I reach out my battered right hand and touch the treble keys with my fingertips. If I am very careful, I can poke out one note at a time. Sigh. It's better than nothing. I start to take a deep breath and wince. Stupid ribs.

Deuce finishes with the kid and comes to stare down at me. He shakes his head. "Damn, girl. Your face is so white and your hair so red you look like a lit match. When did this happen?"

"Wednesday." It's Saturday now. I finally made it down the hill.

He glances out the window. "You drove yourself here?"

"Yes, I sneaked out, said I was going for a walk."

"Sneaked out of where?"

"I'm staying with two women, Dakota and Maryann, up Beaver Creek."

"Mutt and Jeff? One really tall and one kind of short and fat?"

I chuckle. "That's the ones."

"Maryann plays the violin. Not fiddle, mind you. Violin. Classical. She comes here for strings and stuff. Did you know that?"

"No. I had no idea. Is there anything she can't do?"

He grins. "I can think of one."

I close the lid on the piano and start to get up, feel dizzy, sit back down. Maybe I'm really not up to this yet.

Deuce puts a hand on my shoulder. "I'm sorry. I couldn't help myself." He looks out the window, chewing on his lower lip, making his beard move. "You're not one of them, are you?"

"What, gay? No. I like men."

"That's a relief. You be careful they don't convert you."

"They won't."

"Well, I wish I could jam with you, but I've got my accountant coming in, and my books are a mess."

"Oh, sure. My head is fuzzy from the pain pills anyway. I should go back and rest. It's time for more ice." I stand up, groaning.

"P.D., wait. We're not going to jam again for a week or two. Buddy is getting ready for crab season. But I have something for you." He goes back behind the counter, reaches into a display case, and pulls out a box containing a lime green harmonica. "Ever play the harp?"

"No."

"Well, the paper in there will show you where the notes are. I know with your musical chops you'll be blowing the blues in no time. The key of E's perfect for the blues. And pushing all that air in and out will be good for your ribs. Plus you can play it with one hand. Two lips, one hand."

"I-I should pay you for it, but I-I don't have any money." Since when do I stutter?

"Just take it. It's a cheap one. Come back the Wednesday after next, four o'clock. We will rock the house. Go home and practice."

I'm feeling tears. No way. Not crying. "Thanks," I whisper, hugging my elbow against my ribs.

He starts to hug me, then pulls back. "I don't want to you hurt you. Feel better soon, P.D. Remember, a week from Wednesday, day before Thanksgiving. I expect a solo or two."

I nod and go out into the cool sunshine, blinking back tears. In my whole life, nobody has ever encouraged my music as much as people have since I came here.

In the car, I pull the harp out of its case and put the cool green tin between my lips. I blow. Three notes sound at once, an E chord. Moving up the holes, I find A and B7, the other main chords in the key. I go back and forth a few times until I'm smiling so hard it's impossible to blow. It sounds like a party.

And now, on blues harp: PD!

THE NEXT WEEK is a blur—except for Janey's visit. She bops on over after work at the diner one night. Wednesday? Maybe. I've been taking the pain pills because damn, it hurts. In between pills, ice, and naps—where I kind of half sleep, aware but unable to move—I work on this giant jigsaw puzzle Dakota set up on the table for me, try to read, and blow on my harmonica. Sometimes all at the same time.

Playing the mouth harp is not so hard. I can play a couple tunes now. "Jingle Bells" from the instruction sheet. "O Susanna" from my head. "Amen." The thing with single-key harmonicas is you don't have all the notes in the scale, so you have to work around the ones that are missing. Also, the order of notes you blow or suck changes about two-thirds of the way up, so it's blow-suck, blow-suck, blow-suck, suck-blow, suck-blow, and so on.

On the high end, the notes are so piercing Hernando runs and hides. I'm grateful Dakota and Maryann haven't complained yet, but they do seem to encourage me to work on that puzzle, and I'm just OCD enough to spend hours at it. The puzzle is a picture of a wolf on a mountaintop. Everything seems to be shades of tan or brown, except for a little bit of sky at the top, so it's a challenge.

Anyway, I'm dressed in flannel and denim, my hair lying flat, the roots coming out the same brown as this patch of wolf fur I'm working on, when Janey shows up. Everybody knows everybody around here, so the ladies are all huggy-happy. I hate to set down the piece in my hand. I just know I can find where it goes, but we have company, so I smile up at Janey and release my grip on the puzzle piece.

She's like the sun, all bright and shiny with her pink skin and wild yellow curls and a red sweater that fits snug over her curves. She talks in exclamation points.

"P.D.! Jonas told me what happened! I'm so sorry! I knew something was wrong when I didn't see you at the Whale for karaoke and you didn't come into the diner. Especially with the sun out and all. How do you feel?!!"

I shrug. "A little broken, but I'm healing. I'll come sing next week. Meanwhile Deuce at the music store gave me a harmonica and I'm driving my hosts crazy with it."

Maryann shakes her head. "No, it's not so bad."

"Please. Jingle Bells ten times in a row, with assorted wrong notes. You're too kind. Anyway, I can do it with one hand. He wants me to jam with it next week."

"Cool. Why don't you play me a tune now?"

"Well . . ."

"Come on, P.D. I drove all the way up this hill to see you."

So I go to my room and get the lime green harmonica. When I come back, Janey is seated in my easy chair with a cup of tea in her hand. Maryann is watching from her chair by the sewing machine.

I put the thing between my lips, blow a couple of experimental notes to make sure I don't have it upside down, and launch into my greatest hits. Pretty soon Janey's singing along, and then, to my surprise, Maryann has got her fiddle—no, violin—on her shoulder. She plays a round of "O Susanna," then launches into a jig. I toot along and Janey's wailing. I put down the harp and sing, too, in harmony. Then Janey's up and dancing. I start to move, but my ribs curse me, and I sink into a chair. But oh, it's fun. It's a moment, you know. If Tom didn't die and I didn't drive all the way to nowhere, Oregon, move into Donovan's cabin, fall off the ladder and move in with these gay ladies, this would not have happened.

Dakota has brought some more of my stuff here, so now I get out my rented keyboard. After all, we can't play everything in the key of E. I lay it on the table, turn it on, and start doing chords and notes with my left hand. My right hand is itching to join the music. Actually it just itches in general. I un-Velcro my brace, touch my pale fingers to the keys, and discover I can play. I can't stretch my fingers out, but I can definitely do single notes and thirds—that's two notes with an unplayed key in between them. And now the concert is on. Hernando, that little piano lover, is brushing around my legs. If cats can dance, he's doing it.

We're still playing when Dakota comes home from the post office. "Hey, what's this?" she says, smiling, showing the gap between her front teeth. "I'm working all day, and you-all are partying."

"Join us!" Janey hollers.

Dakota disappears into her bedroom for a minute, then comes out with a conga drum. She pulls out a chair, sits, puts the drum between her legs and starts beating out a rhythm.

I'm in heaven.

Of course eventually the pain pills wear off, and my wrist starts screaming almost as bad as my ribs, and we all get tired and thirsty. I want a beer. Maryann offers herbal tea. Whatever. I've got to rest now, but I can't wait to sing and play again, wherever, whenever. I just know that's what God put me on this earth to do.

Maryann invites Janey to stay for supper, but she's anxious to get down the hill to her apartment in town before dark. So it's just us and an eggplant casserole. We're quietly eating when Dakota gets all serious looking and says, "P.D., we have to talk to you about something."

Uh-oh, I think the party's over.

15

THEY LOOK SO serious. So I get all P.D. and try to lighten things up. "I'll go play my harmonica in the woods if it's driving you nuts. I mean, I don't want to—"

"No," Dakota says. "The harp's cool. This is about Thanksgiving."

"Oh. Yeah. It's coming up."

Maryann nods. "A week from tomorrow."

Dakota continues. "Maryann overheard you telling your mom you weren't coming to her house. California?"

I nod, thinking it's none of their business.

"We think you should go. Fly if it hurts too much to drive."

"What? Why?"

I think they're going to get all family-is-the-most-important-thing on me, but they surprise me.

"Here's the thing." Dakota pokes at a sliver on her left thumb. "We're not going to be here."

"Oh. Okay."

"We're driving to Minnesota to spend some time with Maryann's family. Then we're going to South Dakota to see my people. So we're going to be gone a good two weeks. Maybe longer. We're leaving Monday."

Dakota gets up, crosses the room to Maryann's sewing machine table and comes back with a needle. She starts digging at the sliver, wincing as the point draws blood.

"Well, that's okay. I can stay here if it's all right, or I can go back to the cabin."

"Sweetie, you're not ready to be alone," Maryann says. "Especially if there's another storm."

That raises my hackles. She may be a little older than I am, but she's not the boss of me. "I can take care of myself." After all, I have now figured out how to hook my bra. I've pretty much gotten the hang of doing things with my left hand. In another week, I might even be good at it. Or maybe my injured hand will be functional. I just played the keyboard with it. The ribs hurt, but I'm not helpless.

"You're still on pain meds," Dakota says.

"Fine. I'll quit taking them today. I like it here, but I don't need a babysitter."

Maryann frowns at Dakota. "P.D., we've hurt your feelings. I'm so sorry." She scoots around the table and takes the needle away from Dakota, digs for a minute then holds up the bloody sliver. "Got it."

"Thanks, baby." Dakota leans over and kisses Maryann on the mouth.

Maybe it's time for P.D. to go somewhere else. "You guys go on your trip. Don't worry about me. I've imposed on you long enough."

I push back my chair, get up, grab my jacket off the rack by the door and go outside, leaving them to talk about me, make out, or whatever.

It's a clear night, stars so dense there are no black spaces between them, the moon so bright I almost need sunglasses. And it's quiet, just the slightest hum from either the surf or the highway or maybe both. I walk out toward the road.

My surroundings are calm, but I'm not. I'm pissed. I walk north on Beaver Creek Road toward Donovan's cabin, not really thinking about where I'm going, just moving my feet to match the mad pace of my thoughts.

I'm not angry at Maryann and Dakota. They're correct; I do still need a little help. Without them, it's going to be hard. And they have a right to do whatever they want, whether it's kissing in their own house or driving to Minnesota to see the folks. As for me going home to Mom, well, that's what most people would do. They would spend the holidays with family. It makes sense.

I'm mad at my situation. I didn't ask for all this, and people just don't understand. I'm not ready for all that family, all those reminders of Tom being gone, all those people who see me as Cissy, not P.D., who see me as the pitiful widow. Now the pitiful *wounded* widow.

Driving 700 miles to Santa Cruz would hurt like hell. I wouldn't be able to lift my own suitcase. I'm not up for the expense of an airplane trip and the madness of the airport at Thanksgiving. I know Mom would pay for a plane ticket and pick me up at the airport. All I have to do is say yes. But I just don't want to go. Nor do I want to spend Thanksgiving alone. Stupid holidays.

At this point, I've reached Donovan's cabin. I still don't have the damned keys. If I'd been thinking, I would have taken them off the hook by the door.

I walk up the steep driveway, pleased it doesn't hurt as much as it did last time, and walk around the cabin. In the moonlight, Donovan's odd sculptures gawk at me like fairytale creatures.

Around the back of the cabin, amid a scatter of fallen branches, I notice a big empty space where the tree that fell used to be. Dakota has stacked the fresh wood under the steps. I'm looking up at the tarp-covered roof when I hear a low growl.

Oh God. Coyote? Raccoon? Cougar? Bear? I think of all the creatures Donovan warned me about. I think about how I'm down here without a flashlight or anything to protect myself with. I think about how I will sacrifice my injured hand and my fractured ribs to save my life. I think—

I'd better get out of here.

My heart is pounding. I wonder if I will see the creature before it attacks me. I wonder if I will scream before I die. I startle as a twig cracks under my shoe.

Signs at the visitor's center down below say you should shout and make yourself appear as big as possible by standing tall and stretching out. I just want to curl up in a ball and hide. Preferably in a warm bed in a safe house, like the place I just left. Maybe I should go to Santa Cruz and let Mom take care of me. I could take a bus. Maybe she'd come and get me. Maybe—

Wait. I hear it again. Near the woodpile. Shoot. It's not a wild animal. It's Sasha, her eyes glittering at me in the moonlight. Warily, I move closer, expecting her to run or lash out at me with those killer claws. But she doesn't move. "Hi, cat, what's going on?"

She meows, but it's a strained sound, not her usual clear notes.

As I get close enough and Sasha tries to stand, I see why. Her left shoulder is covered with dried blood.

"Oh, Sasha."

She doesn't resist as I gather her into my arms. She weighs so little it doesn't even hurt my ribs. I stroke her head and feel her purring. What else can I do but take her back to Dakota and Maryann?

I can feel Sasha staring at my face as we walk down the dark road. Fear and pain radiate from her shaking little body, and it's my fault. I didn't insist on bringing her in. I told Donovan I'd take care of his cats, and I failed. He called Sasha "my little girl." I know he disappeared on me, but that's not the cat's fault, and I understand from losing my dog Harry how it feels to lose a pet.

I stroke Sasha's fur, no longer afraid of her flying claws. She is so soft. And so small I can feel her ribs. I don't know if she'll survive.

By the time I reach the door of the rainbow house, I'm out of breath and hurting. Thank God it's unlocked. I push on in. Dakota and Maryann are not in the kitchen or living room. I hear murmuring from their bedroom. Please God, don't let them be doing it.

"Hello!" I call.

No response. I am not going to interrupt them if they're— never mind.

Hernando trots out of my bedroom, looking up at Sasha, winding around my feet. Sasha does not respond.

Now's when I could use some of that Mother Earth energy Maryann projects. But no. I take the cat into the bathroom, spread a towel on the linoleum floor and lay her down. In the bright light, I mop away enough of the blood with a washcloth to see she has a deep cut between her neck and her shoulder.

As I press the cloth against the wound, Sasha yowls.

"It's okay, girl," I tell her, but she's not buying it. She yowls again, louder and louder.

"What's going on?" Dakota says from the doorway. Her long wavy hair is loose, her shirt half-unbuttoned. For the first time, she looks like a woman to me.

"I found her by the cabin. She's half-starved, and she's hurt. I think she needs stitches."

"Let me see."

Dakota's body radiates heat as she kneels down, her arm grazing mine as she bends over the cat, probing with her long fingers. Sasha is quiet now, surrendering.

"Well, I don't know. It's pretty much stopped bleeding, and it doesn't seem to be infected. I think it might heal on its own if we put some antiseptic on it and bandage it up a little. Besides, we'd have to drive a long way to find a vet who's open this time of night."

She leans into the cabinet beneath the sink and pulls out gauze, tape and a tube of antiseptic cream.

I hold onto Sasha, but she shows no inclination to move. In a minute, Dakota has her all patched up. We wait to see if she can stand on her own.

Several minutes pass. Dakota and I kneel on the bathroom floor watching. Maryann comes to the doorway, a quilted bathrobe cinched around her waist. "What's happening?"

"Kitty's hurt," I say.

"And starving," Dakota adds. "Watch her. I'll get some food and water."

"I'll get it," Maryann says. Her slippers swish across the wooden floor.

"Come on, Sasha," I whisper. She looks up at me, her expression seeming to say it's just too hard. "Come on. I know it hurts."

Dakota glances at me. I look back into her gray eyes. From the kitchen, we hear the sound of kibble being poured into a bowl. Sasha hears it, too. Slowly, painfully, she rises on her shaky legs and heads toward the sound.

In a minute, she's crunching the hard pellets.

"She's gonna be fine," Dakota says, going into the bathroom and closing the door behind her.

Maryann stands at the kitchen counter, swirling a tea bag in a mug of hot water. "Chamomile," she says.

"Ah."

I don't know what to say to these women anymore. I lean against the kitchen wall, watching as Maryann takes her tea to a chair by the fire. I don't belong here. I love the warmth, the good food, the electricity, and the seeming ability of Maryann and Dakota to fix anything. But it's time to go.

They have been nothing but kind. I need to apologize. They don't know about Tom, don't know I'm living with widow brain, which must be a little like being 13 all over again.

It's so quiet I hear the old school clock ticking on the wall above me.

"Maryann, I'm sorry for being so bitchy. You have been so good to me, but I've got some things I need to figure out. When you guys leave on Monday, I'll take the cats back to the cabin. We'll be fine."

"Okay," Maryann says, gazing into the fire. "No worries, P.D."

FOR THE NEXT three days, both cats sleep on the bed with me. Dakota, Maryann and I maintain a polite distance. I'm not exactly sure what happened between us. Maybe they're pissed at my declaration of independence, embarrassed I caught them making love, or tired of having a houseguest. Maybe they're just worried about me. Maybe they've joined the Pitiful Cissy club. I need to do something to repay them, but I haven't figured out what yet. When I offer to watch over their house while they're gone, they tell me there really isn't anything that needs doing.

In preparation for going back into the no-phone zone, I make calls. Stella, the real estate agent in Missoula, says she plans to add some potted plants and get somebody to weed the garden, if I don't mind. And no, nobody has expressed any interest in looking at the house. It's not a good time of year to try to sell, she says.

"So why are the tenants leaving?"

"Too cold," Stella says. "And the guy lost his job. Also, the wife is pregnant with twins and they need more space."

"That all happened kind of quickly, didn't it?"

Stella doesn't respond.

I'm starting to have second thoughts about taking a chance on selling the house before I go bankrupt. "Maybe we should try to rent it again."

"Mrs. Soares, we still need all those repairs, which you said you can't afford."

She's starting to tick me off. "Well, if you had gotten more reliable tenants . . ."

"I'm doing my best."

"Right. Just sell it as quickly as you can. I'll be waiting to hear from you."

I get another cup of coffee and steel myself for my next call.

I don't feel like talking to my mother, but figure I ought to touch base once more. I'm thrilled when my brother Andy answers instead of Mom.

"Hey, Cissy, where the hell are you?"

"Seal Rock, Oregon. Up in the hills off the coast."

"Nice. Mom says you're house-sitting."

"Yeah." But I'm not there. "What's new with you?"

"Oh, you know. I'm allegedly learning the landscaping biz, but I feel like all I do is weed-eat and haul stuff. It's not like I'm planting or designing or anything. Except at Mom's house. You ought to see what I've done with the yard."

I settle into the easy chair by the woodstove. Dakota and Maryann are out, so I have the house to myself for a while. I miss my freckle-faced little brother, who's not so little anymore. A late-life surprise for my folks, he has always seemed like a kid to me, but he's a man now, old enough to have served in the Army right after high school. Iraq. We held our breath the whole time, but he came home happy to be alive and ready to pursue his dreams. "What did you do with the yard?"

"Oh, Cissy, you should see—"

"Call me P.D."

"That's right. Sorry. I took out all the old junk plants and bricks and planted some new drought-tolerant plants that look good without a lot of work. I put in a path and added a couple benches."

"Sounds nice." I glance out the windows, suddenly sick of pine trees. Santa Cruz is by the ocean, too, but it's warmer and drier.

"Mom's worried about you being all alone. You ought to come down for Thanksgiving. She's planning the usual feast."

I can't deal with the guilt thing this year. Not from Mom or from Andy. "I can't this year. I'm sorry. Listen, I have to go. Somebody's at the door. Happy Thanksgiving, Kiddo. Tell Mom and everybody I love them and miss them."

"Okay. I love you, Cis-uh, P.D."

"Bye."

I click off the phone and set it on the table beside me. Sasha comes up, meowing. I pull her gently into my lap. "Well, it's just us cats for Thanksgiving. Do you like turkey?"

16

It's Monday. Before Dakota and Maryann left around 7 a.m., as the sky was getting light, Dakota loaded my stuff in my car for me. Maryann prepared a care package of all the leftover food from the refrigerator and the pantry. They hugged me goodbye and told me to take my time, but now that they're gone, I figure I'd better get out, too. My stupid stomach is doing the Macarena. It's funny; it was fine the whole time I was here, but now that I'm leaving, it's freaking out again. Nerves. Has to be. I don't know what to do about that except keep going. My stomach doesn't seem to know we're P.D. now, not delicate old Cissy.

I grab Hernando and my new buddy Sasha one at a time and put them in the car, figuring they won't walk up the hill by themselves. Why give up the good life in the rainbow house? I can't blame them.

My tires crunch over gravel and mud. A truck passes, spraying my car with more mud, squeezing me to the side of the road.

Six more months, huh? At the mailbox, I turn right, climb the hill, and think about what I'll have for lunch.

But wait. There's smoke coming out of the chimney. And a blue pickup truck parked out front. Pain streaks through my stomach. Donovan? Was his truck blue? I don't remember. Our interaction was so brief I can barely remember what *he* looks like. If he's here, then what do I do? He can't just kick me out. He's supposed to be gone for seven months. I know, we didn't have anything in writing, but . . .

When I open the car door, Hernando jumps over my lap to get out. Sasha hesitates. I'm sure it looks like a long ways down from her perspective with her bum shoulder. I grab her and float her to the ground. Both cats head for the front door, tails high. Chow time?

As usual, I reach for the front door with my right hand then have to switch to my left because my wrist is still in the stupid brace, all the time praying, "Dear God, don't let anybody be in there. Let the truck be—I don't know—let it not be trouble."

Opening the door, I look around and see nobody. The fire is burning in the woodstove. There's a note on the counter in Dakota's right-slanted scrawl. "Welcome home. We thought it would be nice if it was warm and cozy for you, even if you are stubbornly independent. Call us if you get in trouble." D and M

She left her cell phone number.

Nice. I'm such a bitch for complaining.

I glance into the bedroom. Nobody there either. The furniture is all back in place. The bed is made, with clean pillowcases and a fresh sheet lapped over the quilt. Nicer than I deserve.

The cats are picketing for food, not that it's actually mealtime. But I've got to know about that truck parked out front.

The studio looks the same as when I left it. The wine stain has dried to a soft pink. I go out the back door. At first I don't see anything except the whole nature scene, with some fallen trees in the mix. Pretty sky, looks like it's quilted with clouds.

A voice hails me. "Hello!"

I look down and see a man wearing a blue jacket and a black baseball cap. He's in the process of collapsing an extension ladder.

"Hey!" I call back, going down the stairs. "What's going on?"

"I just finished fixing your roof." He pulls off a glove and holds out his hand. "Rick Jones."

He's the guy from the diner whom Janey called "Uncle Rick." "Hi. I didn't expect to see anybody here."

"Well, I'm a friend of Donovan's family, and Jonas asked me to take care of this. He said you'd be home today, so I wanted to make sure everything was secure. It ain't gonna leak on you anymore."

Looking up, I see perfectly matched shingles and no evidence a tree bashed a hole in the roof. "Wow. It looks great." I take in a deep breath of cold, pine-scented air. "Thank you."

"No problem." He puts his glove back on and picks up the end of the ladder. "I see you banged yourself up."

"Yes, I tried to get the tree off the roof and fell off the ladder."

"Ouch. I've done that a couple times myself. Broke some ribs."

"Me too," I say, patting my side.

He smiles at me. I smile back. He's got the shiniest eyes, ocean blue, bright against his tanned skin. Bedroom eyes, my mother used to call them. His hair under the hat is black, stippled with gray. I get a good vibe from Rick Jones, even though he needs a shave and smells slightly of sweat. He said he was a friend, not Jonas' uncle. Interesting.

"Can I help you carry the ladder?" I ask.

"You've got a dinged-up hand."

"But the other one works just fine."

"And your broken ribs?"

"I can handle it."

He laughs. "Sure. Grab an end."

And I do, but as we walk around the cabin to the truck, I can tell he's carrying most of the weight.

Soon he's got the ladder and all his tools in the truck and is ready to go.

"Thank you again," I say.

"Be safe," he responds. "Stay off the ladder." He turns the truck around and rattles down the hill as I watch.

I follow the truck as far as the mailbox, thinking I probably won't have anything in it, but I'm wrong. I pull out a fistful of bills—mortgage, car insurance, cell phone bill—and a postcard with a picture of the Grand Canyon. Apparently my wandering father is in Arizona. Wish I was.

Okay, cats, here I come. Now my stomach is just fine. Let's all have a snack, then curl up by the fire and figure out what comes next.

AFTER MUSHROOM SOUP, a blueberry muffin and a nap, I feed another log into the fire and come outside because I have already learned that if the sun is shining around here, a body had better take advantage of it.

These first few weeks, I've pretty much ignored the garden. I mean what can you do when you've got killer rain and hurricane-force winds? Now, I'm not sure how useful I can be with my gimpy hand and the ribs that are screaming after my helpfulness with the ladder. Not that I would ever tell Rick Jones.

I smile thinking about him. It's crazy. He probably has a wife and kids, an ex and kids, a 25-year-old girlfriend, or all of the above. Probably hangs out in bars when he's not working. But still . . . I felt something with him that I haven't felt in a long time. Okay, it's lust. I'm surprised at myself, but there it is.

Anyway, let me tell you about Donovan's garden. Picture a circle of shrubs with various sizes and shapes of leaves. I recognize a couple rhododendrons and some rosemary and lilac. Come spring, they'll be blooming in pink, blue and purple, but in November they use all their energy just to stay alive. I see sticks that probably turn into something prettier in the spring and berry bushes with nothing but thorns at this time of year.

Inside the ring of shrubs, I find a weird collection of stuff that my mom would label junk, but I kind of like it. Donovan has cups and saucers up on posts, a sculpted elf with a clam-shell hat, upside-down wine bottles like bunny ears on top of a red stop sign on top of two little tires that stick out like shoes. I think there might be a message there. On the stop sign, above the white lettering, he has glued blue glass eyeballs and under the letters a curved bone of some sort for a mouth.

That's not all. I see a crab net with a wooden seagull inside, the totem pole I mentioned before with four women's faces gazing in all four directions, green bottles of different heights lined up like organ pipes, and a bird bath made out of a pink toilet bowl. I reach into the icy water to flick away a few leaves and pine cones and notice lettering along the rim that says "drink here and eat there," with an arrow pointing toward a wooden bird feeder. The feeder is empty, but I notice some seeds on the ground and decide I'd better fill it up, just in case birds can read. Maybe he's got a bag of birdseed in the house somewhere.

Inside the ring of shrubs and around the stop sign, bird bath and other doodads, Donovan has planted a faux flower garden with petals of fused glass blooming atop stalks of copper wire. It's quite beautiful with the sun shining on it, a nice touch where nothing blooms half the year. But strange.

I'm wondering what it was Donovan thought I could take care of. I mean, I certainly don't have to water, considering how much it rains. Nothing's blooming or fruiting or whatever, except a few mushrooms. The sculptures could use some cleaning, but they'll just get dirty again. He's one weird dude.

AS I MENTIONED before, you don't waste sunshine here. I sit out on the back porch with a book and a glass of iced tea, soaking it up. I'm really enjoying the solitude right now. It's so quiet I can feel peace seeping into my bones. When I pay attention, my breathing is slow and easy. My previously gnarly stomach is sated with Maryann's soup. Even the cats are at peace, sleeping down below in a patch of sunlight.

But then the sun moves and I feel cold. Looking out over the valley, I see the sun is shifting to the west, so I think I will, too. I lock up the cabin and drive down the hill.

Cars dot the parking lot at Ona Beach. The giant puddles from before have evaporated into patches of mud. I walk the paved path past the picnic tables and the restroom, go through the trees and over the footbridge and emerge at the sand. A barking black Lab watches anxiously for its owner to toss a Frisbee, then charges into the surf to get it. A gray-haired couple walk together barefoot along the lacy edge of the waves, bending every few feet to pick up shells or agates. A young mom digs in the sand with her little girl, using red rubber shovels.

The sun is nearly to the horizon, silvering the water and the wet sand where the waves go in and out. It's too bright to stare at but beautiful. I wonder if the eagles are still on the bluffs above the beach. I take off my shoes and socks and feel my feet sink into the cool sand. Back in Santa Cruz, sometimes the sand was so hot it burned our feet, sending us running into the water for relief. Not here. Got to keep moving to keep warm.

The tide is not out as far as it was that other time when I saw the bald eagle's nest, and I don't want another soaking. I keep my eye on the waves and stay close to the wet rocks, wincing when my bare feet hit the occasional crab shell, rock or bit of seaweed. My bruised toe that I hurt the day of the fallen tree still aches, but I choose to ignore it.

Around the bend, I look up. Sure enough, high on the cliff, there she is, all white-headed and gray-feathered, sitting on her nest of sticks and leaves. "Hey!" I shout like an idiot. The lady eagle spreads her wings halfway out, making me nervous. Apparently I'm too big to be prey so she folds her wings back up and returns to contemplating the ocean.

I walk a little farther. The wind has blown the sand into ridges and valleys. The tide is coming in, so I turn around. As I pass the older couple, the man salutes me with his plaid wool cap. I nod and smile back.

That wouldn't happen in Santa Cruz or Missoula.

Back on the wider stretch of beach, I find a sheltered spot and sit on the dry sand, wrapping my arms around my legs, feeling the rough wrist brace scratch against my jeans. It was near here that I handed over the little girl's bracelet to Ranger Dave. I wonder what happened to it. I wonder what happened to her.

The waves roll up, get bigger and break into a happy froth of white, easing across the sand, following the same pattern wave after wave. Beyond the breakers, it's calm blue water all the way to the horizon. I have a hard time believing it could change so much so quickly, but I remember the tsunami pictures on TV from Japan last March. The water rolled in and sucked everything up, turning houses, stores, cars, and people into toys that it ripped apart and took away. It roared right into people's bedrooms. Nothing was safe in its path. Could these benign waves suddenly turn into monsters, just like in Japan?

They talked about tsunamis in Santa Cruz, too. I was 19 when the Loma Prieta earthquake trashed our town. It knocked down houses and stores, including the mall, and killed 63 people in the Bay Area. We were lucky. We just had some broken dishes and a lot of stuff on the floor. Hundreds of people lived in government-issued trailers for over a year because their houses were no longer habitable. But we didn't have a tsunami. It wasn't the right kind of earthquake for that.

Back in 1964, a tsunami hit Crescent City in Northern California and pretty much wiped out the town. That was after the big Alaska earthquake that reverberated all around the Pacific Rim. I wasn't born yet, but we heard about it in school.

All it takes is one earthquake of the right type in the right place. A few minutes warning, and here comes the mother of all waves. But how likely is it really? Even if towns along the coast keep preaching tsunami preparedness and some have installed warning sirens in case the big one hits, I have lived by the ocean nearly all my life and never seen it happen. God, the moon, whatever. The waves know where to stop.

Time to go. With a glance at the sun sinking toward the tinfoil sea, I put my shoes on and walk back to the trail that leads over the footbridge and through the park.

From the bridge, I hear voices and stop to watch a young couple floating down the river in a two-seater kayak. I had hoped Donovan would have a kayak I could borrow, but he doesn't. I searched all over. I don't know how I would have gotten it down to the water anyway.

It makes me giggle to think about such a big guy sitting in a kayak. How would it hold him up? Donovan would need a much bigger boat.

I get so busy watching the kayakers I don't notice Ranger Dave until he's right beside me. "Hi, P.D.," he says, joining me in leaning against the railing.

"Hi. I'd sure like to do that," I say, pointing toward the kayaks.

"You should."

"I guess I could rent a kayak."

He smiles, revealing deep dimples. "I've got a better idea."

"Oh?"

"My daughter Amy and I are going on Saturday. I lead kayak trips down Beaver Creek in the spring and summer, so I've got a whole bunch of kayaks stored up at South Beach. I'd be happy to loan you one and show you the ropes. What's your favorite color?"

"Red."

"Good choice. We'll meet you on Saturday at the put-in across the highway with a red kayak for you and a yellow one for us."

Well, why not? "What time?"

"8:30. We'll paddle along the creek a couple hours, then get brunch at the diner."

He's smiling so broadly. How can I resist? "Okay. Thanks."

What about my wrist? And my ribs? I'll P.D. through the pain. Does he have a wife who's staying home to do the laundry or something?

But he doesn't seem to be worried about anything. "Great. If anything comes up, call me, but I hope nothing does." He pulls a card out of his shirt and hands it to me. Dave Walsh, it says.

He squeezes my shoulder and it's not an oh-poor-Cissy kind of squeeze. It's an I- really-like-you squeeze.

He walks away whistling. I normally hate whistling, but he's pretty good at it. Musical even. I wonder if he sings.

By the time I get into my car, I'm whistling, too.

I'm looking forward to my kayak trip on Saturday and the jam session on Wednesday. But there's more. My phone catches me just before I would have driven out of range. I pull off Beaver Creek Road to answer.

It's Janey. "P.D., what are you doing for Thanksgiving? I heard that Dakota and Maryann were leaving, and I don't want you to be all alone."

As if I would shrivel up and die if I spent a holiday by myself. "I don't have any plans, but I'm okay," I say.

"Well, we're all meeting at the diner for Thanksgiving dinner. Mom likes to do it there because she has the space and the big kitchen and doesn't have to clean her house. It'll be me and Jonas's family and Mom and a few of our friends. I'd love for you to come. Maybe we could sing something if we're not too stuffed with turkey. What do you say?"

In the background, I hear clinking dishes and a murmur of voices. She must be at the diner now. "That sounds good. What time?"

"Noon."

"Can I bring anything?"

"Bring your instruments and a big appetite."

"I'll be there." This new life is getting better by the minute.

"Good. Are you karaokeing tonight?"

"Sure." I still hate karaoke, but I'm here to sing.

I have one more message on my phone that I didn't notice before. Somebody saw my card at the music store. They actually want me to be the paid entertainment for an anniversary party up in the hills above Newport. I call right back and accept. It's this Wednesday, the day after tomorrow. Obviously I'm a last-minute substitute for whoever they really wanted, but I don't care. P.D. has a gig.

17

IT'S A GOOD karaoke night at the Whale. Outside, the weather has turned cold, and clouds hide the stars, but inside, it's warm and loud and fun. Janey and I duet on a whole set of songs. There's a group of Newport Chamber of Commerce people at the big corner table. They clap like crazy.

One older lady suggests we're just like the two women in the movie "Chicago." Janey looks like Renée Zellweger, so I guess that makes me Catherine Zeta-Jones. I might have the voice and the breasts, but I don't have the long dark hair. I could, of course. I'm hiding my roots with my fedora, but with a box of dye I can make it any color I want. It's getting a little too long to stand up like it was doing in my original P.D. hairdo, but I'm starting to wonder if that's the image I want anyway. Maybe I should dye it jet black and get some piercings and tattoos.

Anyway, since the woman brought up "Chicago," I scan the song list and find "All That Jazz." Oh, we ham it up big, even doing the dancing, even though neither one of us can actually dance, my ribs won't let me shimmy, and the wrist brace doesn't quite fit the image. When we return to our table, fresh drinks are waiting for us, a beer for me and a tequila sunrise for Janey.

You can't top us, so young Collin, the MC, takes a break. The older lady asks if we're available for special events. I want to shout, "Hell yes!" but I just smile and say, "Yes. Thanks for asking." I hand her my card. She slips it into the pocket of her blazer. Her name tag says she's Tamara Boyle, chamber vice president. This is good, very good.

Tamara invites us to join them at the big table, so we haul our chairs over and squeeze in. Miss Janey is getting more giggly by the second, thanks to the tequila. Her porcelain cheeks have turned bright red. I'm wondering if she's going to be able to attend her morning music class or serve lunch to the guys at the diner. I'm not her mother, and I know she's got a ride home in Jonas's taxi. I'm sipping my beer very slowly because I have to drive back over the Yaquina Bridge to Beaver Creek and up the hill.

Janey tells the chamber people all about her classes at the community college. She's majoring in music, might transfer to Oregon State next year. Everybody seems to know her family. She and Jonas graduated from the local high school, where she was a star singer and Jonas excelled at baseball and played drums in the jazz band. The chamber people know about the taxi service, they know about the diner, and they know Janey's dad, who ran a tackle shop on the Bayfront before he divorced Diana and moved down the coast to Coos Bay with his girlfriend.

They know Uncle Donovan, too. The only one they don't know is me.

"So, you're staying at Donovan's cabin?" asks Tamara.

"Yes. Up Beaver Creek Road."

"Where is he now?"

I don't want to get into this mess, so I go vague. "He's traveling, working on some projects."

"Whereabouts?"

"I'm not sure."

A white-haired man with black glasses leans across Tamara. "Quite a character, isn't he?"

I smile and nod.

"Have you seen his art?"

I nod again. "Yes, it's unique."

"Hah, that's the word for it."

A younger woman calls across the table, "Your name is P.D.? What does it stand for?"

I shake my head. "Not saying."

"Ah. Well, where did you come from?"

"Most recently Missoula, but I'm originally from Santa Cruz, California."

Tamara breaks in, thank God. "P.D. and Janey might do some music for one of our events."

"Oh, that would be great," the younger woman says.

I'm thinking I ought to pin Tamara down with some dates when I notice Jonas standing by the door. I nudge Janey, who is talking with the man on her other side.

"Oh, Joney. You're too early," she says, slurring her words.

He scowls. "You're drunk. Come on. It's snowing out there."

"What?" says the young woman who wanted to know my name. "Snowing? No way."

"Way," Jonas replies.

Snow? I thought I left that behind in Missoula. Janey and I get up, thank the Chamber people, put on our coats and follow Jonas to the door.

Our new friends are right behind us. Rain is no big deal for folks here, but the locals panic when it snows.

Outside, soggy snowflakes land on my hat and my face and pile up in the parking lot. Jonas offers to haul me up the hill in his taxi, but I've got my car and don't want to leave it here, so we say goodnight, see you on Thanksgiving. At the highway, he goes north, and I head south, back to Beaver Creek.

The snow is coming at my windshield like a cascade of white pins. It makes me dizzy to look. I direct my tires into the tracks left by other cars and start to pray. Yes, it snowed in Missoula. It snowed for months, but I had snow tires and proper clothes. I had a gas-powered heater. Snowplows kept the roads clear. Here, the road crews toss a little gravel on the highway, as if that's going to help.

As I climb Beaver Creek Road, I can feel my tires slipping on the icy asphalt. With the higher elevation, the white stuff on the ground is deeper; the snow coming at me from above is thicker. I must be out of my mind to be driving up here in the snow at this time of night. But I've done snow before. I can do this.

IN THE MORNING, I wake up to a black and white movie, with snow hanging off tree branches, coating the roof of my car, and covering the ground around Donovan's glass garden. The view out the back door is all white: white sky, white pastures, white-flocked pines. Even the creek looks silver-white from here. The snow is not deep, only a couple inches, but it is snow, and under it appears to be ice.

I'm not going anywhere today. The cats seem to be in agreement. Thank God the jam at the music store isn't until tomorrow and my gig isn't until tomorrow night. My drive from Newport to here in the snow last night was pretty hairy; I don't want to do it again.

The cats and I are snug and secure here in the cabin—as long as the electricity keeps going. Dakota left me a good supply of wood, so I don't even have to go outside to keep the fire going. I'll be eating Maryann's muffins, soup and fruit salad for a couple more days. And I've got music to practice for tomorrow's jam and tomorrow night's gig.

As I take off my wrist brace to shower, I wonder if I'm ready for this. My wrist is still sore. When I move it certain ways, such as turning a doorknob or brushing my teeth, it hurts like somebody stabbed me. Yesterday, when I was brushing my teeth, I put the toothbrush in my right hand out of habit, didn't even think about it until I started to brush, and oh man! I cursed and switched to my left hand. So how am I going to play? They want two hours of keyboard and vocals at the party. For the jam, I suppose I could stick to the harmonica and vocals, but I know I'm going to want to play that grand piano. It's a magnet and I'm a little blob of steel. I can't resist.

After breakfast, I get the keyboard and fake book out and start making a list of songs, struggling to write with my left hand. "Background music" was all this woman named Michelle said on the phone. It's an anniversary party for her and her husband. I asked if I needed sound equipment, which I don't have but could probably borrow from Deuce. "No, no," she said. "It's just a small place, a few friends. We don't want anything too loud."

I put together a list of my favorite songs, including a lot of old jazz and some light rock. Billy Joel, Elton John, Carly Simon, Whitney Houston, Adele, Beyoncé.

Then I practice. I don't want to strain my gimpy wrist, but I want to play as well as I can. This gig could lead to more jobs, maybe enough to pay the bills.

Tired of playing the keyboard on my lap, I set it on the work table in the studio, turn on the portable heater, and play while enjoying the snowy view.

The room is all hard surfaces, so my voice reverberates off the windows, floors and walls. I can sing softly and sound big. I love it. Playing is another matter. I tried playing with the brace on, but I couldn't move my fingers enough, so I stripped it off and now my wrist aches. My thumb aches. My fingers ache. This hand is not ready for prime time. As the seashell clock over the cabinets clicks toward 11, I switch to harmonica and wonder if I can I get away with playing some harp songs.

By noon, I have a list, a raw throat and a hand that's screaming for an ice pack. I plan to rest all afternoon. Tomorrow I'll be fine.

18

TODAY IS THE DAY. I don't dare do anything with my right hand. I have to save it for the jam and the gig. I'm tired of this, tired of soreness, tired of having to do things with my other hand, tired of my ribs still aching, especially when I try to turn over in bed. I can't knit, can't do any real chores. All I can do is read, pet the cats, and play my harmonica. The more I play it the more I long to get back to my keyboard.

I try to pick out something wonderful to wear, but I don't have a lot of options, just the same black pants and black silk shirt that I have worn almost every week to karaoke. I can't wear my silver sandals in the snow, but I can take them in my bag and switch out of my tennis shoes when I get inside. Looking at myself in the mirror, I hate my hair, all two-toned and shaggy. Another hat day. They're paying me $100 for tonight's gig. Maybe after that, I can get my hair dyed and styled in town, but tomorrow is Thanksgiving, so I'll have to wait. Stupid holidays.

It hasn't snowed anymore, but it's cold, patches of ice here and there outside. Like on the porch steps. I started down to get the mail, slipped and fell on my butt. Barely kept myself from landing on my wrist again. Jarred my whole body. I decided the mail could wait.

I'm cranky. I'm nervous. Stage fright. I've felt it lots of times, and I'm always fine once I start singing, but that was mostly church, open mics, and family picnics. Nobody has ever paid me to perform alone outside of church before. As P.D. And I'm going into it with a dinged-up wrist and sore ribs.

"Dear God," I pray, "Please be with me this afternoon and especially tonight. Help me to sing and play well and give me a bionic wrist that doesn't hurt. I promise to ice it and rest it tomorrow if you'll just let me be a star tonight. Thank you. Amen.

"P.S., please melt the snow and ice on the roads before I have to leave."

THIS PRAYER THING might work. By the time I get my jacket on and head ever-so-carefully down the steps with my keyboard and music books, it's a little warmer, and most of the snow and ice have melted. I gaze up into the cloudy sky. "Thank you, God."

I imagine him saying, "You're welcome, P.D."

I crawl in second gear down the driveway and down Beaver Creek Road. Snow is piled up along the sides and coats the grass in the shady spots under the trees. I scan the pavement for ice and breathe a sigh of relief when I hit the highway. Thank you again, God.

Before I reach the bridge into Newport, the sky darkens. Charcoal-colored clouds hang overhead. The bay down below is the same color. Another mile north, and sleet is falling onto my windshield in flat cakes of ice that slide slowly toward the hood. Oh Lord. Not now.

Should I turn around? No way. I'm going to jam, and then I'm going up into the hills to play that party. I hope they're going to feed me because there's no time for dinner, and I'm going to get hungry.

Then again, eating Maryann's cooking has made P.D. a little too fluffy. I could stand to lose a couple pounds.

Over the bridge and into town, I see the Whale on my left, Ocean Harmony Music on my right. Look at that, there's a parking space by the door. I slide into it, grab my purse and fake book, get out of the car and get ready to storm into the warmth of cool jazz.

I don't believe it. The store is dark. The door is locked. The sign is flipped to "closed," and there's a handwritten sign taped to the door. "Closed for the Thanksgiving holiday. See you Monday."

What? No! I have been looking forward to this for two weeks. I practiced. I learned to play the harmonica. I drove here through sleet and snow. No. Defying logic, I pound on the door. Maybe Deuce is hiding somewhere in the back. Maybe he closed up early so we could jam in peace. I knock and listen.

Nothing. Nobody comes to the door. I look around. My car is the only one here. I can't see another human being anywhere.

There is no jam.

I want to scream, break windows, jump off the bridge, do something to release my frustration. Where the heck is Deuce? Did he forget? Was it no big deal to him? It was a huge deal to me.

So now I feel like a fool. I'm sitting in my car watching ice fall from the sky, like pieces of glass. Any idiot from a mile away can see the store is closed. In fact, the stores on either side of it are closed, too. What is up with this town? It's just a little snow.

Maybe if I listened to the radio or got online once in a while, I'd know what's going on. I punch the car radio button. Loud rock. Old rock. Christian rock. Country rock. NPR. The fiscal cliff. Apparently our country will go bankrupt if Congress can't agree on a budget. Why don't they just crunch the numbers and set a budget already? Off with the radio.

I have two hours to kill. Maybe the library is open.

In five minutes, I'm there, and yes, it is open. Warmth. The usual collection of teenagers, tourists and homeless people hogging the computers. I put my name on the signup sheet and peruse the nearby shelves. A new book on grief and loss. No thanks. Big-print mysteries. CDs and DVDs. Wait, is that guy getting up?

I've got 30 minutes. First, I check the weather. Snow predicted for tonight. Peachy. It's supposed to turn to rain tomorrow for Thanksgiving, and then it's going to warm up. We might even get sunshine on Saturday for my kayak trip with Ranger Dave.

I've got 143 emails. Of those, 126 are advertising or charity solicitations. Highlight, delete. It takes me three tries because my stupid wrist brace gets in the way. Finally I rip it off and throw it into my bag. My hand feels light and weak, but I can move it.

There's a message from my brother Andy wishing me a happy Thanksgiving and telling me about Mom's latest craze, 12-layer Jell-O creations. Andy has a new girlfriend he's bringing tomorrow. He hopes she won't dump him after she meets the family. Smiley face.

Andy says he ran into Tom's folks. Tom's sister is pregnant. They're going to have their first grandchild in June.

I wince. That was supposed to be us, me and Tom, giving them grandchildren.   Well, that's not helping my mood. Neither is Facebook, a sea of holiday good wishes, pictures of turkeys, pumpkin pies and turkey-shaped cakes, along with the usual babies, toddlers and dogs. Everybody's doing the family thing, and here I am alone in Nowhere, Oregon, trying to be a musician.

I check my watch and feel nerves sizzle through my chest. I've got an hour and a half until I have to go sing and play at the party. I can do this. It should be fun, but I have to admit that I'm crazy nervous.

"Excuse me," whispers a librarian bending down near my ear. "Your time is up."

Crap. I didn't do the one thing I needed to do.

"Just let me look up one more thing." As quickly as possible, I Google-search the music store and get a phone number. I write it on one of the little slips of paper on the table, all the while feeling her leaning over me, smelling the peppermint on her breath. "Thank you."

Back in the car, I call the music store number and get nothing but ringing. Heck of a way to run a business. Deuce doesn't even have voicemail for people to leave messages. I can't call his home because I don't know his last name or even what his real first name is.

So, an hour and 15 minutes. Another five-minute drive and I'm at Starbucks, which, thank God, never closes. I order a tall coffee and a fat cinnamon roll. Dinner. I will diet on Friday, when Thanksgiving is over and I'm not so darned nervous.

AN HOUR AND 30 MINUTES later, I'm lost in the foothills above Newport. What is it with these road signs? White print on a green background, they're tough to read in good times, and it's snowing again. The names all seem to be variations of the same words, and I'm not sure whether I'm supposed to be on Sand Hill, Eden Hill, Rose Hill, or Mole Hill. SE, SW, NE, NW? Give me a break. I park in front of somebody's house and call the phone number Michelle gave me.

Somebody answers, not Michelle, some guy. I tell him I'm the musician and I'm lost. I hear him turn away from the phone and holler, "Did somebody hire a musician?" Then muttering. He comes back and asks where I am.

Long story short, a half hour late, I pull up in front of this house on top of a hill, everything at a slant, every inch of driveway and front parking space filled with cars and pickups. I park three houses down the hill, praying my brakes will hold. I gather up my purse, keyboard, and music books, struggling to carry them with my hand in its brace and my ribs saying, "Hello, this hurts," and schlep up the steep, icy sidewalk. By the time I bang on the door, I'm freezing and gasping for breath. My fedora is crooked, but I don't have any hands left to straighten it.

A fat teenage boy opens the door and stares at me.

"Hi," I gasp. "I'm P.D., the musician for the party."

The kid shrugs. "Come in."

It's an expensive house with an ocean view. A formal entryway. Shoes lined up by the door. Apparently you're not allowed to walk on the white carpet with shoes on. So much for the silver sandals in my bag.

The kid is gone. Alone in the foyer, I set down the keyboard and books, straighten my hat, and pull off my tennis shoes. Barefoot, I haul my stuff into a living room that is hot and loud, smelling of shrimp and beer, and filled with people, elbow to elbow. I don't know a soul. I look around for a space that might serve as my stage. I need a TV tray or something to set the keyboard on. In a house this fancy, you'd think they'd have a grand piano. I don't see one.

I need to find Michelle and get started. I need to earn that hundred dollars. I realize with a pang I haven't warmed up my voice since before I drove to the music store. I try humming a little, the sound disappearing in the general clamor.

Somebody's playing a computer sports game, shouting with every move. A stereo blasts music. Everybody's talking.

I need a beer. No, whiskey. No, hot chocolate in my PJs in front of the fireplace.

Okay, I have to just do this. I start asking people around me. "Do you know where Michelle is?"

Nobody knows. I move toward what I think must be the kitchen, just beyond the buffet table laden with platters of hors d'oeuvres. Sure enough, in the kitchen I find a sweating woman with huge breasts nearly falling out of her low-cut top. "Michelle?"

"Oh hi. P.D., right? Thank you for coming out in this weather. I can't wait to hear you."

"Thanks." I eye the margarita in her hand and wonder if she'll offer me something, but she hustles me out to the living room and points to a corner under the big-screen TV showing a football game.

"I thought we'd have you set up right here." She's shouting over the noise.

I shout back, "Have you got a chair and a TV tray I could borrow?"

She looks at me, puzzled.

"For my keyboard. I don't have a stand."

"Oh. Uh, yeah, I'll be right back."

I lean against the stereo cabinet under the TV, then turn and shut off the recorded music. The din decreases only slightly. Don't need a microphone, she said. Right.

Michelle comes back, dragging a dining room chair, while the boy follows with a wooden TV tray. I thank them.

As they wander away, I sit, turn on my keyboard, set the volume all the way up, lick my dry lips, swallow and start to play.

I can barely hear it.

I start to sing. I can't hear myself. Somebody scores in the game, and people shout. I want to scream, "Everybody shut up!" But no. P.D. is a professional.

I'm doing my best to play and sing in spite of the obstacles when somebody bumps into the TV tray and nearly dumps the keyboard into my lap. He doesn't even say he's sorry.

This is ridiculous.

I leave my station to find Michelle again. She's bent over the oven taking out a tray of little pizza rolls. "Is there someplace else I can set up? Someplace a little quieter?"

She stands, rubs an arm across her sweaty forehead. "Oh. Um, the dining room, I guess."

Getting away from the game helps. I set up in a corner of the dining room. As I start to play, I can see the lights of fishing boats flickering on the ocean through the floor-to-ceiling windows. A couple of people sitting at the table with their drinks turn to listen to me.

"You have a beautiful voice," a woman says in the middle of "You Were Always on My Mind."

"Thank you." I sing on. Well, at least one person is listening.

A bunch of guys pile in, the game apparently over. One of them scowls at me. "What is this shit she's playing? Is it from like the 1950s? We need to rock out. Hey, Michelle, why didn't you hire Steve's band?"

She stands in the kitchen doorway, eating a pizza roll. "They're out of town. I saw this woman's card and thought she'd be good. Mood music, you know."

"Well, I hope you're not paying her." He swigs his beer and goes out through the sliding door to the deck. I see him light up a smoke, his cigarette glowing red in the dark.

"I'm sorry, P.D.," Michelle says. "But do you know anything a little more lively?"

"Sure." I swallow the lump in my throat.

I don't do a lot of rock, but I try. I give them "Proud Mary." I give them "Footloose." I give them some Katy Perry, even a little Lady Gaga. Nobody even looks at me. I feel like a pile of dog doo on the sidewalk.

That same guy walks back in, smelling of smoke. "Give it up, old lady," he says.

I know he's wasted. His face is flushed, his eyes are glittering, and he's lurching around. I shouldn't pay any attention. But I'm hurt. I try to P.D. it off with a fake laugh and yell, "Fine. If you can do it better, come on over and sing."

Wow, my voice is so raspy. He acts like he doesn't hear me as he heads for the bar.

I try to pretend I'm at home. I go through the fake book and play the loudest, fastest songs I can find. I use the automatic settings on the keyboard to get that bang-crash-squeal sound that the kids seem to love. I sing and play till I'm hoarse and my wrist hurts like it's been stomped on, yet the hands on the clock never seem to move.

A little after 9, somebody yells something about cutting the cake, and everybody gathers around a table in the center of the living room. I figure I can stop playing now.

I get up, find the restroom, and help myself to a beer and what little is left on the buffet table, a couple carrots and some guacamole dip. I lean up against a wall observing the party. Everyone here, including my hostess, seems to be younger than I am. I watch Michelle and her husband hold a knife together to cut a slice out of a big white cake and feed bites to each other. For once it gets quiet. I hear her saying, "Happy anniversary, honey." They kiss and hug. People clap and cheer.

I turn around and see a couple snuggling on the leather couch, whispering to each other. A diamond glitters on the young woman's hand. The man reminds me of Tom, same dark hair, same brown eyes, a striped white shirt like he used to wear.

Suddenly I miss Tom so bad I think I'm going to die. This was supposed to be us celebrating our anniversary, year after year until we were in our 80s or 90s.

I need to get out of here, but I can't. I still have 20 minutes to play. As people go off with pieces of cake, I go back to my chair and page through the fake book. I don't have any more rock songs left in me. My voice is toast. I decide since nobody is really listening, I'll play whatever I want for the rest of my time.

I try to sing "Wind Beneath My Wings," but Tom loved that song so much, I have to quit halfway into the first verse. That couple is still cuddling on the couch. I can't even look at them. I switch to instrumentals.

I'm in the middle of "I Dreamed a Dream" from "Les Miserables" when I realize Michelle is standing in front of me with cash in her hand. I roll to a final chord and stop.

"Thank you. That was beautiful," she says and hands me the money, a stack of 20-dollar bills. "People want to dance now, so we're going to crank up the stereo. Do you need any help carrying things out?"

"Um, no. Thanks."

"Well, thank you."

And she's gone. Feeling like I'm in a trance, I close up my music, turn off the keyboard and put it back in its plastic case. I strap on my wrist brace, fastening it as tight as I can. My tendons sigh in relief.

I shove my way through the crowd. Somebody says, "What ya got in there, a gun?"

I force a half smile and keep going to the doorway. I reclaim my coat, put on my tennis shoes, and push out into the snowy night.

What a disaster. But I did play and sing the whole night and I have 100 bucks in my pocket. Maybe I'll use it to buy a microphone. The biggest, loudest mic I can find.

There's a black cat sprawled across the hood of my car, probably trying to keep warm. As I reach out to pet it, it bolts away, leaving little kitty footprints.

I want to beat up that drunk jerk who called me old. I want to take the hostess to the gym to lose weight and find a better group of friends. I want to blubber like a baby. But no. I'm P.D. Proud and determined. To hell with them.

As I ease my car down the hill, squinting through a foot-wide clearing in the window, I remember the business about the shoes and start to giggle. I worried so much about what footwear to put on and it didn't matter. I could have worn Donovan's Gulliver boots. These people think they're so hot with their white carpets and their giant shrimp—which I didn't get to taste. Poor Michelle spent all night sweating in the kitchen while a bunch of drunks trashed her house. She thought she was doing a good thing by hiring me. She didn't have a clue.

Agh! My car hits a patch of ice and slides toward the curb. When I touch the brake, it does nothing. The steering wheel feels loose in my hands. Hyperventilating, I carefully steer into the slide as Tom taught me until I regain control. Whew. I've got to pay attention to the road. Yes, it about killed me when they did the anniversary business, but I'll have to cry about that later. If I die on this hill, somebody will contact my mom and she'll put my real name in the obituary. She won't even mention I was a musician.

Okay, here's the highway. Oh jeez, look at that poor raccoon. Flattened by cars, nothing left but guts and fur. From his perspective, my night could have been a lot worse.

19

I WAKE UP Thanksgiving morning feeling like I drank a barrel of hard liquor and lost a bar fight last night. Surely I'm black and blue all over. I lie here listening to the rain. Rain, not snow. That's good.

I know it's cold outside of this bed. I know the cats want their food. I know I'm not in the mood for Thanksgiving. Could I stagger over to the rainbow house to use their phone and call in sick?

I can't move. I remember last night, my face burning as that guy talked about me. I remember watching Michelle and her husband share that anniversary cake, and that young couple kissing. That diamond ring. I pull my hand out from under the covers and stare at my unadorned fingers. The place where my wedding rings used to be is the same color as the rest of my finger now. It was white and wrinkly when I forced them off and set them in a drawer with Tom's ring.

Damn. I pull the covers over my head and try to go back to sleep.

Sometime later, I hear knocking at the door. Then someone calling "P.D.!"

"What?" I whisper.

More knocking. She's not going to stop.

I roll out of bed, pull on my robe, and shuffle-crawl to the door. Janey.

She's all bright in a red Christmas sweater. "P.D., are you sick? Jonas thought we might give you a ride to the diner."

"Um. I . . ." Suddenly I'm crying. Janey rushes in and puts her arms around me.

"Oh, P.D., what's wrong?"

I can't talk. I want to shout that my husband is dead, I'm almost broke, I hurt all over, and my first professional gig was a disaster. But all I do is cry.

Finally my sobs let up and I raise my head. "God, it's cold in here."

She nods. "Sure is. Get your clothes on. I'll make some coffee to get you started. It's nice and warm at the diner. Mom's been cooking since 5 a.m."

Just like my mom, I think, and I almost start to weep again. "I'm not in the mood for Thanksgiving," I say, my voice a croak.

"Too bad. You're coming." She's already working on the coffee.

Jonas comes to the doorway. "What's wrong?"

"Everything," I say. "I'm cold, I'm in pain, and I miss my husband."

"You're divorced, right?" Janey asks.

"No. He died of cancer four months and 12 days ago."

"Oh, P.D. You never said. I just assumed . . . I'm so sorry. Everyone around here seems to be divorced."

"Not me." I turn away and struggle to get my emotions under control.

If I can't stop this weeping-Wilma act, I'll never be able to face them again. They'll see me as the poor pitiful widow like everybody did back in Missoula. I clear my throat, take a deep breath and manage a wobbly smile. "Let me take a shower, and then I'll come down. Okay? I don't want to celebrate Thanksgiving, but I sure would like to be warm."

Jonas nods. "Warm is good. And you shouldn't be alone. You've got a half hour. If you're not down there, we'll come drag you down."

"He means it," Janey says. "Bring your keyboard and your harmonica. We'll be waiting."

I hold up my wrist in its brace.

"Yeah, yeah. I know you can play. See you soon."

As they head out the door, she ducks back in. "We've got eggnog. With brandy."

I nod and hurry to the shower, peeling off my brace. Getting drunk sounds perfect. After some hot coffee.

I barely pay attention to what I'm doing as I shampoo and wash my body in the lukewarm shower. This is my first Thanksgiving without Tom. I want to be Tom's wife again, cooking his breakfasts, ironing his shirts, standing beside him at city functions, and singing in the choir at church. I want to snuggle with my husband on the couch, sharing a bowl of popcorn as we watch a stupid movie. I want to be there on a warm Fourth of July watching the fireworks from our back yard and on a snowy Christmas morning opening our presents together by the tree.

I was supposed to get 50 years out of this marriage, not 12. I was supposed to have children and grandchildren, not this barren useless body and this frozen cabin belonging to a crazy man who has disappeared.

I think about that guy at church who was always being sympathetic and asking what I planned to do. Blaine. Maybe he wasn't such an idiot. Maybe all those people who oozed sympathy at me weren't idiots. They knew more than I did about grief. They knew you can't put on a happy face and pretend nothing happened. What do they say in the psych books? You can't go around it. You have to go through it. I thought I could fly over it.

It's time for P.D. to give old Cissy a hug, let her cry a little, then move on together. Just like with my wrist and cracked ribs, I have to admit I'm wounded and it hurts. But I refuse to be pitiful.

I'M CALM BUT a little grumpy when I walk into the diner one minute before my half hour is up. I didn't want them coming up to get me. Plus I'm starving.

It smells like Thanksgiving: turkey, sage, cranberries, sweet potatoes, pumpkin pie. About now, back in Santa Cruz, Mom has the table set with the good silver and china, and she's in the kitchen, getting ready to take the turkey out of the oven. The guests are gathering in the living room, watching football on TV. I can hear the announcer's voice.

No, wait. Somebody has a television on here.

Before I can follow the sound into the dining area, Janey comes at me with a glass of spiked eggnog. "Drink up."

She hands me the glass.

I take a sip and sigh as the brandy soothes my sore throat.

Janey starts to put an arm around me. I shake my head. "Don't touch me. Don't be nice, or I will dissolve into a puddle of tears. You will not mention my little cryfest this morning. Okay?"

She backs off. "Got it. Come into the kitchen and help me put out the hors d'oeuvres. Then, when you've got a little brandy in your blood, I'll introduce you to everybody."

"Who's here?" I thought it was just going to be the family.

"You'll see. Come on."

Diana nods to me from the stove, where she is making gravy in a big roasting pan. "Welcome," she says. "Janey, better hurry with that stuff; I hear they're getting hungry."

"We're on it."

By the time we finish lining up plates of deviled eggs, peanut butter-stuffed celery, and cut-up chunks of bread for the spinach dip, the brandy has warmed my blood and my emotions. I'm not usually much of a drinker, but I'm thinking the day might go a lot easier if I stay in a brandy blur.

We take out the appetizers, open bags of tortilla chips, lay out bowls of dip and set them on a big table in the middle of the crowd. People immediately start grabbing handfuls of food, barely taking their eyes off the football game until a commercial gives us a chance for introductions.

So who all is here? We've got Janey and Diana, Jonas, Molly and their twin boys Tim and Ty. Frankie from the Seal Rock store. And this pretty brunette woman about my age with a teenage girl. Turns out they're Ranger Dave's wife Caroline and their 16-year-old daughter Amy. Dave is working for another couple hours, making his rounds of all the beaches from South Beach to Yachats. He drew the short straw, his wife explains.

"Caroline's an artist," Janey says. "She painted that picture over there." She points to a watercolor between the west-facing window and the wall. It shows two little kids playing on the beach. Something about it makes me want to cry again.

"It's beautiful."

"Thank you."

And this," Janey continues, "is—"

"Rick Jones. We've met." The cute guy from the roof. Now I'm wishing I had bothered with makeup. At least I put on my hat.

"Hey, P.D., good to see you," he calls across the chips and dip.

"You too." As I smile, my face feels frozen with dried tears.

"How's the wrist?"

What wrist? "Better."

"So that's everybody," Janey says, turning back toward the kitchen. I start to follow her. "No, stay and socialize."

We're back to the game. Texas vs. Texas Christian, Christians leading at the beginning of the second quarter. I settle into a chair. Tom used to watch football. He was a 49ers fan.

I reach for a deviled egg but freeze with my hand in midair as the door opens.

In walks Donovan freaking Green.

"Hey, everybody! You can start the party now. I'm here."

He seems different. His hair's longer and he's wearing a black blazer over a tie-dyed tee-shirt, but that isn't it. It's his swagger, like he's not Donovan but his more-confident twin brother. Maybe he is. I hope.

As the others all sit and stare, Diana rushes out of the kitchen.

"Donovan, what are you doing here?" she asks, hugging him and rubbing his beard. I see Janey leaning against the doorway, a half-smile on her face, like she's not sure what to do.

"It's Thanksgiving. I wanted to see my family. Besides, I'm sick of the city."

I see people exchanging looks, shrugging, then turning back to the football game. I can feel Jonas staring at me.

Thank God I'm a little drunk. I set down the deviled egg, rise on shaky legs, and walk up to Donovan. "Remember me? I'm P.D. I'm housesitting your cabin."

"P-what?"

"P.D."

"Never heard of you."

My mouth hangs open in amazement as Janey rushes to my rescue.

"Hey, Uncle, don't you remember? You asked P.D. to stay at your place and watch over it while you were in Portland and Tucson.

We thought you'd still be in Arizona, all warm and happy in the sun. You didn't tell us you were coming back."

"I didn't go to Tucson, kiddo. Never left the state of Oregon. I didn't get an invite to this here party, but I figured you do it every year, and that was just an oversight."

Diana explodes. "Damn it, Donovan! We didn't know where you were. For the last *month* we haven't known where you were. P.D. tried to call you, and all your numbers were dead. For all we knew, so were you."

Donovan claps a beefy arm around his sister. "Ah, Sis, I knew where I was the whole time. I did a tour of the galleries, and then I settled in to do some work. Then I wasn't feeling so good, so I took a little time to rest and recover. Now here I am. I'd sure love a glass of your delicious eggnog. Lightened with a little brandy, of course."

She frowns. "You're drinking?"

"Sure. I'm fine. No worries."

"I guess you're eating turkey, too."

"Wouldn't miss it."

Who is this man? What happened to the mild-mannered teetotaling vegetarian I met in October? I catch Frankie rolling her eyes at Ranger Dave's wife. Apparently they're well aware of the quirks of Donovan Green.

I'm thinking I should go clean my stuff out of the cabin before Donovan storms in to take over. I whisper this plan to Janey, who shakes her head. "No. We'll go later. He's off his meds, a little manic, but he's not dangerous."

"He's not?" I think about the broken glass and spilled wine in the studio and all the liquor bottles decorating the garden.

Janey squeezes my shoulder. "Don't worry. We've all seen this before. It'll be okay. We'll go to the cabin later."

Meanwhile, Jonas and Rick are setting up drums and mics for music. My stomach zings a little, remembering last night's fiasco. I tell it to hush. This is going to be completely different.

"Let's eat!" Diana says. We sit, hold hands and say grace. Frankie leads the prayer, thanking God for bringing us all together for this wonderful meal. Then we chow down.

It's an amazing feast, even better than my mom makes. The tables have been shoved together and covered with a white cloth so it looks like one huge rectangular table. Donovan sits at the head, on the south side, and he keeps telling stories. He's loud, colorful, barely stopping for breath, talking about these homeless guys he met and this doctor at a rehab facility and this argument he had with some guy over gathering up car parts at the dump to use for his art. Apparently he was actually down in the garbage when this man showed up with a tractor and threatened to call the cops. "I told 'em, 'One man's trash is this man's art.' But the tractor driver was not an aficionado. He picked up his cell phone and started dialing, so I decided to come back later."

The people around him, half watching the muted football game, smile but don't laugh nearly as hard as Donovan is laughing at his own story, all the while shoveling in turkey and stuffing. I have to admit he tells some good stories. I just wish he remembered who I was.

I sit at the other end of the table with Rick, Janey, her mom, and Frankie. I tell them about going to the jam session and finding nobody there and about my disastrous gig last night.

"I'd have walked out," Janey says.

"I needed the hundred bucks."

Diana shakes her head. "When my kids were small, I cleaned houses and babysat for some of the rudest people I've ever met. If I could make 20 dollars, we could eat. I wish we could hire you to work here at the diner, but we just can't afford to take anybody on right now. This economy . . ."

We all nod. Our country's depression/recession has been going on too long.

"Where's Kelly today?" Frankie asks, looking around for Diana's partner.

"With her family in Portland."

Rick nudges my shoulder. "Knowing your skill on the ladder, I could put you to work doing roofs."

We all laugh.

"I could use a hand at the store," Frankie says.

"I might be interested in that."

"We'll talk. Or if you're looking for something else, I know just about everybody."

"And I only know you guys, so thank you."

Full of turkey and alcohol, with a job possibility looming, I'm already feeling better when the football game ends. Before the guys can switch to another game on another channel, Janey announces it's time for music. We make our stage in the northwest corner, windows to our right, a shelf unit full of antique teapots to our left. I've got the keyboard and harmonica, Jonas has a whole drum set, Janey pulls out a flute, and Rick surprises me by picking up a beautiful Martin guitar. He counts 1-2-3-4 and we're off. "Midnight Special." I can't believe how good we sound together. By our third song, I have forgotten all about dead husbands and families far away. Donovan is still talking, but nobody is listening.

"We ought to take this show on the road!" Janey shouts between tunes.

"What'll we call ourselves?" I ask.

"The DK Band?" Jonas says.

"Nah. Hot rocks," Rick says.

"No," says Jonas. "How about P.D.G, pretty damned good?"

"Seal Rock," suggests Janey.

"Yes!" Everyone's talking at once.

"Seal Rock Five?"

"Seal Rock Sound," I venture.

"That's it!" "Yes!"

The Seal Rock Sound plays for about an hour before somebody says it's time for pumpkin pie.

That's when the building starts to shake.

20

I HEAR THE RUMBLING before I feel the shaking. Hard shaking. God is rattling the diner like we're dice in a cup.

"Oh my God," Diana says.

"It's the big one," Rick mutters.

I'm losing my balance. I reach for the shelf behind me, but it's falling down. I drop to my hands and knees. Everything is falling, flowers off the counters and windowsills, teapots off the shelves, pictures off the walls. Dishes and glasses rattle, glass breaks, dust rains down from the ceiling tiles.

I hear Jonas' boys wailing and Jonas shouting, "Duck and cover! Just like in school."

I'm from California. I know about earthquakes. I lived through the biggest one in modern times, but I've never felt one like this. It goes on and on.

"Get under the table!" Rick yells, and we scramble through the chairs to get underneath. As I crouch down with my hands over my head, I feel Rick beside me.

Bam! The cymbal falls off the drum set. A coffeepot falls. I hear water dripping onto the floor.

Out the window, I see power poles and trees swaying, the overhead wires spinning like jump ropes. Something cracks and falls hard on the table above us. It has to be the ceiling fan. A shelf unit crashes down near the entry. The boys are shrieking, someone's cursing, and from out near the kitchen I hear Donovan shouting, "Yeehaw!"

I suspect we're not going to be eating pumpkin pie.

Finally the shaking stops and Rick eases back. "You okay, Babe?" he asks Diana.

"I think so."

"P.D.?"

"Yeah. I'm fine. We have to get out of here." I know from my experience in California there will be aftershocks.

The power is off. It's twilight inside the diner. Plants, potting soil, broken dishes and shattered teapots litter the floor. As I crawl out and see the wires dangling where the ceiling fan hung, I kneel on a fork. "Ow!" I haul myself up on wobbly legs, grab my hat, and start for the door.

The building starts shaking again.

"Oh God," Diana wails.

"Everybody out," Rick orders. "Get away from the building."

He grabs one of Jonas's boys and carries him out, then goes for the other one, but Ranger Dave's daughter Amy already has him in her arms. We all follow, tripping over our feet in the moving building until we're in the parking lot.

"Jeez Louise," Jonas mutters in the sudden silence as the shaking stops.

"Amen," says Frankie, glancing southward. "I guess my store's a mess now." She rubs at a red spot on her cheek where something must have scraped it.

I reach down and massage my knee. A spot of blood has leaked through my good black slacks.

"Where's Uncle Donovan?" Janey asks.

He's not with us.

"I'll go," Rick says.

"No!" Diana says, but Rick's already pushing his way back in.

I feel the ground begin to sway. I don't know whether it's me or an aftershock. I reach for something to hold onto and Diana puts her arm around me. "Quite a party, eh?"

I hear yelling from inside. Rick is telling Donovan to get out and he won't go. "Leave the fucking glass!" Rick yells.

"No. This is good stuff."

"Come on, crazy man." Although he's almost a foot shorter, Rick manages to drag Donovan out the door. The big man is clutching an armload of broken glass. Blood trickles from a cut on his hand.

So we're all assembled in the parking lot. I grabbed my purse but not my coat. It's not snowing anymore, not even raining, but it's still gray, and I'm guessing it's about 40 degrees at the most.

"What do we do now?" Molly asks, rocking one of the boys in her arms like a baby.

"Go home?" Jonas says.

"We should help Diana clean up," Frankie says.

Rick shakes his head. "It's not over yet."

He's right. It's not. As Amy's cell phone chirps, I hear a siren from far away, maybe Waldport, the small town about 10 miles south.

In a trembling voice, Amy reads the text message on her phone. "A tsunami warning has been issued. Move to higher ground immediately."

"We're safe here," Jonas says.

"My apartment isn't," says Janey, her white face gone even whiter.

"Where is my dad?" Amy dials Ranger Dave's phone and gets no answer.

"If I know my husband," Caroline says, "He'll be on the beach, looking for people, making sure everyone is safe. Everyone but himself."

Jonas shakes his head. "Don't worry. We've had tsunami warnings before, and nothing ever happened."

"I know," Caroline says. "But this was an awful big earthquake."

I stand there, shivering from the cold, my knee bleeding, my ribs aching, my stomach hurting. I'm not sure what to do or where to go. Another siren starts up now. A fire truck, I think.

Jonas lights a cigarette with shaking hands and takes a drag. The smell comforts me. My dad used to smoke.

Donovan, still holding his bloody clutch of broken glass, comes up to me. "Did we go out on a date?"

I stare into his glassy eyes.

"Yes, we did. Café Mundo. I sang at the open mic."

"You sang?"

"Yes."

He shakes his head. "You look different."

"So do you," I respond, but he's looking at Diana now.

"Give me my house keys, Di. I want to get to work."

"I don't have them."

His eyes bug out. He looks like he's about to hit her. "Give me my fucking keys."

"I told you, D. I don't have them." She glances at me, but doesn't give me away.

"You can't go anywhere right now anyway," Jonas says, patting his arm.

"Why the hell not?"

The ground shakes again in answer. I think this might be what it's like to ride a surfboard.

"Feel that, Uncle? Stay here with us."

He shakes him off. "I'll break in if I have to. It's my house."

In my mind, I inventory what I left in the cabin—clothes, cosmetics, library books, knitting, food—and give it all up. God knows it might be a mess up there now anyway. If Donovan wants to eat what's left of the soup and a few bites of fruit before it goes bad, I don't really care. I hope the cats are okay, figure they're smart enough to hide out somewhere safe. "I have the keys," I say, pulling them out of my purse.

He yanks them out of my hand. "What the hell were you doing in my cabin?"

Diana rushes to protect me. "You asked her to housesit."

"Bullshit."

I back away. The man is crazy, drunk and twice my size.

And a tsunami is coming.

Shouting curses, Donovan gets into his truck. Tires squealing and gravel flying, he zooms out of the parking lot, barely missing the D & K Diner sign as he heads north toward Beaver Creek.

NOBODY KNOWS what to do now.

Rick sits in his truck with the door open, clicking through the stations on his radio until he comes to one broadcasting news. The signal is faint and hissy. I move closer to hear.

"An earthquake measuring at least 8 on the Richter scale has occurred off the central Oregon coast. We are hearing reports of damaged buildings, power outages and possible injuries throughout the listening area. One man is reported dead. Aftershocks continue to rattle the coast. The Oregon Department of Transportation reports that the Yaquina Bay Bridge may be coming apart at the south end. The bridge is closed until further notice. Get away from things that might fall on you. If you are in your car, stay there. Watch for fallen wires and falling trees.

"In the wake of today's earthquake, The National Weather Service has issued a tsunami warning for all of the Oregon Coast. If you are anywhere in the tsunami inundation zone, that is, everything west of the highway, along the bays and some low-lying areas beyond, go to higher ground immediately. Do not stop to pack or prepare; just go. We have less than 20 minutes before the first wave hits.

"To repeat: An earthquake measuring at least 8 . . ." The voice goes silent, leaving nothing but a loud hiss.

They weren't kidding with all that tsunami preparedness stuff. Now I wish I'd paid more attention.

I'm shivering so hard I can't stand still. "P.D., get in the truck," Rick says. My own car is parked nearby, but screw it, I'm getting in with Rick. The others scatter to their own cars now. Jonas and Molly strap the boys into their car seats in the mini-van. Janey squeezes into the back seat between them. Diana glances back at me and Rick, then takes the front passenger seat.

As I climb into Rick's truck, I feel the ground sway again. I try to pretend I'm on a sightseeing boat on a warm, sunny day, even as I stare out the windshield at the houses across the highway and the waves beyond, expecting the water to come rushing at us any minute.

We all sit in our cars, as if waiting for someone to tell us what to do next.

"It's fucking cold," Rick says. Before I can say anything, he's out of the truck and running into the restaurant.

The ground starts shaking again. "God, please don't let the roof fall down on him," I pray.

It shakes and shakes. When it stops, the house across the highway is leaning to the south, partially off its foundation. The reader board in front of the diner is swinging loose, about to fall off. I hope it misses my car. I hope it misses Rick.

I'm staring at the door, hoping to see him, when my stupid phone rings. My mother. They must have broken into the football game with the news. Or maybe she just wants to say Happy Thanksgiving. I cannot talk to her now. I silence the ringer and type a text to my brother's cell, which I know is always belted to his hip. "I'm okay. Talk to you later. P.D." As I push send, the phone flashes a "searching for service" message. Oh well.

Rick emerges with his arms full of coats, purses, hats and gloves and goes from car to car passing them out.

He hands me my jacket, gets in, shuts the door and starts the engine. I stare at him. "Where are we going?"

"Beach."

"But—"

Rick roars down the road and parks at a vacant lot across the highway between the diner and the store. It overlooks the beach from a safe height. At least I hope it's safe. Jonas is right behind us while Caroline and the others follow on foot. Residents of the houses on either side are already gathered here, looking down on the beach at Seal Rock with its monstrous rock formations.

Usually the water comes up close to the cliff, making spectacular splashes around the rocks, but today as we get out of the truck and look down, there is no water. The beach extends way beyond the rocks.

"Jesus," Rick mutters.

"Low tide?" I ask.

"No. It's pulling out in preparation for the big surge."

"Oh."

The shaking has stopped. The water has pulled way back, exposing miles of bare sand, rocks, tree stumps, chunks of wood, seaweed, and fishing nets. Several sea lions lie beached like boats run aground. I realize I'm holding my breath.

Jonas stands nearby, smoking. "I should try to go home while I still can. I can go the long way up Beaver Creek through Toledo or something. Dawn has been on call all day, and I'm supposed to be on duty tonight." He turns back toward his car. "I'll take Janey to her place."

"No," Rick says. "Stay put. If you go right now, this surge is likely to catch you and drown your whole family. Janey's apartment is right in the tsunami zone. I don't think anybody is going to be calling for a taxi tonight anyway. Sorry, kids, you can't go home."

Jonas takes a deep shuddering breath and nods. He glances back at the car, where Molly is trying to calm their sons.

"Look!" cries a red-headed woman from one of the houses.

Jesus. A wall of water is coming our way. It's not like a wave; it's more like a lion crouched and coming at us on giant paws, its teeth bared. It starts way out, but it's coming fast. I want to turn and run. We think we're safe up here, but the water is so high.

Unconsciously, I back up toward the road. Off to my right, I see Caroline making the sign of the cross. Suddenly we're all grabbing hands as she starts to pray. "Dear God, please—" Her voice breaks.

Frankie takes over, a quiver in her own voice. "Dear God, all powerful and loving God, please protect us from these giant waves. Watch over our homes and especially watch over our loved ones. Take special care of Dave, who is such a good husband and father and a devoted public servant who would give his life to save someone else on the beach. Please bring him home safe. In Jesus' name, we pray. Amen."

We all whisper amen, but keep holding hands.

"Here it comes," Jonas says.

"Damn. There's somebody on the beach," Rick says. "Idiots."

I see them. A man with a camera and two kids standing on a log.

We all start screaming. "Get back! Get back! Run!"

But it's too late.

You know how waves usually curl up, break and roll to a stop at a certain point? How they look like can-can dancers swirling their skirts one at a time down the line? Not this time. This wall of water, this mother of a wave, just keeps coming until it rams against the cliff, splashing us all, coming so close I swear I could reach down and touch it. The giant black rocks that line Seal Rock beach like teeth disappear.

Salt water in our hair and running down our faces, we hear roaring, crashing, breaking sounds and feel the ground shake beneath us from the power of the wave. It's a wave that will not be stopped. It must be pouring through every little opening, every creek, river, and bay.

"Oh Lord," moans a woman nearby.

In the blur of crashing water, I see dark spots where the people were and then I don't see them anymore.

With a loud sucking sound, the wave pulls back out to sea, almost as far as before, but this time it's taking pieces of stairways and buildings. Off to the right, I watch as the water washes a balcony off the front of a house, along with patio chairs, flowerpots, a hose, everything in its path.

Right here where we stand above the Seal Rock beach, there isn't much for it to take, but south in Waldport there are homes right on the sand and boats in the marina. To the north, in Newport, the wave would hit more boats, the aquarium, the shops along the Bayfront, houses, apartments, restaurants, galleries, the performing arts center, a Montessori School—Oh my God.

In the silence, Diana asks, "Do you think Donovan made it to the cabin in time?"

Nobody answers. We're all thinking the same thing. Probably not. The wave would rush up Beaver Creek and cover the road, floating his 4 x 4 pickup like a child's toy.

"I have to go," Rick says. "Should have gone sooner." He gives Diana a quick hug and kiss before climbing back into the truck and driving away.

"He's a volunteer firefighter," Frankie explains.

In a minute, three red trucks emerge from the Seal Rock fire station. Two head south on the highway, while one truck goes north toward Newport.

"Here comes another wave," Jonas says.

We all back up a little and watch in silence as another surge hits, this one bigger than the last and loaded with furniture and pieces of wood. Again, we get wet. Again, we hear roaring, cracking, and crashing. This time rocks and trees from the cliff go out with the tide.

I swallow. "I'm not sure we're safe here anymore."

"It's going to take my house," says a white-haired lady standing behind us.

Diana hugs her. "It'll be okay, Flora," she says, but I don't think any of us are sure of that.

I don't know how long we stand there. It's getting dark. I can't stop shivering. Amy keeps trying to call her father, but she can't get through. I keep looking at Caroline, thinking that by tomorrow she might be a widow like me. Most of the women standing here are single, either divorced or widowed. It occurs to me for maybe the first time since Tom died that I'm not that special in my widowhood. I'm not the only one. Right now in view of what is happening, it seems like a small thing, something I can get past and move beyond, just as these other women have.

The aftershocks have gotten farther apart. In fact, I haven't felt one for a while.

It's a long time between waves. I guess it takes a while to gather all that water. The third surge, almost two hours after the original earthquake, is a lollapalooza. We have backed up all the way to the edge of the road and can't see what's happening directly below. From the ripping, crashing, banging sound of it, it destroys part of somebody's house. I hope it's not Flora's.

Finally the waves get smaller. They pull back less, don't come in quite as far. By the time it's truly dark, the tsunami seems to be over. The waves come and go in their usual lazy fashion, as if nothing has happened.

Except that most of us can't go home.

21

WE HUDDLE IN QUILTS and blankets in the living room of Diana's house up the hill from the restaurant. Things have fallen down here and there in the house, but it's relatively unscathed, except we have no power, no water, and no telephone service. With every report on the battery-powered radio, the news gets worse. Twenty-three dead, then 38, then 49, with hundreds injured and dozens missing. Extensive earthquake damage in the cities along the I-5 corridor more than 50 miles inland.

Electricity is out everywhere. Gas and water lines are compromised so they've been shut off. The Alsea Bridge to Waldport and the Yaquina Bridge to Newport are both closed until they can be thoroughly inspected. The south end of the Yaquina appears to be at least a foot lower than it used to be and there's a crack across the pavement. Here in Seal Rock, we're an island between the bridges.

Buildings along the coast from Brookings to Astoria are damaged or destroyed. The tsunami is over and the aftershocks are becoming less frequent, but we are being told to go somewhere safe and stay there. "Do not try to drive anywhere," the announcer emphasizes. I drove my car up from the diner, dodging debris in the narrow road to Diana's house. I wonder what it's like on other roads.

Diana heated chicken noodle soup on her woodstove. We ate it with French bread and butter and sweet red wine she found in the back of a cupboard.

We're safe, but I can't stop trembling. The woodstove provides some heat, but not enough, and I keep seeing the wall of water in my mind.

Molly put the boys to sleep in Janey's old bedroom. The rest of us are awake, except for the Border collie sleeping under the table.

After a while, I hear nothing but hissing coming from the radio. I turn it off.

"Might as well try to sleep," Diana says. "Tomorrow's going to be a big day."

Janey groans. "How can I sleep when everything I own is being washed out to sea?"

"Oh, baby. Be thankful you're alive and we're together."

But Rick and Donovan are not here. Nor is Ranger Dave. I feel like we shouldn't be hiding here when they're in danger out there somewhere in the dark.

In the silence, I hear Jonas' voice from the hallway door. "Timmy says he wants a turkey sandwich."

Diana laughs. "Well, maybe next year. Today's turkey isn't safe to eat anymore. Maybe we could salvage a couple of pies tomorrow."

"Pumpkin pie. Don't forget the whipped cream," Molly calls.

My stomach gurgles at the thought.

IT'S A LITTLE AFTER midnight. Everyone else is asleep or at least I think so from the snores and heavy breathing. Diana and Jonas's family occupy the bedrooms while Frankie sleeps on the sofa, and Caroline, Amy, Janey and I lie on the floor.

It won't be light for another seven hours, but I can't stand it. As quietly as I can, I get up, find my purse and coat and head for the door. The dog starts to follow. "No. Stay," I whisper. He lies back down.

As I'm turning the handle, Janey asks, "Where are you going?"

"I've got to do something. I've got to help somehow."

"I'm coming with you."

Somebody stirs, and the dog is on his feet again. I pull Janey out the door, putting my finger on my lips to shush her. We don't talk until we're safely in my car.

I try the radio. Nothing.

"I can't believe this is happening," Janey says.

"Me either. Let's go up Beaver Creek first and check on Donovan."

The highway is surprisingly clear—until we get near Ona Beach, where the road dips to near sea level. I slow down to 5 miles an hour, grateful my car is small as I dodge chunks of wood, road signs and garbage cans over a surface glazed with mud and sand.

"Is that part of a picnic table?"

It is. I swerve around it and lose control of the car. We're doomed. But God hears my unspoken prayer as we spin across the road. The car stops sideways in the northbound lane. Ripples of water shine in the headlights. "Thank you, God," I whisper, carefully easing up to the turnoff to Beaver Creek Road.

The road here is under several inches of water. Even with my headlights on high, I can barely distinguish the pavement from the wetlands on either side. I'm terrified my car will start floating. I understand why the guy on the radio said not to drive, but now I'm here and there's no way out of it but to keep driving through this flat area until we start climbing the hill. The higher we go, the dryer it will get.

If the world weren't falling apart, this would be a beautiful night. The sky has cleared, the stars are out, and a rainbow surrounds the half-moon shining over the ocean. I'm thinking how great it is that we haven't had an aftershock for ages when I suddenly have trouble controlling the car and feel water lapping against the tires. I keep going, afraid to stop, until Janey whispers, "Oh my God. Look."

"What?"

"It's a body."

I don't want to stop, and I don't want to see a dead body, but it might be Donovan. I put on the brake, and we both jump out, flashlights in hand, water sloshing over our ankles as we wade toward the dark thing lying on the side of the road. There's not another soul around for miles. I'm thinking we should have stayed on the floor at Diana's house, but that's not P.D. If I'm going to be P.D., I can't hide from trouble and let the men handle everything.

Rick might have already searched for Donovan, even found him and taken him to a shelter. But maybe not. He'd have to go where the fire trucks went. This isolated road would not be their first stop.

Janey reaches the body first.

"It's not him."

It's not even human. It's a dog, a golden retriever. Drowned, its tongue hanging out of its mouth, its eyes glazed with death.

Janey squats beside it, stroking its sodden fur, and starts to cry. "You poor beautiful thing."

I will not cry. I will not cry. We have to move on. "Come on, Janey. We can't do anything for him right now."

"We could bury him."

"Where? It's all water. We have to find Donovan. Let's go."

Back in the car, wet from the knees down, I drive up the hill, breathing a sigh of relief when I feel the tires take hold on nearly dry pavement. We're safe from tsunamis here, but what about the earthquake? I pray we find Donovan at his cabin cheerfully drinking wine and gluing pieces of glass together by candlelight.

It's so weird going up this road now. It feels like forever since I drove down it this morning feeling all sorry for myself, my face soggy with tears, thinking I had nothing to be thankful for. I had lights, food, and friends. I was safe. Elk grazed along the road; there were no dead dogs. Or dead humans.

We cross from paved road to gravel. As I try to stay on the narrow lane curving uphill, fences seem to be catawampus, and houses seem to be leaning, but I'm not really sure of anything.

We both hold our breath as I turn off the road and push the car up Donovan's steep driveway.

His truck is not here. The garden appears to have been trampled, but the house is dark. There's no electricity, but he would have lit a fire, wouldn't he? Or some of those candles he had stashed everywhere.

"Oh no," Janey says. I can tell from the quiver in her voice that she's about to cry again.

"Don't panic yet," I command. "He might be in there sleeping, or he might have gone somewhere else."

"Japan."

"Oh, come on. He probably decided to go someplace safer."

"He was drunk and crazy when he left."

"Well, maybe he went looking for a bar. Come on, let's check the house. I don't have any keys, but we can peek in the windows."

As we climb the porch, I hear a meow and turn, expecting Hernando. But it's Sasha. She lets me pick her up. She's scared too, I guess.

"The window's broken," Janey says. "Give me something to knock out the glass, so we can get in."

I try the door. "Wait." It's not locked. In my hurry this morning, did I forget to lock it? Or was Donovan here? Did somebody break in?

Flashlight aimed like TV cops hold their guns, I open the door and walk in, letting Sasha down to the floor as Janey follows me. I have this spooky feeling somebody's going to jump out at me. Maybe Donovan will spring out of the dark and attack. But as I swing my light around, I don't see anyone. I do see cupboard doors open, dishes and soup cans tumbled onto the floor, a broken coffeemaker, my books fallen off the table by the easy chair. Donovan's fish clock is face down on the floor. In the bedroom, the shelf has fallen down, but everything else looks the same.

"He's not here," Janey says.

I glance back at Janey. She looks like a terrified Shirley Temple. "Maybe he's in his studio." I ease the door open.

I don't see anything different. At first.

Janey points to the cabinet I couldn't unlock. The door is open now. Our lights shine on a mishmash of metal and glass. Some of it looks like the china from the restaurant.

"Listen," Janey whispers.

Singing. Somebody is singing. Sounds like an Irish tenor. Sounds like Donovan. We crouch by the window and see him sitting in the chair on the back veranda, waving a glass and singing at the top of his lungs. Relief floods through me as Janey giggles.

"Shh!"

"Sounds like he's feeling just fine."

Unbelievable. Thank you, God.

"P.D., how did he get here? I didn't see his truck."

"I don't know. But I'm not about to ask him."

"Me either. Now what?"

"Let's get out of here."

We tiptoe out, closing the door behind us. I pour a little food for the cats then decide to get the rest of my stuff. "Help me pack."

It's cold in the cabin. The last chunk of wood in the fireplace has turned to ash. That's Donovan's problem now. We scurry around grabbing my stuff out of the bathroom, bedroom, living room and kitchen and hurry back down the steps. Donovan doesn't miss a note.

IT'S 1 A.M. AS we slip and slosh back down the hill past the leaning fences, into the standing water, past the dead dog and stop where Beaver Creek Road meets Highway 101. As I consider the mess around us, I'm thinking there's brave and then there's stupid.

"I think we should go back to your mom's house."

"No," responds Miss Janey. "Let's look for Dave, and then let's try to get to my apartment."

"Janey, we can't get over the bridge, and I don't know where we'd look for Dave."

"All the beaches from Newport to Waldport."

"Are you kidding? It's dark, and God knows what's on the beaches now."

"The tsunami is over."

"Maybe."

"Come on, P.D."

Well, I know I wouldn't be able to sleep if we did go back. "All right. We'll go up the road a little ways, but if it gets this hairy again, I'm turning back." Feeling as if I'm steering a boat, I ease my car onto the highway heading north. Around the bend, the water recedes, but it's still slippery.

The next beach up is Lost Creek. I turn into the parking lot high above the sand. There isn't much to this park, just a bathroom up here and a narrow path down to a shallow beach. It's almost all under water even during an ordinary high tide.

When we get out of the car, we hear the waves lapping against the cliff and see the moonlight sparkling off curls of black water.

"We can't go down there," I say.

Her flashlight offering only a tiny circle of light, Janey starts down the path to the beach. She doesn't get far before she slips and almost falls on a patch of mud, grabbing at the chain link fence. "Whoa. I guess not."

"Let's try South Beach." It's a much bigger park, with campgrounds, trails and a wider beach.

But we find sheriffs' cars with flashing blue and red lights blocking the entrance. I pull to a stop and open the window as an officer shines a flashlight in my face. I can't look straight at him, it's so bright.

"Where are you headed, ladies?" He looks like the weightlifter who spotted me at the gym.

Janey leans across me. "We're trying to find a friend, a ranger, Dave Walsh. If we could just drive in and look around . . ."

"Sorry," says the sheriff. His name tag says Loomey. "We're not allowing anyone past the barricades. There's extensive damage in there, and it's just not safe."

"Well," I ask. "Is there any way to find out if Dave is okay?"

"I'm sorry, ma'am. All I can tell you is we know Dave and we haven't seen him or heard from him around here. Right now, a lot of people are missing. We've got folks searching all over the coast. If he's injured, he might be at the hospital. He could be at the emergency evacuation center at the community college. You might want to go up there. Otherwise you probably ought to turn around and go home. The bridge is closed to all traffic, and it's not safe to be driving around here in the middle of the night."

"We can't just sit around," Janey says.

"I understand, but there's not much else you can do." He turns off his light and walks away. I know he's just doing his job. God knows, he may have left a house in shambles, might have missing friends and family, too. But I want to hate him.

ALL OF THE TSUNAMI evacuation guides have told us not to drive, but here I am in my car. When we get to the community college, the parking lot is full. I park at the end of the line on the entry road. Inside, we blink in the lights that must be powered by some kind of emergency generator.

Janey, a student here, leads the way into the commons area. Either this relatively new building is especially sturdy or they did a fast job of cleaning up the earthquake damage because nothing looks out of order. People in sleeping bags are scattered among the tables and chairs, between candy and soft drink machines and magazine racks. Some are asleep, some are talking quietly. One couple is trying desperately to hush their sobbing toddler.

We walk up to a big table covered with plates of cookies, cups of juice, and pots of coffee and tea. "Welcome," says a woman with a gray felt hat over her white curls. "You can have a snack and relax anywhere you like. Please sign in so we know who's here."

I gaze around the room, inhaling a blend of cookies, punch, and wet clothes. "We're not staying. We're looking for a friend."

"Oh. What's her name?"

"His. Dave . . ."

"Walsh," Janey says.

"Would he be with his family?"

"No." I follow her pearly fingernail down the handwritten list.

"Janey!" someone calls from the sleeping bags.

"Hey," Janey stage-whispers to a young man about her age. "Is your house—?"

"Toast."

"I'm sorry. I haven't seen mine yet."

The woman has finished her search. "No. I don't see anyone by that name."

"He's a ranger," Janey says. "Probably in uniform."

"Sorry."

"Well, thank you for checking."

"I hope you find him." As we turn, she adds, "Maybe you should stay here. I see you're already injured."

She's looking at me. I had forgotten about my wrist brace. "Oh. I did that before. Fell off a ladder. It's almost healed."

I try to smile, but my face feels frozen. I'm exhausted. This day started hard and never ended. My ribs ache. It's the middle of the night, but I can't curl up and rest. Not yet. I'm not sure what I'm supposed to do, but I have to do something. I send up a silent call to God. Hello, remember me? I need a little direction here.

I don't know if it's God, but the first thing I'm moved to do is get me a cup of coffee and a cookie. I suspect such things are going to get pretty scarce with no electricity and half of the coast under water.

I wonder who put all this together. Who baked the peanut butter and chocolate chip cookies? Were they sitting in somebody's freezer waiting for a disaster or were they baked for somebody's Thanksgiving party? "Thank you," I say, grabbing two peanut butters.

"Thanks," Janey adds through a mouthful of chocolate chips.

"Stay safe," the woman says as we steal away with our snacks.

As I drink my coffee, I wonder if this is a bad idea because then I'll need a restroom, but the coffee tastes wonderful, offering warm comfort all the way from my mouth down my throat to my belly.

We push out the big glass doors into the dark.

"I think we're out of options. Maybe we should go home," I suggest as I drive back down the hill to where the college road intersects with the highway.

"We can't give up yet."

I see flashing lights and barricades up ahead at the bridge. We're not driving over it, that's for sure. "How about the jetty? Can we get to the beach from there?" Even as I say it, I know it's a dumb idea.

Janey shakes her head. "No way. People die on the jetty in normal times. Just last year, a couple got washed off the rocks. One minute they were there; the next they were gone. Besides, the jetty probably got torn up by the tsunami."

These waves look pretty, but you can't trust them. Right now I hear them banging into the sand like my mother used to bang pots and pans when she was mad at my dad. Nothing like a pissed-off ocean.

So here we are at 1:30 a.m., sitting at the turn. I've got all my stuff in my car, except the keyboard, which is back at the restaurant, maybe in pieces. Donovan has taken the cabin back, so I really have no ties at this moment, except to these people I have met within the last few weeks.

An aftershock shakes the car as we hold on to the dashboard. When it subsides, I look over at Janey, a curly-headed shadow in the dark car. "Let's just go back to the college and rest until daylight."

She stares out the window at the blinking lights by the bridge. "I know we're not supposed to go there, but . . ."

"What?" I know what I would want. "I know. You want to see your apartment. But Janey, we can't drive over the bridge."

"I know. But I have an idea."

22

A FEW MINUTES later, I park in the Oregon Coast Aquarium lot closest to the marina. I choose a space in the middle where nothing could fall on my car during an aftershock and hope the tsunami is really over.

We walk through what's left of the marina and the brewery next door. In the moonlight, we see boats on their sides, light poles on the ground, a pile of rubble where the bait shop used to be. I smell spilled beer and fish guts. Our shoes crunch on mud, sand, and bits of wood. We dodge car parts, chairs, lamps, and tables. People wander around with flashlights, talking in the quiet voices folks use at funerals. I hear someone sobbing. In the dark, we meld into the crowd and walk toward the foot of the bridge.

That's when Janey's phone rings, painfully loud. We didn't tell anyone we were leaving. Of course they would panic to find us gone. But I can't believe the phone is working.

I can only hear Janey's side of the conversation.

"Mom. Hi. We're okay. We went to look for Donovan. He's at the cabin. He's just fine, drunk and happy."

She pauses.

"Yeah."

"No, we're okay. We—Mom? Mom?" She stares at the phone. "No service. And my battery's getting low."

"Turn it off." With no place to charge our phones, we are all going to run out of battery power soon. And not just in our phones. My little car has about 10 miles left before it switches from electric power to gas, and I have less than half a tank left. That won't get me very far.

Where would I go anyway? Even if I could get my car across the bridge to the highway east, it's 50 miles to Corvallis and I-5, and all of the gas stations depend on electricity to operate their pumps. Plus, the roads might not be open. According to the radio, there's earthquake damage everywhere in western Oregon, not just here on the coast.

It won't be long before nobody can drive unless somebody finds a way to bring in some gas. My electric car might give me a slight advantage. But not for long.

We hear a commotion behind us and turn to see a couple of people dragging something out of the ruins of the bait shop. It's a human body, naked, limp like it has no bones. In the dark, I can't tell if it's a man or a woman, but it has long hair, so it isn't Dave. My heart is beating too fast. Breathing in the stench of mud and death, I move toward the group, wanting to see who it is, to see if there's a chance he or she might be alive.

Janey tugs my arm. "Come on."

While the other people are distracted, she leads me to a set of concrete stairs that go up to the bridge.

They're steep and slippery. But we get to the top and turn north toward town. A policeman sees us and yells, "Hey! Stop!" Ignoring him, we run right down the middle of the bridge. I've never done anything like this, running away from a police officer who's telling me to stop. I think we're breaking the law, but we're not stopping, come hell or tsunami. The cop is too busy to chase us.

We don't get far before another aftershock hits. I never did like amusement park thrill rides, so I'm not liking this either. We both grab for the railing, hoping the bridge doesn't fall apart and dump us in the bay. A breeze latches onto my hat, and the fedora leaves my head, sails over the rail and falls. I watch, helpless as it disappears in the darkness, probably floating under the bridge, through the jetty and out to sea. Maybe it will land in Japan.

Meanwhile, we've got to get off this bridge. As soon as the shaking stops, we start running again.

Halfway across, my shoe catches on a crack in the pavement. Before I can stop myself, I'm falling, landing on my stupid sprained wrist. Pain shoots from my fingertips to my shoulder blade as I scream. My voice is lost in the thrashing of the water under the bridge. I lie there, fighting to breathe, chanting, "Shit, shit, shit." It hurts so bad I think my wrist must be broken now.

"Are you all right?" Janey yells.

"Yeah, sure," I answer as I pull myself back up, glancing back toward the cops. "Let's go." I'm shaking. This may be the stupidest thing I've ever done, but we're here now. Going back would be just as hard as going on. Besides, if I need to go to the hospital, it's on the other side of the bridge.

If I hadn't done all that time on the treadmill at the gym before I fell off the ladder, I don't think I could make it. Poor Janey is gasping for breath before we get to the end of the half-mile span, where we face another line of police cars, their blue and red lights blinding in the surrounding blackness. Janey leads me slipping down the stairs on the other side. Finally we're in Newport.

It doesn't look the same.

From what we can see in the light of the moon and our flashlights, light poles lean this way and that, signs lie on the ground. A lot of the buildings seem to be cockeyed and have broken windows. I see what looks like a fire in the distance, somewhere near the electric company headquarters. This is bad, but I'm thinking it's nothing compared to what we'll see closer to the beach.

I hear voices and see shadow people clustered in front of an apartment building and gathered at the Chevron station. We keep walking along Highway 101, which serves as Main Street for most of the towns on the Oregon coast.

A little way up the road, I see lights off to the right: The hospital, lit up with backup generators. I point it out to Janey, even as our legs keep moving past it.

"Should we check to see if Dave is there?" And maybe use the bathrooms, get some more coffee, and get warm for a minute?

She shakes her curly head. "You go if you want to. I have to see my apartment. I have to know." She barely has enough breath to speak.

"No. We're not splitting up." It is so eerie out here in the dark. I'm afraid any minute our flashlight batteries will die or we'll trip over something. I'm worried about my wrist. As we walk, I wiggle my fingers, move my hand around inside the brace. It probably isn't broken, but it hurts so bad I'm surprised it isn't glowing red in the dark.

It's another two miles before we reach the street that leads to Janey's place on Coast Street in Nye Beach. It's after 2 a.m. now.

Despite the coffee and the fear hammering in my chest—or maybe because of it—I want to curl up somewhere and go to sleep. Every bench, every porch calls me. But the closer we get, the faster Janey walks, breathing hard, powered by her need to see if she has a home left.

Two blocks west, our feet hit sand. Debris begins to block our path. Little things at first. Pieces of wood, a rubber boot, a metal napkin dispenser, restaurant menus, steel posts from a parking lot. A child's jacket is plastered to a fire hydrant. Another block, and the rubble gets bigger. A coffee table. A wooden chair. An overturned Volkswagen.

Janey stops, moving her light along the buildings on either side of Third Street. I hear her make a high-pitched sound, like a wounded animal. "That's where Uncle Rick's place was."

Piles of wood, bricks and plaster, and cars sit in the middle of what used to be buildings. Dear God. And we haven't gotten to Janey's place yet. I put my good arm around her shoulder, and we forge on, stepping around pieces of houses and God knows what.

"Jesus," I mutter as we reach the last street before the beach. Restaurants, stores and art galleries are gone, water running through the rubble. The sign for the Coast Inn, proclaiming "vacancy" "HBO" and "free Wi-Fi," is no longer attached to a building.

Around us, I see people picking through what's left. It takes me a minute to realize what they're doing. They're looking for folks who are trapped and for dead bodies. I wonder about the old man at the Coast Inn and the people who were staying there. God, please help them, I pray as we turn north toward where Janey's apartment is supposed to be. It's uphill a little ways. Maybe—

"Janey? P.D.?" a deep voice calls in the dark.

It's Rick. I suck in a chilly breath and thank God.

WE TAKE SHELTER in Rick's arms, clutching his wet fire jacket. He's got mud on his face and smells like salt water and blood.

"What the hell are you doing here?" he asks, pushing us away.

Janey is crying. "I had—I needed—I couldn't sleep not knowing where anybody was or what had happened to my apartment. And oh God, your place—"

"It doesn't matter. You shouldn't be out here now. There's not one building you can trust to not fall on your head. We're finding people who are hurt, people who are dead. We're worried about fallen wires, toxic spills, and fires. Go home, girls. Please. I don't want anything to happen to either of you."

"Rick!" another firefighter calls.

"I have to go. You—oh, Jesus, don't go back over the bridge. Go to the shelter at the high school and stay there."

As he turns away, Janey says, "We found Donovan."

"He's okay?"

"Drunk as a skunk, singing his songs."

Rick's grinning white teeth shine in the dark. "Good. Now go!"

On the beach, the ocean swells into waves that smash on the sand. How do I know they won't come any farther? How do I know we're safe here? I want to go inland, but Janey won't stop until she sees her apartment. After that? I don't know.

I don't want to be a wimp hiding at a shelter when people are dying. For the first time, I miss my hospital job, where in my small way, I was helping people who were suffering. I was the connection between them and the doctors. Would it really be so bad if they called me Cissy or my actual name? If we ever get out of this mess—

I follow as Janey leads us three blocks north on Coast Street. The debris thins a bit. "There it is," she says, stopping in front of her two-story apartment building.

I don't know what vagaries of waves and location saved it, but as near as we can see with our flashlights, the building is still standing. The bottom floor looks pretty trashed, windows and doors broken out, everything inside upended and wet, but upstairs where Janey lives seems pretty unscathed.

The metal stairs dangle unattached. She stands there, looking up.

"I don't think so, Janey."

"I've got to get to my place."

"Not that way. It's not safe. It could fall down in the next aftershock. Take it from the woman who fell off the ladder and was lucky she didn't break her neck." I finger my wrist brace, now dirty, its Velcro fastenings loose. It's tight against my swollen wrist.

She puts her foot on the first rung. I grab her arm. "No. Please. Wait until morning."

"Leave me alone, P.D." She shrugs me off and starts to climb as an aftershock hits. The loose stairs swing in the air and threaten to detach completely. Janey drops to the ground, shaking with sobs.

I hold her and try to comfort her. Sometimes I forget how young she is. At 22, she could be my daughter. "I'm sorry. At least we know it's still here. I'm thinking everything inside is pretty much as you left it. We just have to wait a little while to get upstairs safely."

She nods, crying so hard she can't speak.

Finally, drawing deep gasping breaths, she lets me lead her away from the apartment.

"Let's just go to the shelter. Okay?"

She clears her throat. "Okay. But I want to check Jonas's house. It's on the way."

"Where?"

She sighs. "Inland. Out of the tsunami zone."

Behind us, something pops, then bangs. Fire lights the darkness from the area where Rick just went.

"The dry cleaners," Janey says, changing direction, pulling me toward the light.

One of the few buildings that was still standing is on fire. I wonder if it might explode. Didn't I see a propane tank close to the building?

"Janey, we have to get away from here."

"But Uncle Rick is there."

The fire grows rapidly, flames licking the black sky, the sound joining with the ocean to create such a roar I can't hear anything else. The firefighters bring water trucks around, set up hoses, start to spray. The buildings on that block are all close together, some of the shops dating back to the early 1900s, many with residences on the second floor.

I strain to see Rick amid the men in uniform. The area is lit up by the fire and by the lights on the trucks, but with the firefighters wearing their helmets and all, it's hard to tell who's who.

"Please clear the area, ladies," a young fireman orders.

We step back into the darkness, our eyes still fixed on the fire. I know we need to leave, but I just can't, and Janey isn't moving either. I feel like I should grab a helmet and help somehow. Go through the rubble. Carry things to safety. Something. I'm physically fit and wide awake. Unlike these other people, I have nothing to lose here.

"Roof's about to go!" I hear somebody shout.

"Everybody clear?" a man asks.

"No! Rick went in to get the owner and his wife. They live upstairs."

"He didn't come out yet?"

"Negative, Chief."

"Shit. I'm going in."

"Chief. That's not what—"

"Don't tell me the rules, kid. I helped write 'em."

As the burly man in yellow turnouts is about to step through the broken door, a section of roof crashes down.

Over the roar and crackle of the fire, I hear the men cursing. The chief hesitates at the entry. Then, "To hell with it, I'm going in."

"Chief. Not advisable."

"My man is in there. Plus civilians. Get the bus ready."

"Yes sir."

We feel the heat of the flames now. We can see the light on the sweating faces and piles of dry-cleaned clothes in plastic wrappers soaked and smoldering. My heart is pounding, adrenaline racing through my blood. I just met Rick Jones, but I feel connected to him. And those poor people inside, they might be dead.

Oh God. The chief's coming out, dragging someone. "That's not Rick, is it?"

Janey shakes her head. "I don't think so. I think it's Mr. Wu."

"Is he dead?"

"I hope not."

They load the man into the ambulance. In the lights, I can see now that he's too small to be Rick. I hear him talking in Chinese. Nobody knows what he's saying, but it's a good sign. He's yelling something over and over. I suspect it's about his wife.

Time passes. Too much time. The fire spreads to the bar next door despite the steady stream of water. The smoke makes it hard to breathe. I start praying. "Lord have mercy, Lord have mercy, Lord have mercy." Janey joins me with "Christ have mercy, Christ have mercy, Christ have mercy. Lord—"

This time it is Rick. The chief has his arm around him, half carrying, half dragging him out the door. He's protesting, saying something about the wife being still inside.

"You can't do anything for her now," the chief says as a firefighter gets on Rick's other side and helps lower him to a gurney. The chief turns to another guy. "We've got a recovery situation in there."

The Chinese guy understands and begins to wail.

As they load Rick into the ambulance beside Mr. Wu, Janey and I rush forward.

"Get back!" a guy yells at us.

Rick turns his head our way, opens his mouth to speak, then closes it as if he can't get any words out. He reaches a hand in our direction. They close the doors and drive away.

"Forget the shelter. I'm going to the hospital," I tell Janey.

"Me too. I'm going to check Jonas's house on the way and I'll meet you there."

We retrace our steps, shining our flashlights on the ground, stepping over books, toys, a woman's purse, pieces of cars and pieces of buildings until we reach relatively clear pavement. When we get across the highway, Janey continues east while I turn south toward the only building I can see with lights on. My flashlight is starting to flicker. "Get some batteries at Jonas' house!" I call.

"I will." She stops. "Hey, P.D.? Thanks."

23

I BLINK IN THE LIGHT as I enter the crush in the emergency waiting room. The hospital sure looks different from when I was here almost applying for a job. At the hospital where I worked in Missoula, we had this big lobby with an information desk and a half dozen cubicles where admissions clerks like me checked people in. The hospital, five stories tall and covering several acres, was so big people got lost all the time. We had volunteers walk them to where they were going. It would be hard to get lost here.

Folks are lined up to the door waiting to check in. People sit, stand, and lie on the floor amid children crying and old folks bent over in shocked silence. I see people bleeding, limping, holding their bellies, pressing ice packs against their faces. Their clothes are torn and muddy, their eyes red with shock. I wonder how many have lost their homes or loved ones. One minute, people were eating turkey and watching football. The next minute, they were fighting for their lives.

I literally cannot walk through without gently shoving people. I want to cut to the front and ask the harried nurses if they've seen Rick, who would have come in the ambulance entrance, but I'm thinking these people's needs are bigger than mine.

As for my wrist, it hurts, but it can wait.

I want to find Rick. I want to know what happened to Dave. I want to jump in and help. And I really need a restroom. I head there first. It's a mess. I gather up wads of paper towels and toilet paper and throw them in the wastebasket. The toilet takes three tries to flush. In a couple days, I suspect it won't work at all. How long would it take to set up Port-a-Potties? Where would they come from?

The hallway outside the restroom leads to admitting, where I find just as big a crowd. I almost shout Rick's name when I see a firefighter in uniform, but when he turns his head, it isn't him. Maybe he knows where he is. I push my way through.

"Excuse me."

He doesn't hear over the noise.

I try again, louder. "Excuse me!"

A tall guy, he looks down. His face is smudged with dirt, his eyes bloodshot. "What do you need?"

"I'm looking for a volunteer firefighter named Rick Jones. He was hurt. They were bringing him here. Do you know where he is?"

He sighs. "I don't know, ma'am. I know him, but I haven't heard anything about him. Sorry."

"Thanks. By any chance do you know a ranger named Dave Walsh?"

"No. Sorry."

I hesitate, staring at the bloody handkerchief wrapped around his left hand. "Are you injured?"

"Just a cut that needs stitching. No big deal. I'll take care of it later. I'm actually waiting to finish the paperwork for my son. He— he's in surgery right now." He looks away.

I wonder where the mother is, if she's hurt or got caught somewhere and couldn't get to her family. No, it's Thanksgiving— Thanksgiving! They would have been together. She's probably in the surgery waiting room. Which is most likely a madhouse, too.

The line at admitting must be 30 people long. I want to do something. I know that Rick is being taken care of. I have told people that same thing countless times, that they need to wait and be patient, somebody will talk to them later, they need to let the doctors work, yada yada yada. This is different. But what right do I have? I'm not family. I'm not his wife, not even his girlfriend. Shoot, I barely know him.

"Excuse me, everyone," shouts a balding man in a wrinkled white shirt. I can tell by looking at him he's the hospital boss and wishing he had any job but this one right now. "If you do not need to be in this area, we need you to go somewhere else. There's some space in the non-emergency waiting room, and we've got coffee in the conference room. Please, if you don't have to be here, you need to leave."

As he turns toward the emergency waiting room, probably to make the same announcement, I step forward. Before I even know what I'm saying, I tell him, "Hi. Until recently, I worked in admitting at St. Patrick's Hospital in Missoula. If there's some way I can help, I have some training and I want to do something."

He stares at me for a minute. I can imagine what he thinks of my two-tone hair and my grubby face. I wait for him to tell me to clear out, but no.

He nods. "Thanks. I appreciate it. We can't pay you anything, but if you can lend a hand . . . What's your name?"

I almost give him the real deal, then stop myself. "P.D. I'm P.D. Soares."

"Come on."

THE HOSPITAL IS NOT equipped to handle this many people or any major trauma. There's a helicopter pad outside to take patients to other hospitals. That's probably the safest way to travel right now. In my weariness, I lean against a wall, shut my eyes for a millisecond and imagine myself in a helicopter flying high above the shaking earth and the out-of-control ocean. In the sky, it's safe . . .

"P.D.?" says Shirley, who is in charge of admissions.

I guess I fell asleep in my chair for a minute.

It's daylight outside now, and I've been working for hours. I'm basically their extra hand, doing whatever I can do without being an official employee. Sworn to uphold patient privacy, I'm making copies of insurance cards, helping people fill out health history forms, attaching ID bracelets. I'm leading people to X-ray, waiting rooms, coffee, telephones, wherever they need to go. And I'm listening to their stories about things falling on them, about waves coming into their houses or carrying them away in their cars and smashing them into buildings, about clinging to shelves and rafters and stairways, sure they're going to die. About screams and crashes and cold and wet and dark, about praying, about a family on the beach and kids at the playground being swept away. About bodies being found on the beach when the tide went back out. Dear God. Whatever problems I thought I had are nothing.

Occasionally an aftershock rattles the hospital, sometimes the power flickers. The computers are iffy, causing the clerks to curse, but we're working our way through the line.

The heaters aren't working, but having so many bodies in one place keeps it warm enough.

I wind up being the one to help the tall firefighter with his paperwork. He tells me he talked to a nurse friend about Rick while he was waiting. He hesitates. "Are you family?"

"No. Just a friend. I don't know if he has any family around here."

"I don't think he does. I know he's divorced. Anyway, he's in surgery, got hurt pretty bad when the roof fell in at the dry cleaners, but they expect him to recover."

"Good."

"P.D.!" Shirley calls.

"Gotta go," I tell the firefighter. "Find me when you're done with the forms. Thanks for telling me about Rick."

"Thank you for your help. Surgery is . . . ?"

I point down the hall. "Follow the signs."

As I hurry back into the admitting office, I send up a quick prayer. "Please God, let Rick be okay. And that fireman's little boy." I look at the never-ending line. "Let them all be okay."

At 8:00 a.m., new workers arrive, and Shirley tells me I can go home. Except I can't. I can't go back over the bridge, and Donovan has taken his cabin back. I can't even sleep in my car. Assuming Rick's out of surgery by now, I climb the stairs to the second floor. I know it's not visiting hours, and I know the nurses might kick me out because I'm not family, but I also know that nothing is normal today, so they're probably not enforcing the rules.

I pause at the nurses' station. "Rick Jones?" A skinny man in scrubs checks a list.

"Room 216."

Before I get there, I glance into another room and see the other firefighter hovering over a bed beside a woman I assume is his wife. It's none of my business, but I slow down and peek. The child is lying flat and still, his head bandaged, oxygen tubes hooked into his nose. The father has taken off his fire jacket, just a tee shirt underneath. The mother has makeup smudged under her eyes, her dark hair half falling out of its upswept do. Her Santa Claus sweater bulges in the front; she's at least six months pregnant. Merry freaking Christmas.

Room 216 is at the end of the hall. Rick is in the bed closest to the door. An older man sleeps in the bed by the window, his back turned to us.

Rick removes his oxygen mask and snarls, "What are you doing here?"

In that minute, I remember all those days I spent beside hospital beds in Missoula, watching Tom deteriorate. I remember the feel of the hard chair, the cold metal bed railings, the plastic trays of plastic food on plastic plates. The tubes, the monitor blinking his blood pressure, heart rate and oxygen level, the plastic bag on the IV stand leading to the needle in his hand. The awkward silences spent staring at muted television screens while rubber-shoed doctors and nurses bustled down the hall. The windows, beyond which the world went on as if nobody was dying.

I remember Tom lying there with his eyes closed, so still I couldn't be sure whether he was asleep, unconscious, or dead—except for the numbers on the monitor that showed his heart was still beating, his blood still circulating, his lungs still taking in oxygen. And then that day when the numbers turned to zero and Tom's body became an empty shell . . .

I don't want to do this again.

"P.D., I asked what you were doing here."

I shake my head, trying to force a smile and failing. "I don't know. I volunteered to help out downstairs and kept wondering how you were. I was worried."

He looks different with his hat gone, his hair thinning, his face covered with black and white stubble, and his muscular arms sticking out of a blue-flowered hospital gown.

"Didn't I tell you last night to go home?"

"Yeah, well, I can't get back across the bridge, and Donovan forgot he ever loaned me his cabin, so I might as well be here. How are you?"

He coughs so hard it must hurt and then leans back against the pillow. His voice is hoarse. "I'm fucked up."

Typical male answer. "Could you be more specific?"

"You want a list?"

"Yeah." I pull over a blue plastic chair and sit down.

"Okay. I inhaled a boatload of smoke—" He stops to cough again—"got a dislocated shoulder, a collapsed lung, a concussion, and had to have my spleen taken out. Plus miscellaneous cuts and bruises. That specific enough for you?"

"You should have been *on* the roof instead of under it."

He's not laughing. "I don't think so."

"What about your house?" I ask.

"What about it? It's gone. I'll live on my boat, I guess. I don't really care."

Change the subject. "You wouldn't believe how many people are here."

"I might. So, did the whole town burn down while I was unconscious?"

"I don't know. I've been here since last night."

Awkward silence. We have no TV to distract us today. Rick starts coughing again. I pour some water from the plastic pitcher into the plastic cup on the nightstand and hand it to him. He drinks, sputters into another coughing jag, drinks, and gasps.

"P.D., I don't really want any visitors. I just want to get out of here and get back to work."

"Not today, I suspect. Listen, is there anybody I can contact for you? Wife, kids, parents, sisters, brothers . . ."

"Nope. My son is in Bend with his mom. I'm not bringing them here, and I don't want to see my brothers. My mom either." He grunts in pain as he tries to sit up.

I jump up to adjust the bed and realign his pillows.

"Don't fuss over me!"

"I'm just trying to help."

"I know. You're so helpful. If I weren't worrying about you and Janey back at the scene, maybe I would have been paying more attention to what I was doing."

I stand, almost knocking the chair over. "You're blaming us for you getting hurt? You ran into a burning building."

"That's my job. Look, I just need to be alone, all right?"

"Okay. Feel better."

He puts on his oxygen mask and closes his eyes.

I FOLLOW THE SIGNS to the chapel and slump into an empty chair, staring at the non-denominational etched glass pictures of coastal scenes. The room is all hardwood floors and mahogany, the walls hot-chocolate-brown, the flowered chair cushions stiff and new. There's a candle and a box of Kleenex on the round table in front of me and a rack on the wall with brochures with titles like "Coping with Grief" and "When a Family Member has Cancer."

I try to summon a prayer, then remember chanting "Lord have mercy . . ." last night by Janey's apartment. Where is Janey? She was supposed to meet me here, but I haven't seen her. I check my phone. No service. Maybe she stayed at Jonas' house, but I have no idea where that is.

I go out to the hall, where there's a telephone for patient use, but did anybody leave a phone book? No. I guess they figure if you're making emergency calls to family and friends, you know the numbers. I lift the receiver to my ear. Dead. Back to the chapel.

Most of the people who have come to feel like family are on the other side of a bridge I can't cross. Rick is upstairs in a hospital bed and doesn't want to see me. I don't know where Janey is. Dave is still missing. The rainbow ladies are somewhere in Minnesota. Donovan is probably sleeping off his drunk at his cabin. Then he'll wake up and eat the food I brought in for myself, not even remembering who the heck I am. I hope he feeds the stupid cats.

Shoot, I miss Hernando. I even miss Sasha. I picture her rolling in the sun amid the glass flowers.

People are saying we could be without power for weeks or even months. Water and food are going to get scarce. Businesses will be closed indefinitely. I don't know how many people are dead or injured. A lot, I fear.

Meanwhile here I sit, P.D. with the two-tone hair, unfettered, unemployed, a washed-out wannabe singer who could be home in Missoula knitting hats and mittens for Christmas presents. If I could get there. My car is still on the other side of the bridge with all my stuff inside.

I should just find a way to get to the car and drive the hell out of here. I'd have to find a road that will let me avoid the damaged bridges and make my way to I-5.

But if I stay here and help, I might be able to do some good

I'm too tired to think. Let me just rest my head on my hand for a minute . . .

Voices nearby wake me up. Someone's crying. I open my eyes, struggling to remember where I am and why. My neck hurts from bending the wrong way. I'm hungry and thirsty.

Sun streams through the etched glass, glinting off the windows of the two-story house across the road. It could be any ordinary day here. I could pretend nothing is damaged outside, everything is as it was when I woke up Thanksgiving morning feeling sorry for myself because I was widowed and my gig went badly. Dear God, please make this not have happened.

I want to go outside, but first I wash up in the restroom and seek out the coffee and cookies in the conference room.

No luck. The room is deserted, with empty cups and paper plates scattered around the tables and counters. Nothing is left on the cookie trays except crumbs. I pump an inch of cold coffee out of the bottom of the urn, close my eyes and drink it like medicine.

Maybe the cafeteria . . .

The sounds of rattling dishes cheer me as I round the corner. I'm used to hospital food. In Missoula, I ate an awful lot of meals in the hospital cafeteria, both as an employee and as a worried wife, grateful for the free coffee, healthy food, and ever-cheerful workers who ignored the pain and death going on in the rest of the hospital. This one black guy was always singing as he worked. He called me "Beautiful," greeting me with "How you doing, Beautiful?" He probably called all the women that, but it helped. It really did.

I'm thinking bacon and eggs, maybe hash browns, but the kitchen is closed. A half-asleep woman with an apron over her jeans and tee shirt hands out cups of coffee and plastic-wrapped sweet rolls. I accept them gratefully, sinking into a chair at an empty table overlooking the garden. As I devour the roll, the room starts to rock, splashing my coffee out of the cup. I hold onto the table until it stops.

    I've got to get out of here.

24

AFTER THE DIM coolness of the hospital, the sun feels good as I shove out the door into the parking lot. I'm not sure what to do. Janey is probably trying to get into her apartment. I'll go that way.

In spite of everything, it feels wonderful to be up on my two strong legs, walking toward the beach.

At first, the changes are subtle. A leaning fence. A cracked window. Flowerpots fallen off a porch railing. The town's few stoplights are dark, stop signs on sawhorses sitting at the intersections. Everything's closed in the middle of the Friday after Thanksgiving. Black Friday. The day everybody goes shopping. Not this year.

I'm assuming the music store is closed, too, just as it was on Wednesday, but I'm going past it anyway, so I'll stop and check. Gosh, it was only yesterday, about 24 hours ago, that I was singing and playing my little keyboard with the band that had just named itself Seal Rock Sound, and now . . . Sweet Jesus, I can't believe this happened.

My wrist hurts. Sometime in the night while I worked in admissions, I took off my brace because it was getting in my way. Now it's gone, probably discarded because it was dirty and used and nobody knew whose it was. My wrist is swollen again and feels stiff. I take a deep breath, run my fingers along my ribs. A little sore, not too bad. I'm luckier than a lot of people. I'm alive, and as far as I know, all the people I loved who were alive the day before Thanksgiving are still alive and well.

I feel the harmonica I slipped into my coat pocket yesterday morning banging against my hip. I've got my wallet and my keys in the other pocket, lighter now that Donovan took back the keys to the cabin. Just car keys and a key to the house in Missoula. Neither one does me much good right now.

Driving through town in my car, it always seemed like everything was close, but it doesn't feel that way on foot.

It's getting cold. Clouds have taken over the sky, turning everything gray. Wind tosses around the signs and litter scattered by the earthquake. As I pass the Thai restaurant, my shoes crunch on broken glass. The sign proclaiming the specials lies shattered on the pavement.

I'm tired. My little nap was nothing like a good night's sleep. When will I be able to crawl into a soft bed and sleep soundly again?

The porn shop. Chamber of commerce. Pig N Pancake restaurant. The Blue Whale Pub. Everything has the same beat-up look, signs trashed, windows cracked, walls not quite straight.

As I approach the music store, I see the door open and hurry, hoping to catch up with Deuce. There's a battered pickup truck out front I assume is his. It makes sense that he'd be here, checking on his shop.

But when I get closer, I don't see Deuce. I see three young men, possibly still in high school, grabbing stuff and carrying it out to the truck. Looters emptying the store in broad daylight? They could be friends of Deuce, but I don't think so. I hear them talking.

"Hey, look at this."

"Ah, cool. Get it. And grab that bass."

"Jason needs a drum set."

"Yeah. Let's get it."

Now, I'm P.D. I'm brave. I'm strong. But I'm only one person and have only one usable hand. Walking in and confronting them alone would be a bad idea, and I don't see anybody else around. My phone is useless.

Okay, God, what should I do?

I'm almost at the doorway when one of the guys, a heavyset kid with Hispanic features, notices me. He seems worried for a second, then puts on a brave face for his Anglo looter friends. "Can we help you with something, Lady?"

They're just kids, and I doubt they carry guns, but I'm still a little nervous. I force a smile. "I was looking for Deuce. Have you seen him?"

A tall kid pauses, shoves his bangs out of his eyes. "Uh, no. I don't think he's around today."

"Well, he said he'd meet me here right about this time."

"Well, he ain't here."

"So I see. Is there much damage?"

"Not too bad. We're just straightening up."

"Deuce will appreciate that when he gets here. I'm surprised he's not already here. He was pretty adamant about meeting now." Okay, okay, P.D., keep it up. End with a zinger. "So guys, I'm new around here, and I need to find the police station. Can you tell me where it is?"

The boys glance at each other, then the kid with the bangs grins. "Oh yeah, just up the road in the city hall building. You can't miss it."

"Thanks. Stay safe," I say as I walk away. I wait until I get to the stoplight at the end of the block before I look back.

It worked. Thinking either Deuce is coming or I'm going to get the police, they have all gotten into the truck and are driving away. They took some things, but it could have been worse. I dig out a pen and write the truck's license number on my Starbuck's receipt from the other day. As soon as they're out of sight, I go back to the music store, lock the door and slam it shut. Not that that's really going to keep anybody out.

At the police station. they're crazy busy and don't have the staff to worry about this. But a man at the front desk takes my information and thanks me for my help.

Time to find Janey.

IN DAYLIGHT, I can see the damage near the beach. Tourists won't be strolling down Coast Street eating clam chowder and buying glass floats here for a while. If ever.

The place is crawling with people shoveling mud and sand off the streets and parking lots, sweeping trash and glass out of the buildings that still stand, shoring up those that are leaning, and going through the rubble that used to be homes and businesses. Some of the buildings are just plain gone, wiped away like sandcastles at high tide.

The blackened remains of the dry cleaning shop are still smoking. The near wall of the bar next door is burnt, the beach side pushed in so the whole structure appears ready to fall.

I pass a bookstore where the shelves have fallen every which way. Books sit turning to mulch in a foot of water. The owner stands in the doorway, his eyes full of tears as he smokes and stares at the wreckage. Books don't mean much in this situation, do they? What will he do now? What will any of them do?

Near the ruins of the Montessori school, soggy children's drawings of dogs and purple houses lie plastered to fused glass art pieces that remind me of Donovan's garden.

A seagull screeches overhead, flies around in a circle and lands in the middle of a group of seagulls congregated on the street. I wonder what they think about all this. I know, they're birds. I'm tired, I'm not thinking straight. But their world has changed, too. I mean, they usually line up on the fence between the parking lot and the beach, but the fence isn't there anymore, its poles scattered.

Janey's apartment building is a little bit higher up, so the damage isn't quite as bad as it is in the heart of Nye Beach. More earthquake, less tsunami. But still, it isn't good. The stucco walls are visibly cracked, the windows broken. Downstairs, an older couple is hauling stuff out onto the sidewalk. A shattered mirror, broken chairs, twisted lamps, shards of glass figurines, dripping cushions and rugs. They toss it all into a dumpster. Two teenagers are helping, maybe their grandsons. None of them are crying, just working as quickly as they can, as if the waves are coming back, as if another quake will shake the rest of the building down. As I watch, the woman comes out clutching a pile of framed photographs against her chest. One of the boys waves a swimming trophy. "Grandma, where should I put this?"

"In the truck, I guess."

I'm about to step forward and offer my help when I hear "P.D.! Hey!"

It's Janey, hailing me from her front door on the second floor. "Come on up."

"How?" The stairs are completely off now, lying on the ground.

"Jack and Cece—" she points down toward the neighbors—"gave me a ladder to climb in the window. Around the other side."

"A ladder?" Like I want to climb another ladder. I'm still healing from the last time I tried it.

"You can do it, P.D. It's sturdy."

The old man, Jack, waves at me. He's got a bloody scrape on his balding forehead.

Okay, I'm doing it. Just, God, it would be nice if you refrained from aftershocks until I'm off the ladder.

This is a taller ladder than the one at the cabin, and my puffy right hand isn't much help, but at least it's not raining at the moment, and I'm not going anywhere near the roof. One, two, three steps, four. I pause and look down at the ocean. It seems as calm as always, but the beach is littered with stuff. I see televisions, computers, tennis shoes, papers, books, pots, a ukulele . . . Some people are down there collecting whatever they can, whether or not it was theirs to begin with.

As the ladder starts to sway, I hurry up the last few rungs. I don't want to think about climbing down. Janey pulls me through the glassless window into her bedroom. Instead of rubble, I see boxes and suitcases. She's packing. The closet is empty, the clothes thrown on the bed. I grab a yellow blouse and start folding. "Moving, huh?"

She shrugs. "This guy who works for the city said the building is going to be condemned, that they'll knock it down when they get around to it."

"I'm sorry." I toss the blouse into a box and pick up a brown sweater. "Are you supposed to be up here?"

"No." She stares at a pair of gold high-heeled shoes, moans, and tosses them into the box.

"Where'd you get the boxes?"

"I still had them from when I moved in. I haven't even been here a year."

"Where will you go now?"

"Back to my mom's."

"How are you going to get all this stuff there?"

"I've got a plan."

I don't ask my next question, which is how she's going to get it all downstairs. I keep folding clothes and putting them in boxes, using my gimpy right hand as little as possible.

Janey closes up the boxes and stacks them near the window. When the bedroom is empty, I follow her to the kitchen. She throws open a cabinet door and stares at a collection of unmatched plates, bowls and glasses. "It took me a week to pack this stuff before. Do I even need it?"

"I don't know."

She slams the door shut again, the first time I've ever seen her angry. "Screw it. I'm taking a few keepsakes and whatever food isn't rotten, and getting out of here. Crap. Just when you think you've got your life together . . ."

I move toward her, about to put my arms around her, but she pushes me away. "P.D., if you hug me, I will cry, and we don't have time for that."

I smile, remembering I said the same thing to her just yesterday. "Got it. You want this kitty-cat cookie jar?"

"It's not broken?"

"Nope."

"Cool. Can you wrap some towels around it?"

As I'm cushioning the cookie jar, I say, "I didn't see you at the hospital last night."

"No. Sorry. I stayed at Jonas's place, cleaned up a little and then I fell asleep. As soon as I woke up, I headed over here."

"How is his house?"

"Not bad. Some stuff fell down, but no big damage. Did you see Rick? How is he?"

"Grumpy."

"Good."

She hands me packages of spaghetti noodles, flour, sugar, and canned goods. I keep putting things in boxes until she declares we're done. She opens the fridge. "Yuck!"

I smell the beginnings of food starting to rot.

"You want a Pepsi?"

"Sure."

She grabs a couple cans and shuts the door on the stench. We pop off the tops and chug the lukewarm soda. I'm not a big soda drinker, but it tastes fantastic right now.

From a lower cabinet, she pulls out a plastic bag full of nuts, dried fruit and chocolate. "Gorp. I bought it to go camping and never went."

"Perfect. Got any other food in there?"

"I've already packed most of it to take to Mom's house."

We stare out the front window at the wreckage that once was Nye Beach. I can imagine how excited Janey must have felt when she moved in here, her first place of her own, right by the water. I can see even now that she put a lot of effort into decorating it, and her downstairs neighbors seem like nice people. Now it's going to be bulldozed.

"Janey! You ready?" calls a male voice from downstairs.

She runs over to the window. "Ready and waiting."

To my amazement, a tractor thing with a lift on it backs up to the house, and the lift rises to window level. I can't see the driver, but I hear him call, "Load her up."

"Come on, P.D."

So we start piling boxes onto the lift. "Who is that?"

"My friend Keith from school. Great baritone. He works at the lumber yard. He borrowed the lift to help me move. He also has a huge truck."

"Amazing."

"Small towns, P.D. You know everybody, and in a pinch, everybody helps."

It doesn't take long to empty the apartment. Keith takes me and Janey down on his lift, so I don't have to worry about the ladder. We squeeze into the front of his truck for the short drive to Jonas' house, a pale blue ranch-style home near the high school. We load everything into the garage, thank Keith profusely, then relax in the living room with some of Jonas's beer. It's a comfortable house that reminds me of my house in Missoula. Unlike Donovan's cabin, it feels like a home, surrounded by other homes, a real neighborhood where kids can grow up and play on the front lawns.

In this moment, I know that more than anything, more even than singing and playing my music, this is what I want. A home. A safe, sound comfortable home. Preferably with other people in it.

"I'm hungry," Janey says, bringing me back to the present.

"Me too." I'm getting buzzed on the beer. It's mid-afternoon, and my last real meal was yesterday's turkey dinner.

"You know what doesn't spoil?" She's grinning.

"What?"

"Peanut butter!"

We feast on peanut butter and strawberry-jelly sandwiches, apples, and chocolate chip cookies from Molly's cookie jar.

Finally full, we sit in silence on Jonas and Molly's soft tan sofa as another aftershock rocks the house. I think about bolting for the doorway, but it seems like a small one, so I just close my eyes and ride it out. When I open them, Janey is staring at me. "Okay, P.D., now what?"

25

THE HOSPITAL IS COLD, dark and crowded. Today the doctors are treating the folks who decided their problems could wait until morning and the ones who are just being rescued from the rubble. Emergency workers are still searching for people who might be buried or trapped, hoping to find them before it's too late.

Outside, clouds cover the sky, and it's starting to get dark. Days are short here in November. I dread the night like a lid slamming down on top of us. At least in daylight, we can see.

Janey is with me this time. She's hoping they have working phones so she can talk to her mother. I plan to visit Rick again, even though he didn't want visitors, and then go back to work in admissions. I've got to do something. I can't just go on with my life as if this disaster didn't happen. Also, I'm putting off facing the challenge of getting back to my car and deciding where I'm going to live.

I can't keep mooching off my friends. Logic says I should high-tail it to Missoula. This place is going to be a mess for months, probably years. I don't have a job, I don't have a home here, and I don't have lifelong connections like Janey has with people like Frankie at the store and "Uncle" Rick. Maybe I won't stay in Montana, but right now it seems like the right place to go. The house will be vacant on Dec. 1, in just a few days.

"Janey!" calls one of the clerks in emergency as we pass through.

"Zelda!" Janey exclaims. "You're still working?"

"Yes, I am," says the young black woman. "But not for long." She cradles her pregnant belly.

"Wow, you got so big."

"I know. I thought it was twins for a while, but it's just one boy. One huge boy. Already taking after his dad." Zelda shakes her head. "What am I thinking? Are you guys here to see a doctor? Are you hurt or sick?"

"No, no. We're going to visit Rick Jones upstairs. Plus I was hoping to find a working telephone to contact my mom."

"Oh. Well, the phone in the hall works off and on, but every time I look, there's a line. I heard about Rick. He's going to be okay."

"And he's cranky," I add.

Zelda looks at me, confused. Janey hurries to introduce me. "This is my friend, P.D."

"P.D., P.D., I heard that name recently. Oh, I know. You volunteered to work in admissions last night. I heard you did a great job."

"Thanks. I just wanted to help. I worked at the hospital in Missoula."

"Right. You should apply here."

The door opens, and two men come in, carrying another man between them. Blood drips from his face and neck onto the carpet.

Zelda jumps up to open the door to the emergency room. "Gentlemen, go right in. We need a gurney!" she calls. As the door closes, I see a man in scrubs running to help.

We continue to the hallway, where there is indeed a line for the phone, but that's a good sign because it works and somebody is actually talking on it. Janey gets in line. "I'll meet you up there. What room?"

"216."

As I climb the stairs, I wonder if there's anyone I should call. I should let my mother know I'm all right. I should call Missoula, tell the realtor I'm planning to move back into my house, to stop trying to sell it. But the other people haven't even moved out yet, and the market is miserable. That can wait a couple days.

Upstairs, I inhale the smells of cotton sheets, alcohol, cleaning solutions, and stale food. I hear someone weeping. A nurse hurries down the hall with a tray of pills in little plastic cups.

Rick sees me coming.

"P.D. is back," he growls.

"Yes, I am. How are you?"

"Bored out of my mind. Tell me what's going on outside."

"Well . . ." Taking my place in the chair between Rick's bed and the curtain hiding the other bed, I describe the scene in Nye Beach and tell how Janey and I climbed the ladder to get up to her place.

"You guys are crazy," he says. "The house could have fallen down with you in it, and you'd both be lying in beds like this one."

"No."

"Yeah." He sounds angry, but I see hints of a smile. "You don't do well at following directions, do you?"

"Maybe not." Yes, it's a full-blown smile now, and I'm suddenly glad I'm here. "But hey, it wasn't my idea this time. When I got there, Janey was already upstairs throwing her stuff into boxes."

"She's a stubborn little girl. Like Shirley Temple. You remember her?"

"Sure. From the old movies. My mom loved her."

"Mine too. She would have loved to have a kid like Janey. Too bad my mother only got boys."

I relax, sitting back and crossing my legs. "How many brothers do you have?"

"Three. We Jones boys got quite a reputation in our younger years."

"Really?"

"Oh yeah, but now we're all middle-aged. Heck, I'm the baby, and look at me."

"You don't look too old to me."

"About the same as you, I'd guess, but not as pretty."

I feel myself blushing. Nobody has complimented me like that since I lost Tom. I'm thinking I look pretty scruffy about now, unwashed and still in yesterday's clothes.

"Thank you. So, do they all live around here?"

"Two fled to the valley for better jobs and better schools, but my oldest brother, Steve, stayed in the area."

"Are your parents still living here?"

He shakes his head. "No. Well, my Dad's dead. My mom moved to New Mexico with her new husband. We don't get along."

"I'm sorry."

"Yeah, well, it happens."

I've been staring at his left hand hanging off the edge of the bed, tanned, callused, and hairy. I reach over and wrap my fingers around it now, and he doesn't pull away.

Our eyes meet for a minute, then I look away, not sure what to do with the feelings I'm having. I suspect he and Diana are a couple, but it's just nice to hold somebody's hand.

"What's your actual name?" Rick asks.

"It's P.D. now."

"Yeah, but what was it before, and why'd you change it?"

"I'm not saying what it was. I changed it because I was trying to be less pitiful and more bad-ass."

He stares at me, then bursts out laughing, holding his side with his hand. "I guess that's why you dyed your hair orange, too. Bet you even got a tattoo."

I smile and slip my shirt down off my shoulder.

"Tom, huh? P.D., you don't have to change your name and dye your hair to be bad-ass. It comes from inside. Me, I'm bad-ass through and through."

I gaze into those blue eyes and laugh. "Yes, I'm sure you are."

We're kind of smiling at each other, and I can sense Rick getting ready to ask me another question when he looks past me and lets go of my hand. "Hello, Miss Janey Peacock. Did you bring me any pumpkin pie?"

"Let me check my purse. Nope. Sorry, Uncle Rick. So, how are ya?"

"I've been through worse. And they've got pretty good drugs here. I'm not feeling any pain right now."

"Then hook me up. I could use a hit of whatever you're taking."

"Sorry, that's only for grownups."

"I AM a grownup."

"Not to me, baby."

As they banter, I wonder if the flirting is just the drugs talking.

"Did you get hold of your mom?" I ask.

She nods. Her curls are matted, straight in some areas, kinked cockeyed in others. "Yeah. Mom's pretty ticked that we ran away in the middle of the night, but she's glad we're safe."

"I'll bet she's pissed," Rick says. "I'm mad at you, too, Janey. Do you have any idea how dangerous it was out there?"

"Maybe. Anyway, Mom and Jonas and Molly have been trying to put the diner back together. In addition to things falling down and breaking all over the place, they've got water damage from broken pipes, so the floor's all messed up. Frankie and Caroline have been working on the store, which is an even bigger mess."

"Shit," Rick mutters, shaking his head. "Diana's okay though?"

"Yes, she's fine. Don't worry."

"Any word about Dave?" I ask.

"No, but listen to this, you guys. After we slipped out, Amy went to the beach by herself looking for him. She almost got killed by a stray log that knocked her down just in time for a giant wave to push her halfway to Toledo. A cop found her. Her knee is trashed and she's bruised up, but somehow she's not hurt worse. Dave is still missing. Nobody has seen him since he left for work on Thanksgiving morning."

"Damn," Rick whispers.

In the silence, I find myself thinking there goes my kayak trip tomorrow. I know. That's crazy. I guess I just want everything to go back to normal.

"So, bottom line, Mom wants me and P.D. back in Seal Rock as quickly as possible because it's not safe here on this side of the bridge."

"Safe as anyplace else," I say.

"Safer," says Rick. "You've got access here to a hospital, lots more resources, and Highway 20 out of here. There's nothing south of the bridge." He tries to sit up straight and groans. "Oof. Hey, Janey girl, can you use that phone out there to check on my boat? I left it in Toledo with Ronnie getting it fixed up. Guess I need to live on it now that the ocean has taken my house."

"Sure."

"What about your brother, the one who still lives in the area? Where is he?" I ask.

"He's running our family ranch up Highway 20."

"So you could go there."

"I don't think so." He looks at Janey. "His wife doesn't like me very much, blames me for messing up my marriage by hooking up with a certain other woman."

"Did you?" The words jump out before I can stop them.

"Yes, I did." He glances at the doorway. "Thank God. Rescued by the nurse. Time for my sponge bath?"

"I'm here to change your bandages," the young nurse says.

We're leaving. I pat Rick's foot under the sheet. It takes me right back to Tom in the hospital in Missoula. No. I can't let those memories rush in. This is a whole different situation. "I'll see you tomorrow," I say, leading the way out the door as Janey bends over to hug Rick.

In the hallway, I tell Janey I'm going to volunteer in admitting again.

"I'm going to do my homework."

"Why? The college won't be open anytime soon."

"I know. I just want to do something normal."

At the admitting office, Shirley beckons me in. "Hell yes, we can use your help." She hands me a monster stack of papers. "Can you file these?"

"Sure."

As I grab them, she notices my wrist. "How long has your hand been black and blue and swollen like that?"

I go to the files, struggling to organize papers with my left hand. "Oh, about three weeks, I think, since I sprained it falling off a ladder. I zapped it again falling on the bridge yesterday, and I lost my brace somewhere last night. Compared to the problems other people have, it's no big deal. It'll heal."

She reaches into a drawer under her desk and pulls out one of those instant ice packs. She snaps it to release the cold and hands it to me. "Go sit down. Ice it for 15 minutes before you start work. I'd make you get an x-ray, but I'm not sure the machine is working."

As I sit in the waiting area and apply the magic ice, I can feel my tendons scream "thank you." The line at the phone is not bad, so I join them to call my mom. When she doesn't answer, I leave a message that I'm all right and will call again when I can.

When I come back, Shirley hands me a new brace. "Put this on, and don't take it off."

"Yes ma'am." It feels good having that support around my injured limb, like a hug.

I get to work, doing as much as I can with my left hand. There aren't as many patients tonight, but enough to keep us busy. Finally about midnight, Shirley tells me to go home.

"You look exhausted, P.D. We don't need you getting sick. So go get some sleep."

I nod. She's right, possibly psychic. My throat hurts, and my head aches.

As I'm putting on my coat, she says, "Wait" and hands me an employment application. "Fill this thing out, okay?"

I tuck it into my pocket. Later. I'm too tired to think.

26

BEFORE I OPEN my eyes in the morning at Jonas' house, I know I'm sick. My throat is raw, and my nose is running. I might have a slight fever. Plus my wrist is killing me.

In the dim light filtering through the red and white curtains, I look around. I'm lying in a twin bed with Spiderman sheets and a Spiderman quilt. Stuffed animals, toy trucks, children's books and Legos fill the shelves and tops of the dressers. Janey is asleep in the matching bed two feet away.

I slept in my underwear. It's cold in here with no heat. I hate to put on the clothes I wore to Thanksgiving dinner for a third day. I was upset and in a hurry when I got dressed. I wouldn't choose these black jeans and this long-sleeved yellow tee shirt as what I'd want to wear indefinitely. I look like a stupid bumblebee. I feel filthy, but I'm guessing we don't have hot water for a shower.

Heat. Electricity. Food. Clean water. We take it all for granted most of the time, just like we assume we can turn on our phone, computer, or TV and connect with the world instantly, but here I am in my dirty underwear with no lights, no heat, no hot water, and no way to find out what's going on.

They're not going to want me at the hospital sick like this. I could wear one of those masks, but I'm still contagious. In normal times, I'd call in sick and spend the day in bed, reading or watching TV, but these aren't normal times.

I reach up to touch the ruby heart necklace I wear most of the time, the one from Tom. It's not there. Damn. I left it on the sink at Donovan's cabin. I took it off for my shower and didn't put it back on because it didn't match my yellow top and I didn't have time to think twice about it. Stupid. It's probably still there, but how am I going to get it back?

The earth begins to rumble again. You know how you shake up the Italian dressing before you pour it on your salad? That's what it feels like, as if a giant hand is shaking us and we're the flecks of garlic and pepper bouncing off the sides of the bottle.

Windows rattle, a windup clock falls off the nightstand, stuffed bears and dogs tumble onto the floor, and something goes bang in the bathroom. I cling to the headboard, hoping nothing falls on me.

This is a big one. It could be starting this whole mess over again. Another quake, another tsunami. More fires, more buildings falling down just when everybody is starting to get things cleaned up. Come on, God, enough already.

Janey falls off the bed just before the shaking stops. "Whoa. Good morning," she says, straightening her polka-dotted night shirt, nudging a stuffed elephant out of the way. "So glad I cleaned up."

"Good morning."

"You sound stuffed up."

"I'm sick."

"That sucks." She gets up, slides her feet into fuzzy slippers and heads for the bathroom. "There's shampoo all over the floor!" I hear her scrubbing up the mess with a towel.

At least she has all her stuff here. I've got nothing. I get up and start putting on my gross clothes. If the house is going to fall down around us, I'd rather be wearing more than blue bikini panties and a beige bra.

Janey comes out, yawning as she pulls on her jeans. "Did you make pancakes? With blueberries maybe?"

"I wish."

"They have lots of disgusting cereals in the cupboards. Or maybe near the cupboards now. Milk not guaranteed."

I find a box of tissues in the kitchen and carry it to the table as Janey splits what's left of a box of Cheerios into two yellow plastic bowls.

"The milk is rancid," she says, "but I found a can of peaches. You want to share it?"

"Yes, please."

I sit blowing my nose as she opens the can with a hand opener she finds in the back of the silverware drawer. We drop the sliced peaches on top of our Cheerios. It's not too bad. I'm so clogged I can't taste anything anyway, and I'm so cold I can't stop shivering. It's probably about 40 degrees outside and 45 inside. I grab a gray hoodie hanging off the back of a chair, slide it over my injured arm and then over the good one.

It's odd invading somebody else's house. This is my third one since I came to Newport. First Donovan's cabin, then the rainbow ladies' house, now Jonas' place. Four, if you count the time I spent on Diana's floor. Used to be I wouldn't peek at anybody's private stuff, and I certainly wouldn't eat their food or wear their clothes, but things are different now. If you need it and it's there, you take it. I wonder if Molly's clothes would fit me.

I remember those boys at the music store yesterday. Only yesterday? Did Deuce ever show up? Is he all right?

I'm so tired. I want to go home. To my own house with my own stuff. I want to hang out with people who have known me for more than a month. Of course my furniture isn't in the house anymore, and people back in Montana would call me Cissy, but let me enjoy my fantasy for a minute.

My head hurts. "You got any aspirin?"

Janey skips off to the bathroom and comes back with a box. "Look, Tylenol Cold."

"Perfect. Thanks."

I wash down two capsules with a few sips from the last bottle of water in the fridge. What are we going to do for water when that's gone? I go to the sink, turn on the tap. Nothing.

Janey has found a portable radio. She turns it on and spins the dial around until she gets a fuzzy news report.

"Aftershocks continue following the 7.9 earthquake off the Oregon coast on Thanksgiving. The largest one struck about 20 minutes ago and was estimated at 5.9, shaking up an already shaken population, causing additional damage. But the good news is that no new tsunami is expected.

"The death toll now is up to 193, with more than 200 people still missing up and down the coast from Crescent City to Vancouver, British Columbia. Only 10 percent of the coastal towns have electricity, and residents are struggling with shortages of gas, food and clean water. On the central coast, trucks from Corvallis will be bringing water to the shelter at Newport High School at approximately noon today. The Red Cross has set up a food distribution station there for anyone who needs it."

"I never thought we'd be victims like those people we see in disasters on TV," Janey said.

Me either.

"FEMA representatives will arrive on Monday to start the long process of helping homeowners and business owners file claims and get help coping with the damage. Most of the main roads have at least one lane clear, but the bridges are still closed. The city has arranged for ferry service on the Discovery tour boat from the Bayfront to the South Beach marina, starting at noon today, but space is limited."

Janey looks at me. I nod.

"In view of the continuing emergency situation, we urge anyone who doesn't have to go anywhere to stay home or at a shelter.

"Weather today is expected to be typical for November, wet and windy, with a high of 48, low 39, winds 25 to 30 miles an hour."

The report begins again. Janey turns off the radio.

I keep blowing my nose; I never run out of snot. My head is throbbing. But I can't just sit here. This is just a stupid cold.

"Want to take a ferry ride?" I ask.

"Sounds like fun. But we can't go till noon. I guess I'll go visit Uncle Rick."

"Say hi for me. Tell the folks in admissions I won't be there today. I can't take my germs over there."

"Maybe you should go back to bed."

"Maybe I will. Wake me up at 11:00."

I crawl back between the Spiderman sheets, close my eyes and try to pretend I'm home in Santa Cruz. It's 1976, I'm six years old, and it's warm and sunny. Mom is in the kitchen baking cookies and humming along with Carole King on the radio as I drift off to sleep.

"RICK'S GONE!"

Startled awake, I stare through my fever at Janey in the doorway with her hands on her blue-jeaned hips.

"What?"

"He left the hospital. Disconnected his IV, got dressed and left. The nurse found a note saying he has better things to do than lie around in a hospital bed."

My nose drips. I reach under the pillow for the tissues I have stashed there. "Well, maybe he does."

"P.D., he just had major surgery. When the drugs wear off, he'll be in killer pain. The nurse told me they had expected to keep him there for a week. Stupid stubborn man."

"They all are." I sit up, feeling slightly better now that my own drugs have kicked in. If the earth shook during my nap, I didn't notice it. "So now what?"

"I don't know. Maybe Rick went to his boat. If his friend brought it down from Toledo like he told me he would, it's probably moored at what's left of the South Beach Marina. Across the bridge."

"Everything's across the bridge." I start putting on my shoes. "Let's get on that ferry. We can look for Rick. I've got to get my car. You can hook up with your mom."

"What are you going to do?"

It might be the cold pills, it might be the daytime nap in a child's bed, but suddenly everything seems very clear to me. You know those moments when you look around and think *Whoa, so this is where I'm at*? "I'm going back to Montana for a while."

"What? No."

"Well, I've got no home and no job here. I can't keep freeloading off my friends, especially now."

Her face got red. "You're not freeloading. P.D., we love you. You're sick; you're not thinking straight. You said you don't want to live in Montana anymore, now that your husband isn't there. You missed the beach, remember?"

"I know, but my renters have moved out, and I can't afford to live here without their rent payments. It's time for me to stop running and face who I really am."

"You're P.D.!"

"Yeah . . . Maybe I'm really Cissy, which is what they called me back there."

"Cissy? You're not a Cissy."

"I know." I shove my feet into my shoes and stand. I feel hot, sticky and weak. But there's no sick leave in the midst of a crisis. "Should we make the beds?"

"You got germs all over yours."

"Oh well."

We pull the covers up anyway, leave our dishes in the sink, and go out, locking the door behind us.

IT'S A LONG WALK to the docks. Wind-driven rain blasts my face, soaks my hair and drips down my neck. I pull up the hood on the borrowed sweatshirt I'm wearing under my coat.

I, P.D., am officially not having fun.

The last part is downhill at about a 40-degree angle. Is that right? Well, steep enough that if I don't pay attention, I'm going to fall forward and roll all the way into the bay. There's no tsunami damage at the top of the hill, but people are busy fixing fallen fences and broken windows from the earthquake. I wish I had stock in glass right now.

It's a different picture at the bottom of the hill. Boats are scattered all over like kids' toys, on their sides, upside down, humping each other in the water. We walk through mud, sand, wood and trash. We pass more buildings knocked down, flooded up, beat to bits. It looks like a junkyard.

"Where do we go?" Janey asks.

I'm wet down to my skin, and I can barely see. "Beats me. Is there a place where people used to board the tour boats?"

"Used to be."

There's wood everywhere from the busted-up docks. But I see a line of people down toward the bashed-up hotel on the east end. "Let's go over there."

"Okay." Janey adjusts the straps on her backpack and leads the way. Our shoes squinch on the sand and debris.

"How much will it cost?" I ask.

"Don't know. Do you have any money?"

"A little."

"I think I have five dollars."

The line is longer than it appeared from afar. We ask the couple at the end if it's the line for the ferry. They nod.

"The boat just went out full," the guy says. "They can only take 30 people at a time."

I look ahead to the front of the line, trying to count. We might just make it.

"What's it cost?" Janey asks.

"They're not charging," the wife says. "One blessing."

We take our places in line. I see a white tour boat threading its way through the debris.

"You live south?" the man asks.

"Yes and no," I say.

"My mom does," Janey explains. "My apartment is condemned."

"Sorry," the woman says.

A woman with two little boys turns around from in front of the couple. "Janey?"

"Dawn! Oh my God." Janey runs up to hug a young woman who I later learn works for Jonas driving the taxi. "Is your place okay?"

Dawn and the kids are soaked, water plastering their blonde hair to their pale faces. "So-so. It's pretty beat up, no windows, no heat, so I'm going to stay with my sister for a while. How about your place?"

"Still standing but doomed."

"Shoot. I haven't heard from Jonas."

"He's with my mom in Seal Rock. That's where we're headed."

"Oh." Dawn bends down to the little boy tugging on her pants. "Pretty soon. The boat is coming. I know you're cold." She hefts him up into her arms.

"They're getting so big," Janey says.

"Yeah, they are."

"Oh. This is my friend P.D."

Dawn smiles at me. "Nice to meet you. Are you a singer, too?"

I shrug. "Trying to be. Were you driving the cab when it happened?"

A cheer rises from the front of the line as the white boat approaches our side of the bay. It's not big, maybe 60 feet long, with an open deck around an enclosed cabin and a small upper deck. Designed for bay cruises where the passengers could sip champagne while looking for whales and taking pictures of the scenery, it was never intended for this.

A guy in a yellow slicker orders us to wait until everyone on board has a chance to get off.

"See, honey, they're coming," Dawn tells her son, brushing a glob of snot off his upper lip. She looks at me and Janey. "I was in the cab when it happened. I was parked at Coast and Third trying to keep warm. Business was super slow. And then, whoa, everything began to shake, and things were starting to fall down, and I didn't know what to do. All I knew was I wanted to get to my kids, who were back home with my roommate. Then all of a sudden, bam, a power pole fell across the hood. I peed my pants I was so scared. The windshield was shattered and I was afraid it was gonna fall in on me any second. I just turned off the car, crawled out, and ran home. I kept falling down. I'll never forget it." The line is moving forward now. "Hold on to me, kids."

"Well thank God you're okay," Janey says.

Dawn frowns. "When we went back by there yesterday, the cab was gone. I think the wave got it. Tell Jonas I'm real sorry."

"He'll understand."

Janey and I are the last ones aboard. The guy in the slicker tells the people behind us that they have to wait for the next run. "Ladies," he says to us, "squeeze in wherever you can. It's going to be tight, but it's a short ride."

Dawn and the kids disappear into the cabin, but we're out on the deck, crammed ass to belly, still getting pounded by the rain. I can feel this tall guy towering over me, his elbows practically in my face. My nose keeps running, and my tissues are so used up they're in shreds. I blow, cough and breathe noisily through my mouth. I'm a mess, and I'm probably making everybody around me sick.

I'm surprised when the man hands me a handkerchief. "You need this more than I do."

"Thank you." I blow my nose.

We spend the ride gawking at the debris floating by, expecting any minute to see a dead body. Anything that could be on a boat—fishing poles, ropes, seats, buckets, lamps, slickers, dead fish, anything—is floating in the murky green water now. I think I see human waste, too. If the sewer lines are broken, that's going to be a problem all over pretty soon.

I can't stop shivering as we dock at the South Beach marina and walk up a board placed between the boat and the shore. I tell myself we're almost there. We can get in the car and turn the heat up. We can even turn on the radio or play a CD.

"I don't see Rick's boat," Janey says.

"Maybe he's at your mom's house."

"I hope so."

A half mile farther and I see my car. Oh Lord.

28

My little white Volt is covered with mud. Papers, trash bags and plastic coffee cups cling to the tires. The window on the passenger side is shattered and the back hatch is open.

"P.D., somebody broke in!"

"Yep." I look up at the thunderclouds overhead and feel the rain pounding on my cheeks. "God, what have you got against us?"

Everything on the passenger side is soaked. My suitcase is open, my clothing spread all over. My camera and the bag in which I kept my jewelry are gone. So is my ice chest. I guess it's a good thing I left the keyboard back at the diner. I feel in my coat for the harmonica, comforted by the rectangular lump in my pocket.

"Should we report it?"

"To whom? And how? The police can't do anything now; they're still looking for bodies. Let's just see if it starts. I have my doubts, since they left the back door open, which means the light was on."

I go around to the driver's side and get in, feeling dampness wick up through my pants. Janey gets in on the other side, wincing as the icy water soaks her jeans.

"You can sit on some of my clothes if you want to."

She reaches back and feels among my jeans and shirts. "They're all wet, too."

I turn the key, praying *please God, please let it start*. But it doesn't even turn over. Dead battery. "Shit!" I almost hit the dash with my bum right hand. Janey grabs my braced-up wrist just in time.

"Thanks. Well, I've got jumper cables, assuming they didn't get stolen, too. All I need is somebody with a working car."

"Couldn't you just plug it in?"

"Where? Besides, there's a separate battery like in regular cars, and that's the one that's dead."

This looks more like a salvage yard than a parking lot. If I need to borrow some parts, I'm in luck, but electricity, not so much.

I'm sick and shivering, sitting in a wet car.

"Maybe there's somebody at the aquarium," says Janey.

"Yeah, cleaning out the dead fish."

We get out of the car and hurry up the walkway that leads through the trees along a little creek to the aquarium entrance. It's dark and locked. We lean up against the cracked glass doors and try to see inside.

"Can I help you?" says a voice behind us.

I turn and see a guy with a security badge pinned to his heavy blue jacket. Maybe, just maybe . . .

"Hi," I begin, stopping to cough. "My car is out in the parking lot, and the battery's dead. I'm wondering if you or somebody could give me a jump."

"The aquarium's closed."

"Yes, we know. I hope everything is okay in there. But right now we're just trying to get back to Seal Rock."

He shrugs. "Okay. Come on. I've got my car."

Thank you, God. The uniformed cop-wannabe pulls his Buick sedan up to my car.

"What the heck?" he says when I open the hood and he sees the odd-looking engine.

"It's a hybrid electric car," I explain. "When there's no power, it uses gas."

"Huh," he says. "But we can charge it like a regular car?"

"Yes. If you wouldn't mind."

He gazes at my license plate. "Guess cars are different in Montana."

In a minute, my car is running and we're heading south, an icy breeze thrumming through the broken window. Behind us, barricades still block the bridge. The entrance to the state park is still closed. Ahead, the road is clear, and we don't see any other cars. Beside me, Janey is shivering. I drive as fast as I dare.

As we approach the diner, I see a van with a rainbow painted on the side parked out front. Dakota and Maryann are here.

Part of me is glad to see them, but a bigger part of me resents Dakota's way of stepping in and taking charge. Still, I wouldn't mind one of Maryann's hugs about now.

Entering the diner with Janey, I barely have time to notice things are looking pretty straightened up, if a little bare, before Diana rushes out of nowhere and grabs Janey, spinning her around. "Oh, my baby, I'm so glad to see you. I was so worried."

"I'm okay, Mom. You're choking me," she says, pulling away. "How are you? Is Rick here?"

Diana brushes tears out of her eyes. "I'm fine. Isn't Rick still in the hospital?"

"No. He unhooked himself and left. We don't know where he is."

She goes white. "Dear God."

"He'll be okay, Mom. He's tough."

"Hey!" Dakota calls from the ladder where she's putting the ceiling fan back up. She tightens a last screw and comes down, bending over to hug each of us. As she lets go of me, she presses the back of her hand against my forehead. "You've got a fever. What's going on?"

"I've got a cold. That's all."

"It might be the flu, P.D. You feel really warm, and you're all flushed. Plus you're both soaking wet. You could end up with pneumonia."

"I'll be fine." Let's change the subject. "I thought you weren't coming back for another week."

"We weren't. But when we heard what happened here, we figured we'd better get home and check on the house and our friends."

"Might have been smarter to stay away."

"Naw. Maryann wouldn't hear of it. She's a do-gooder through and through. Besides, she's packed away enough food and water for an army just in case something like this happened. If people are hungry, she wants to be here to feed them."

"Where is she now?"

"At the house cleaning up. She was almost done when the aftershock hit this morning and she had to start over."

Janey asks, "Did you have much damage?

"No, just stuff falling down. Plus a couple of scared pussycats waiting for us."

"Sasha and Hernando?" I ask.

"Them's the ones. Hungry little critters."

"So Donovan hasn't been feeding them?"

"Donovan? Isn't he in Tucson?"

Janey and I look at each other. "That's a long story, or maybe not so long," I say. "He came back at Thanksgiving, acting drunk and crazy. He demanded his keys back, didn't even remember he had invited me to stay there, and he moved back in. When last seen, he was on the balcony drinking and singing to the moon."

Dakota shook her head. "Oh boy, not again. Well, P.D., you can come stay with us, curl up in your old bed, and sleep off this thing you've got. Hop in the van and I'll take you up."

"I can drive myself." I really don't want these ladies mothering me again. And how come nobody filled me in about Donovan when I was moving into his place? He seemed so normal, a little quiet and subdued, but normal. Sweet even. Nobody told me he was crazy.

Dakota studies my fingers, still swollen and discolored where they're sticking out of the brace. "How's the wrist?"

"I fell again on the bridge, have to start over."

"Sounds like you've had a hard time."

I pull my hand away. "Yeah, well, Janey's apartment will probably be condemned. We had to sneak in to get her stuff. Rick's place was totaled." Get the attention off of me already.

"Bummer."

"And somebody broke into P.D.'s car," Janey added. "Smashed the window. Took her camera, went through everything. It's all wet in there."

I glare at her, like *shut up*. "It could be worse," I say. "People are dying or hurt bad, which makes our problems seem pretty small."

"Still . . . Let me finish up here and I'll go back to the house with you."

Janey's mom has already got her working, wiping off the tables and chairs. As she cleans, she tells on me. "P.D. wants to go back to Montana."

The girl needs a muzzle.

Dakota finishes attaching the pull chain on the fan and spins the blades. "Montana? It's snowing there, kid. Stay here." I can't stop my teeth from chattering. She climbs down, slaps the dust off her hands and latches up her tool box. "You've got to go to bed. Come on."

Well, it wouldn't hurt to get dry and warm and eat a good meal before I leave town.

She pauses at the door. "Diana, dinner at our house. We've got a generator, and we've got food."

"We'll be there."

Outside, the rain and wind hit me again as we hurry to our cars.

"I think I should drive you," Dakota says.

"No. I have to stop at Donovan's first." I sink into the wet seat and shiver in the wind coming through the broken window.

She talks through the missing window. "What for?"

"I left my necklace there."

"We'll get it later."

"No. It's the only jewelry I have left. I don't want Donovan making a sculpture out of it."

"Okay, but I'm coming with you. When he's manic, he's unpredictable."

Remembering how he was right after the earthquake, I nod. "Fine."

I SWEAR MY CAR is driving me as we climb the hill, Dakota leading the way in the rainbow van. It's hard to believe the water was so high night before last. Now the road is glazed with mud and littered with tree branches and leaves. We pass the spot where we saw the dead dog. The dog is gone.

The whole world looks gray. Gray sky, gray rain, gray all around me. Even the trees are grayish green. I can't stand the silence. I turn on the CD player and want to weep in gratitude when I hear John Denver singing "Rocky Mountain High."

Too clogged up to sing along, I pat the steering wheel with the beat, not noticing until I almost hit her van that Dakota has stopped halfway up the hill. Her long arm points out her window, and I look to the left of the road. There's Donovan's red pickup, mired in the sludge. Did he actually walk all the way up to the cabin? Angry as he was, maybe he did.

We drive on past the rainbow house and turn up the steep driveway to Donovan's place, parking out front.

The garden is wrecked, the wine bottle sculptures smashed, the ceramic flowers lying in the muddy grass as if a herd of elk trampled them. Somehow it doesn't look like earthquake damage.

The dark house seems unoccupied, just as it did Thursday night.

"Maybe he's out back," I suggest.

We walk around past the wood pile and peer up at the balcony. No Donovan.

"Maybe he took off," Dakota says.

"Maybe." In which case, I can go in, claim my necklace and get the heck out of here. I start up the back steps, then notice the door to the studio is open. "Dakota?"

She comes up behind me. "Go back to the car."

"No. I'm not 12." I shove past her and push the door open. "Dear God."

Donovan is lying on the floor, surrounded by broken glass, blood pouring from his hands and wrists. His face is pale, his mouth open.

I get down on the floor, check the pulse in his neck and listen for his breath, the way they taught me in first aid training at the hospital. "He's alive, but barely. Can you go call 911 on your phone? Pray they get out here fast."

"Let me take care of him and you go."

"No!" I guess I look fierce. For once she lets me take charge.

Only after Dakota drives away do I remember the bridge between here and the hospital is closed. Would they let an ambulance through?

Dakota isn't gone a whole minute before Donovan appears to stop breathing. Is he dead? I bend closer, trying not to lean on stray pieces of broken glass. I can't hear any breath sounds. I'm clogged and coughing, but I can't think of what else to do except start CPR. I'm glad I learned it, but our instructors never said what to do if you have a cold at the time. Somehow in the videos, there's always a crowd of people, not just one sickly woman full of snot.

Here's a comforting thought: If I make Donovan sick, no big deal. He already wants to die. Okay, that's the evil side of P.D., the one that will make a joke out of anything. God, please help me do this. He's a good man with a troubled mind. He's Diana's brother, Janey's uncle.

First, compressions. My stupid brace is in my way again. I strip it off, place my hands on his massive chest and start pushing. Yes, my wrist hurts. So what?

After 30 compressions, it's time to blow.

I wipe my nose, pinch his massive red-veined honker, open his mouth and start breathing my germy breath into his mouth, counting, breathing, pushing on his chest, and praying.

Come on, Donovan Green. I watch his chest, fill my lungs and breathe into his mouth. His chest rises. I shift position so I'm crouched over him and start pushing again.

Then I blow. What's taking Dakota so long? What am I going to do if he dies? My wrist is killing me. How long can I keep this up?

As long as I have to. I come up, gasping for air. "Come on, Donovan, you idiot. Breathe!"

One more time.

To my amazement, it works. It actually works. After eight rounds of breathing and pushing, Donovan gasps and pulls in a ragged breath. He opens his eyes and stares at me. Amazed, I stare back, wondering what to do now. He mumbles something I can't understand.

"What?" I lean down so my ear is close to his mouth.

"Damn. I'm still alive."

I laugh, I don't know why. I laugh and hug this big crazy man. "Damn straight you're still alive." Then I start to cry. I don't know why I do that either. As I'm hunting for something to wrap his bleeding wrists, the fire truck and ambulance from Seal Rock arrive, and three men run up the steps, Dakota behind them.

Donovan tries to sit up, but as soon as he starts to get vertical, his eyes roll back and he passes out. I back away and let a paramedic take over, filling him in on what little I know as he checks Donovan's blood pressure and pulse, starts some oxygen, and wraps his wounds with bandages.

"We have to transport him," he tells the other guys.

"You can't get over the bridge, can you?" I ask.

One of the firefighters answers, "No, Ma'am. We have to either drive around or fly emergency cases over the bay. Luckily, the airport's on this side of the bridge, and we've got a Coast Guard helicopter on standby. I don't think this guy can wait."

As they take Donovan out the front door, I have this big attack of *deja vu*, remembering the times when paramedics from Missoula took Tom out our front door. I fight not to start crying again.

Dakota puts her arm around me. "You did good, P.D. He'll be okay."

"I know," I squeak.

"Let's go home. I bet you could use a nice hot bubble bath and clean clothes before dinner. You also need some ice on that wrist."

"Yeah," I will let Dakota mother me for a minute. But I'm not staying at her house any longer than I have to.

On the way out, I check the bathroom and find the necklace Tom gave me right where I left it. It's a tiny ruby heart on the most delicate gold chain I've ever seen. I put it on, not an easy task with a club for a hand, and swear to never remove it again.

28

BACK AT THE RAINBOW house, I wake up from a nap, feverish, congested and confused. It's almost dark, a red candle flickering on the nightstand. Was all this a dream or did it really happen? Oh wait, what are those knick-knacks doing on the floor? And that picture is crooked. It's all true, the earthquake, the tsunami, the night in the dark, working at the hospital, the dead Chinese lady, Rick getting hurt, Donovan almost dying, all of it. It's Saturday, only two days since the earthquake and tsunami, but it feels like months have passed.

Maryann dried some of the clothes from my suitcase by the fire while I slept. I can finally wear something besides my filthy Thanksgiving outfit. As I dress in clean jeans and a white blouse, I hear voices from the living room. I quickly fluff my hair, brush my teeth and go out.

"Hey, sleepy," Dakota says.

"Hey."

"How are you feeling?"

"Sick and sore." I look around at Diana, Janey, Frankie, and Dakota gathered around the candlelit table as Maryann carries bowls and platters from the kitchen. The lights are off, probably conserving gas in the generator. "Do we know anything about Donovan?"

"Good news," Dakota says. "The fire guys stopped by to let us know. He's in stable condition, but he'll be staying at the hospital a while. His wounds were superficial, but his blood sugar was through the roof."

"He's diabetic?"

Diana nods. "Diabetic and bipolar. High highs and low lows. When he's manic, he eats and drinks whatever he wants, despite the fact that it makes him sick. My mother was the same way. Which made growing up in our house very interesting. I think my first words were '911.'"

"Grandma was plum crazy," Janey adds.

"But he's going to be fine," Dakota says. "Sit down. Dinner's almost ready. Can I get you some tea? We heated the water on the woodstove."

"Thanks."

"Hey," Janey says. "Look what Mom brought you."

She points toward the sofa in the living room. There's my rented keyboard, looking as good as ever. I swallow hard. "Thank you."

"You can play me some songs when you feel up to it," Diana says.

But for all the trauma and drama, you'd think this was just a party at the rainbow house, maybe a welcome home for Maryann and Dakota. Maryann has produced a vegetarian feast out of her emergency stash and the fruits and vegetables she and Dakota brought home from their trip. We have more than enough food because Jonas and Molly decided not to come. The boys are having a hard time, so they're staying at Diana's house. They plan to take the ferry to Newport in the morning. Diana says Jonas needs to get back to work, driving his van until he can buy another cab. Amy and Caroline are at home up the hill a few miles south, praying to hear something about Dave.

As she passes rice, squash, mushrooms, melons and biscuits, Dakota asks me, "How's your touchy stomach doing?"

I laugh. "Surprisingly, it's just fine."

"It was stress," she says.

"Did you try those herbs I recommended?" Frankie asks.

Oops. "Not yet. But I will."

"They work, honey. They really do."

"Shall we say grace?" Diana asks.

I set down the biscuit I'm buttering and grab Dakota's bony hand on my left while Janey avoids my gimpy wrist and rests her hand on my right shoulder.

"Dear Lord, thank you for bringing our wanderers home safely. Thank you that Donovan is safe again. Please help him find peace. Please help Rick to heal from his injuries. And please, watch over Amy and Caroline and bring Dave home safe, too. Watch over everyone suffering in the aftermath of this earthquake and tsunami. Thank you for this wonderful food and wonderful friends. Through Christ our Lord, Amen."

"Amen." I feel Janey squeeze my shoulder as we finish.

"Now eat before it gets cold," Maryann orders. "I can't heat it back up."

A half hour later, as we linger over Maryann's oatmeal raisin cookies, several conversations are going at once, and I'm not participating in any of them, just sitting there, trying to breathe between bites. Janey leans over and asks, "P.D., are you still thinking about going back to Montana?"

I choke on my cookie. As I cough so hard my eyes water, I try to figure out what to say. Right at this moment, I don't want to leave. I want to stay here surrounded by friends and good food. I don't want to be alone. Plus the last two days have tickled an idea in the back of my mind.

I'm thinking about becoming a nurse. There must be a reason why God keeps leading me to people who need medical care. I could go to school part-time while I work at my old job back in Missoula. By the time I graduated, the house would be sold, and I could live anywhere I wanted. Maybe even here.

As my coughing jag eases, I take in a few deep breaths and drink a sip of tea.

"You okay, darlin'?" Frankie asks.

"Yeah," I whisper, mopping my eyes with my napkin.

"So, are you going back to Montana?" Janey repeats.

"Yes. At least for a while." Which reminds me. I never called my real estate agent to tell her not to sell the house. I stand so abruptly I almost knock my chair over. "Dakota, can I use the phone?"

"Sure."

"It's long distance."

"No problem. Actually it's local calls that are all jammed up. I think you can call out of state."

I run to the bedroom, dig in my bag for Stella Brasch's number, then grab the old-fashioned wall phone and dial.

Everybody's watching me now, but I have to do this, should have done it a couple days ago.

Voicemail. Of course. I wonder what Stella is doing when she's not answering her phone. As everyone listens, I leave my message: "Stella, this is P.D. Soares with the house on Keith Avenue. I have decided not to sell it. I'm going to move back in. I'm sorry for your troubles. I'll sign whatever papers you need me to sign when I get back there in a few days. Thank you. Bye."

Okay, we have a plan. Behind me, no one is talking. They're all staring at me.

IT'S SUNDAY, and the others are all going to an ecumenical prayer service at the firehouse while I stay in bed in my pajamas, propped up with three pillows. I've got pomegranate juice, a box of tissues and a couple of Maryann's *Country Home* magazines on the nightstand. Hernando is curled up against my hip, while Sasha is cleaning her paws at the foot of the bed. The generator is turned off to save fuel. The fire in the woodstove is keeping the house warm.

It's my last day here. Tomorrow, sick or not, I'm going to pack up my stuff, what's left of it, cover my busted car window with something, and say goodbye to tsunami land. Missoula, here I come.

I'm tempted to call some friends in Missoula to tell them I'm coming back. But then I think about how I'd have to say, "Hi, it's Cissy," and Lord, I can't do that. I am so sick of that name. Prissy Cissy. It doesn't feel like me anymore. Somewhere along the line, I have truly become P.D. They're going to have to get used to it. But I would enjoy seeing them again. I miss singing at Mass. Even snow sounds like a nice change from all this rain. At least people know how to deal with it there. I can get a job and start working toward having enough money to pay the bills and have a little left over. If I want to pursue nursing, I'm sure there's a school there, probably a bigger and better one than the little community college in Newport.

I can find places to sing and play in Missoula, and I can practice on my own piano. Someday I might come back here, but I'm not going to make a singing career in this tiny town. As for the Seal Rock Sound, the band we formed on Thanksgiving, that was just a momentary dream born of eggnog and too much turkey. Janey will be going off to a four-year school pretty soon, Jonas is busy with his work and his kids, and Rick, nobody knows where he is.

I touch the ruby heart on my necklace. Being in Missoula would make me feel closer to Tom, even though he's buried in California.

After the prayer service, the others are going to work on fixing up Frankie's store. Whatever fresh food she had will have to go into the trash bin, where it will sit and stink. I doubt the garbage trucks will be coming on their weekly rounds any time soon. Frankie and her friends will fix the broken shelves, clean up the junk on the floors, and organize the cans and packaged goods. They talked about painting the place while they're working on it. Might as well. If they can find paint on this side of the bridge.

As for the diner, it's almost ready to reopen, but there's no food or electricity. Or water. There aren't likely to be any customers right away, not with the roads blocked in both directions. Kelly, Diana's partner, hasn't come back from Portland; the roads are too messed up.

How will I get out of here if the roads aren't open? Well, Dakota gave me some maps last night that showed all the forest service roads in the area and ways I can get to a main highway where the damage isn't too bad. So that's what I'll do. It might be kind of rugged, but I've been driving up this hill long enough to almost get used to narrow, unpaved roads. While the generator was on yesterday, she charged the car enough to get me to I-5. God knows where I'll find gas.

With luck I'll get to the valley and sleep in an actual motel with electricity, maybe even TV. Microwave, coffeemaker, hot water, and privacy. I can't wait. Of course maybe they don't have power there yet either. Guess I'll find out. I'll sleep in my car if I have to. Eventually I'm going to get to someplace unaffected by the earthquake.

My eyes are getting heavy. All I want to do right now is sleep.

AFTER LUNCH, ALL slept out and full of Maryann's vegetable soup, eaten cold, I sit in the easy chair by the fire while Dakota stands just outside the front door sanding a new porch rail to replace one that broke off in the earthquake. Maryann is knitting by candlelight, humming what sounds like "Amazing Grace."

With Maryann's humming and the shushing of sandpaper on wood for background, my mind wanders. There's something I'm curious about. I go out and watch Dakota's hand moving back and forth on the wood.

"Is Dakota your real name?"

She looks up. "It is now."

"You mean you legally changed it?"

"Yep."

"What did it used to be?"

She stops sanding and grins, tooth gap showing. "Annabelle. Annabelle Marie Wells."

I laugh. "Seriously?"

"Oh yeah. I was Annabelle till I was 18. By then I'd gotten all my friends to call me Dakota. I told 'em I'd beat 'em up if they called me Annabelle. But teachers, pastors, grandparents, I couldn't stop 'em. As soon as I was old enough, I had it legally changed."

"Why Dakota?"

"I was born there and I liked the sound of it." She goes back to sanding as I ponder this. Since I'm asking questions, I try another one. "Did you know you were . . ."

"Gay? Oh yeah. I've always known. How about you? Your parents didn't name you P.D."

"No, they didn't."

"Your real name isn't that bad. I saw it on your mail. Why change it?"

"I'm not that other person anymore." It's cold. I turn to go in. "I'm beat. Maybe I should go back to bed."

But she isn't letting me off that easy. "You can't run away from your real self, you know." She's looking at me all serious now.

"You did."

"No, I became my real self."

"That's what I'm doing, too."

Dakota rests her hand on my shoulder. "Are you sure?"

"I'm sure. I'm not running away, Dakota. I'm going back to Montana."

"Because you don't have the balls to stay here."

"What?"

"Forget it. You do what you need to do. I need a cigarette."

As she lights up, I go back in and stand by the woodstove, my face hot as I think of all kinds of things I want to tell Dakota aka Annabelle. I'm grateful for her help, but if I want to change my name or leave town, that's none of her business. I was just passing through and got caught in this mess. I'm going tomorrow, even if I am sick.

I'm about to start packing when Janey bursts in, Dakota behind her. "P.D., they found Uncle Rick! He's back in the hospital. He ran his truck into a ditch and the cops found him passed out. He's got some kind of infection. He's really sick. Oh P.D., he could die!" Janey is all teary-eyed.

I want to say I don't care, that I'm leaving, that the last thing I need is another man dying on me. But I do care. Damn it. I care about Rick and all these people more than I want to admit.

"He'll be okay," I tell her because that's what people always say.

"Does your mom know?" Dakota asks.

"Yes. She's taking the ferry over to be with him."

Suddenly it clicks. Rick and Diana. That's why Janey calls him "Uncle."

I CAN'T SLEEP. It's too quiet. But my mind is a three-ring circus. In one ring, I wonder what Dakota looked like as a tough little girl named Annabelle, wonder why she and Maryann moved here to Beaver Creek, wonder if she's right about me running away.

In another ring, I picture Rick in a hospital bed in intensive care, pale, unshaven, hooked up to machines, maybe dying alone. I feel his hand holding mine at the hospital. Or is that Tom's? No, Tom's hands didn't have calluses and cuts. It was Rick's hand. When we were standing together watching the tsunami, I felt connected to him. But now I remember Diana was always nearby, too.

And in the center ring, I think about getting into my car in the morning and driving away, saying goodbye to these people, possibly forever, starting over in Missoula without my husband.

Somewhere in the back of my mind, I know it's almost Christmas, that people away from the Oregon Coast started putting up decorations a few days ago. The stores will be full of holiday music and people frantically buying presents. Do I want to spend Christmas alone in Missoula? Should I drive south to Santa Cruz instead?

With a shudder, I realize Santa Cruz might have earthquake and tsunami damage too. Nature didn't stop rumbling at the California border. I haven't even asked anyone. My family lives high enough to be safe from the waves, but this earthquake was bigger than the Loma Prieta quake. Santa Cruz could be just as trashed as Newport. I've got to call Mom in the morning.

For months, I've been acting like I'm the only person in the world who has troubles. Maybe Dakota is right. I need to stop running away from my life as a widow—and start thinking about other people for a change.

I have to go to the bathroom.

As I pass the living room, I notice a light. In the flickering glow of a lantern, Maryann sits sewing. I'm guessing she can't sleep either. I don't know much about Maryann. I never asked. I'm a selfish ingrate.

29

TOWARD MORNING, I sleep for three blessed hours. I awaken to the hum of the generator and the smell of waffles and maple syrup. I'm hungry.

Today is the day I drive away from here.

I get up, use the bathroom and go to the kitchen, tying my borrowed bathrobe around me. "Good morning," I say, my voice still hoarse. At least my nose has stopped running.

"Good morning, P.D.," Maryann says. "Hope you're hungry."

"I am."

"I heard you up last night."

"Couldn't sleep."

"Me either."

Her eyelids are puffy and her brown hair is disheveled. None of this has been easy for her. She's just always there, quietly doing things for everyone else. Like right now, she's pouring me a cup of coffee.

"Thank you. Where's Dakota?"

"Outside." She nods toward the window. I see Dakota duct-taping a piece of plastic over my car window. I'm about to go help when I see her walk off toward the back of the house. Too late.

I sit at the table and take a sip of coffee. So good.

Now is my chance to talk to Maryann.

"I'm sorry I haven't gotten to know you better," I begin.

"Well, it's crazy times."

"True. So . . . what did you do before you came here?"

She smiles. "I was a kindergarten teacher."

"Oh. I'll bet you were a good one."

"I loved it, loved those little kids."

"Why did you quit?"

She pulls out a finished waffle, adds it to a stack keeping warm in the oven and pours more batter on the iron. "I didn't quit. I was asked to leave after they found out about my, um, lifestyle."

"Because you were gay?"

"Right."

"Is that even legal?"

"Oh, I don't know. They came up with all kinds of reasons, budget cuts and such, and I decided not to fight it. The worst part was trying to explain to my kids why I was leaving."

"They didn't wait until the end of the school year?"

"Nope." She cracks eggs into a cast iron skillet as Dakota comes in.

"Your car's all ready if you insist on going."

"You guys have been so much help I don't know how to thank you."

"Just be well and happy," Maryann says, scrambling the eggs while Dakota washes her hands at the sink.

"And know you're always welcome here," Dakota adds.

Damn. Now I want to blubber. But no. No tears. P.D. is strong. Determined. Hungry.

AFTER BREAKFAST, it all happens quickly. I call my mother and learn she's okay. I kiss the cats goodbye, throw my stuff into the car, accept peanut butter and jelly sandwiches, oatmeal cookies, and herb tea from Maryann, get in, start the engine, and say thank you for everything, I'll be in touch. Maryann and Dakota watch, arms around each other, as I roll down the driveway. At Beaver Creek Road, I pause, consider driving to Donovan's house for one last look, decide against it and turn left toward the highway and civilization. In a quarter mile, I'll hang a right and start my adventure on the forest roads heading east.

It's more than 50 miles from here to civilization via the highways. How many hours will it take me on the forest roads? What if I get lost or run out of power and gas or get a flat tire in the middle of nowhere? Might other people be traveling the same roads? I guess I'll find out.

It's sunny and cold today. In the meadows, the grass is tall and green. The black and white cows cluster together as if nothing has happened. Humans go crazy when natural disasters hit, but nature simply adjusts, I guess.

Halfway down the hill, I see Donovan's truck where it has sat since the night of the tsunami. Getting it out of there seems like a low priority when people are hunting for human bodies. I assume someone looked inside, saw no one there and moved on.

That makes me think about Dave. No one has heard anything about him. Could he really have been swept out to sea, just gone? Dear God, please let Dave be somewhere safe. He's a good man. His wife and daughter need him. Let him be just stuck on the other side of the bay working. And while you're in the neighborhood, please help Rick Jones and Donovan—

My cell phone interrupts my prayer with the little jingle that tells me I have voicemail. That means somebody fixed the tower or rigged up a temporary connection. Hallelujah. I pull into the parking lot at the boat launch to check my messages. As I turn, my tires slip on the mud and I almost land in the creek before I regain control and stop, facing the water. The mud is so thick you could shovel for days and not reach pavement.

Framed by alder trees and blackberry vines, the olive green water ripples along as always, but now it carries garbage cans, ice chests, a camper shell off someone's truck, boards and signs, plastic bottles, shoes, hats, and lots of little things I can't identify from the car. An oily sheen floats along the top. Debris clings to the trees and the banks across the creek. To the west, the bridge over Beaver Creek still stands, silent witness to what has happened.

Sun pours through the windshield, but it's cold in here, especially with no glass in the passenger side window. I've got to get it fixed as soon as possible. I wonder if my car insurance will cover it. But right now I need to find out who called me.

"You have two messages," the voice tells me.

"P.D., this is Shirley Madden at Pacific Communities Hospital. Did you turn in your job application yet? We could really use you. We've lost some of our staff in the disaster, and business is booming. If you could come in tonight, I'd really appreciate it." She gives me her number and says, "Please call back."

Okay. I'm going to have to break it to her that I'm leaving town. But part of me wants to go back to the hospital and get to work. I don't know what it's like in ordinary times, but I never felt as comfortable in Missoula. It was such a big hospital with so many rules.

Maybe I should wait one more night to leave, put in another shift at the hospital. But my car is packed, and I can't drive it across the bridge. I don't want to leave it at the aquarium to get broken into again. Anybody could reach right in through the missing window.

Message number two is my mother, but I lose the connection before I can listen to it. Just as well. I already heard what she had to say. Minor damage, broken docks. She's worried about me. I should come home. I should be with my family instead of with strangers in Montana. She keeps calling me Cissy.

Everybody expects me to make decisions, but then they don't accept what I decide. Why do people do that to widows? They give you about a week to grieve, and then once the funeral is over, they're asking, "What are you going to do? You should sell the house. Move back in with your mother. Get a new job. Start dating." Yes, some of my friends suggested after only a month that I start looking for a new man.

All you really want is your old life back. You can't bear the thought of building a life without the man who was supposed to be your partner until you were too old to care anymore. It hurts so bad you can barely stand up, but people keep asking for decisions. That and "How *are* you?" with that horrible tone full of pity.

Leave me alone.

That's why I ran away, why I wanted to be P.D. So I could find my new life without everybody expecting things from me. Maybe I won't stay in Montana. Maybe I'll just let Stella sell the house. I'll take the money, get my stuff and come back here where I can do some good. I'll take the job at the hospital, rent an apartment and start over. But I can decide that later. Right now, it's time to move on.

In a minute.

I STARE AT THE brownish-green water in the creek. This is where I was supposed to go kayaking with Dave and his daughter Amy last Saturday. I picture us floating along between the trees and bushes, pointing out birds and beaver dens, startling a blue heron or a snowy egret, waving at people on the shore. There would be no tsunami debris. My arms would feel strong as I worked the paddles. My wrist might hurt, but I would power through it. Dave said he'd get me a red kayak, and he'd choose a yellow one.

I open my window and breathe in the fresh air. I swear I have never seen such a blue sky as we have here when the sun comes out. Even if they do call Montana Big Sky Country. Around me, pines wave in the breeze. A seagull coasts on the wind, its orange beak open as it squawks, sounding almost like it's laughing. A dump truck roars by on the highway, downshifting for the curve just south of Ona Beach.

I see something yellow out there, to the left of the trees. Could be a kayak. Or part of one. Could be a rain slicker. Could be someone under it. I hope not.

I'm getting out of the car for a closer look.

My left shoe sinks in the mud. I can feel mud oozing over the top. What's the good of saving one shoe if the other is ruined? I put my other foot down in the mud and stand. After a brief struggle to get my balance, I ski toward the creek, leaving massive footprints in the mud.

A foot from the water, I stop, rivulets lapping near my toes.

I don't see it now. Maybe it was just a piece of paper floating by. I need to get going. Missoula is 700 miles away. But my feet are literally glued to this spot.

The mud makes a sucking sound as I lift my right foot. Wait. I hear a moan. I freeze, hold my breath, and listen. Another moan. Human. Not far away. My heart jumps.

Slipping and sliding with both feet into the icy water, mud gushing up around my knees, I move toward the sound. I see the patch of yellow, which is indeed a kayak, lying upside down in a shallow cove. As I get closer, the moans get louder and I see bare bluish feet sticking out.

God, please help, I think as I take another step, clear my throat and call, "Hello?"

"Help me," a weak male voice responds.

"I'm coming." I splash quickly through water, now up to my hips, pushing pieces of wood, bits of rope, netting, buoys and fast food wrappers out of my way.

The kayak is caught in the refuse on the bank. As gently as I can, I lift the end and tug it out of the mess enough to see that lying underneath it is Ranger Dave, his face covered with mud and red stubble. His blue eyes stare up at me. "P.D.," he whispers.

"Yeah. I need to help you get out of here."

"I can't move."

"At all?"

"No."

Any fool knows you don't move a person who might have a spinal cord injury. I have to call for help and pray there are still paramedics around who can get him to the hospital.

I squeeze his bruised shoulder. "Can you feel that?"

He winces. "Yes. But I can't feel my legs."

"Okay. Hang on. I'm going back to the car to call for help."

Please God, let the phone work, I pray as I wade back toward the parking lot. I curse myself for not putting my cell phone in my pocket. When I trip on a rock and fall into the water a second later, I'm glad it's safe in the car.

It works. I call 911. Then I call Dakota and Maryann to tell Dave's wife and daughter. I slither back to Dave.

It's a long wait. I don't know where the ambulance is coming from. It's Monday, which means he has probably been here since the tsunami on Thursday. I'm guessing he was securing the kayaks at Ona Beach when the wave came and washed him inland. Maybe he was helping kayakers in trouble. Or maybe he was caught in a wave and grabbed the kayak. He'll tell us eventually, but right now it doesn't matter.

I support his head and do my best to rinse the mud off his face. It's a good face, handsome with its three days of red stubble, with freckles and laugh lines around his eyes and mouth.

"It's going to be all right," I keep telling him as we wait. I don't know what his injuries are yet. Clearly something has happened to his neck or his back. He's probably hypothermic. Starving. Dehydrated. Bruised. There may be broken bones and internal injuries from getting bashed around. I'm no expert. I'm starting to wish I was.

"Caroline? Amy?" he whispers.

"They're both fine, Dave, just worried sick about you. I sent a message to them."

"Thank you. I-I don't know if I'm going to make it."

"Sure you will. You're strong." I glance back toward the road, praying to see the ambulance. "I wonder what's taking them so long."

"They're b-busy."

"That's true. Oh, hey." A car has just turned into the parking lot, skidding to a stop. Caroline and Amy get out, Amy on crutches.

"Dave!" Caroline calls.

"Over here!" I reply as Dave begins to weep.

While Amy waits near the car, Caroline slides across the parking lot and splashes through the water till she sees the kayak. "What were you doing, kayaking?" she screams, tears running down her face.

Dave smiles. "Sure."

I can see her about to grab him in a big hug and have to stop her. "Caroline, be careful. He says he can't move."

"Oh God."

"I know. The paramedics are on their way. God willing, he'll be all right, but we shouldn't move him or jar him."

"Okay."

I see her future as the wife beside the hospital bed, no longer the artist with the happy family. I want to tell her how sorry I am, but she wouldn't want all that pity any more than I do.

30

LATER WE'LL WONDER what would have happened if I hadn't stopped here and found Dave, but right now we don't have time to think. The ambulance arrives. I explain Dave has a possible spinal cord injury. The two men, whom I recognize from Donovan's house, grab the backboard and rush into the water.

I stand in the mud watching until he's strapped on and loaded into the ambulance.

As they're closing the doors, I ask a paramedic, "Are you flying him to the local hospital?"

"Yes. Although he probably won't stay in Newport." As Caroline starts to climb into the ambulance with her husband, he puts a hand on her shoulder. "I'm so sorry, but I only have room for one passenger on the chopper. If you and your daughter want to drive the back roads, it will take a while, but you can get there."

"Mom?" Amy says.

"Amy, you can ride in my car with me," I say. "I have to get to Highway 20 anyway. I'll get you to the hospital as fast I can."

"Let's roll," the ambulance driver calls.

Doors closed, everybody loaded, red lights flashing, the ambulance heads toward Highway 101 while I load Amy and her crutches into my little car and begin my journey east over the forest service roads that Dakota mapped out for me.

WHAT CAN I TELL YOU about the route? Muddy. Narrow. Blackberry vines scraping the sides of the car. A little pavement, mostly gravel. Sometimes hanging on the side of a cliff, other times driving in ruts hoping my car won't ground out on the grass in the middle. Feeling sure I am lost. Certain I'm going to crash into a ditch and destroy my car. If Amy weren't sitting beside me reading the directions and worried sick about her father, I probably would turn back. I pray more than I have in ages.

Still sick, I get started coughing and spew phlegm all over my hands as I drive. Despite the cold weather and my wet clothes, I'm soaked with sweat. I'll be lucky if I don't need a bed at the hospital for myself by the time we get there. If we get there.

When we hit pavement and start seeing houses on Elk Creek Road, which comes out on Highway 20 way east of Newport, I want to get out and kiss the pavement.

"Oh, thank you, God," I whisper. I'm almost halfway to I-5 and clear sailing to Montana, but I have to go back to the coast first.

"Please hurry," Amy says.

It's the first time she's said anything in many miles, but I know she must be scared spitless. "We're almost there, sweetie."

I drive as fast as I dare, speeding through the 30 mile-an-hour curves at 50, praying my way through every milepost marker. Ninety minutes after we left Beaver Creek, we reach Highway 101 at Newport. The sign proclaiming Newport "The Friendliest" lies broken on the side of the road.

The streets are relatively clear now, and a city crew is realigning a light pole where we turn toward the hospital. Parking in a visitor space, we hurry toward the emergency entrance, Amy hopping as fast as she can on her crutches. The powerless electric doors are propped open. It's cold inside, where several people huddle in their coats, waiting.

Zelda at the desk remembers me. "P.D., right?"

"Right. We're here for Dave Walsh. The helicopter just brought him in. This is his daughter."

She scans her clipboard. "Oh, yes. Amy?"

"Uh-huh."

"You can go right in. Sorry, P.D., you have to wait outside."

Amy starts toward the door, but turns back. "Thank you, P.D."

"You're welcome. He's going to be okay. I'm sure of it."

She swallows. "I hope so."

Then she's gone, and I'm on my own in the emergency waiting room.

"P.D., you know what I heard?" Zelda says in a low voice, beckoning me closer. "I heard that Mr. Walsh rescued a whole family in his little kayak. They were drowning in Beaver Creek and didn't have the strength to swim against the tide. He pulled them aboard and got them to land. I guess he got caught by the next wave. Man."

"I can see him doing that. He's the kind of guy who would always put others first."

"I know. I'm so sorry he got hurt."

"Me too." A man is coming up to the desk with a little boy holding a bloody towel over his hand. No more time to talk.

As I settle into a chair with an old copy of People magazine, a nurse calls the young couple sitting across from me. I wonder what their story is.

This stuff in the magazine is stupid. Trivial. Who cares what some actress wore to the Academy awards or whether a singer's "baby bump" is showing? All along the west coast, cities are ruined, people are dying, and we're running out of food.

The mud on my wet shoes is flaking off on the dirty hospital carpet. I take them off and peel my soggy socks off my feet. The rough carpet feels warm against my skin.

I picture what's happening on the other side of the door. Dave will be hooked up to monitoring devices. He'll have an IV. They'll do X-rays, an MRI if that's available. Maybe he'll need surgery. He'll probably be flown to a bigger hospital in Portland. It's going to be a long day and night for him and his family. But at least he's getting care now, and we know where he is. One less missing person.

I SIT WITH THIS stupid magazine in my lap for 15 minutes, 30 minutes, 45 . . . I can't sit here anymore. I need to tell Shirley I can't work tonight. I might as well check in on Rick and Donovan, too. Then I need to hit the road.

I give Zelda my cell phone number and stop in the bathroom to freshen up. I can't believe I look so ordinary after all that has happened. My clothes still feel damp, but it doesn't really show. My hair is two-tone, my brown roots pushing out the red that has faded a little every time I showered.

As I dig around my purse for my comb, I touch something that feels like my wedding ring. It must have fallen out of my wallet where I was keeping it with Tom's picture. I'm lucky it wasn't in the car with my other jewelry. I slide it onto the chain with the ruby heart. It feels heavy and cold against my neck.

The young woman working the admissions desk tells me Shirley is on a break. I climb the stairs to the second floor and stop at the nurses' station to ask about the two people I have come to visit.

"P.D.!" someone shouts from down the hall. Deuce from the music store rushes toward me, his arms wide open for a hug. He smells of cigars and hand sanitizer.

I pull back, blushing at the sudden closeness of this bony old hippie. "Hey, Deuce. Oh my gosh. How are you?"

"I'm excellent. And you? Still got the gimpy wrist?"

I look down at the brace. I had forgotten about it for a while. "Yes, but it's healing."

"Good. We need you back on the piano."

"Is the store open?"

"Not yet. But soon. Hey, the cops told me about how you interrupted the looters. I appreciate it. I'll bet I know who they were, but I have insurance, so I'm not going to worry about it. If I see them playing one of my instruments, I'll know where they got it. Anyway, I'm going to make the jams a regular thing. I'll put it in the paper and everything."

"Cool." I look around. "Are you visiting someone? Did the tsunami get your house?"

"Nah. Nothin' like that. My wife decided to have our baby last night. Another boy. He fumbles in his jacket pocket and pulls out a cigar. Want one?"

I laugh. "No thanks. Congratulations. How many kids do you have?"

He chuckles. "Five. The old lady's a fertile one. I figure when the young'uns get a little older, we'll form a band and tour the world."

"Good idea."

"So, what are you doing here?"

"Visiting a couple friends who got hurt during the disaster."

"The earthnami? That's what my eight-year-old calls it."

"Yes, the earthnami."

"Deuce!" a female voice calls.

"Oh, that's the old ball and chain. She wants her coffee. Hasn't been able to drink it for months, so now she can't get enough. I'd better go. See you soon, I hope."

He walks off with that long swooping gait of his as a nurse looks at me questioningly.

"I'm looking for Donovan Green."

"Room 212. I don't know if he'll talk to you, but it's worth a try."

"Thanks."

Why do I want to see this guy anyway? He's crazy, one moment loud and obnoxious, the next mean, the next trying to kill himself. But he can also be kind and funny and creative. I saved his life. I guess that connects us somehow.

Donovan is lying on his back, staring at the ceiling. He looks too big for the little bed. He's hooked up to an IV. His wrists are bandaged where he cut them.

I clear my throat. "Hi."

He turns and stares at me. "P.D." His eyes fill with tears. "I'm so sorry."

"For what?"

"Everything. Kicking you out. Making you save my sorry self."

I grab his beefy white hand. "It's okay."

"No, it's not. I'm done screwing around. A nice girl like you shouldn't have seen me like that. I'm going to take my meds, stay on my diet, and never drink again."

"That's good to hear." What is there to say now? "Are you—" I'm about to ask if he's in any pain, but he interrupts.

"I'm tired of being alone. I can't do it anymore."

"You're not alone. You have a great family."

"Yeah. They don't want to be around crazy Uncle Donovan."

"Sure they do."

"No."

"Hey, at least you're never boring."

"I guess not."

More silence. "I ran into Deuce from the music store, I don't know if you know him." He nods. "His wife just had a baby last night, a boy. Number five. He says he's going to form a band with his kids and tour the country."

"That's nice." He closes his eyes. "I'm so tired."

"I know." That's my cue to leave.

As I stand, he reaches out. "P.D., come back again, okay?"

"Sure."

In the hall, I run into a nurse bringing pills. I stop her. "How is he really doing?"

"Are you family?"

"Yes," I lie. "He's my uncle."

"Well, he'll be fine. Physically. We're releasing him to a facility in the valley tomorrow where he can work on his other issues."

"Rehab?"

"Yes."

"Good. Listen, do you know what room Rick Jones is in?"

She grins. "Another uncle?"

"No, just a friend."

"223. He just got out of intensive care. He may not be awake."

"Thanks."

It occurs to me that if I'm going to spend this much time bopping from room to room, I might as well get a name tag and work here.

Rick is asleep when I tiptoe into the room. The other bed is empty. I stand by the window, looking out at the parking lot, the highway, the buildings, and the ocean. I can't quite see the damaged part of town, but I know it's there. Things seem pretty normal in here, life just standing still.

Oh, how I remember those hospital days with Tom. Sitting until my back and legs hurt, looking out the windows of the various rooms he occupied, pacing up and down the hall. Sometimes I cried, sometimes I wanted to run away. Sometimes I just got in the car and drove around Missoula. I remember when I'd go to a store or a park, I felt so out of place. It might be sunny, with kids playing on the slide or the swings, Moms giving them juice boxes and crackers, a radio playing country music somewhere, but my life was none of that. In a way, I felt more comfortable at the hospital.

I pull a chair over next to the bed.

Rick is a handsome man, pale under the stubble, where Tom was more swarthy. There's a bandage on his forehead, probably from crashing his truck. I wonder where it was, how fast he was going.

His fingernails need trimming. His left hand, the one closest to me, is bruised from multiple IVs. His breathing sounds raspy, but the numbers on the monitor are good. I guess he has beaten his infection.

I want to touch him, to feel his forehead, to run the back of my hand over his beard. But this is not Tom, whom I had the right to touch anywhere I wanted. This is a near-stranger. We shared a tsunami together—an earthnami—but we don't really know each other. Besides, he's Diana's boyfriend.

I should go downstairs and talk to Shirley. She sounded pretty desperate. She'll ask me about the application. I don't have it anymore. I tossed it in the recycle bin at Dakota and Maryann's house.

I'm standing, ready to leave, when Rick opens his eyes. "Hey."

"Hi. How do you feel?"

"Stupid."

"Well, besides that. Any pain?"

He breathes in and winces. "Some."

"I'll get your nurse."

He puts his hand on mine. "No, wait. I'd like to be awake for a little while, even if it hurts." As I bend toward him, my wedding ring clinks against the bed rail. He squints, confused. "Is that a wedding ring? I thought you were divorced or something."

I didn't tell a lot of people here the truth. I didn't want to be poor Cissy the widow, but what's the point in hiding it now? "It is a wedding ring. My husband died a few months ago."

Rick rubs his finger over the smooth gold band. "I'm sorry, P.D."

Tears gush up from my heart. I try like crazy to stop them, but a few leak out.

"Damn. I didn't mean to make you cry."

"It's okay. I thought I was over this part."

"Baby, you never get over it completely. My dad has been gone for 20 years, and my mom still bursts into tears. It's okay."

"No. It isn't okay. Why'd he have to die?"

"How come I didn't? Only God knows those answers, and he doesn't share much information. I think there's a box of Kleenex on the nightstand."

"Thanks." I grab a wad of tissues.

"I'd ask you what he died of, but I don't want to start another gusher."

I smile through my tears. "It's okay. Cancer."

"Damn."

I stare out the window, not really seeing anything.

"Hey, P.D."

"What?"

"What the heck is your real name? I've been trying to figure it out while I'm lying here, but I just don't know; none of them sound right. Prunella?"

I laugh and cough and wipe at my tears. "No."

"Well, come on. Tell me. I'll keep it a secret."

"Will you?"

"I'm a fireman. If you can't trust a fireman, who can you trust? Is it Peggy?"

"No."

"Paris. Like Paris Hilton."

"Definitely not. You're not going to let this go, are you?"

"No ma'am. Just tell me."

"Oh my God. I haven't told anybody. I was trying to leave that person behind."

"Come on. I almost died. How can you deny me something so small?"

"Oh, play the guilt card."

"You bet."

His smile is so disarming, I give in. I learn over the bed and whisper my real name in his ear.

"That's pretty. I like it. You get rid of that red hair, and you might be the kind of girl I'd be interested in."

I'm sure I'm blushing to my brown roots as I pull back and stare into his sea-blue eyes. "I heard you're already taken."

"Well, yeah. But if I wasn't—"

Thank God an aide comes in. "Are you P.D.? You're wanted downstairs."

"Rick, I've got to go."

"Give me a kiss."

I blow him a kiss, leaving him smiling as I hurry to the stairs and run down to the first floor. Zelda beckons me to the window.

"They're life-flighting Mr. Walsh to a spinal cord unit in Portland."

"Oh, jeez. Is he still paralyzed?"

"I'm not allowed to discuss his condition with you. You know that, but it doesn't look good. His wife and daughter are going to borrow a friend's car and drive up there. They wanted me to give you this."

She hands me a slip of paper folded in quarters.

Dear P.D.,

There are no words to thank you for finding Dave and saving his life. He may be paralyzed, and that possibility terrifies us, but he is alive. We still have our husband and father, thanks to you. And thank you for driving Amy here. She said you were amazing. If you need a place to stay, you are always welcome to stay with us.

Love,
Caroline and Amy Walsh.

Here come those stupid tears again. "Thank you," I whisper to Zelda.

I take a deep breath and pull myself together as I approach the admissions desk, where Shirley is on the phone. She signals for me to come closer, finishes her call and smiles. "Got your application filled out?"

"Not exactly. You got another one?"

31

I KNOW, I KNOW. I was going to Montana to live. It's the practical thing to do. If I don't sell that house soon, I'm going to be a bag lady. I can't be paying on two homes, and I'd be lucky to find one here that even has electricity and running water at this point. Paying first month and deposit on a rental will drain my savings to nothing. But I don't care. This feels right. I let Shirley put me on the schedule for next Monday, a week from today. I saw her write down a big P period D period.

Now I have some explaining to do.

It's too chilly outside to stand still, but I'm too restless to sit in the car, so I walk west toward the beach. For the heck of it, I try my cell phone. I've got one bar. Close enough. I dial and listen to the phone ringing in Montana. I'm about to give up when Stella Brasch answers.

"Yes?" She sounds out of breath, distracted.

"Stella, it's P.D. Soares."

"Okay, good. I got your message. This is a—um—I'm in the middle of something, but I have good news. We have an offer on the house."

"Oh!"

She puts me on hold.

I take in a deep breath of cold air as a little girl on a pink bicycle passes by me, her blonde hair flying under her pink helmet. She waves, and I wave back. Stella has an offer? I gaze up at the sky. Really, God?

Stella is back. "I know you wanted to move back in, but—"

"No, no. I accept the offer, whatever it is."

"Great. Where shall I send the papers?"

"Keep them with you. I'm on my way to Missoula. I should be there day after tomorrow."

"The people want to move in right away."

"Fine. I want to take one last look, and then it's all theirs."

"So you can turn it over to them by next Saturday, which is the first?"

"Yes. I'll stop by your office on Wednesday to sign the papers."

"Great. Thank you. Sorry, but I've got to go. I've got people here."

"I understand. I—" The phone clicks in my ear. Okay.

My heart's beating faster than usual, and it's not just that I haven't worked out lately. I'm a little bit in shock. My house is sold. The new people are moving in next weekend. And I said I would be in Montana by day after tomorrow. I need to empty my storage locker while I'm there, but what am I going to do with all that stuff? I'm homeless.

I could babble with myself all day, but as I walk closer to the beach, I know I'm on the right track now. I'll just rent a storage locker here until I can find a new home of my own. I'll have a job. I'll have money from the house. No problem.

Wow. There's not much left of the dry cleaners now, just a blackened pile of wood and plaster. The Nye Beach art galleries, restaurants and gift shops are mostly gone, a wall standing here and there, smashed cars and overturned toilets where people used to eat and enjoy the ocean view. The street is still coated with sand and junk.

A hard-hat crew is knocking down what's left of the Coast Inn, tossing the pieces into a dump truck. Up the road apiece, Janey's old apartment has yellow "keep out" tape around it now. Across the street, two men are putting a new window on the front of a house. Piece by piece, they'll put this town back together, but it won't be the same.

I send a text message to Janey telling her I'm going to Montana to get my stuff and will be back by next Sunday. She texts right back with a string of happy faces.

Beyond the buildings, waves lap calmly at the sand as if nothing unusual ever happened. As I watch them, I know, for the first time since Tom got sick, exactly what I'm going to do. It feels good.

I COULD DO A LONG travelogue about my lonely drive in my muddy little car across the Columbia Gorge, through southeast Washington, across Idaho and into western Montana. It was scenic, but a lot longer than I remembered, with several detours around earthquake damage, and I'm glad it's over. Rain and snow, miles of open spaces, a night at a Motel 6 in The Dalles, and then more driving, mostly with one healthy hand on the wheel and one injured hand in my lap.

As I roll into Missoula past motels and casinos, past the university into my old tree-lined neighborhood, I feel a pang, not doubt about my decision but a little regret. I prefer the coast, but I do love this place, love its rolling hills, its dramatic weather, and its cowboy culture. With 44,000 people, it isn't too big, but it has everything I need. I thought it was going to be our home forever. Our children and grandchildren would grow up here. We would be Montana people.

As I see signs for places like Orange Street and Rattlesnake Gulch, memories come flooding back. There's our church, the stores where we shopped, Tom's doctor's office, the hospital, the school where we talked about sending our children, and the city hall, where Tom worked. The town is decorated for Christmas, with colored lights on all the buildings and silver garlands wrapped around the light poles.

In the shelter of my car, I forget how much colder it is here than it is on the Oregon coast. The temperature sign at the bank says it's 26 degrees. I will sure be glad to get reacquainted with my heavy winter coat, hat, gloves and boots, all boxed up in the storage locker. But first I have to see the house.

It feels so natural to turn left on Arthur and take another left on Keith, drive halfway down the block and park my car in the driveway, as if I could just go in, toss my purse on the chair nearest the door and grab myself a snack out of the refrigerator.

But of course it isn't like that.

Stella must have replaced the broken mailbox with the plain white one that stands out front now. The garden looks a little sad, nothing blooming this time of year. The real estate lock box still hangs off the screen door. I open the door and use my key to go in.

Phew. It stinks of smoke and urine, and I can see where the carpets are stained. Everything has been removed from the living room except a cable TV cord. In the kitchen, the yellow walls have black marks from the fire, especially around the stove. Our refrigerator is still here. I'll let the new people have it.

Curious, I start opening drawers and cupboards, not finding much, a few plastic forks, a pizza coupon, a couple matchbooks from a local bar. Bedrooms, closets, and the garage are all basically empty.
The lights still work, so someone has paid the electric bill. The new people will pay it next month.

I really don't see much of anything to indicate Tom and I were ever here. My footsteps echo in the empty rooms. It's just a house, an empty ordinary house.

In the master bathroom, I stop to use the toilet, laughing at myself as I shut the door out of habit. Who would see me? When I finish, I wash my hands and dry them on my pants.

I can't help looking in the medicine cabinet. It's one of those where the doors slide open, so there's a blind spot in the middle. I reach up in there, not expecting to find anything. My fingers touch a pill bottle. I pull it out and sink to the edge of the bathtub as I read the label. "Thomas M. Soares, take one to two capsules every four hours as needed for pain." Two bright red capsules are left inside.

"Oh my God," I whisper. I hold the bottle against my shirt as my heart breaks one more time. Tom is gone. If I could just touch him one more time, just hear his voice, feel his arms around me—I sob so hard it's a wonder I don't die from it. Then I pull myself together, wiping my face with the last of the toilet paper. At least he's not in pain anymore. He will never hurt again. That makes it worth letting him go. It has to.

I inspect the whole house, then walk around the back yard. There's the fence board Harry gnawed to splinters when he was a puppy. There are the rose bushes I planted and pruned so carefully. There are the stepping stones Tom placed to make a path through my garden. There's the garbage can on which he spray-painted our house number.

I can hear the neighbor's children playing on the other side of the fence. If I think about things too hard, I'll start crying again. But Cissy lived here. Now I'm P.D., and I have to move on.

Nobody has pruned my rose bushes this year. I don't know if it will work, but I grab hold of the first one, placing my fingers carefully between the thorns, and break off a branch, then go to the next bush and do the same, until I have six of them. I get a tee shirt out of my suitcase, soak it from the faucet and wrap it around the rose cuttings. With luck, I can make them bloom in my new home.

It's time to go. I shut the gate behind me, walk through the side yard to the driveway and get into my car. "Goodbye," I say as I drive away from Keith Avenue forever.

32

Sometimes God looks down on us with our little plans and giggles. I'm sure of it. Oh, I think I have it all together. Before I go sign the real estate papers, I have lunch at my old favorite place, Ruby's. I order the "Porky" sandwich with fries like I used to do when I was overweight Cissy. While I'm waiting, glancing over the local paper, I spy a familiar person coming in the door. Before I can hide, he spies me back.

Yes, friends, it's Blaine, the guy who was driving me nuts trying to fix my life back at my old church when I was Cissy. Here he comes, staring at my hair.

"Cissy?"

"Blaine. I don't really go by that name anymore. It never really was my name. Just call me P.D." He looks confused, so I go on, loving it. "I'm moving to Oregon. I came to sign off the papers on my house."

"Are you sure?" He slides into the seat across from me. "It's not wise making such big decisions too soon after losing a loved one."

"I'm sure. I'm a big girl, Blaine. I can make my own decisions." And get the hell out of my booth.

"Were you involved in that big earthquake and tsunami?"

"Right in the middle of it."

"Good Lord. Thank God you're safe. I can't imagine why you'd want to go back there."

I shrug. "I know, but I do."

"Will you stay in town long enough to come to Mass or maybe choir practice tonight? Your friends would love to see you."

"They just want to see who I used to be, Blaine. I'm not that woman anymore. I'm single, 42, not married, no children, no ties. Missoula is a nice place, but it's not my home."

"Sounds to me like you're just running away." He's got that concerned amateur shrink expression on his face.

I look him straight in his bespectacled eyes. "I was for a while, but now I know where I'm going. I have work, friends, and family waiting for me."

"Well, I wish you the best."

"Thank you. You too. Good seeing you." The waitress sets my lunch in front of me and I reach for a French fry.

Thank God he takes the hint. As he goes off to eat with his grownup kids, I dig into my fried potatoes and my fried pork sandwich and love every bite. Bye, bye, Blaine.

BUT SHE WHO GLOATS will get indigestion. Here's the part where God gets a good laugh. The second Stella Brasch sees me coming in the door, I know there's a problem. I can see it in the way she takes off her blue-framed reading glasses and her beady eyes dart around nervously, looking for backup. She pretends she doesn't know me. "Can I help you?"

"I'm P.D. Soares."

"Oh, sorry, I didn't recognize you." She sighs, a bit overdramatically. "I have bad news."

"Don't tell me that."

She leads me into a cubicle with cat pictures and real estate award certificates on the walls and tells me to sit down.

"Ms. Soares, there's a hang-up with the financing. The buyers' loan fell through. Would you consider a rental deal with them until they can qualify?"

My lunch turns into a wad of misery. "When did you find this out?"

"First thing this morning. I'm so sorry. But maybe it's a good thing. You talked about wanting to move back in and live there yourself."

"Not anymore. I just said goodbye to that house. I was counting on the money from this sale. What happened? You told me the husband had this great job and everything."

"Yes, but he just started and hasn't gotten paid yet. He was unemployed for the last eight months."

"How about the wife?"

"She took maternity leave, had to stay out longer with complications. But she's working part-time now."

"Swell." I feel my face turning hot with anger. I'm not letting this incompetent bitch ruin my life.

"Do you want me to put the house back on the market?"

I stare at her white-tipped pink fingernails. "No. I'm going to find somebody else to handle it."

She glares at me. "After everything I've done for you?"

I'm so mad the words just pour out. "Look. Somehow you let the renters trash my house in a few months and let them move out with virtually no notice. You accepted an offer from people who wanted to move in yesterday and who turned out to not have the money to buy it. Now you want me to rent it to them in the hope that they might actually get a loan somewhere down the road. You didn't return my calls and never acted like you remembered who I was when I did reach you. It's time for another real estate person." I know I'm being too loud and too harsh, but I can't stop myself.

She slams closed the file on her desk. "I'm sorry you feel that way. None of it was my fault."

"Right. Can you please go remove that lock box?"

"Is tomorrow okay?"

"Whatever. I won't be here."

Stella stares out the window at the traffic on Orange Street, then turns back to me. "Are you sure you won't consider a rent-to-own contract? They still would like to move in this weekend if possible. That means you wouldn't have a gap between rent payments. We can even raise the rate a little."

"I don't think so."

While I liked Missoula a half hour ago, I'm not too fond of it now. I don't know what to do. F-ing Blaine jinxed it. He'd love it if I showed up on his doorstep and said I have no job, no home, no money, will you please take me in and advise me. Maybe the church could take up a collection for poor P.D. No, no, Cissy. The Widow Soares.

"I'm sorry it didn't work out," Stella says.

"Me too." I walk out in a huff, all P.D.-haughty, which lasts until I get out the door. As soon as I'm closed up in my car, I scream as loud as I can until my throat is raw and I'm out of breath. I notice my rose cuttings on the passenger seat. I want to rip them into little pieces.

Too tired to do anything else, I drive to the crummy side of town and get a $45 room in one of those cheesy motels people rent by the week. Swell. I'm back to living in a motel. At least I can go to my locker and get my warm coat. Then I don't know what I'm going to do.

It's 7:30 p.m. I'm sitting cross-legged on the bed in my pajamas eating stale cheese and crackers from the junk food machine by the motel office when Stella Brasch calls me. I'm tempted to not answer, but I don't want to leave any details undone in our non-sale.

"P.D.," she says. "Listen, the buyers would like to meet you. They think if you knew them, you'd be more willing to let them rent the house for a while. Can we get together at 8:30 tomorrow morning? I know you were counting on a sale, but these are good people, and they will buy it if you give them a chance, if you can hang in there for a few months. They even want to fix it up, so even if the worst happens, you'd be in better shape than you were before. What do you say? We'll buy you breakfast at the pancake house."

Shoot. I don't have a better plan. You've got to give Stella credit for being persistent. And she called me P.D. this time, not "Ms. Soares." "Fine. Can we make it 8 o'clock?"

"Of course. Thank you."

I can't imagine being able to sleep tonight. I figure I'll be tossing and turning, thinking about everything until the wee hours, adding up the numbers to see if I can afford my new life in Newport, but I'm so tired, I close my eyes and don't know anything until a garbage truck out front wakes me up at 7:30. I've got thirty minutes to get to the restaurant. Why did I ask for 8 o'clock? Just to one-up Stella. Meeting at 8:30 would have been fine.

A quick shower, a comb through the hair, put on the first clothes I can find, and I'm out the door. Luckily the pancake house is practically across the street.

The buyers, the Cunninghams, are ridiculously nice. They have the cutest baby girl. As the waitress leads us to our table by the window, they make a crack about Montanans and their cowboy coffee, and I like them immediately. They're just like Tom and me the way it was supposed to be, smart, in love, well-employed, with a beautiful child. All they need is the house. By the time we order our blueberry pancakes, I know I'm going to let them have my place. The wife, Melanie, can go all Cissy on it. She's already raving about the roses and the kitchen cabinets and coming up with colors to paint the walls, colors I love.

They're from California, too, wouldn't you know? Stella sits there beaming. She's got all the papers handy, so as soon as our plates are cleared and the waitress wipes the syrup off the table with a wet rag, Stella starts handing out forms and pens with the real estate company's logo on them. We laugh and sign.

We part like old friends. I even hug Stella. I invite them all to come visit me in Oregon.

Pretty soon I'm alone again, grabbing my stuff out of the cheesy motel, wetting paper towels to re-wrap my rose cuttings, gassing up the car and hitting the road, still broke, except for the Cunninghams' first month's rent and cleaning deposit, which I have to use to pay the mortgage. I have just enough money left to rent a U-Haul truck with a trailer for my car, get my stuff out of the locker, and make the trip back to Newport, where half the town is in ruins and the other half is closed. Everything else is going on the credit card.

I get a big, muscular teenager from the storage place to help me load the truck. I might be strong, but there are some things you just need more than one hand for. I don't know who's going to help me on the other end, but the same company has a place south of Newport, so I reserve a locker there and get the address of the U-Haul office to turn in my truck.

First thing we load is my piano. I'm so glad to see it I want to sit down and play it right here in the storage yard. I would, sprained wrist and all, if the kid wasn't here. It will need a good tuning when I get back to the coast. I hope Deuce can help me find somebody who'll do it for free. Maybe I'll learn how to do it myself.

I don't take everything. It won't fit in the truck or my new life. I got rid of most of Tom's things before I left last summer. Now I have to let the rest go. The kid looks at me like I'm nuts when I close up the truck and tell him, "You can keep the rest. Sell it, take it to Goodwill or haul it to the dump, I don't care."

"Really?" I see him eyeing Tom's fishing pole and video games.

"Yep."

Adios, Missoula.

33

AT MY FIRST SIGHT of the ocean, I want to cry. The sun is low over the water, turning it silver. I've spent most of my life by the ocean, and now I'm coming home. Thank you, God.

At the intersection of Highways 20 and 101, I glance at myself in the mirror. My hair is a little longer than the first time I came here, and it's all brown now. Tawny, it said on the box. I dyed it last night at the motel where I stayed in The Dalles. I think I like it. The color sets off my brown eyes and my Italian-Irish skin—olive with freckles, if you can picture that.

I also went shopping while I was there, filling my car with bottled water, canned food, soaps, shampoos, cleaning supplies, propane for the generator, and other things people will need here.

When I registered at the motel in The Dalles, I used my real name. The clerk checked my driver's license, and for the first time in ages, I matched the picture. I'll need to get an Oregon license—as soon as the DMV is back in business. I was going to get one before, but then the tsunami hit, Donovan evicted me and—all water under the bridge. Literally.

The traffic lights in town are still not working. Stop signs on sawhorses face all four directions. I see cars parked outside the J.C. Market. Could it be open?

No Christmas decorations here. It's too soon after the tragedy, and the city doesn't have the manpower to be putting garlands on light poles when buildings are falling down.

Of course the big questions are whether I can get over the bridge and where exactly I'm going to stay tonight. I'm driving this giant truck containing all my possessions and pulling my car on a trailer behind me. The storage place and local U-Haul dealer are both south of the bridge. And how am I going to move all this stuff by myself? Yes, I should have figured all this out before, but I didn't. I was too busy plowing through the snow and rain in my own version of a covered wagon heading west.

I drive my rig across the highway, park in the grocery store lot a few slots down from a Red Cross truck, and pull out my cell phone. Time to swallow my P.D.-pride and ask for help. Thank God the phone is working.

Janey sings her greeting on the second ring. "Helloooo."

"It's P.D. I'm back."

"You really came back? Yay! Where are you?"

"I'm parked at the J.C. Market. I'm in a U-Haul with all my stuff."

I hear her shouting to her mom. "P.D.'s here!" Then some talk I can't understand.

"Janey. Can I get over the bridge in this thing?"

"No. It's still closed, but now they've got a ferry big enough for cars. Brought it down from Seattle."

I picture myself trying to maneuver this truck and trailer onto a ferry. It won't be pretty, but I'll get it done. "Okay. I'll go that way. How is everybody?"

"Oh, we're good. Mom's going to help me find a new apartment. Jonas and his family are back home. The kids were pissed because we ate all their cookies. Mom and Kelly are going to re-open the diner pretty soon, and Frankie is making good progress on the store. Wait till you see the new color scheme."

I shouldn't be chit-chatting. I should be getting on that ferry, but I'm nervous, I guess. "How's Donovan?"

"He's in rehab in Corvallis. Doing pretty well. The nurses say he keeps asking for you."

"Me?"

"He says he has something important to give you."

"Huh. And what about Rick?"

"Ah, stubborn Uncle Rick. He's doing okay. He went home to his boat yesterday, but he has to take a full month off of work and firefighting, and he's pretty grouchy about that. Mom has been taking care of him. She swears he's worse than one of her kids."

The sky has darkened. Raindrops sprinkle the windshield. "Janey, I'd better get going before the storage place closes. Any chance you could meet me there and help me unload this thing?"

"Sure. No problem."

As I start to maneuver my rig out of the parking lot, I see a yellow cab passing down the highway and recognize the driver. Jonas is back at work. That's a good sign.

I'm not the world's best driver. I'm used to my little Chevy Volt, not this gigantic truck. As I drive it onto mud-caked Bay Boulevard and follow the signs to the ferry, I'm sure I'm going to smash every car on the side of the road, wipe out a few pedestrians, and hit a couple buildings. Somehow, miraculously, I make it onto the boat. Two guys wearing orange vests guide me into a parking place.

I sit in that truck in the middle of a handful of parked cars as we move slowly through the murky water. The harbor is still a mess, with missing and broken docks and boats lying every which way. As for the stores and restaurants along the bay, they're pretty much all destroyed. I think about the early 1900s photos I've seen on restaurant walls. They show only a few buildings and a dirt road. It's almost back to that now. It's going to take a long time to deal with the damage from the earthquake and tsunami.

It's 4:30 when I roll off the boat on the other side of the bay. Nearby, the bridge is lit up with big lamps. I see workers and equipment. How long will it take to fix it, I wonder as I hurry down the highway to the storage place. The office closes at 5:00.

As I pause in the center lane, waiting for an opening to turn in, I notice a familiar van with a rainbow stripe on the side. Dakota is here? What the heck? Turning in, I see other cars. As I park and get out, my legs stiff, Janey, Diana, Dakota, Maryann, and Frankie offer hugs.

"Welcome home," Diana says.

I never expected this.

"We heard you needed a little help," Dakota says. "Give me your keys. You go do your paperwork."

The old black guy who works here beckons me in. Soon, I've got the form filled out and the first month paid. Dakota has backed my car off the trailer and is ready to move the truck.

"Number 120," I say, and everyone heads toward the far back row of lockers as I pull my lock and key out of my purse.

By 6:15, the locker is full, the truck is empty, and I'm ready to drive it across the highway to the U-Haul place, which seems to still be open. Even if it isn't, I can leave the truck there and come back in the morning to finish up. I'll be coming back here anyway to sort through my stuff and figure out what I want to use now and what I'll save until I find a place to live.

Meanwhile, we're all going back to the rainbow house for dinner.

"You're staying with us," Maryann says. "Don't argue about it."

I'm not.

THE FOLLOWING SATURDAY, I sleep late in my room at the rainbow house, enjoy a mushroom omelet and banana bread, and take a walk on Ona Beach. It's strange being here after all that has happened. I find myself looking for Ranger Dave, even though I know he won't be coming back here anytime soon, if ever. The park is not the same, the picnic tables half gone, half knocked over and broken apart, the grass coated with mud. Park crews have padlocked the damaged bathroom and blocked the path with red cones. I ease along the creek until I come to where the footbridge to the beach lies in pieces.

I pick my way across the creek over rocks and debris, remembering how Dave and I stood here talking about going kayaking. I wish that day had turned out just as we had planned it, gliding along in our red and yellow kayaks, sun sparkling on the water and warming us through our jackets. Dave and Amy would show me how to row in a straight line and point out the beaver dens, birds, and plants. We'd wave at other kayakers going by. And afterward, we'd pig out on biscuits and gravy or marionberry pancakes at the diner.

Nuts.

I look east up the river toward the highway and the boat launch area where I found Dave under the kayak, half-dead and unable to move his legs. I know I saved his life, but it doesn't seem like enough. I have to put him in the hands of God, his doctors and his family, but it's not easy.

Next Monday, I'm going back to the hospital to start my new job. I'm really thinking about enrolling in the nursing program at the community college once I get a little money saved up. Might they want a 42-year-old widow/part-time singer who can't seem to stay away from hospitals?

A wet golden retriever comes rushing toward me and jumps up to give me a soggy kiss. I hug him against me as his teenage owner comes running up. "Oh, I'm sorry, ma'am. He got loose."

"It's okay." I don't even care that he left muddy paw prints on my jacket. Maybe I'll get me another dog.

The boy runs toward the beach, and the dog follows.

I trail behind them, taking off my shoes. The fine gray sand feels cool and soft on my feet. It looks the way it always did, littered with pieces of driftwood and seaweed, plastic bottles and bits of rope. Now I guess our stuff will be washing up in Japan.

I head south around the rocks and look up to where the eagle's nest was. The tree that held it is gone.

I try to picture the waves coming all the way up to the top of the cliff and washing over the paths, the grass, the parking lot, and the road. I try to remember seeing the ocean pulled back farther than any of us had ever seen it before and then coming toward us as a wall of water ready to smash anything in its path. It doesn't seem real. Today the waves look small and choppy, like dancers waving their lace-trimmed skirts. Now I will always wonder what keeps the ocean in its place—most of the time.

I missed the ocean when I lived in Montana. All my life, the sea had been nearby. I could wake up and smell the salt in the air, hear the roar of the waves, feel the sand on my feet. These beaches in Oregon are colder and rockier than the ones around Santa Cruz. Only naive visitors spread out their towels and try to get a tan on the sand here. When they start to turn blue, they run for their sweatshirts. But it's still the same Pacific Ocean I have known all my life. If once in a while, it gets manic, like Donovan, I guess I just have to forgive it and get out of the way until it calms down.

34

It's Sunday, and I haven't been to church in months, not since I left Montana last summer. I was pretty mad at God for everything that happened, but I'm thinking maybe it wouldn't be so bad to go to Mass one of these days.

So when Janey said, "Hey would you like to go to church with us tomorrow in Newport?" I said yes. The Peacocks are Catholic, like me.

My hostesses are not into formal religion.

"Church, huh?" Dakota says when I tell them. "Not for me. God's in the trees, the ocean, the rocks, and the animals. So have a good time. Say hi to the bloody guy on the cross."

"Dakota!" scolds Maryann from the kitchen sink.

"How about you?" I ask her.

"I used to be Catholic. Gave it up when they gave me up."

"Oh. I'm sorry."

"Not your fault. Some of my best friends are Catholic."

"Yeah, they can't help it," Dakota says.

Janey and Diana pick me up at 9:00 Sunday morning, and we ferry across to Newport for Mass at Sacred Heart Church.

Unlike the vast modern church near our house in Missoula, this one is small and utilitarian, its red brick walls rising to a shingled roof with a bell on top. Boards cover a couple of windows broken in the earthquake. Inside, the pale wooden pews creak as we slide in next to Jonas's family about five rows from the front on the right-hand side.

The only light comes from the uncovered windows and from candles flickering on the altar and in front of the statues of Mary and Joseph. The church is nearly full. In the midst of tragedy, people seek comfort in religion.

We kneel on the padded kneelers. I stare up at Jesus on the cross as the others bow their heads and pray. I don't know what to say. I should say "thank you," I guess, that I'm here and alive and starting over with these wonderful friends.

I watch the "choir" of three women settle into their chairs off to the left as the pianist arranges her music. I feel like I should be up there. If I'm going to go to church, I should be singing. Right? But I don't want to just re-create my old life. I want to start fresh.

I bow my head and close my eyes as Janey and Diana sit back on the pew. "God, you brought me this far. You have taken me through death, injury, earthquake and tsunami. Please guide me on this new path. Watch over Tom in heaven. Amen."

I make the sign of the cross as the music starts and the priest walks in. Beside me, Janey and Diana are singing. I grab a hymnal out of the rack and join in. I know this song. It feels good to sing again. On the second verse, I add an alto harmony. Janey pokes my ribs, and I realize they don't hurt much anymore. Thank you, God.

During the prayers after the sermon, the priest reads a long list of people who died or went missing in the earthquake and tsunami. I catch my breath as he reads a name I recognize. The fisherman from our jam session at the music store. Damn.

The elderly priest has to stop twice to compose himself before he can conclude his prayer. I hear someone sniffling behind me. I glance back, nod at the woman in sympathy. I see a few people on crutches, one with a neck brace, one with her arm in a sling. Tamara from the Chamber of Commerce recognizes me from the karaoke bar and forces a tearful smile.

This has been a hard time for all of us. But as the collection basket comes my way with the next song, I notice people are putting lots of cash and checks in it, sharing even though their livelihoods may have been destroyed. Life has changed for everyone, not just me. I toss in a five-dollar bill, wishing I had more.

After Mass, the priest announces the usual social hour with coffee and donuts is canceled due to the repairs going on in the hall. As we join the people shuffling into the aisles and toward the door, the tall redhead who played the piano stops us.

"Janey! Hi," she says, bending for a hug. "I could hear you two singing all the way from over there. I need you both in the choir."

"Oh, Lizzy," Janey says. "I don't know if I have time. But hey, have you met my friend P.D.? She just moved here a couple months ago, just in time for all the fun."

"Nice to meet you," Lizzy says as she shakes my hand. I pretend it doesn't hurt. I'm embarrassed at how dirty the wrist brace is, but I'm not taking it off this time. I want my wrist to heal properly, however long that takes. "You have a great voice."

"Thank you. I sang in the choir at my old church."

"Well, come join us. We practice on Wednesday nights. Maybe if you come, Janey will come, too."

Janey shrugs. "Maybe."

Lizzy's bottle-green eyes reflect light from the altar candles. They match her green velour shirt. I think she's about my age. I can see she needs more than three singers. We had 18 in our choir in Missoula. "Well, let me get a little more settled in, and I'll think about it."

"Please. We really could use you."

"P.D. plays piano, too," Janey says.

"Really? That would be great. I'm doing all the Masses now that we lost Gracie."

I hold up my gimpy wrist. "Maybe in a few weeks."

She doesn't ask how I hurt my wrist. I'm sure she thinks it was the earthnami. I wonder what happened to Gracie. I'll ask Janey later. Or maybe I don't want to know.

What I do know is I'd like to put my fingers on the keys of that piano.

Somebody in the choir calls Lizzy's name.

We say our goodbyes and head out to the parking lot, where Diana is waiting for us in her van.

"Did Gracie get caught in the tsunami?" I ask as Janey gets into the front seat and I climb into the back.

Diana chuckles. "She moved to Florida a couple months ago. "I'll bet she's sitting in the sun right now. Anyway, we're meeting Jonas for brunch at Izzy's, okay?"

"Great," Janey and I say together.

Izzy's is where I first hooked up with this family, where I met Donovan Green. I thought he was just a big teddy bear then. I had no idea he could turn wild.

FERRYING OVER the bridge later in Diana's van, I look out at the dirty water and the guys working on their boats. Most of the wreckage has been cleared by now, with empty spaces where docks used to be, but there's still an overturned boat up against the rocks and plenty of litter floating in the wake of a fishing boat puttering toward the open ocean.

We waited almost an hour to board the ferry. If I'm working in town, this bay crossing is going to be a drag. I need to get a place on the north side of the bridge. Now that I know I'm staying, I'm anxious to put it all together as quickly as possible.

"I need to stop at Rick's boat," Diana says as the ferry docks on the south side of the bay.

Diana parks the van at the marina and leads the way down the makeshift ramp to the Melinda Sue.

We find Rick on his hands and knees scrubbing mud off the deck. He looks up and smiles at the three of us in our Sunday clothes. "Hey."

"Hey yourself," Diana says. "Are you trying to bust open your incision? You're supposed to be resting."

"I am. This is resting for me. You can't expect me to do nothing forever."

"You're the most stubborn man I've ever met."

"And that's why you love me."

Janey follows her mother on board. "Hey, Uncle Rick. I smuggled you some pizza from Izzy's." She pulls a Styrofoam box out of her big purse.

"Thanks." He notices me hanging back. "Come on board, P.D. I won't bite. I thought you moved back to Montana."

I climb awkwardly over the side and stand beside Janey. "Changed my mind. I'm staying here."

"Good. Listen, I'd offer you three ladies a beer, but Diana won't let me have any. She wants me to drink *tea.*"

"It's better for you."

"I'm not English or Chinese. Anyway. How was church?"

"Good," Janey says.

"Lots of people dead or injured," I add.

"Yeah. I know." He looks off toward the bridge and beyond. Where dozens of boats used to be lined up in orderly rows, only a few remain. "But we made it." He pulls Diana close to him and plants a kiss on her cheek. "Right, Darlin'? Will you marry me now?"

She laughs. "Get away from me."

We chat while Rick eats his pizza. Diana cleans up the cabin and feeds him his pills.

Standing out here in the fresh air, feeling the boat rock in the gentle current, I feel good. This is where I belong.

"Time to go," Diana declares. "I've got work to do at the diner."

Back in the car, I'm staring out the windows at the trees, rocks and ocean going by when Diana shouts, "Oh!" so suddenly I think we must have a flat tire or we're about to hit a deer. I brace myself. She says, "I completely forgot. P.D., I've got a letter from Donovan for you."

"For me?" Great. He wants rent money or to yell at me for squatting in his cabin. Maybe he thinks the damage is all my fault.

She hands me a sealed envelope on which he has drawn a picture of a singing frog with red hair sticking straight up.

"Looks just like you," Janey says.

"Uh-huh." I slide my finger under the flap to open the envelope and pull out a card with more frog pictures and a note.

As I open the card, a check for $1,000 falls out. "Oh my gosh."

"What is it?" Janey asks, leaning over the back of the seat. I show her the check. "Wow. What does he say? Wait, maybe it's none of my business."

I scan the note, which covers the entire inside page and continues on the back, then read it out loud.

"Dear P.D.,

Forgive me for being such a jerk to you. I was off my meds and out of control, but you didn't deserve to be kicked out of your temporary home when I promised you could stay there until May. I wouldn't have blamed you if you let me die. I know you're going through a tough time, and I made it worse. I am so sorry. I hope you feel better soon, and I hope this money can help you find a comfortable place to sleep. I'd offer you the cabin again, but I suspect you're sick of the place. Besides, my cats have moved to Dakota's house, and my art . . . there's nothing to protect anymore until I can get home and get back to work. I do remember going to hear you sing that night at Café Mundo. You are very talented as well as beautiful, and I hope I can get to know you better in the future.
Warmly,
Donovan J. Green.

Janey grins at me. "He likes you, P.D."

"He barely knows me."

"Just be careful," Diana says, as she turns off the highway and up the hill toward the rainbow house.

"I will." Heck yes, I'll be careful. I have seen the highs and lows of Donovan J. Green. But it's intriguing. And the check will get me into a new place to live. Meanwhile, I think I know what I'm going to do this afternoon.

I NEVER THOUGHT I'd be weeding a garden made of glass, but that's what I seem to be doing as I gather bits of red, yellow, green and blue glass from among Donovan's broken glass flowers. Some of the flowers just need to be set upright again while others are on the ground in pieces, along with the wine bottle sculptures. Wearing leather gloves to protect my hands, I put the glass and metal pieces in trays I found in the studio, sorting them by color. Perhaps Donovan can make something new out of them.

You might ask why I care. I don't know. There's something about Donovan that calls to me. Plus I want to finish what I started.

It's cold out, even with a sweatshirt, ski jacket and knit hat. Wind sighs through the trees. But the sun shines through dark clouds, creating a warm golden light. I stand and stretch my hands up toward the sky. I miss my exercise. Maybe I'll go back to the gym next week—if we have electricity. But there's work to do here today. When I finish the garden, I'll tackle the studio, the stains on the carpet, the scattered glass and tools. Then I'll see what I can do in the other rooms and on the porch where Donovan seemed so happy drinking and singing in the midst of the tsunami disaster. Diana said he's coming home next weekend. I'm not sure yet just where I'll be, probably in the rainbow house until I find another place.

Sun glints off the trays of red and green glass. It's almost Christmas. I haven't made any plans for the holiday. Nor have my friends here. We're all too busy putting our lives back together.

Dakota brought me some Christmas cards that came in the mail, forwarded from Missoula. I'm sure my friends are confused about where I am and why they haven't heard from me. Some of my California friends don't even know that Tom died. If I were the old on-top-of-everything Cissy, I would have sent them all cards with a note inside about what happened. But I honestly didn't even think about it.

I got a card from my mother, too. She wants me to come home for Christmas, but I have already told her I'm not coming, that I need to stay put for a while. It's not that I don't want to see my family; it's that the earth hasn't quite stopped shaking for me. I'm still doing a little bit of duck and cover, but I can see that it's almost safe to come out.

Meanwhile, I am about done with the yard. Time to tackle the cabin. It freaks me out a little to think the last time I was here, I was on the floor giving Donovan CPR in the midst of a mess of blood and broken glass. I was sick and miserable myself, but I saved his life. I put his card on the nightstand by my bed at the rainbow house. I know he's got problems, but there's a good person inside that giant of a man.

The kitchen looks pretty good. Some food spoiling in the fridge. I bag it up to toss in the garbage. I dust and sweep a bit, put Donovan's knick-knacks back on the mantel, straighten the covers on the bed, and admire Rick's patch job on the ceiling. It's hard to tell there used to be a big hole there with a tree hanging through it.

The studio is a different matter. I get myself a glass of water and stand in the doorway studying the mess. I can sweep and sort the glass, but I'm not sure how I'm going to get the blood and wine off the rug. When I try to scrub it with a towel, the stain just spreads. I'm thinking maybe Donovan should just throw the rug away and get a new one. Or dye the whole thing red.

I find bits of glass everywhere, the biggest pile around where I found him, but some bounced all the way across the room. By the time I get through sweeping, scooping and crawling under the table, my ribs hurt, but the room looks a lot better, and I have a big collection of colored glass that Donovan should be able to make into something. A mosaic maybe.

As I'm taking a last look to see if anything else needs doing, Dakota knocks on the door.

"Hey. Dinner's about ready. You comin' down?"

"Be right there." Chicken and dumplings have been simmering at that house for hours, and I'm not about to miss it.

35

Two weeks later, I'm taking my break at the hospital, reading the classifieds in the local paper, when I see an ad for a rental that looks perfect: "Two-bedroom 1940s cottage overlooking the Bayfront. Garage, fenced yard, owner relocating, small pets okay. $1,050."

It's too bad I can't afford to buy a home at the moment. You can get an earthquake-damaged fixer-upper for a steal right now. Maybe the owners of this place will be willing to sell, and I can get the same kind of deal I gave the Cunninghams back in Missoula. My renters sent me a Christmas card gushing about how happy they are in my old home.

I circle the ad. I've got five more minutes on my break. I pick up my phone. As I start to dial the number in the ad, the phone rings.

"P.D.!" Janey yells. I hold the phone away from my ear. "I found this great house for rent, overlooking the Bayfront. It sounds fabulous! Will you come look at it with me after work tonight?"

That's my house. "Wait. The one for $1,050? I was just about to call on that one."

"Well . . . want to share it?"

I look up at the cloudy sky and know God is smiling somewhere above the clouds. "Yes. What time are you going there?"

"You get off work at 5, right?"

"Right. Meet you there at 5:15?"

The house is perfect. Inside a wooden fence with cutouts of fish and sea stars, granite stepping stones lead through a garden full of rhododendrons and azaleas that will burst into bloom in a few months. A big white cat rubs around our ankles. Wind chimes shaped like little glass fish tinkle in the breeze. The house itself looks like something out of a fairy tale with its shingled siding, moss-covered roof and bright yellow door.

A smiling woman in her 70s opens the door and beckons us into a sunny living room with a worn leather sofa and recliner and a scarred-up wooden table and chairs. I see an empty bookshelf and boxes piled against the walls.

"Come in, come in. I'm Sylvia."

We introduce ourselves. "Janey." "P.D."

"P.D. What does that stand for?"

Janey says, "She doesn't tell anyone that. It's just P.D."

"Well, I kind of like that. Leaves it up to interpretation. Let me show you around. You know, the ad just came out today, and you're the first to respond." As we follow her, I notice Sylvia limps. Her feet are swollen over her black tennis shoes.

I love this place. I love it all. It's funky and functional. The kitchen with its vast white-tiled counters and polka-dotted linoleum reminds me of my grandmother's house. There's a pantry on the back porch, which leads to a sweet garden with benches and a bird bath. I know exactly where I'll put my roses, which Maryann has kept alive since I brought them home from Missoula.

The house is old. I see cracks in the sheetrock that might or might not be from the earthquake, and there's no dishwasher in the kitchen, but I still love it.

Janey and I keep looking at each other, and I know we're thinking the same thing: Yes!

"How could you leave this place?" I ask.

"Oh," Sylvia sighs, hauling herself up the back step and leading us to the dining area. "Sit down. Would you like some lemonade?"

We would. As we sit, she pours lemonade from an etched pitcher, then sets out poppy seed scones on a crystal plate.

"I love your house," Janey says.

"Well, you know, I do, too, but I can't live here anymore. I've got some health problems, and that business with the earthquake and tsunami was the last straw. I'm going to move in with my sister in Portland. We're both alone now, and it just makes sense." She takes a scone. "Help yourself."

I want to say "I'm sorry," but if she weren't moving, this house wouldn't be available.

The scones are delicious. Maybe Janey and I could share the house with Sylvia. But there are only two bedrooms.

"So," Sylvia says. "Are you two mother and daughter?"

Janey and I laugh.

"No," I say. "We're just friends. We both like to sing and know some of the same people, so we naturally got together."

"Oh, that's nice. Neither of you married or have kids?"

"Not me," says Janey.

"I was married. No kids. My husband died earlier this year."

Sylvia nods. "I'm sorry. I lost my guy 15 years ago, and I still miss him every day. Well, it's good you girls have each other."

The cat meows at the front door. As Sylvia struggles to rise, I jump up to let the cat in.

"Her name's Marshmallow."

Janey giggles.

"Are you taking her with you?" I ask.

"Oh yes." The cat jumps into her lap, and Sylvia rubs her face against the soft white fur. "I wouldn't leave my baby behind."

"Your ad says pets are okay."

"Yes. I don't think a home is complete without a furry companion. Do you girls have a dog or cat?"

"Not yet," I say, looking at Janey. She smiles. "But maybe soon."

"Well, that's wonderful. What do you do besides sing?"

"I'm going to OCCC," Janey says, "and I work at my mom's diner in Seal Rock."

"I just started a job at the hospital similar to what I did in Montana. I work on the admissions desk. I'm thinking about going into the nursing program at the community college next year."

Janey shoots me a surprised look.

"Aha. I admire you girls. Lots of energy and gumption. Too many seem to be helpless without husbands. So, what do you think? If you want to rent the house, it's yours."

"Don't you want to check our credit or anything?" Janey asks.

"Oh, I will. My son will make me do that, but I have faith that you two are trustworthy."

"We are," she says.

"Well, good. I'm leaving some furniture behind. Don't need it at my sister's house. This table and the sofa will stay. The bedroom furniture goes. Is that all right?"

"Sure, that's great. We have our own," I say. I left most of my furniture in Montana. Too many memories. I look around the room. The spot where the bookshelf is now would be just right for my piano. It's going to be tight. This house only has two bedrooms, the living room/dining room combination, the bathroom, and the kitchen, but it's enough.

For all her informality, Sylvia has some pretty formal-looking rental forms and credit forms for us to fill out, and she's got a list of rules and regulations, none of them obnoxious. As we write, she uses the wall telephone in the kitchen to call her sister.

"It's me. I've got renters for my house already," she says. "Yes, two girls. They seem very nice. I feel good about passing my house on to them. Well, if you can get Jeremy down here this weekend to help me with my stuff, I'll move in on Sunday, in plenty of time for Christmas. Yes, yes, I have Mother's ornaments. Umhm. Umhm. Yes. Okay, I have to go."

She comes back to the table. "My sister Julia is a talker. I guess I'll get used to it."

By 6:30, we're finished. I've got a copy of the house key in my pocket. Sylvia offers us some more scones to take with us, but we politely decline and hurry out.

"I can't believe this," Janey says outside. "This is way better than where I lived before the tsunami. I was going to move to Corvallis next year, but I think I'd rather live here and commute."

"Good. I wondered about that. This is going to be fun."

"A blast."

We caravan the short drive down to the bay and get on the ferry just before it leaves. On the south side, driving with the radio on, I find myself singing along with "Jingle Bell Rock."

36

CHRISTMAS IS NOTHING like Thanksgiving. Janey and I sang at midnight Mass, but we got up early to start cooking and welcome our guests. We're all jammed into the little house overlooking the bay. Rick, Donovan, Jonas and the kids relax in the living room near our scraggly little Christmas tree while Janey, Diana, Dakota, Maryann, Molly, and I gather in the kitchen. I know. It's totally sexist, but it works.

Salads, olives, pickles, salami, and Maryann's fresh cranberry sauce sit on Sylvia's old table covered with an embroidered tablecloth I inherited from my grandmother. I'm about to take the turkey out of the oven when the doorbell rings.

It sounds like a church bell. Janey and I look at each other and laugh.

"Did you even know we had a doorbell?" I ask.

"No!"

"You gonna answer the door?" asks Dakota as she pops the cork out of a bottle of *pinot gris*.

But Jonas beats me to it. I turn to see my mother and my brother in the doorway, their arms loaded with gifts. I am speechless. Nobody else knows who these people are, so I have to pull myself together.

"Mom! Andy! I can't believe it."

"Surprise!" says Mom, handing her gifts off to Jonas to put under the tree. "If you won't come to us, I guess we have to come to you."

I wipe my hands on my apron and rush forward to hug them. Oh my God. She may drive me crazy sometimes, but my mother gives the best hugs. When I'm in her arms, all feels right. Andy bends down and wraps his big old arms around me. Crap. Tears are pouring out of my eyes. Mom's crying, too.

Finally I pull back and notice Mom's Buick parked out front. "You drove?"

"All 733 miles," she says.

"Thank you so much."

"How are you feeling?"

"I'm fine, Mom. Really, better than I've been in a long time."

"She's been planning this trip since right after Thanksgiving," Andy says.

Tricky Mom.

But all these other people are waiting for introductions. "Listen, everyone, this is my mother, Pauline, and my brother, Andy. This is, oh God, so many people." I look around at these friends I have come to love, and the tears keep coming as I introduce them all.

Pretty soon everybody is talking at once. I hear questions about where Mom and Andy live and what route they took and comments about the tsunami damage they saw along the way. They talk about how this disaster compares to the 1989 Loma Prieta earthquake back in Santa Cruz. Dakota offers drinks, and Maryann serves hors' d'oeuvres as I scoot back to the kitchen. I can't let the turkey burn in the midst of all this. God forbid it not be perfect; my mother is here.

I pull the roasting pan out of the oven and place it on the old-fashioned cutting board set into the tile. The turkey skin is crackling on top, grease oozing out as I pierce it with a knife. I can smell the sage and apple stuffing as I untie the strings and reach for a spoon.

"Can I help you with that?" a deep voice behind me asks.

I look up into Donovan's kind face.

"I'm a pretty good turkey carver," he says.

"Oh? Okay." I set Grandma's big white platter beside the cutting board and hand him my knife and fork. As he lifts the turkey out, I grab the roasting pan to make the gravy.

"That's my job," my mother says, pushing through.

I yield my place at the stove. Her gravy has always been better than mine. I'm not too proud to admit it.

"Everything smells so good," she says.

"Thanks."

Donovan hums "Deck the Halls" as he slices slabs of white meat and places them on the platter.

"I like your little house, and I like your friends," Mom says.

"Thank you. We haven't finished unpacking yet. For today, we just shoved everything into the bedrooms and shut the doors. But we like it." I rest my face against her shoulder. "I am so glad you came."

"Me too. And oh, hey, I got a card from your father."

"Where is he now?"

"He says he's in Las Vegas but plans to come visit you in the near future. Oregon sounds good to him, he says. So, who knows? Maybe Rambling Jack will settle down."

Donovan looks confused.

"My dad doesn't like to stay in one place very long."

"Ah. Well, I look forward to meeting him."

"You might really like each other."

"Hey!" Rick calls from the living room. "Is that bird done yet?"

I glance out and see Diana snuggling against him on the love seat. "Just about."

Sylvia's table isn't quite big enough now. We have 12 people. Janey's setting up a card table. I didn't even know we had one. A kids' table. I have finally arrived, I think.

With lots of helping hands, the food is quickly set out in a colorful mixture of dishes from Janey's family and mine. We grab hands to say grace, and everyone looks at me.

I pull in a deep breath. I remember Tom doing this in years past. God, how I miss him. But he has moved on, and so must I.

"In the name of the Father, and of the Son and of the Holy Spirit. Amen. Dear God, thank you for bringing us together here today. Thank you for bringing my California family together with my Oregon one. Please bless this food and these people. And please, if you can manage it, don't let us have any earthquakes or tsunamis or any other disaster today. Amen."

"Amen," the others echo as one of the boys, Tim I think, screams, "Amen!" and his mother shushes him.

"Let's eat," Janey says.

We settle into our chairs and start passing dishes. Soon our plates are full. Of course somebody has to mention how it gets quiet when people's mouths are full. My mother says, "Honey, it's all delicious."

"I didn't do it alone."

Diana is looking at her cell phone. "I just got a message from Caroline. She and Amy are still up in Portland with Dave. He's doing okay, she says, considering. He claims he's still going to be kayaking this summer, and he's got a red one waiting for P.D."

I fight the tears that clog my throat. We all know he'll be coming home in a wheelchair.

"Good for him," Jonas says and raises his wine glass. "Here's to Dave."

We clink glasses and drink.

I can almost see Tom in the room with us. I reach for the necklace he gave me, feeling the ruby heart and my wedding ring warm between my fingers. "Never stop singing," he told me. I won't. Nor will I ever forget him.

I'm startled when Donovan leans close. "Are you the one who cleaned up my house and garden?"

"Guilty."

"Thank you."

I look up into his kind Santa Claus face. "Well, thank you for the money and the card. I love your garden."

"If you'd like, I'll make you something for your new home."

I squeeze his giant hand. "That would be wonderful."

I notice Diana watching us. I know she's worried Donovan will go crazy again, but I'm liking this version of him a lot.

"How do you like your new job?" Andy asks. The conversation scatters in four different directions as we eat until we're stuffed. We still have the pumpkin and marionberry pies Diana brought. This time, if the earth sits still, we might actually get to eat them.

"I'm so full," Jonas says. "That was good."

"It was." I'd love to sneak out to the gym and work off what I just ate, but I finally saw a doctor about my wrist, and he says I have to wait two more weeks. It wasn't just sprained. I had a hairline fracture in one of the bones, but it will be fine.

"I think it's time for some music," Janey says. "P.D., do you know any Christmas songs?"

"A few dozen."

"We really have to start our band, The Seal Rock Sound."

"Absolutely."

Rick nods. I look at Maryann. "We need a fiddler."

She shrugs. "Why not?"

I take my seat on the piano bench, scooting over to make room for Janey to play the right hand notes as the others retire to the sofas and the floor. Except for my mother. As we hit the opening chord for "Jingle Bells," she interrupts.

"I'm going to start on the dishes, Cissy."

"Cissy?" Rick says.

"Who's Cissy?" asks little Ty.

"Hold on," I tell Janey. I turn around on the bench. "Mom, you can't call me Cissy anymore. That was my little girl name. Now I'm a grown-ass woman. You know what name you gave me when I was born. It was a good name, and it wasn't Cissy. But it's not me anymore."

I stand up and face my friends and family. "I know you're all dying to know what my real name used to be. Well, someday I might tell you. Meanwhile it's whatever you want it to be. Piano diva. Plucky dame. Paradox. Prune Danish."

"Postage due," says Dakota.

"Peking duck," says Diana.

Now we're all laughing.

"Potty dance!" shouts Jonas.

"Pipe dream," says Maryann.

"Prima donna," says Janey, poking me in the ribs.

Rick leans close and whispers in my ear. "It's Priscilla Donatella O'Leary Soares, but I won't tell anybody. My name isn't really Rick."

"What is it?"

"I'm not sayin'." He gives me a quick kiss on the cheek. My face is as hot as that turkey was in the oven. He's right about my name, but I'm not admitting it, even though Dakota, Mom and Andy know what P.D. stands for. I'm sure they'll spill the beans eventually.

"No, not even close," I say out loud. "Any other guesses?"

Seeing my mother's mouth start to form my actual name, I shake my head as Donovan jumps in. "Pure delight." He gives me a look that makes me blush.

"Okay," I say. "Spell it out however you want, but call me P.D. Now let's sing!"

Acknowledgments

Where does a novel come from? A little of this and that, life lived, people met, ideas that pop in from God knows where. It flows from my mind to my fingers to the computer to the manuscript. But turning it into a book requires help.

Thank you to my critique group partners, Dorothy Mack, Bill Hall, and Theresa Wisner, who plowed through the early drafts and rewarded me with cake when I reached the end.

Thank you to all the people who have planned for and written about the real earthquake and tsunami that is expected to hit the Oregon coast one of these days. Let's pray it never really happens and pray for those who have already experienced tsunamis in Japan, Indonesia, Alaska, and other places.

Thank you to my beta readers who offered far more help than I asked for: Simonne Braden, Kristin Cole, Bonnie Dodge, Jacqueline Evans, Sue Humes, Tamara Meaux, Lacie Semenovich, and Christine Robertson. To my most loyal fan, Patricia Stern, a big hug.

To Fred, thank you for giving me the freedom to write.

About the Author

Sue Fagalde Lick spent many years earning an honest living writing for newspapers in California's Bay Area before moving to the Oregon coast with her late husband, Fred. When not writing books, essays, poems and blogs, she assumes an alternate identity as a singer, guitarist and piano player. Sue lives with her dog Annie just above the tsunami zone in South Beach, Oregon.

Also by Sue Fagalde Lick

BLOGS

www.childlessbymarriage.com
www.unleashedinoregon.com

BOOKS

The Iberian Americans: Portuguese, Spanish and Basque immigrants in America

Stories Grandma Never Told: Portuguese Women in California

Azorean Dreams: a Portuguese-American Romance

Childless by Marriage: What if you want children, but he's unable or unwilling?

Love or Children: When You Can't Have Both

Shoes Full of Sand: a memoir

Unleashed in Oregon: Best of the Blog

For more information, visit www.suelick.com.

Made in United States
Troutdale, OR
06/22/2024